THE GEEZER FACTORY MURDERS

THE
GEEZER FACTORY MURDERS

A NOVEL BY

Corinne Holt Sawyer

DONALD I. FINE BOOKS
New York

DONALD I. FINE BOOKS
Published by the Penguin Group
Penguin Books USA Inc., 375 Hudson Street,
New York, New York 10014, U.S.A.
Penguin Books Ltd, 27 Wrights Lane,
London W8 5TZ, England
Penguin Books Australia Ltd, Ringwood,
Victoria, Australia
Penguin Books Canada Ltd, 10 Alcorn Avenue.
Toronto, Ontario, Canada M4V 3B2
Penguin Books (N.Z.) Ltd, 182-190 Wairau Road.
Auckland 10, New Zealand

Penguin Books Ltd, Registered Offices:
Harmondsworth, Middlesex, England

Published in 1996 by Donald I. Fine Books,
an imprint of Penguin Books USA Inc.

1 3 5 7 9 10 8 6 4 2

PUBLISHER'S NOTE
This is a work of fiction. Names, characters, places, and incidents either are the product
of the author's imagination or are used fictitiously, and any resemblance to actual
persons, living or dead, events, or locales is entirely coincidental.

Library of Congress Cataloging-in-Publication Data

Sawyer, Corinne Holt.
   The Geezer Factory murders : a novel / by Corinne Holt Sawyer.
   p.   cm.
   ISBN 1-55611-497-4
   1. Benbow, Angela (Fictitious character)—Fiction.   2. Wingate, Caledonia (Fictitious
character)—Fiction.   3. Retirement communities—California, Southern—
Fiction.   4. Women detectives—California, Southern—Fiction.   5. Aged women—
California, Southern—Fiction.   6. Widows—California, Southern—Fiction.   I. Title.
PS3569.A864G44   1996   96-6831
813'.54—dc20   CIP

This book is printed on acid-free paper.

Printed in the United States of America

*To my sister Madeline Campillo, without whose help this book
could not have been written.*

*And to all the little furry, four-footed beings who have
filled my life with love:
Chester, Gussie, and Bum,
Anastasia, Amanda, Samantha, Ronson,
Annie, Souris, and Heather,
Tiger, Gus, Him, Her, and Prince Igor,
Mi-Tu, Miss Peeper, Sammy, the Fat Black Object,
Sally, Y.Y. Flurch, and Freddo.
You are with me still, if only in memory.*

CHAPTER

1

OLAF TORGESON, THE RED-FACED and corpulent administrator of Camden-sur-Mer, that gracious old hotel-turned-retirement-home situated on prime ocean-front property just thirty-five miles north of San Diego, rubbed his hands together with satisfaction. On that beautiful May day, he had no inkling that murder and madness waited in the wings; instead he was aware only of a sense of warmth and happiness.

"This has been a remarkably successful year so far," he told his long-suffering secretary, Juana Ortega, who sat listening patiently as Torgeson gloated, beaming expansively out of his office window toward the gardens. "Remarkably successful!" he went on. "Five new tenants in as many months—three scheduled to move in this very week, and one already happily in place. Of course the fifth one . . ." He frowned mightily. "Well, it's too bad Mr. Cherry passed away shortly after his arrival. All the same, since we don't return but half of a new tenant's entry fee after the first month, it wasn't all that bad, from our point of view. After paying the refund to his estate, we were left with a tidy sum for our general fund."

"But poor Mr. Cherry!" Miss Ortega said timidly. "Just think. He was only here a few days over a month before he passed away. I feel so sorry for . . ."

"Of course you do, Miss Ortega," Torgeson assured her earnestly. "And so do I. But it's a cruel truth that in the retirement-home business we most welcome two sorts of tenants—the hale and healthy who have all their wits about them, and the enfeebled who won't last long enough to use up that down payment. Because we hardly break even on just the monthly rent fees, let alone show a profit for our owners, what with all the services we give and the constant repairs on this old building. So while it sounds very unpleasant, I'll admit that if the truth were known, the best thing for us, businesswise, would be to have all new tenants pass away quickly, so we could have at least half of that down payment and then get an entry fee from someone new. See what I mean? The faster the turnover of residents, the larger the profit for our owners."

Miss Ortega shuddered in spite of herself and Torgeson brought himself up short. "Oh, I don't mean that it's not regrettable when a resident passes away. Of course it is. Dear old Mr. Cherry is a case in point; terribly sad, terribly sad." He sighed heavily to underscore the point. "And if we had only the frail and infirm as tenants, it would become impossible to interest a new prospect in . . . I mean, our little home here becomes much more attractive when we have lively residents who are willing and able to attend the programs, take part in the activities, head up committees, welcome newcomers . . . It makes for a marvelous atmosphere. Look at the lively chatter out in the lobby before meals. Almost all our residents get together there to visit and share the news. In a lot of ways, this is like a small village," Torgeson went on expansively. "A big, extended family. And that's a real magnet to prospects. I enjoy watching visitors' faces as they meet some of our more active residents, like . . . well, for instance, like that pair of nuisances, Angela Benbow and Caledonia Wingate. I confess I haven't always been grateful for those two and their . . . their meddling. I've even tended to blame them for some of the things that have happened here, although usually the problems weren't really their fault. But nuisances or not, their fellow residents genuinely like the two of them very much and to be fair, it would be duller around here without them. Besides, even when we've had serious trouble—like that unfortunate death at Christmas—somehow it hasn't hurt our business. With a very few exceptions, our residents have remained loyal to us. Loyalty from the residents," he went on, rocking back in his chair expansively, "is almost as important to a retirement home as good food—and heaven knows, the meals here are one of the biggest attractions, don't you agree?"

Juana nodded with genuine enthusiasm. The staff as well as the residents had little to complain of in the gourmet meals the chef, Mrs. Schmitt, served up every day. "But about Mrs. Benbow and Mrs. Wingate," she ventured timidly, "you call them nuisances, but I . . . I rather like them myself. They're so . . . so vital. Interested in everything and everybody." She was nearly whispering because she hated to contradict him. He never hesitated to suggest that her job depended on her pleasing him, and with a woman's sure instinct, she knew that meant agreeing with his opinions, even if he were to declare that the sky had just turned green. "Yes, Mr. Torgeson," she'd have said. "So it has. How very unusual." So she disagreed now only very quietly.

It didn't seem to matter. Torgeson was beaming out his window again, smiling at the fresh faces of the roses that nodded in the May sunshine. His mood was too good for him to notice that, on this occasion, her opinion did not echo his. "And let me tell you something, Miss Ortega. Getting new tenants is not the best of it. Neither is my turning a profit for my bosses. Do you want to know what the best thing of all is?"

He waited a moment, so she filled the pause by breathing, "So, what *is* the best thing of all?"

"The best thing is that the institution up on the hill—our rivals at The Golden Years—they're losing tenants to us! These last three transfers are all from The Golden Years!" Once more he rubbed his hands together and his ruddy cheeks glowed his pleasure. "And to think that only a month ago I was fretting that we were losing the race to them. That they were filling their vacancies while we had empty apartments. But here we are with this sixty-some-years-old building with all its frayed wiring and leaky plumbing . . ."

"It doesn't leak all the time," Miss Ortega protested. "And this building is so beautiful. So graceful with the old-time Spanish architecture and the lovely big lobby. That place on the hill is so . . . so plain and so grim! At least," she added hastily, "from the outside. You know I've never gone inside!"

Torgeson smiled his approval. "Of course not. But I did when they first opened, and frankly I was repulsed. It's completely utilitarian and bone-ugly. Inside as well as out. Surprisingly, some people seem to prefer all that stark efficiency to charm and grace. But shiny and dust-free as they are, they've been having problems we never even dreamed of!" His smile became huge and positively lupine.

"Of course I feel for them." He rubbed his hands together gleefully a second time. "I feel their pain," he insisted, but his beaming face belied the sentiment of his words. "However to be frank, their bad fortune is our good fortune! Three defections from The Golden Years in one week! And all coming here to us! Who'd have thought . . ."

and he rubbed his hands together yet a third time, unable to conceal his delight, nor trying very hard to do so.

It had all started some weeks before when Tootsie Armstrong, one of Camden-sur-Mer's long-term residents, had surprised her friends (as well as a dismayed Torgeson) by announcing her intention to move out of her comfortable little apartment and transfer to the retirement home newly built across town near the San Diego Freeway. And she was not the first. A relatively new tenant, Calvin Bugle, had also moved to The Golden Years a month earlier, but since Calvin had been complaining about everything at Camden-sur-Mer from the moment he arrived, his decision to switch residences was no great surprise. Besides, Torgeson took comfort in the thought that Bugle had stayed long enough so that only about one-third of his entry fee had to be refunded; the books would show a profit when the Bugle apartment was let to a new tenant. But Torgeson had been genuinely bitter when he learned that Tootsie Armstrong was—as he put it— deserting to the enemy. She had lived a long time at Camden-sur-Mer in apparent content. How could she prefer The Golden Years? It still rankled, even though weeks had passed since the move.

A more unlikely matchup one could not imagine between resident and residence than the pairing of Tootsie Armstrong with The Golden Years. Despite its romantic-sounding name, The Golden Years was—as Torgeson often commented—an ugly edifice: a squat, three-story, red-brick building with the utilitarian exterior common to orphanages, prisons, and other necessary but unpleasant institutions. The architect had added not a pillar, not a scrolled eave, certainly not a stone gargoyle to break the starkness of the facade; there was not even a bas-relief motto chiseled in marble over the front door—the Camden post office looked positively frivolous by comparison. Perhaps when the shrubbery around the foundations grew larger and fluffier, perhaps when vines climbed the brick, the building's outlines would be softened. But at the moment, its style was distinctly "early Chicago warehouse."

The interior design was every bit as forbidding: Formica, stainless steel, Naugahyde and vinyl, and glossy white, washable enamel covered every available surface in the lobby, the meeting rooms, the dining room, and the hallways. In such public and communal areas there were no window draperies where microbes could hide, no ornaments on tables or pictures on the walls to catch the dust, no carpeting to get stained by spills from beverages held by trembling senior hands. The dining room was anything but cozy; sounds echoed through its expanse of chrome, glass, and plastic as through a cave, even when the room was fully occupied. In short, everything that met the eye at The Golden Years was practical, antiseptic, and completely cheerless. One assumed, of course, that inside the private apartments, the residents' own furnishings and personal effects created the illusion of individuality and warmth, but those were not characteristics one could associate with the rest of the place.

The reason Tootsie seemed such a bad match with the place was that she was anything but crisply modern and neatly efficient. "Haphazard" was a good word to describe her style; or "impractical and fanciful," or even "frowsy and disorganized." Other women at Camden-sur-Mer were carefully groomed; Tootsie looked as though she had recently been in a high wind, clothing askew and iron-gray curls unruly. The other women walked as steadily as aging joints and occasional arthritic twinges would allow; Tootsie toddled in a gait made unsteady by the spike-heeled shoes she insisted on wearing ". . . because they make my legs look so nice"; as a consequence, she would frequently teeter and had to be steadied by anyone within reach. The other women at Camden-sur-Mer wore little dresses or carefully matched slacks suits; Tootsie picked up whichever article of clothing came first at hand when she reached into her closet, whether it matched what she had already selected or not. "For a week at a time she looks perfectly fine," her fellow resident Angela Benbow once complained, "and the very next day she's likely to show up in sequins and burlap!"

Tootsie's thinking was as chaotic as her sense of fashion. "Scatterbrained" was the word her friends most often used about her. She leapt from topic to topic without introduction or transition, so that it was sometimes hard to follow her in conversation, and she constantly jumped to conclusions—frequently the wrong conclusions. Angela Benbow was a formidable conclusion-jumper herself, but she often said that Tootsie was as likely to add up two and two and make twenty-two, as she was to make four.

On the other hand, Tootsie was a warmhearted, generous soul with nothing but kind intentions toward her fellow man. In a tightly knit community like a retirement home, where everybody knows everybody else and everybody gossips about everybody else, a slighting word can be misinterpreted as a grave insult and mild annoyance can build to a feud. So Tootsie was popular with the other residents because she never took offense and never spoke ill of anyone.

All the same, Tootsie—to the surprise of her fellow residents—had decided to leave her comfortable apartment and abandon the pleasant routine established over her years at Camden-sur-Mer in favor of moving to the new retirement home up the hill. "But why?" Angela Benbow had asked her, when Tootsie announced her decision to a little group of her special friends one day when they had gathered in the lobby before lunch. "Why in the world do you want to move at all, let alone up there?"

"Well, I met these delightful people from The Golden Years. The Dusenbergs. I've gone over to their place for meals, you know, and to play bingo with them and to see a special concert a couple of times. They're awfully nice to be with, and it's very pleasant up there. Really. And then The Golden Years offered me a cut rate on rent. Well, I couldn't ignore that. Everything costs so much these days, and being on a fixed income, I really do have to think about expenses."

"A cut rate?" Emma Grant, tall and gaunt, perked up and adjusted her hearing aid, as though to be certain she had heard correctly. "Now that is interesting. We've had two rate increases in the past three years here. I might be interested in that new place myself, if it costs less."

"That reduced rate is just for my first year. And it's only if one signs up by June. It's just to help them fill up some of their rooms while they're getting started," Tootsie said apologetically. "Unless you made up your mind in a hurry you could miss out on the offer. Anyway, it isn't just the money, you know. It was the idea of being near my new friends, the Dusenbergs. I really enjoy their company—not that I don't like being with all of you, of course. It's just . . . Well, when I was down here and they were up there, they only came to see me maybe once a month and I only got up there maybe two or three times all together. They've been urging me to consider the move because we could visit each other more often if we lived in the same place. So . . . ."

"I think you're being terribly silly," Angela Benbow snapped. Angela might be a woman of tiny stature, but her voice was the kind that made people sit up straighter and listen more attentively. As an admiral's wife she had heard, admired, and imitated her husband's tone of command; now as an admiral's widow, the mellowing effects of age and the demands of communal living in a retirement home had generally softened her, brought her to assume a more tactful approach to her fellow man. Once in a while, however, she slipped and spoke with as much acerbity as ever. "Even sillier than usual," she added now, unaware of the fact that Tootsie cringed a bit. "I mean, who would move if they didn't have to? It's such an upset. I moved often enough when my husband was alive to know all about the joys of moving day; the Navy moves their officers around every few years. And even when the service takes charge, there's all kinds of sorting and packing and unpacking and rearranging you have to do. I wouldn't go through all that if I didn't have to. And you don't have to. Think about it, Tootsie. You've decorated your apartment here just the way you like it, you have your friends here, your daily routine . . . If you move up to The Golden Years you'll have to start all over again."

"Angela's absolutely right," Caledonia Wingate chimed in. Angela had been about to continue, but Caledonia—a woman of Junoesque proportions—was serenely unaware of the fact that she was rolling into the conversation like a juggernaut. Caledonia Wingate was also an admiral's widow, and Angela didn't intimidate her one bit; Caledonia simply rumbled along, ignoring Angela's obvious desire to speak herself. "Moving's a terrible pain, any way you slice it, and I've had plenty of moving in my life, too, so I know. But there's more to it than that. Up at The Golden Years, you'll be away from the ocean. Way away! Living here you always get a nice little breeze off the sea. Up there, it's easily three or four degrees warmer, and you'd only get a sea breeze on a really windy day! And what I think is, there's no point in living in a coastal town like Camden unless you live within sight of the sea."

"Oh, yes! The view!" The comment came in a rapturous sigh from little Mary Moffet. Ordinarily she listened, rather than spoke, when she was with her friends; she was painfully shy, partly because of her stature, she being the only person in all of Camden-sur-Mer who was smaller than Angela Benbow. Being tiny had never slowed Angela's assertive presence one iota, but it seemed to inhibit Mary, who shrank back as soon as she'd spoken, as though hoping that perhaps her remark had gone unheard.

But Angela had heard and (to Mary's relief) nodded her agreement most vigorously. "Mary's right. That wretched view! On the one side, the rear end of a motel. On the other side, the city's main office building. And across the back, the San Diego Freeway. Honestly! At least here, if we're bored with television, we can look right out at the ocean."

But Tootsie was not to be swayed from her decision. "The freeway can be interesting too," she said defensively. "All the different cars in bright colors, and now and then a wreck . . . My friend Jenny Du-senberg swears she saw a family of illegal aliens crawl out of a stalled pickup truck, one time, dodge through the traffic, climb the steel-mesh fence, and jump off into a city street and run away. Now tell me that's not interesting! As for looking at the ocean, well, that's not so wonderful, either. It doesn't *do* anything. It just *is!*"

"The waves . . ." Angela began.

"What about them?" Tootsie said. "They just go up and down, up and down. Exactly the same thing all day, every day!"

Just at that moment, the recorded Westminster chimes sounded over the lobby's loudspeaker system, and lunch was served. Since nothing short of an earthquake registering at least a 6.1 on the Rich-ter scale could have deterred the residents of Camden-sur-Mer from their meals, and since Tootsie's friends sat at several different tables in the dining room, general discussion ceased. All the same, Tootsie's friends were concerned and brought up the subject of her move at every opportunity.

They might as well have saved their breath. Within the week a Mayflower van pulled up at the side door of the main building and Tootsie's possessions were loaded in, driven away, and presumably set up again in her new quarters at The Golden Years. The residents watched the move and commented on it, but within another week, Tootsie had passed out of their collective and individual conscious-ness. Her decision to move had been, by comparison with the usual day-to-day news they shared, a mild bombshell, it is true. But even a minor sensation eventually subsides, and Tootsie was gradually for-gotten until three weeks to the day after her departure, she returned.

That particular morning hadn't begun especially well for Caledo-nia. Nothing special, just that Caledonia was a night person and morning was never her best time. She might turn the lights off in her garden apartment at midnight out of deference to her neighbors whose bedroom windows faced her across the expanse of grass and flowers. But the blue eye of her television set often shone on, un-winking, till well toward dawn as she watched Jay Leno and David Letterman, Conan O'Brien and the all-night movies, Ted Turner's various news stations, the Home Shopping Network, and sometimes even the nationwide weather reports. As a result, she stayed abed in the morning as late as she dared. Breakfast was served at Camden-sur-Mer, however, only from 7:00 till 9:00. So if Caledonia wanted to be served her breakfast instead of stumbling around her kitchenette with eyes half-closed, groping for the Wheaties and fumbling for the milk, she had to rise by at least 8:35 so she could get to the dining room in the main building before the big double doors were closed again until lunch time.

"If you don't want to cook for yourself, there are a lot of nice restaurants in Camden," Angela said once, tired of hearing Caledonia complain about having to get up at what she called "an ungodly hour . . ." to be fed. "You could always go out to eat breakast at some time that would suit you."

"When the food here is better than in any restaurant? And closer. I only have to walk a few steps to get to the dining room here. Besides, I pay for three meals a day as part of my fees here each month. I'm not going to pay again at a restaurant."

"Why not just skip breakfast?" Angela asked.

Caledonia swept her hands broadly outward across the vast expanse of her caftan, the garment she habitually wore because it hid her generous outlines, and laughed hugely. "Please! Do you think I've ever voluntarily skipped a meal in my life?"

Thus it was that Caledonia was stumbling grumpily up the walk that ran down the garden's center, intent only on getting to the main building without tripping over anything, when Tootsie Armstrong appeared on the sidewalk in front of her. "Oh, Caledonia, I'm so glad I found you," Tootsie chattered. "You're the very person I was coming to see. Or rather, I wanted to see you and Angela both. In fact, I stopped by her apartment first . . ." she gestured back toward the main building where Angela's apartment was located. "But she isn't in. Do you think she's gone out walking or something?"

"Very possible," Caledonia growled. "Incomprehensible to me that she or anybody would want to march around, gawking at the scenery and working up a sweat at this hour, but she's one of those who goes walking after she's had breakfast. So I suppose . . . why'd you want to see us?"

"I need your help." Tootsie's usually cheerful face was creased in a deep frown. "There are such odd things going on . . . Maybe you won't think it's serious, Caledonia, but it's very upsetting to me. I've even thought of leaving . . . Leaving up there and coming back here, I mean. Nobody up there even seems concerned, but it's making me so nervous . . ."

Caledonia had stopped walking when Tootsie began to speak. Now she began to move again, slowly and majestically, toward her objective: the dining room and her breakfast. "What exactly is it that's making you so nervous?" Tootsie tottered along beside Caledonia, stumbling over an uneven concrete square in the walk so that Caledonia had to reach out a huge arm to steady her. "Wore those silly little high heels again today, didn't you?" Caledonia asked, glaring in the general direction of Tootsie's feet.

"Well, you know," Tootsie apologized, "they make my legs seem . . ."

"You have on slacks today, Tootsie," Caledonia snorted impatiently. "Nobody can see your legs, even if they were inclined to look, at this hour. Listen, come with me and let me have coffee and something to eat and we'll talk at the table, when I have my head screwed on the right way. I can't even think yet."

The two entered the dining room and Tootsie seated herself meekly at Caledonia's table. She might be in some kind of distress, but she recognized Caledonia's need to fuel the furnace with calories—and to light the fires of intelligence with an adequate dosage of caffeine. She smiled appreciatively when Chita Cassidy, the waitress on duty that morning, recognized her and welcomed her back, and she accepted the offer of coffee for herself, but she said very little till Caledonia had downed at least two cups and poured out a third. Then Caledonia sighed gustily and leaned back in her chair. "All right, Tootsie. I can see and hear just fine, now. And even think a little. So I'm ready to listen to whatever is troubling you. You've got a problem with your new apartment?"

"Oh, not with the apartment itself. It's quite wonderful. A two-room suite—so different from the one-room studio apartment I had here. And lots of closets and shelves . . . I never had enough space for things here. Half the things I owned were left in the basement storage bins packed into boxes."

"Well then, is there a problem with your plumbing? Something's always going wrong with it here, and . . ."

"No, not really. It's a new building, after all. Oh, I miss having a tub, but . . ."

"No tub? Good heavens!"

"We just have showers. They're nice ones, but I do miss soaking in a lovely, hot bath once in a while. No-no-no, the bathroom is nice."

"Is the food good?"

"Well, it's all right, I guess. Very healthy, I suppose. It's not as tasty as the food here, and it isn't served very graciously, but it's not that."

"Then what on earth is it, Tootsie dear? Oh, hand me the sugar bowl from the next table there behind you, will you? This one seems to have emptied itself completely."

Tootsie obliged, and then she began to fidget in her chair. "Oh dear, Caledonia. This is so difficult. You're going to think I'm quite loony, I suppose . . ."

"I've always thought you were a little eccentric, dear, but most of us are, you know. The older we get, the less we care what others think, and the more we tend to do what we please no matter how odd it looks. Another thing about getting on in years . . . we've heard everything, one time or another, and we're very hard to shock. So go ahead and tell me and I promise not to laugh or gasp or . . . well, anyhow, go ahead. Tell me."

Tootsie sighed deeply. "All right. It's ghosts. I think that place is haunted."

"Ghosts!"

"Oh, yes. I can't think what else it could be, you know. So I believe there are ghosts up there at The Golden Years. And it's about to drive me crazy. I'm not sure I'm going to be able to stand it."

Caledonia frowned and killed a minute by buttering a sweet roll while she thought. "Listen, Tootsie," she finally said, "I'm not making fun of your concerns, believe me. But I don't even believe in haunted houses, so you can imagine that the notion of a haunted brick factory doesn't seem very credible to me."

"A . . . brick factory?"

"That institution you live in now. Ghosts belong where there are bay windows and widow's walks and circular staircases, not in the midst of all that stainless steel and glass. October in New England, that's where ghosts belong. A cold wind swirling the falling leaves, sleety rain, clouds scudding over the face of the moon, old graveyards with mossy tombstones tilted at angles . . ."

"I knew you'd think I was crazy! But what else could it be? First of all, there are the voices. I hear them sometimes out in our courtyard, very late at night after everybody's in bed and asleep. Our building is a hollow square, you know. Some of the apartments look out at the street or the freeway, but some of them look inward toward the court-yard. Just as your rooms here at Camden-sur-Mer do, except that this building is a U and our building is a squared O."

"Yes-yes-yes . . ." Caledonia waved an impatient hand. "You have a courtyard. A paved courtyard you mean?"

"No. It's mostly a lawn with some shrubbery. No flowers, like here. Maybe they'll put some in someday. But now it's mainly just grass and bushes. Some of the men use a corner of the lawn for a putting green, and there are three or four people who play croquet every day. And that's where our swimming pool is, of course."

"A swimming pool! Pretty fancy stuff, Tootsie. But a haunted swimming pool? That's hard to believe."

"No, the swimming pool isn't what's haunted. Or, well, maybe it is. I can't tell. All I know is I'll be sitting there watching TV and I'll hear people talking and I'll look out and I can't see anybody out there at all. And then there are the lights . . ."

"Lights?"

"Yes. Yellow lights. Out there in the courtyard."

"Lights so people can swim at night?"

Tootsie shook her head. "We're not allowed to use the courtyard at night because it might make too much noise. We go to bed early, you know. So there aren't any lights around the pool or over the croquet field. Do you call it a field, or is it a court?"

"I haven't the faintest idea. But listen. About those lights. Aren't they just safety lights like we have here along our garden sidewalk? You know, to keep people from tripping at night."

"No. I mean, we had safety lights, all right, but they were turned off because the people in the ground floor apartments complained that the lights shone into their windows all night long and kept them awake. Besides, the lights I'm talking about move. They bob around. They move over things . . . across things. I saw a movie once about ghosts and when one ghost tried to pick up a book, he couldn't. His hands just kind of slid over the surface. And that's what this reminds me of. The light kind of slides over things, like it was a ghost trying to touch . . ."

"Tootsie, I'd bet anything you like that there's a reasonable, every-day explanation that doesn't involve ghosts at all."

"Maybe so," Tootsie said skeptically. "But I haven't told you the most worrying thing of all. The little child crying. Almost every night. At least I think it's a little child. Kind of moaning and bawling . . . a hoarse little voice outside my room in the corridor. As soon as I hear that sobbing sound, I run as quick as I can, but when I open the door and look out, there's nobody there! Caledonia, I'm scared to death! It has to be a ghost. What else . . ."

"How about the wind? Or some motor starting up, like a refrigerator in the kitchen, maybe? Some motors whine, you know." Tootsie shook her head and didn't bother to answer. "Or—I don't know quite how to put this without sounding insulting and I don't mean to— could you be imagining the sound?"

"Please! I'm not imagining all this. It's a real sound."

"What did your friends up there say about all this?"

"Oh, dear!" Tootsie was wringing her hands. "I mentioned it to the Dusenbergs last week and neither of them had noticed anything unusual. Of course their room faces the freeway, not the courtyard, so maybe they wouldn't have. I should have asked someone else too, I suppose, but I was afraid they'd laugh at me."

"Oh, dear, Tootsie, if I had a nickel for every time someone laughed at me I'd be a millionaire. You mustn't let that bother you. Besides, we laugh at you, Angela and I, and you don't mind that, do you?"

Tootsie shook her head. "Of course not. Because you and Angela don't mean anything by it. You laugh at me in a nice, friendly way, if you know what I mean. But I don't want people I've just met to think I'm crazy or anything. So I haven't asked many questions. I've just kind of hinted. As much as I dared. And nobody seems to have noticed anything unusual. But it's scaring the living daylights out of me, I can tell you."

Caledonia poured herself a fourth cup of coffee. "Well, I suppose you have reason to try to find out what's really going on. But what makes you think Angela and I are the ones to help you, Tootsie dear? I mean, suppose there really is some kind of haunting going on at your new home. Angela and I aren't into psychic research. Never pretended to be."

"No, but you solve crimes."

"Well, crimes, yes. Or rather, to be accurate, we've been able to help out with a police investigation a couple of times."

"There you are! And ghosts can't be all that different, can they? Well, I know ghosts are different, obviously, but finding out about them should be the same. Mind you, I don't want you to let on you're investigating. I don't want people to know I'm worried about anything so . . . so weird. So please don't tell anybody what you're doing."

"Gee, I don't know, Tootsie . . . How would we find out about your ghosts from this distance? Especially if you don't want us to question the residents up there. And we'd have to go up there day after day to do whatever we could do, and . . ."

"Oh, I've got that all worked out. You'll move in. Oh, just for a day or two," Tootsie added hastily as she saw Caledonia's look of dismay. "There are a couple of guest apartments on the ground floor that a prospective resident can stay in while he or she looks the place over. You could claim you want to move in, stay a few nights in the guest apartment, and pretend all your looking around was because you might become tenants."

"Just a day or two, you say?"

"Oh, I should think so. And they're very nice little studio apartments, those guest quarters. Caledonia, please . . . I'd be ever so grateful . . ."

Caledonia grinned. "Tell you what. At least I'll talk it over with Angela, that much I can promise. And if I can talk her into it, we'll do it. We'll pretend to be prospects and move in up there for a short stay while we nose around."

"Oh, Caledonia! That would be such a relief!"

So Tootsie, bubbling with gratitude, departed. Caledonia returned to her own apartment and settled down to phone Angela's quarters every fifteen minutes or so until she got an answer about midmorning, followed by an invitation to come over and talk about ". . . whatever it is you want to discuss . . ."

Caledonia didn't take long to explain Tootsie's problem and Tootsie's request. She wasn't a bit surprised that Angela registered reluctance and no little skepticism. "What makes Tootsie think we can play ghostbusters anyway?" Angela asked. "It all sounds so bizarre. California and ghosts just don't go together. I mean, it's like saying you were worried about a haunted sushi bar. It's more funny than frightening."

"Exactly what I told her," Caledonia nodded. "There's obviously some natural explanation. Or else Tootsie is seeing things."

"Cal, do you think maybe Tootsie is starting to show signs of senility? I mean, I don't like to admit it, but I look for signs of the start of senility in myself all the time. Don't you? When I can't remember someone's name, I think 'Is this it? Is it starting now?' If I forget an appointment . . ."

"Angela," Caledonia said gently, "don't talk about things like that. All of us are scared to death we'll get Alzheimer's. But it doesn't do a bit of good to worry about it, so we might as well just keep doing whatever we want to do for as long as we can, don't you agree? Anyway, that's really beside the point, isn't it? I mean, the point is, whether Tootsie's getting silly in the head or not, something is going on up there at The Golden Years that's frightening her. And she wants our help in figuring out what it is, whether it's ghosts or not. I'm not fond enough of Tootsie Armstrong to walk into the fiery furnace for her, so to speak. Come to that, I probably wouldn't even walk across a hot sidewalk barefoot for her. But she was one of our special group of friends here for years and years, and maybe we owe her . . . I suppose I could do it by myself, but it's never half as much fun doing things alone. So how about it. Are you interested?"

"Of course I'm interested," Angela said, just as Caledonia had known she would. With her curiosity and her indomitable spirit, Angela would have taken a happy interest in the details of her own execution. But Angela was nobody's fool, and she put her finger directly on the heart of the problem. "The difficulty is, I'm not sure there's anything we could do about whatever it is. I mean, suppose it really were some kind of . . . you know, some supernatural thing? Not that I believe in ghosts, of course. I don't. But just suppose. We're not expert in anything like that."

"To be fair, we're not experts at anything," Caledonia said cheerfully. "But we do understand senior citizens, being at that stage of life ourselves, and we have had experience with people who were up to no good. I think we could come up with some practical solution to Tootsie's little problems, whatever they are."

Angela nodded. "Well, I suppose we could. This place here is getting a little bit dull anyhow. I mean, before lunch yesterday, the whole conversation was about which new flowers had bloomed and what the gardeners were going to do about the snails. So I suppose . . ." The truth was, Angela was absolutely fascinated. But for a little while she kept up her show of reluctance. It would be helpful later on, if everything went wrong with their project, to remind Caledonia that it wasn't Angela's idea. That Angela wasn't the one who wanted to plunge in. "Anyway, if you insist, Caledonia, I can hardly say no," was Angela's way of shifting the responsibility.

"Oh, I insist," Caledonia grinned. She could afford to be generous and take the blame for their enterprise.

"And now I should go to the council meeting . . ." Angela picked up her purse and headed for the door of her apartment.

"The council meeting! Of course!" Caledonia smacked her broad forehead. "I'd lost track! That meeting's today?" She strode for the door. "I wouldn't miss this for anything. What're we waiting for?"

Ghosts and detective work and Tootsie's possible senility and the chance to snoop around at The Golden Years were all forgotten as Caledonia charged out of Angela's apartment, heading down the four steps to the lobby, Angela skittering along at her heels and plunging across to the chapel-theatre-conference-room where the Residents' Council was holding its twice-monthly meetings.

CHAPTER

2

THE RESIDENTS' COUNCIL OF Camden-sur-Mer was the invention of Olaf Torgeson, who found it difficult to deal with his residents individually and directly. It was far more convenient, not to mention less upsetting to his ulcers, to learn his tenants' suggestions second-hand, funneled to him through a single spokesman, and he was well pleased that Trinita Stainsbury, one of the few residents who consistently agreed with his opinions and who referred to him as "our beloved administrator" and "our dear Mr. Torgeson," appointed herself the chair of the Residents' Council and, as she simpered to Mr. Torgeson, ". . . their spokesperson, rather than spokesman. We must keep abreast of the current fashion for changing the Teutonic base of our English language, mustn't we?"

"Beg pardon?" Torgeson was completely mystified, and a pedantic explanation that the Germanic form *man* correctly translated to "person," not to "masculine person," simply left him more muddled than ever. Fortunately Trinita kept right on talking, presenting the latest of the residents' concerns, and he had no need to say anything intelligible. He just let her talk. When she finished and handed over a copy of the petition she had come to present—a request that the cracked tile in the front entryway be replaced or repaired—he was able to thank her warmly and usher her out with a huge smile. As for the request for maintenance, it was handed to Juana Ortega to file with the other residents' petitions and it was, like most of the others, quickly forgotten.

As a general rule, Torgeson stayed far away from the Residents' Council meetings himself. He had learned his lesson two years before when the little fountain near the foot of the garden needed to be repainted. It consisted of a circular concrete pool, from the center of which rose a group of three giant seahorses nearly five feet tall. The graceful curve of their outsized bodies was complemented by the stream of water that bubbled from each of their mouths and arched into the pond below. Some long-forgotten administrator at Camden-sur-Mer had decreed that the fountain be covered in whitewash, but it had been many years since the paint was refreshed, and the fountain's surface now looked positively leprous, with patches of gray concrete showing wherever the white paint had flaked off. And Torgeson, moved by who-knew-what human impulse, had come before the council to find out if his tenants had any suggestions for the new paint job.

"We could," he said expansively, "paint the pool beneath a soft blue and the bodies of the seahorses a kind of aqua green, you know? That might be very attractive . . ."

"Watermelon!" Mrs. Pollard said loudly.

"I beg your pardon?"

"Watermelon. I heard that Elsa Clinch—you know, the one with the English accent on CNN? I heard her say pink would be all the rage this season. Paint 'em watermelon pink."

"But Mrs. Pollard," Torgeson said, "pink water? Pink seahorses?"

"Personally," Janice Felton said from the other side of the room, "I've always thought those hot pinks and cerises were too jarring. I'd suggest a kind of melon or mango. A little on the coral side, you see?"

"That's silly," Mr. Markham snorted. "Whoever heard of coral seahorses? Whoever heard of a coral ocean?"

"How about the Coral Sea?" Janice Felton asked huffily. "What about that?"

"Coral's too orange, in my opinion. Who wants an orange fountain? Brown's better," George Julian said. "Nice neutral color. Like the carpet we got for our apartment. Doesn't show the dirt, goes with everything . . ."

"A brown fountain?" Torgeson said helplessly. Things were, in his opinion, getting completely out of hand.

"Why not brown?" Mr. Grogan spoke up from the corner. "Goes just right with those beasts in the middle—the vomiting vermin!"

"Mr. Grogan!" Trinita Stainsbury grasped her gavel. "Mr. Grogan, you aren't even a member of the council! By rights you don't have an opinion."

"Got plenty of opinions," Mr. Grogan snarled. Others might have a drinking problem—Grogan had a sobriety problem. In his cups, he was unpredictable and unsteady, but at least he was mellow and occasionally even amiable and amusing. Between drinks he was sour-tempered and positively volcanic in his irascibility. "Got opinions, and I'll give 'em if I want to!"

Trinita banged the gavel loudly. "Order. Order! Mr. Grogan, I meant you don't have a voice in this meeting."

"Get that man out of here," Mrs. Pollard whined. "He makes me nervous."

"Yes," George Julian agreed, "get the sergeant-at-arms to escort Mr. Grogan out."

"We don't have a sergeant-at-arms," Trinita said. "We'll just have to appeal to his gentlemanly instincts. Mr. Grogan . . . Mr. Grogan . . ." A loud snore came from the side of the room where Grogan sat slumped in his chair, perhaps not quite sober after all and certainly dozing. Grogan's snore was echoed by another from the other side of the room; Jim Goodwin had also fallen asleep, not because of drink but because of age. He had a tendency to nap in all but the most lively entertainments and had been known to nod off right in the middle of a conversation.

"Let 'em sleep," Mrs. Pollard suggested. "Now about that fountain. You don't like pink, so how about painting it lavender? That's such a beautiful color. Not purple, mind you, but a light shade like spring lilacs . . ."

"Oh, dear no. Purple is so . . . so garish," Janice Felton protested. "But if you were to tone the color down to, say, periwinkle blue . . ."

Torgeson left the meeting with a horrible headache, determined on two things: first, simply to refresh the original coat of plain white, and second, never to attend another council meeting if he could avoid it. At his direction, the maintenance crew painted the fountain shiny white, but the very next night after everyone else was asleep, someone—and Torgeson always suspected Mr. Grogan but never could prove it—someone tiptoed down the garden with their own cans of paint and gave the seahorses big blue eyes with long black eyelashes.

So, for the sake of his ulcers and his blood pressure, Torgeson did not ordinarily attend the council meetings. But today's meeting was to be a very special one, devoted to the controversial subject of allowing the owning of pets by the residents, and Torgeson had a big stake in the council's adopting the plan. It was an idea Torgeson had come up with some weeks before at a time when he was feeling particularly desperate. Usually there was a waiting list for the occasional vacancy at Camden-sur-Mer, but for some reason the last few apartments to be vacated had remained empty. Of course competition from the newly opened Golden Years could account for some of it, but Torgeson had noted a pattern among his list of prospects: one after another they had expressed dismay that they could not bring Fido or Fluffy with them to their new home. As one had explained, her cat was a companion and a friend; she'd much sooner have given up one of her children—now grown up but perpetually ungrateful—than to give up her beloved pet. Torgeson had gone back to his office, the unsigned contract still in his hand and a new idea in his head.

He rather tentatively broached the notion of allowing residents' pets to Trinita Stainsbury first. "I've heard that some retirement homes . . ." and "What do you suppose our residents would think if . . ." Trinita expressed enthusiasm, but Trinita would have expressed enthusiasm if Torgeson had suggested putting a thatched roof on the main building, establishing classes in kickboxing, and hiring Madonna as the new receptionist; if her dear Mr. Torgeson suggested it, it had to be a good idea. So her dear Mr. Torgeson knew better than to predict by Trinita's responses what others would say. Instead he dropped the subject for the moment. He let Trinita pass the idea along to other residents and he kept a wary ear open as he walked through the dining room or the lobby. Thus he soon realized that there was deep disagreement among his residents on the subject; he was going to be in a lot of hot water with the tenants whichever way he decided. So his solution was to pass the buck to the Residents' Council. Let them take the criticism, he told himself. Thus it was that Torgeson formally requested the council to come up with a Pet Plan and warned them that he would be breaking his own precedent to attend their next meeting. He didn't bother to tell them that he intended to fortify himself for the ordeal with at least a jigger of whiskey and with several extra-strength Excedrin.

There were no absentees for this council meeting. Angela, usually among the early arrivals, found that the little theatre off the lobby was already packed with council members and several miscellaneous residents who had decided that this was too important an issue to leave to their elected representatives without supervision.

"Caledonia, you haven't been to a meeting since you were elected," Angela scolded as she and her best friend hurried across the lobby toward the meeting. "Why today?"

"Because they're going to bring dogs into this place over my dead body."

"Cal! I thought you liked dogs! I'm frightened of them because I was bit by a dog when I was little. But you always said you liked . . ."

"I love 'em. But not here. Not in a communal-living situation with senior citizens. I mean, think about it. Dogs bark. All night long, sometimes. We can't have that. We need our sleep. Now shush . . ." She put a finger to her lips as they entered the little chapel and slid into seats at the rear of the group that was already gathered.

"Order. The meeting will come to order." As they took their places, Trinita Stainsbury, standing at the lectern in front of the group, was already tapping her gavel and intoning her mantra. "Order, please. Order."

"We're completely in order, thank you," Caledonia growled, but she kept her volume low and spoke behind her hand.

"You know why we're here," Trinita began, laying down the gavel and patting her chestnut coiffure, recently dyed to match the earth tones she was favoring in her clothing this season. "So let's wade right in and start the discussion."

"No discussion needed," Mrs. Pollard said firmly. "I vote yes."

"There's no motion on the floor," Trinita said. "What are you voting for?"

"For pets, of course," Mrs. Pollard said.

"No-no-no," Janice Felton waded in. "Some people are allergic. And the noise . . . all that barking . . ."

"What barking?" Sadie Mandelbaum asked blankly. Sadie was profoundly deaf and hadn't been troubled by a barking dog in years.

"Who's going to pick up the garbage, if somebody's dog tips over my trash can?" Jim Goodwin said. "I live in the cottages and we have trash cans out behind . . ."

"We know, we know. But put the lid on tight and a dog won't be able to knock it over," Sheila Robertson said. "He might not even smell food scraps inside . . ."

"Sure he can," George Julian said. "Just because you can't, it doesn't mean a dog can't. They got noses that . . ."

"Will you furnish all the dog owners with pooper-scoopers?" Jim Goodwin asked. "The missus and I like to walk across the lawns here. And especially if somebody were to bring in a big dog, like a Great Dane or a Saint Bernard . . ."

"Perhaps we could set weight limits on the dogs we'd admit,"

Mrs. Pollard suggested. "What would be reasonable? Twenty pounds?"

"Saint Bernards drool," Betty Wisdom put in. "I vote we don't admit anybody with a pet that drools."

"We already have pets here, you know," Tom Brighton said gently. "People own fish and birds . . ."

Caledonia spoke up, and even using a reasonable tone, her voice rumbled out and silenced the others. "If you could keep a dog in an aquarium or a cage, I might vote yes. But I'm going to have to say that bringing into a communal-living situation an animal that barks and sheds and poops and raids the trash is just plain impossible."

Torgeson listened as the debate continued for another five minutes or so, and his sense of dismay mounted. He had not thought through the problems, simply assuming that what was good for his cash-flow problems would be judged good for the institution as a whole. But he could already anticipate added maintenance staff, the cost of pooper-scoopers, the expense of tight-lidded trash cans, perhaps even a suit against Camden-sur-Mer if some large dog should show its affectionate nature by jumping up against one of the frailer residents and knocking him or her down . . .

"All right, all right," he intervened to cut discussion short. "I can understand your problems with having residents' dogs here and I yield to your wisdom. The suggestion is withdrawn."

"Well, now," Janice Felton said, "that takes care of the matter of dogs, but cats are quite different of course."

"You bet they are," George Julian said with a snort. "Haughty, cold-natured, sneaky . . ."

"Nonsense," Janice snapped. "They just show affection in a different way. My Bootsie loved me as much as any dog could. Bootsie was black with white paws, and . . ."

"Don't come when they're called," Mrs. Pollard said. "Don't pay any attention at all when you tell 'em 'No.' Fact is, I think they understand perfectly well and they do the opposite just to be contrary."

"I never had a cat," Caledonia Wingate said, "and I don't even like 'em much, so I'm no authority, but at least a cat wouldn't jump up and breathe hamburger fumes in your face and get muddy paw prints on your dress. Nor bark all night."

"And you don't need a pooper-scooper. Cats do their own pooper-scooping, you know," Tom Brighton laughed. "If you want to allow pets at all, I can see a certain logic to a cat being brought into a communal-living situation."

"But allergies . . ." a voice said.

"Don't cats suck the breath out of you while you're asleep?" someone asked.

"Nose-in-the-air attitude," George Julian muttered. "Sneaky, underhanded . . ."

"Well, I may not be a cat person," Caledonia rumbled, "but I'm positive that's a lot of foolishness."

"Of course it is," Angela put in tartly. "Cats aren't sneaky. They just move quietly. At least most of them do, and . . ."

Olaf Torgeson could stay out of the discussion no longer. "The Golden Years," he put in emphatically, "has benefitted from their policy to allow residents to own pets. And they have filled a higher percentage of their recent vacancies than we. If we don't do something, and do it soon, you're facing a rate increase here! And that's the bottom line!"

There was a lengthy silence as residents looked unhappily at each other, and at last Trinita Stainsbury spoke the words of capitulation. "Does anyone want to put all this in the form of a motion?"

There was a buzz of whispers, another silence, and at last Tom Brighton got to his feet. "Madam Chairman," he said.

"Chairperson," Trinita corrected automatically.

"Madam Chairperson," Tom went on smoothly, undeterred by the interruption, "under the circumstances, I'm going to move that we try bringing in a cat or two. No dogs, mind you. But I suggest that the next couple of residents to take vacancies in the garden apartments be allowed to bring their cats with them."

"If they own cats," George Julian said, *sotto voce* but perfectly audible, "and the more fool they!"

"And I'll leave the details to our administrator . . ." Tom bowed slightly toward the now beaming Olaf Torgeson, ". . . but I suggest that the council meet again in six months to evaluate the test run. At that time, if there have been serious problems, we can terminate the experiment. How does that sound?"

Council members and non-council members, all talking at once, expressed general approval, with many rising from their seats and beginning to edge toward the exit. "Wait, wait," Trinita Stainsbury pleaded. The gavel banged again and again. "Order! The meeting will come to order! We need a formal vote on the motion. Order!"

"Oh, tie a can to it, Trinita," Caledonia said. "The matter's settled and you know it. We're just talking through our hats now because none of us has ever tried mixing a retirement home with pet owning. After a trial run of six months, we'll all be much smarter and we'll know whether we can live with the policy or not."

"We're going to know much sooner than that, Cal," Angela whispered. "If we move into The Golden Years to help Tootsie Armstrong, we're going to see how it works right away."

"That's right! I forgot. Well, I suppose we better notify our management here we'll be gone for a couple of days, and go pack our bags."

"All right, but you do the notifying," Angela said, "because I'm going to be busy the rest of today deciding what clothes to take along with me. What would the proper attire be for going ghost hunting, anyway?"

CHAPTER

3

THE GOLDEN YEARS MIGHT contrast sharply with Camden-sur-Mer in architecture and atmosphere, but at least as a group, the residents at the two retirement homes were very much alike. Angela and Caledonia, introduced around by Tootsie Armstrong in what Tootsie called "our commons room," where several residents were playing cards or backgammon, reading, or just chatting, noticed there were far more women than men, and everywhere one looked one saw gray hair and bald heads, glasses and hearing aids, canes and walkers.

"Everybody's so *old!*" Angela whispered again to Caledonia. "I never noticed that at home—at Camden-sur-Mer. I mean, we *are* old, of course, but . . ." She shrugged and Caledonia grinned. But she knew what Angela meant. Strangers who happened to be old, encountered one at a time, were just gray-haired strangers. Old people who were friends and acquaintances were just friends and acquaintances who were getting on in years. But a herd of people, all of whom were old, were unmistakably, overwhelmingly *old people*.

Tootsie Armstrong led them to a vacant sofa on one side of the room and said "Sit here and let me introduce you to a couple of special friends. Well, not friends, I suppose, more like acquaintances, since I've only known them a couple of weeks. How long does it take before you can really call someone a friend? I never quite understood . . ."

"Tootsie," Caledonia commanded, "friend will do fine as a description. You just bring your friends over, okay? Oooof!" The rush of expelled air was because Caledonia, expecting to sink into the arms of soft upholstery, had met unyielding leatherette and some sort of solid steel springing that gave not an inch, even under her bulk. "Sit down carefully, Angela," she cautioned, "if you don't want a fractured coccyx."

Tootsie returned shortly with a man and woman in tow. "Harvey and Della Ridgeway," she explained. "They live on the top floor. We often sit together at meals."

"Pleased to meetcha," Harvey Ridgeway said. He was one of those men with an upper and lower torso that don't seem to match—smallish legs and hips covered in trousers that cinched tight under an apple-shaped belly that strained the cloth of his brightly printed Hawaiian shirt. "You girls from Iowa too, maybe?"

"Pay no attention to Harvey," his wife said comfortably. She was as lean and angular as her husband was rotund. "He always wants to find people from back home. He just hasn't got used to being a Californian yet. Tell you what I mean . . . we retired two years ago come June, and I've had to listen for two solid years to Harvey grouse because there's no snow."

"Don't seem natural," he nodded, "to go right out and start the car in the middle of January without havin' to shovel to get there."

"Have you been here at The Golden Years for long?" Angela said, getting right down to business. "How do you like it? Comfortable and cozy here?"

"Nearly four months. But I'm not sure we mean to stay," Della Ridgeway said.

Caledonia pricked up her ears. "Something wrong with this place? If we should want to move in, we'd need to know . . ."

The Ridgeways looked at each other. "Well . . ." Mrs. Ridgeway began tentatively.

"Della, I'm gonna tell 'em," Harvey interrupted. "Just to start with, I don't like the food very much. No taste, you know? And small, small portions, but you can't get seconds if you're still hungry."

"Harvey likes his food," Della explained. "My complaint is that they rush you through meals so fast. I understand that they want the staff to clean up the place—swab it all down with Pine-Sol and then get the tables set for the next meal. But meals should be a time when you can sit and chat with friends . . ."

"Della don't eat very fast. She pokes at her food," Harvey Ridgeway said tolerantly. "Your friend Mrs. Armstrong says you have wonderful food down the hill there at Camden-sur-Mer. Can't imagine why she wanted to move up here, if the food was . . . and why you two girls would want . . ."

"And there are so many rules here," Della Ridgeway went on in an unhappy whine. "Don't bring personal things to the dining room or they'll be confiscated, don't bring food back to your rooms, be on time or you won't get anything to eat . . ."

"What do you mean no personal things in the dining room?" Caledonia said. "I don't understand."

"Well, like your favorite jam or a jar of honey," Harvey Ridgeway said. "Because leave them on the table and the waitresses have to move them aside to clean, they say. But even if there's a good reason, we still got rules for everything . . . a steady stream of do this, do that, don't do the other thing . . ."

"Well, but aren't all retirement communities a little like that?" Angela said. "Or at least I think they have to be, when so many people live together and eat together. Community living takes some getting used to. Some adjusting, and . . ."

"But so much?" Della Ridgeway asked. "I tell you, I feel like a little girl back in boarding school."

"It's certainly not very homelike," her husband said unhappily.

The Ridgeways' complaints were cut short as Tootsie returned alternately pushing and pulling along a smiling, handsome man whose generous, snow-white hair was so wavy and soft that Angela had, as she admitted later, an instant impulse to run her hands through it. "And here's my special friend, Conrad Stone. Connie and I both sing in the choir in chapel each Sunday," Tootsie said, nudging the man forward. "You know the Ridgeways, of course, Connie, but these two are the ones I brought you over here to meet. These are would-be transplants from down the hill, just like I am . . ." And there were introductions again, all around.

Stone surprised Angela by leaning down and giving her shoulders a big squeeze before he pulled a chair over to join the group. He plunked himself into it, next to Angela, and beamed broadly at her and at Caledonia. "Delighted. Really delighted. Truly! It's grand to meet two such lovely ladies. And I do hope you two will indeed consider joining our happy home. Such wonderful folks here . . ." Angela was next to him, and again she was surprised when he reached out to take her hand in his for a moment as he added, "We could always benefit here from the addition of two lively young ladies. The more the merrier, I always say." And he laughed as though he'd made a joke of some kind.

Angela was smiling back at him, but Caledonia frowned, and she

pulled the conversation back to the original point. "How do *you* like
it here, Mr. Stone?" she asked. "The Ridgeways aren't completely
happy with the dining room . . ."

"That really doesn't bother me," Stone said airily. "I'm not a heavy
eater myself." He patted his trim waistline. "Learned to avoid salt
and fat years ago, of course, for my health, and food just doesn't taste
as good without salt. I mean, who wants baked potatoes without butter and maybe some sour cream? So I eat lightly anyhow, and I don't
mind the food here, even though it's very . . . well, it's plain food.
Unimaginative and plain."

"Plain and skimpy," Harvey Ridgeway muttered. "Doggoned meas-
ly portions . . ."

"Food aside," Caledonia pressed on, "how about the rest of this
place? Are you happy here?"

"Well," Stone said, "I'm not all that pleased with the building
itself. Because it's new and designed for . . ." he waved a hand around
at their stark surroundings, ". . . for functional simplicity, as you see.
So they're reluctant to make modifications. To build things we want
built, and to alter things. I'll give you a for instance. I have a cat,
and I'd like a cat door cut into my . . ."

"You have a cat! Now I'm interested in that," Caledonia said.
"How does that work out?"

"Well, that's one of the reasons I came here in the first place instead of considering your lovely home. Here we can have our little
companions—you know, like birds or hamsters or white mice . . ."

"Mice!" Angela's voice was nearly a squeal. "Mice?"

"They're in a cage, of course," Stone laughed. "I think there's only
one residing here right now. At least, only one pet mouse. And if
there are any of the other kind, I haven't seen 'em—probably because
there are several cats here. No dogs are allowed, of course, but . . ."

"Well I should think not!" Caledonia said.

"Caledonia!" Angela nudged her friend hard. "Please! Don't interrupt. We want to know how it's working out, this having pets."
She turned her full attention to Conrad Stone and his beautiful white
mane. "Because I don't know whether you heard, but we're testing
out the same policy down at Camden-sur-Mer. So I'm anxious to
know if it's been a problem here."

"Nobody has complained," Stone said. "It seems to be okay with
everybody. As for me, I certainly know I wouldn't stay in a place that
wouldn't let me keep my Puddin'." A foolish smile crept across his

sculptured features. "That's his name. Puddin'. Beautiful, sleek, black animal, and we're really fond of each other. But he hasn't settled in here yet. He seems restless. I think he'd be much more comfortable if he had his own door, so he could come and go as he pleased. As it is, when I'm away from my apartment, he's confined to quarters, as it were. But no matter how I argue with the management, they won't consent to have a cat flap cut into my door. I've offered to pay for 100 per cent of the work, and . . ."

"You could get your cat flap if you lived in Camden-sur-Mer," Angela said eagerly. "They always redo an apartment for a new tenant, and I'm sure you could have the alterations made, assuming you paid for the carpentry yourself, as you say. You should ask about moving, because of the change in policy. Starting next week, I believe."

"I already have," Stone said. "I inquired there first, when I was looking for a place to call home in my last years. Your place certainly has it over this for beauty, with all those Spanish arches and wrought iron and stucco, that red-tiled roof, not to mention that wonderful garden with the huge old trees and the flowers. I was very disappointed when I heard they had a no-pets policy. But it makes your place much more attractive, if you're going to allow . . . Highly possible. Highly. I'm really interested in . . . in fact, I think I'll phone your Mr. Torgeson for an appointment about a possible move down there, to your home," and he beamed at Angela.

"Cats, mice, hamsters . . . Good night nurse! This place is a menagerie!" Caledonia was muttering in a steady undertone and when Conrad Stone paused for breath, she turned to him and demanded, "Tell me, does everybody here have some kind of pet?"

"Goodness, no," Della Ridgeway undertook to answer. "That needn't stand in your way if you don't like animals and are thinking about moving here. Cats are only allowed if you live on the ground floor. So they can go in and out easily, you know. But Harvey and I, for instance, are up on the third floor, and we couldn't have a cat, could we, Harvey?"

"Right. All the same," Harvey nodded, "and nothing to do with pets, mind you, but we've been thinking about going down to talk to your Mr. Torgeson, too."

"But why? If you don't have a cat yourselves?"

"Well, I'll tell you, Mrs. Wingate . . ." Harvey Ridgeway leaned back expansively and a button on his bright shirt popped open, revealing a wide swath of bare skin. "Your friend Mrs. Armstrong's been talking about the chef down there at that place of yours, and about that dining room, and I gotta tell you, we're tempted. You wait till you've had a meal here and you'll see why."

"Thinking of leaving us, Harvey?" It was Ralph Dusenberg, Tootsie's friend. He, Tootsie, and his wife Jenny were joining the group, and Ralph had caught the last bit of Harvey Ridgeway's comment. "You don't want to take him too seriously, folks. He's always threatening to leave."

"No, sir, Ralph," Harvey Ridgeway said. "This time I mean it. I've about had it with this place for a lot of reasons."

"You remember Angela and Caledonia from when you visited me in Camden-sur-Mer, don't you?" Tootsie Armstrong said, bringing the Dusenbergs into the group. Jenny Dusenberg was a small woman, well preserved and waspish, while her husband was large, florid, and expansive. ("Bet he was a salesman," Angela said later.)

"Certainly. So nice to have you here, girls." But Ralph Dusenberg was thinking about Harvey Ridgeway, not about Angela and Caledonia, and he went right on, "I'd think twice about a move, Harvey. It's expensive. They won't give you back any of your entry fee after three months, and you'd owe another fee going into a new place."

"It ain't a matter of money," Harvey Ridgeway said sulkily. "It's a matter of living where I feel comfortable. The six months I've been here, I've felt like a stranger and I ain't settled down yet. And I'm not sure I ever will settle down, if we stay."

Jenny Dusenberg could see that her husband was about to argue again, and moved between him and Harvey Ridgeway. "Well, if you girls are thinking of moving, I'm glad you're thinking of coming here and joining us. Maybe Della and Harvey aren't happy, but we like the place—it's so orderly and neat and always spotless—and we'd be glad of more people who'd be good company. Like you two."

"Ah, yes." Conrad Stone picked up one of Angela's little hands in his again in a proprietary way. "These two girls may be my neighbors yet—and if they don't decide to move in here, I may move down to be near them." And he beamed first at Angela, then at Caledonia.

"You're thinking of moving too?" Jenny Dusenberg said. "I don't believe it. I thought you enjoyed it here."

"Oh, I do, in a way. But I'm really thinking of Puddin'. I did mention that's the name of my cat, didn't I?"

"You surely did. More than once, if I remember right," Caledonia said impatiently, heaving herself heavily to her feet. "Look, Angela and I have a bit of unpacking to do. And a little exploring. Finding our way around the place. And I'd like to get started before lunch time. So if you'll forgive us, we'll be seeing you all later. Perhaps this afternoon? Or tonight after dinner? So nice to meet you all . . . Come on, Angela . . ." And she swept off, not even waiting for an answer, her flowered silk caftan swirling around her and stirring a breeze as she hurried away.

Angela, pattering obediently along behind her huge friend, was a bit surprised to have Caledonia stop short in the hall, instead of entering her room. "You want to come into my place?"

"What for?"

"Well, I suppose you left those nice people so abruptly because you wanted to talk," Angela said reprovingly. "You didn't even wait for them to say goodbye back to you. Honestly, Cal, you were right next to rude."

"Sorry if I was obvious, but I was really repulsed by that Conrad Stone. What an oily . . ."

"Why, I thought he was charming!" Angela protested.

"Oh, you'd think Dracula was charming, if he kissed your hand before he bit your neck," Caledonia said disgustedly. "I saw that man put an arm around your shoulder as you were introduced. I saw him squeeze your hand. More than once! He was so blatant about his shining up to you, I couldn't help but wonder what he was up to."

"You're just jealous because he didn't put his arm around *your* shoulders," Angela said with spirit. "You'd sing a different tune if he'd been sitting next to you."

"Oh, don't be so silly, Angela! You're an incurable flirt! You should ease up a little. You know nothing at all about this man, but you simper at him and you encourage him . . ."

"Honestly, Caledonia, you sound like my mother. What could possibly happen?"

"The man could be a serial killer, that's what could happen. He could be a con man who lives off women's pensions. He could be married with a wife somewhere. Or maybe he's a bigamist. Not one wife but two or maybe three or four . . ."

Angela turned her little nose as high into the air as she could without dislocating her neck. "Of all the nonsense I ever heard, Caledonia, that's the worst. You shouldn't take such a dislike to a complete stranger from two minutes in his company. Besides, people here know him even if we don't, and they obviously don't think he's a bad

person. You really must try to be polite to Conrad Stone. Being so
friendly and open, he could be a valuable source of information. He
doesn't mind talking."

"He sure doesn't," Caledonia growled. "Okay, I'll behave if you
promise to flirt less. Now come on."

"Where? I thought you wanted to talk."

"No, we can talk later. I told those people we were going exploring,
and that's what I want to do. So let's do it." Angela shrugged her
agreement and they set off. They located the echoing expanse of the
dining room, an exercise room with a lot of equipment standing ready
but unoccupied, and a tiny auditorium. They found a small chapel, a
miniature beauty parlor, and in the long front hallway two doors, side
by side, one marked SHELDON CALLEY, DIRECTOR, and the other
marked ENTER HERE. Angela stuck her head in and saw a secretary typing with ferocious speed at a small computer, her desk mounded with
papers and reference books. "Sorry . . . got the wrong door . . . no problem," Angela burbled as she backed out. The secretary looked back to
her computer screen without a word and went on with her typing.

And at last they found the courtyard with its little swimming pool,
a paved area where several lawn chairs were set up, two concrete
shuffleboard courts, and expanses of grass on one of which a croquet
game was being played.

"It comes as a little bit of a surprise, doesn't it?" A cheerful, chubby
woman had come out of the building behind them carrying a book
and wearing a broad-brimmed hat. "Nobody would guess this was
hidden inside our pile of bricks, would they? You two are the new
visitilators staying in the guest rooms, aren't you? Saw you in the
commons room earlier. Can I help you find something or someone?"

"We're thinking of moving in here, you know," Caledonia said,
resorting to their cover story as an introduction, "and we were exploring to see whatever there is that we hadn't found before. I mean,
like that exercise room . . ."

"You enjoy exercisationary activities?"

Caledonia started to say "What was that?" but decided that might
be taken as rude, so she merely went on with the conversation. "On
the contrary. I hate exercise. That was just one of the places we
bumped into in our explorations. Good thing though; I'll know which
part of the building to avoid. By the way, I'm Caledonia Wingate and
my little friend," she gestured at Angela, who had turned lazily away

and was drifting over to watch the croquet game, "is Angela Benbow. We're living down at Camden-sur-Mer, but we thought about moving up here to . . ."

"Oh, that's such a lovely place! They didn't have a vacutancy when I needed a place, which is why I ended up here."

"You like it here?" Caledonia saw no reason she shouldn't pursue their inquiries with this friendly little woman with the odd vocabulary. "Do you have any complaints about it? Anything unusual, strange, uncomfortable that bothers you?"

The chubby woman shrugged. "I guess it's okay. Other people seem to like it. Oh, by the way . . . I'm Nancy Bush," she went on cheerfully. "Funny coincication, isn't it? Here I am, named for two Republican first ladies, and I'm a Democrat. Well, I am most of the time, anyhow. I'm certainly big enough around to be both a Republican and a Democrat rolled into one, aren't I?" and she chuckled happily.

"Oh, I'm not one to criticize if someone has accumulated a few fat cells over the years," Caledonia said comfortably, patting her own meaty frame through the pleats and folds of her caftan. "I guess you're not addicted to exercise, either, right?"

Another chuckle churned itself out through the rolls that made up Nancy's chin. "True, and I guess these meals here aren't helping," she said. "I eat every single scrap on my plate, even when it's not very tasty. I saw you talking to the Ridgeways, so I suppose you got an earful about the food. Harvey Ridgeway's favorite conversatilary topic. But he's got a point. Your Mrs. Armstrong arouses my appetitation every time she talks about your menus there at your place. If you want my advice, you try our dining room more than once before you make up your minds to sign a contract here. You may decide not to join us at all."

"Oh, I figure Harvey Ridgeway had to be exaggerating, you know? It can't be as bad as he says. A retirement home has to pay attention to the food because that's one thing we old people really care passionately about. So surely . . ."

"Well, it's not just meals. Those guest rooms you're in are on the front of the building, and that's not awfully pleasant. The nicest places face inward, to the courtyard, like Connie Stone's place." Nancy waved a pudgy hand toward the line of doors and windows across the full width of the courtyard from where they stood. "But those rooms were all taken when I moved in. So were the ones on the front, looking out at the street. I ended up having to take one on the second floor in the back. All I have a view of is the freeway, and the noise is just deafenating. There's a constant whoosh and roar . . ."

An electronic crackling sounded over their heads and behind them, and a loudspeaker, hung over the main door leading back into the building, snapped on. A woman's brisk voice said, "Lunch time, everyone. Lunch time . . ." and there were four bells, "Ding-ding-ding-ding." The croquet players hastily set aside their mallets and hurried toward the big doorway, Angela hard on their heels. "You'd better come along," Nancy Bush said breathlessly. "They really don't like it if you're late. I got such a scolding from our head waitress the other day!" And she rushed off without waiting to see if Caledonia followed.

"Angela!" Caledonia called and beckoned her friend to come. "Hurry up! I'm told we need to be prompt at meals to avoid a tongue-lashing."

"Oh, dear," Angela said, bustling up. "I didn't realize how near it was to noon. I really need to wash up. Well, you go on into the dining room and I'll just join you in a minute, after I . . ." They were passing the dining room door, on their left as they entered the uncarpeted hallways, and Angela veered away as though to head for their rooms.

"Here! You're headed the wrong way!" A tall, broad-shouldered woman, her muscular frame swathed tightly in a pale green waitress's uniform, gestured Angela from the dining room door.

"Well, I thought I'd stop by my room and . . ."

"No time! No time! Can't you see the meal is beginning?" The woman gestured again commandingly. "You're the visitors who might move in, aren't you? Well, you'll get used to our schedule shortly. We don't fool around when it's time for our meals. We change our clothes and wash our hands early enough that we can be on time. And I suggest we start today the way we intend to go on. That's the best way, don't you agree? So you just come on in right now with your friend. I've put you at the table over there by the kitchen door."

Angela was not easily intimidated, as a rule, and under other cir-cumstances she might have fought back, asserted her independence. But she might want to ask questions of this . . . this prison matron, she thought defiantly. Best to behave. So she meekly followed the pointing arm, and she and Caledonia seated themselves at the small table the pointing hand seemed to indicate. It was bare except for paper placemats, at which she wrinkled her nose in distaste.

"I think this meal may be something of a disappointment," Angela whispered.

"Maybe," Caledonia whispered back, "but it had a great beginning. I mean, I loved it when that female lion tamer took charge of you. And I certainly intend to give the food a fair . . . Oh, gosh! Oh, gosh!"

Caledonia's nose was the one to wrinkle now as lunch was set in front of her on a picnic plate of heavily plasticized paper containing in its separate compartments one chicken croquette drowning in white gravy, a little heap of boiled zucchini, a smallish serving of rice, and a slice of Wonder Bread with a pat of margarine. "The nicest word I can find for this," Caledonia said after she tasted one forkful from each compartment, "far and away the nicest word is *bland*."

"Tasteless," Angela said, nodding unhappily.

"Sawdust and library paste! And here comes dessert already," Caledonia said, "even though we've barely started on the main course." A scurrying waitress dropped two small paper plates onto the table beside Caledonia and Angela, each plate containing a thick-crusted wedge of what appeared to be apple pie. "Well, maybe it tastes better than it looks," Caledonia said, cautiously taking a forkful into her mouth.

She tasted, she chewed, and an expression of extreme distress crossed her broad face. "This crust is the very best grade of cardboard! Angela, are you going to eat your slice of bread? It seems to be the only completely edible part of this lunch." She sighed. "Who ever thought I'd be reduced to a diet of bread and butter?"

"Margarine," Angela reminded her. "Oh, dear, this is really very poor! No wonder Harvey Ridgeway complains. Why do you want my bread?"

Caledonia spread the margarine lavishly on both her bread and Angela's, then reached over and grabbed the sugar bowl and sprinkled mounds of sugar onto both slices. Angela was staring, so Caledonia explained. "We were really hard up, when I was a kid, and there was no jelly available, most of the time," she said. "I used to eat bread-and-sugar back then, and it'll hold me till dinner now, I think. But if dinner's no better than this, we're either going to have to solve Tootsie's little mystery in a flaming hurry, or we're going to have to hire a taxi to take us home to Camden-sur-Mer for at least one meal a day, so we can survive!"

Unlike Caledonia, who insisted on a nap after lunch just as she would have were she at home, Angela claimed—just as she would have were she at home—that she didn't feel tired enough for a snooze. But somehow, on this particular day, the bed in her guest quarters looked irresistibly inviting. It was probably all the fuss and effort involved in packing her bags, taking the limo (at Caledonia's insistence) to The Golden Years, and meeting a lot of new people, compounded by her having to lie, which she always found a strain—a combination of the labor of remembering the lie and her deep sense of guilt. Furthermore, after that wretched lunch, she was feeling the malaise of dyspepsia coupled with annoyance. Whatever the cause, Angela made an exception to her usual rule and curled up under a moss green Velux blanket that had been folded across the foot of the bed, and within seconds she was deeply asleep. In fact, to her surprise, she slept nearly two hours, and only woke to the ringing of her bedside phone.

"Were you asleep?" It was Caledonia's booming voice. "You let the phone ring four times and that's not like you. What's on your agenda for the afternoon? Want to do some more exploring?"

"I really should finish unpacking my bags," Angela said, dodging the question about whether or not she'd been napping by simply ignoring it. "When we arrived, we just dumped our suitcases here in the rooms and went to meet Tootsie. I need to hang things. I don't want everything to get all wrinkled . . ."

"Yeah, I was going to mention your luggage. We're only going to be here a couple of days, and I thought you brought an awful lot of stuff with you for just . . ."

"Well, I wanted to be sure I had enough things to wear no matter how long we stayed or what we decided to do. I mean, they might have a dressy party, or . . ."

"They'd forgive us if we just came in ordinary clothes. They know we're only visiting. Honestly, the way you fuss about having the right piece of cloth on your back! Okay, you unpack and you call me when you're ready for a little stroll around. Or better yet, you come and find me. I'll be out in the courtyard talking to people and getting acquainted. Nobody we've met so far has mentioned mysterious lights or ghostly weeping, and I want to get busy asking questions, because the sooner we get to the bottom of Tootsie's little problem, the sooner we get to go home!"

"You go ahead," Angela said, and her voice was sulky. She had been waiting for Caledonia to say something mocking about the amount of luggage she'd brought, and here it was, just as she'd anticipated. Caledonia had packed in one huge pullman case; Angela had brought three overnight bags, a duffle, a tote, and two makeup cases, all stuffed to overflowing. She'd known Caledonia would have some scathing comment, of course, but how could one be sure one wouldn't need a silk suit or a pair of slacks or even a floor-length skirt for evening wear? "I wanted to be inconspicuous," she muttered to herself as she smoothed a ruffled blouse onto a hanger, "and dressing just right is a sure way to avoid unfavorable attention. Caledonia doesn't understand."

The truth was, Caledonia understood all too well. It was just that she felt differently about clothing than Angela did. Recognizing the problems of dressing smartly if one is a woman of size, Caledonia had long ago abandoned fashion in favor of comfort and had hired a dressmaker to duplicate a favorite floor-length caftan in a number of colors and fabrics; she wore nothing but caftans from that time on. For her, packing for four days involved only folding four caftans and as many changes of underclothes into her suitcase, tucking in a light wrap for cool California evenings and a spare pair of sandals, and finding a corner of the bag for her toilet articles, secured in a plastic zipper bag. Angela's little vanities amused Caledonia. "Well, let her slave over the unpacking," she told herself. "I'll just go ahead with our investigations. I enjoy asking questions at my own pace and in my own way anyhow. Maybe I'm too blunt, but Angela can be so roundabout that people don't even know what she's really trying to ask and sometimes she gets strange answers that aren't very helpful.

I'll just go meet a few folks on my own . . ." and she stumped out to the patio area, warmed by the May sunshine of midafternoon.

There were two men paddling lazily in the swimming pool, while over at one side of the lawn area, two women and a man were knocking croquet balls through wire wickets with what seemed to be total indifference to direction; perhaps they were just beginners at the game, or perhaps, Caledonia thought, they were as bored by croquet as she would have been. Nancy Bush was curled up in a deck chair, reading a book under a big lawn umbrella, doubly shaded by a wide-brimmed hat tied on with a scarf knotted under her dimpled chin. Not one to take chances with sun or wind, Caledonia noted silently. Nancy looked up and waved an indolent hand. Caledonia waved back, but looked further, hoping for someone new to meet and to question.

Across the first grassy expanse and near the pool, Caledonia saw a woman she hadn't met before. The woman was as carefully shaded from the sun as was Nancy Bush, her chair drawn close to the center of another lawn umbrella. Unlike the probably dyed blonde Nancy, the woman was completely gray—at least, that was the impression she gave, because she matched her iron-gray hair with slate-gray slacks, a blue-gray blouse, dove-gray shoes, and gray-rimmed glasses. The only spot of color about her was the work on which she was crocheting industriously without looking down. "I wonder how she does that?" Caledonia marveled. Not being a crafts person herself, she had always wondered at crochet needles that dipped into an opening between strands and pulled through a loop of exactly the right size. She had always admired the patterns that seemed to grow of their own volition, adding shapes and swirls and clumps and knots in just the right places, as though they were quite independent of the person holding the crochet hook. The gray woman seemed more concerned about the men in the pool than about her . . . her . . . her . . .

"What is that thing? Is it going to be an afghan?" Caledonia asked, drawing a chair close under the same umbrella. "Oh, I should have asked if I could join you. May I?"

"Of course." Still not watching the pattern or her hook, the woman smiled pleasantly enough. "Please do sit down. And yes, this will be an afghan. For my sister back East. It'll take me all summer to finish so she'll have it for Christmas—just in time for their first snowstorm, I suppose. I'll think of her," the woman said in a smug tone, "trying to keep warm—and I'll enjoy every minute of the sunshine out here twice as much. Honestly, I can't understand why she stays back there . . . why *anybody* would stay there after they retire." She shook her head and then squinted up at Caledonia a moment. "Oh, yes, I know who you are. You're one of the two new residents, aren't you?"

"Yup. Angela Benbow, my friend, she's the little one," Caledonia said cheerfully. "I'm the fat one. I'm Caledonia Wingate. But we're not residents yet. We're trying the place out, that's all so far. And so far we're having doubts. That lunch today was pretty bad. Is the food always so . . . so inedible?"

"I'm Regina Madison, by the way," the gray woman said, putting down the crochet needle for a moment as she extended a hand. "And no, it isn't. I mean, the food is usually quite acceptable—sometimes even tasty, although it's too . . . well, too *healthy* to have a lot of fascinating spices in it, you know. But it's good plain food, as a rule, I'd say."

"I was talking to the Ridgeways and . . ."

"Oh, Harvey! He doesn't like anything around here," Regina Madison said. "Excuse me. I have to change yarn . . ." and she broke off the tag end of the color she was working on and picked up a ball of a contrasting color. Loop-plunge-loop-plunge-loop-loop-pull . . . Once more the hook began its rhythmic bobbing and ducking. The crocheting was back on autopilot and Regina Madison turned her attention once more to Caledonia. "I suppose I shouldn't criticize Harvey," she said. "He's a good soul. Not like some . . ." She narrowed her eyes and appeared to nod in the direction of one of the men paddling around in the pool. "Some are downright mean-spirited. Take George Tulley there. The skinny one in the plaid trunks. I don't know why he moved into a community-living situation at all, he's so cantankerous. Always wants things his own way . . . Now he's got it in for our cats! Wants the rules changed so our cats can't roam here in the courtyard!"

"You're a cat owner, too?"

"Oh, no, I'm just cat-sitting for the Rosens today. I'm feeding and exercising their Socks . . ."

"Socks?"

"Pippi Longstocking. Socks for short, though she had her name long before the Clintons were elected and brought their cat to . . . Wait a sec. I can't see her now and I'd better check . . ." And to Caledonia's surprise, Regina picked up a pair of opera glasses and trained them on some bushes at the far side of the courtyard, beyond the croquet players. "Ah, yes, she's still there, just taking her ease in the sunshine."

Regina must have seen Caledonia's startled expression, because her tone turned a little defensive. "Don't look so surprised. If you live here long enough, you'll have some kind of binoculars yourself! Everybody does. Those who live on the street side of the building watch people going in and out of the Jack-in-the-Box down at the corner or peer into the city offices. They tell me they can practically read the computer screens at the clerks' desks. The folks who live on the freeway side of the building keep track of the traffic and the fender benders; we have one woman—this Frederica Hendley—who can read lips, and she loves it when there's an accident and she can put her field glasses on it. Then at mealtime she gives us a rundown on what the policeman said and what the driver said. Like, one driver claimed he was watching one of those portable TVs and that's why he rear-ended a big truck! We all had a wonderful laugh over that. Having binoculars is a kind of universal hobby here."

"Oh, I know about having binoculars. No need to apologize. Everybody at Camden-sur-Mer has them, too. But they're watching the ocean—the fishing boats, and the sailboaters, and the dolphins feeding out by the kelp beds. It never occurred to me that you might watch ordinary people doing ordinary things. We mainly watch the scenery, through our field glasses."

"Well, we don't have much in the way of scenery to look at here. But people-watching has its pleasures, too," Regina Madison said without a hint of shame or repentance in her tone. "Once you live here . . . Oops . . . this ball of yarn's almost finished. Hold on while I fish out another and attach it . . . There. I started to say that, once you're here, even if you're not watching something as lively as the freeway, you'll want binoculars. I'm a case in point. I have a room on the second floor looking out this way, and from there I can watch the comings and goings right here in the courtyard. And I don't mind telling you I do. All day long. Though it's much more interesting at night. Such . . . such fascinating things. You'd be surprised!" Her voice was silky with some hidden satisfaction.

"Like what? Give me an example," Caledonia said, trying not to sound too eager.

Well, like . . ." Regina lowered her voice and leaned toward Caledonia, "there's a woman here with one of those apartments across the courtyard—a real hussy. She has a boyfriend. A man from right

here at The Golden Years. He lives up on the second floor next door
to his widowed sister. I know that he and that woman—" she gestured
across the courtyard "—they're what Winchell used to call 'an item'
because I see him coming and going from that woman's place at all
hours. But for some reason they're trying to keep the affair a secret."
She smiled with smug satisfaction. "Some secret. Everybody knows
about them by now. I can't mention them to a soul who hasn't already
heard the gossip. Except his sister. It's his sister he wants to keep the
secret from, or so we think."

She must have caught a hint of distaste in Caledonia's expression,
for she hurried on, "You must think I'm awful. That I spend all my
time spying on my neighbors. I do other things with the glasses as
well, you know. For instance, I keep track of Simon Peterson
there . . ." She had finished attaching the new yarn, so she had a free
hand to wave toward the stouter man in the pool, now floating on
his back in contentment. "Not in a gossipy way, mind you. Not like
I keep track of that supposedly secret romance! It's because Simon
has a heart condition, and he confided that he's terrified he'll have
an attack and nobody will find him to help him. And if he couldn't
phone for help . . . Well anyhow, I kind of train my glasses over on
his windows now and then." She pointed to the farthest left of the
ground-floor apartments facing the croquet game. "That's his place.
If I see Simon's shadow moving across the drapes, I know he's alive
and able to get around. If I don't see him for several minutes, I give
him a call." She giggled like a schoolgirl. "I've called him out of his
shower and I've waked him from a nap many a time. But he doesn't
mind. He's grateful. And in the night if his lights are on and I look
over there and can't see him . . . well, I phone then, too."

"Kind of interferes with his privacy, doesn't it?" Caledonia said
curiously.

"Oh, well, that's just one of the things we all give up when we
move into a retirement home," Regina said without much concern.

"Not necessarily," Caledonia said. "I have plenty of privacy in
Camden-sur-Mer. Of course we don't peer into each other's windows
with field glasses, either."

Regina remained undismayed by Caledonia's obvious distaste.
"Well, Simon finds it reassuring. He used to be afraid he'd get sick
or fall and couldn't get to the house phone to call for help. Now, he
says, he's got an insurance policy. Me."

"I'm surprised you can see into his windows at all. Wouldn't it be more efficient if somebody on the first floor, here on his own level, looked into his windows to check up on him?"

"But it's mostly public rooms and offices on the main floor. Or apartments like your guest rooms that face the street. There are only six residence apartments on the ground floor that face the courtyard, and they're all in a line."

Caledonia glanced around and realized that only one expanse of brick wall was broken at ground level by a line of windows and doors, marking individual apartments. Her eyes idly rose to the second and third floors all around, and after a moment she burst out laughing, for in several of the windows she could see pairs of round, unwinking glass eyes staring down at her. "Several of your fellow residents have been using binoculars to follow along with our conversation, I see," she said.

Once more, Regina's smile had a secretive smugness about it. "Oh, yes. We do like to know what's going on. And you, being new, are bound to be an object of curiosity. They don't mean anything by it, my dear. This is really a very pleasant place to live, you know."

"You think so? You haven't observed anything . . . well, anything strange, for instance?"

"Strange?" For once Regina Madison laid her crocheting down, and her hands were idle in her lap. "How do you mean?"

"Well, you know . . . like . . . well, like unexplained lights in the garden at night."

"Unexplained lights? You don't mean the flashlights, do you?"

"Well, it could be flashlights, I guess. Are you saying that you *have* seen lights?"

"Of course." Regina spread the top of her tote bag further open so Caledonia could see, nestled down among the bright balls of yarn and the gleam of steel crochet needles, a small, black metal flashlight. Caledonia pulled the flash out, looked it over, and replaced it.

"I should think everybody at The Golden Years carries one," Regina said. "There aren't any real lights out here at all, if you've noticed. I don't think they want us to go out here after dark. Probably afraid we'd want to play shuffleboard or take a swim and we'd disturb those who go to bed early. But that means if we do come out here at night—oh, for instance to visit a neighbor—we'd better carry flashlights."

Caledonia grinned. "Well, well, well. Nothing mysterious about lights bobbing in the garden at all, then."

"Of course not. Did someone suggest there was?"

"Oh, no," Caledonia said hastily. "Not at all. It was just a figure of speech. Sort of." She changed the subject as fast as she could to that universal standby topic, the weather. Then as quickly as possible, she made her excuses and drifted away, as much as one with her bulk could be said to drift. She stood near the croquet players for a while and exchanged a few words with them. Jane Something, Emma Somebody, and Chester Whatever. They introduced themselves, but Caledonia didn't really catch the last names. Croquet is such a leisurely game there was plenty of time for an introduction and greeting between shots, though the players were carefully and politely quiet while a shot was actually made; of course, considering how erratic their game was, they might as well have gone on talking. Caledonia was not herself much of a game player. Bridge, of course. And now and then some surprisingly amusing children's game would be organized by someone or other, some game like Crazy Eights or Old Maid or Oh Hell, and Caledonia would compete ferociously, laugh uproariously, and enjoy herself enormously. But games played when one was on one's feet, in a vertical position—like shuffleboard and golf, tennis or badminton, and even a placid game like croquet—were not her cup of tea. All the same, she was sure she could have bested any one of the croquet players she was watching, and she strode off after a while, feeling a little superior, her mood definitely upbeat, to find Angela.

"I'm sure Tootsie's mysterious lights are just flashlights," she told Angela a little later as they sat together gazing into the advancing twilight through the sheer draperies covering Angela's window. "That's what this Regina Madison thinks, anyhow. And I think so too."

"Don't turn on the lamps. Let's just look out from this darker area into the lighter," Angela said, "and we'll be almost invisible, even if the drapes are just sheers. Mama and I used to do that when I was a little, bitty girl. I like the feeling of being able to see people going past in the street when they can't see me . . ." She roused herself from remembering and returned to the present. "Anyhow, go on about the flashlights. Do you believe that's what it is? I mean, that's so obvious. Why wouldn't Tootsie figure that out?"

"Well, you know, I had to ponder that for a while. But I imagine Tootsie wouldn't think of flashlights right off the bat. Afer all, she hasn't seen a flashlight beam for years. She's lived at Camden-sur-

Mer since I've been there, and that must be—gosh, maybe eighteen years now, right? Twenty? And we have lights up and down our garden at night so nobody has to use a flashlight. Besides, maybe these don't look like the ones Tootsie was used to in the old days. Those were always so weak. Regina showed me her flashlight, and it's one of those fancy new ones with the extra-bright light. What're they called? Xenon flashlights? Halogen? Krypton?"

"I think Krypton is what makes Superman weak," Angela said skeptically.

Caledonia shrugged. "Whatever. The point is, flashlights are a lot brighter now than they used to be. And Regina Madison says everybody here at The Golden Years carries one."

"We should still be on the lookout tonight, all the same. We have to be sure. I mean, what are people doing out in the courtyard after dark anyhow? We ought to take a good look . . . I've been thinking and I decided we ought to take turns in the hallway . . ."

"Let's talk about it after dinner," Caledonia said, her voice alive with hope and anticipation. "Dinner! Any minute now, and I can hardly wait! We'll do our planning later."

Unfortunately, dinner—like the lunch—was served on a paper plate, though one bearing a pretty pattern and not divided into compartments. "At least we don't look like kids at a picnic, the way we did this noon. Plates with dividers demand hot dogs and potato chips!"

"Don't give the kitchen any ideas," Angela said unhappily. "Look at this glop!" She forked into a pile of meat shreds, piled up beside some green beans and a ball of glued-together rice so sticky the mound retained perfectly the shape of the circular scoop that had laid it onto the plate.

Caledonia gingerly tasted the meat on her own plate. "Oooooh . . . ICK! And I haven't said that since I was a little kid. This is awful . . . all vinegary! What *is* this stuff?"

"That there's barbecue," the waitress said. She had come to their table to dump off a plastic basket of four dinner rolls.

"That's not barbecue!" Caledonia retorted. "Barbecue is a slice of tender brisket or a rack of ribs, all smoky from slow cooking over a pit of coals and flavored with a sauce that's been basting . . ."

"That there's barbecue, all the same," the waitress insisted. "It's just been chopped up some."

"But it's been soaked in vinegar!" Caledonia protested.

"That there's the barbecue sauce," the waitress said. "We mix it in when we chop up the meat. You don't like it?"

"Like it! Like it? Listen to me, child. The only reason you'd soak meat in vinegar this way is to hide the taste if it's starting to turn!"

"Cal!" Angela's tiny toe found Caledonia's shin under the table with a warning nudge. "Thank you for the explanation," she said sweetly to the waitress, who nodded and went about her chores. "Cal, please . . . we don't have to stay here, so it doesn't matter. And you shouldn't go around making the cook and the waitress angry just because you don't like their version of barbecue. You might want to ask them questions later."

"But barbecue shouldn't taste like this. It shouldn't even *look* like this! Why, in Texas or Arizona or . . ."

"Now, Cal, when Douglas was stationed in Charleston, we learned about Deep South cooking, and believe me, what they call barbecue is all just like this. All sour-y and chopped fine and . . ."

"Okay, okay—but what am I going to eat?" Caledonia groaned. "All right, all right, I won't make a scene. Just pass me the sugar bowl and that basket. It was bread and sugar for lunch, and I guess it'll have to be dinner rolls and sugar for supper. I've got to keep my strength up somehow."

Caledonia's mood was not improved when the waitress informed her that dessert was a single chocolate-chip cookie. "I don't mind a cookie with my ice cream," Caledonia said despairingly, "but not *instead* of ice cream!"

She grumbled all the way to their guest quarters and Angela's attempts to plan their evening's investigations did nothing at all for her temper. She emphatically turned down Angela's first suggestion— that they hover in the hallway, just inside the door to the patio. "We can't see enough from there. And some resident is bound to spot us hanging around in the hall. Then they'll ask us what we're doing there and we'll have to think of some lie . . . Remember, Tootsie doesn't want us to be obvious. No, that won't do."

She also growled an emphatic refusal to Angela's suggestion that they ask a second-floor resident for the loan of a room and window overlooking the patio area. "Angela, I don't call that keeping the secret, do you? I mean, we'd have to come up with some explanation, and I surely can't think of any innocent reason to sit in someone else's room in the dark, glaring out at the courtyard. You'll have to do better." At last, Caledonia agreed grudgingly that they might do best if they took turns sitting quietly in the courtyard itself, perhaps in one of those chairs under an umbrella, shaded from the dim moonlight as the umbrellas' users had been from the sun in the afternoon.

"You brought something dark to wear, I hope," Angela said. "I have black slacks and a black blouse and even black sneakers. And of course a black windbreaker. Did you bring . . ."

"I'm not an idiot, even though you seem to think I am," Caledonia said. "Of course I did. I have a long-sleeved maroon caftan and a navy shawl I'll throw on."

"Do you want to change now and take the first watch?" Angela said. "Maybe from now till midnight, and then you come and wake me and . . ."

"Absolutely not. If you want to get started right now, you'll have to get started on your own. I've got an errand to run."

"Cal! What . . ."

"I'm going down the block to that Jack-in-the-Box that Regina Madison said was down on the corner. And I'm going to get a Jumbo Jack with cheese and a double order of fries. I wouldn't walk that far except for some emergency—but when you think about it, this qualifies as an emergency. I'm certainly feeling desperate. So you go sit in the dark under an umbrella if you want to. I'm going to get myself a decent meal, bring it back here and eat it . . . probably with a double milk shake on the side. When you've had enough of the patio, you come and get me and I'll take over. Okay?"

Angela sighed. "All right. I'll go first," she said. "But I can't approve of the Jack-in-the-Box. That's not playing the game. If we want to keep our investigations a secret and pretend we're going to move in here . . ."

"Let 'em see me! All they'll be is jealous, not suspicious. Angela, if I was ever so silly as to move in here, I'd be at Jack-in-the-Box every night. I'm just doing what comes naturally, and nobody's going to guess that just because I'm eating a hamburger, I'm here to look into mysterious goings-on! So I'm off to make myself more human with some real, honest-to-goodness food. Yes, fat and all. You'll see . . . I'll be much easier to get along with once I've finished a burger. And fries. And a shake. As for you, you just run along and change into your spy outfit. I'll expect a report later. After I get back." And she turned on her heel and marched out toward the front of the building and relief from hunger.

CHAPTER

5

I T WAS CHILLY OUTSIDE, and Angela shivered as she huddled in the dark, curled up in a large deck chair and hidden under a lawn umbrella away from the pallid glow of silver light that the moon tried unsuccessfully to spread across the courtyard. Nobody entering the darkened courtyard or looking down from the windows could spot her, provided she stayed very still. So though she felt fidgety, she pulled herself tightly into a little ball in her chair as she counted the minutes and tried to kill time daydreaming. The glowing dial of her watch showed 9:00.

Half an hour passed, or rather seemed to pass, and yet the dial showed only 9:10. "This thing must be broken," Angela muttered crossly, shaking her wrist. She ran through the lyrics of songs she knew from musical comedies, humming the melodies softly under her breath. She recited poetry to herself. She tried to remember the names of the other children in her sixth-grade class, the ones with whom she'd put on a play for assembly. They'd agreed on doing their own version of *Sleeping Beauty*, and they'd agreed to determine the exact casting by voting during a study period.

Naming Prince Charming had been an easy matter. There was no other boy so tall for his age, so gloriously blond, so rosy cheeked as Royal Hanson, and he won a unanimous vote. The catch had been that Angela wanted to play the role of princess, but the first two times the class voted on a female lead, the class elected someone else. Angela however had named herself chairman of the meeting, and under the amused eyes of her teacher, who struggled with a grin that grew broader and broader, Angela banged her borrowed gavel and declared each unfavorable vote to have been invalid: not everyone voted the first time, and the second vote was too close to being a tie. The class would have to vote again. The class apparently saw the handwriting on the wall, and on the third election for princess, Angela won. This vote, of course, she declared to be legal and final. And that was how she achieved the lead in the sixth-grade production of *The Sleeping Beauty*.

Now she sat in the dark, reliving the past, feeling embarrassed at the memory of her youthful brashness, and struggling to bring back the names and faces of the students who played the wicked witch, the king, the king's court, and the villagers who sang and danced around a maypole in the grand finale. She could see that makeshift maypole in her mind's eye, and the improvised costumes. But the children's faces would not come to her—except for the narrow face and silken hair of Patty Walsh, her chief rival for the role of the princess, and the rose-red cheeks of Royal Hanson, her Prince Charming; the other faces remained blank. And perhaps she dozed a bit as she struggled to fill in those blanks. At any rate, the next time she glanced at her wristwatch, the illuminated dial read 10:30. That was well past Angela's usual bedtime, and she yawned, stretched . . . and froze.

A bouncing spot of light had appeared at the far end of the garden, near the entrance from the main building. It nodded up and down, caressed the shrubbery and slid along the grass toward her. Closer, closer—then there was a rustling noise in the shrubbery, and the light jerked convulsively in the direction of the sound.

"Wha—What's that? Who's there? Oh! Oh!" The voice, that of a young man, kept on muttering and exclaiming—apparently cursing under his breath. Angela could not make out all the words and a number of the words she did hear she didn't understand, which was probably just as well. "One of them cats! I nearly stepped on . . . Why people don't keep 'em out of the way at night . . ." The muttering and the accompanying string of unfamiliar and unintelligible words continued as the light bobbed away, moving toward the row of lighted windows and doors that marked the six patio apartments at the far end of the courtyard.

There was no doubt, of course, that the light was a flashlight, exactly as Caledonia had conjectured. And it was being carried by a young fellow whose outlines as he passed the cowering Angela had become relatively clear to her eyes, adapted as they were to the darkness. He was carrying a couple of boxes in his arms—largish, square boxes, each only about two inches high and as familiar and identifiable in silhouette as though they had been spotlighted.

"It's pizza!" Angela muttered to herself. "Somebody's suffering hunger pains after that wretched evening meal and they're treating themselves to a late-night snack. Or maybe they're giving a party. Though I suppose it's a little late for folks our age to be giving a party. A little late for a snack, too. All that cheese would give me a stomachache, late at night."

"Ow! Wow!" There was another explosion of not-so-muffled anger and the light jerked as the delivery boy caught his foot on something that made him stumble and juggle his burden frantically, trying to hang onto his boxes and his flashlight without spreading pepperoni around the lawn, as Angela could see plainly, since the boy was now between her and the apartments' lights and clearly outlined. "Some kind of metal . . . a great big staple . . ." he was muttering. The boy had apparently tripped over one of the croquet wickets left driven into the lawn when the players quit their game for the evening. The wire, Angela thought, would be quite invisible in the dark. "I'm gonna quit this damn job! Layin' booby traps . . . cats and metal arches and . . . Ow-ow-ow . . ." He kept his hobbling dance going, and the spot of yellow light bobbed and nodded and swiveled in time with his limping gait as he struggled along.

One of the doors opened to his knock—not a very emphatic knock, Angela thought. More tentative. But then, she supposed, one wouldn't want to disturb the neighbors at this time of night. She craned her neck but she couldn't actually see who it was that opened the door and took the pizzas inside. She watched as the boy accepted what she supposed was pay for his delivery, without so much as a "thank you," the lighted doorway darkened again when the door swung shut, and the flashlight beam began its bobbing return across the patio area—closer to the edge this time, so the boy could avoid the area where who-knows-how-many wickets still lay in wait.

At last the boy and his flashlight disappeared into the main building and presumably went on out the front door to a waiting van. Angela uncurled herself painfully and stretched to a standing position with difficulty. Her muscles ached. "I keep forgetting," she reminded herself, "that I can't leave my knees bent up tight for very long at a time anymore. Used to be I could sit scrunched up like that all day while I read a book, then stand up and run to the dinner table. Now for every fifteen minutes with bent knees, I limp for an hour. It isn't," she muttered as she hobbled her way into the main building, ". . . it isn't that I mind getting old. It's that I mind the things getting old is doing to me. I don't like wrinkles, I don't like glasses and hearing aids, I don't like having to write things down to remember them . . . It isn't the number of years; it's the number of things that get weak or that hurt to use. That's what old age is."

Back in the hallway she checked to be sure she wasn't observed. It wouldn't be easy to explain skulking through the darkened courtyard dressed all in black. But the hall was hushed and empty as she stopped at Caledonia's door and knocked for admittance. Caledonia answered promptly. "Who is it?" she asked, peering out into the ill-lit hallway. "Oh, it's you. Come on in. I can't even see you out there in the dark, after I've been staring at the TV. My eyes apparently don't adapt as fast as they used to."

Angela stepped inside into the light as Caledonia went on, "And you know what? I think that's probably what Tootsie's disembodied voices are. I've been thinking about that while you were doing your super-spy routine in the garden, and I'll bet what Tootsie heard were just ordinary people out in the courtyard, people just standing and talking—no funny business or anything. But Tootsie had been watching the TV, and when she looked outside into the dark, those people out there were invisible to her. She just hadn't given her eyes time to adjust. And the longer I thought about that, the more certain I was that was the answer. Don't you agree? I think . . . Angela, you're shivering!" Caledonia had become aware that her tiny friend was hugging herself and trembling.

"Of course I'm shivering," Angela said tartly. "It's really chilly out there. California weather spoils you. Thins your blood. I used to shovel snow at ten degrees below, but now I really feel the cold!"

"Of course you do. You're not nearly as well insulated as I am. Here." Caledonia pulled the blanket off the foot of her bed. "Wrap this around you."

Angela accepted the blanket and wound it around herself. "Ooooh, that feels good. I'll be all right in a minute, I suppose. And you'll be glad to hear you don't have to go outside into the cold yourself. I've done the work for both of us. I mean, that bouncing light was a flashlight, just like you said it could be. It was a delivery boy bringing in pizzas." And she told in great detail the story of her wait in the dark and her observations.

Wisely, Caledonia let Angela ramble on with details that would ordinarily have irritated her. But she felt that tonight Angela had earned the right to embroider a narrative. At last the story wound to its close, and Caledonia nodded with satisfaction. "There you are. I knew there had to be a simple answer. Since there aren't any such things as ghosts, I mean. So we've solved two of Tootsie's mysteries, her invisible talkers and her bobbing lights, by using observation and logic. There's really nothing to ghostbusting, is there?" There was a little pause and then Angela sighed windily. "Still chilled?" Caledonia was solicitous.

"Oh, I'm feeling better. Except that I'm a little disappointed. I thought the answer to our mysteries might be more . . . well, you know, a little more complicated. More interesting."

"Rub your arms. That'll help," Caledonia said.

"How will that keep me from being disappointed?"

"Oh, don't be so silly. You know what I meant. It'll help your circulation and help with your feeling chilled. I can't do much about your feeling disappointed. Of course," she added after a moment, "we still haven't solved the problem of the crying child in the hall, have we?"

"Oh, that was probably just the pizza delivery boy crying after he stumbled over a croquet wicket," Angela said. "It certainly must have hurt him."

"No, it wouldn't be that. Don't forget that when Tootsie looked out into the hall she couldn't see anybody." Caledonia's voice took on those hushed tones one uses for spinning yarns of haunts and specters while sitting around a Scout campfire at night. "Nobody was in the hall who could have made the sounds."

"Oh, it's just another of those silly little explanations like . . . like . . . well, maybe by the time Tootsie could teeter over to the door on those high heels of hers, whoever was weeping out in the hall had time to get out of sight around the corner. Something like that. Nothing interesting at all. And now you're ready to give up and go back to Camden-sur-Mer, aren't you?"

"Now-now . . . You're just grumpy because you're tired," Caledonia said soothingly. "Look, we're both anxious to go on home where we can be comfortable. I'm even more anxious than you are, I expect. If it weren't for that Jack-in-the-Box and its burgers, I'd be starving and frantic. All the same, I was thinking . . ." she patted little Angela on the shoulder comfortingly, ". . . I was thinking that we did promise Tootsie to clear things up for her, so I'll tell you what—why don't we stay here at least one more day to see if we can't discover something about Tootsie's crying ghost."

Tired and cold though she was, Angela beamed. "Oh, Cal. I thought you'd want to leave. Give up before we'd finished. I mean, we both want to leave, naturally. But I don't believe in deserting a job half done. And you know I love solving puzzles. Oh, I'm so glad you don't want to go home without at least trying one more time to finish up. For Tootsie's sake."

"You're smiling," Caledonia said with satisfaction. She had achieved her objective, cheering up her little friend. "That's the spirit—no pun intended."

Their second day passed very much like the first. Angela and Caledonia found breakfast acceptable—how can even a bad cook spoil scrambled eggs and buttered toast—and through the morning they put themselves wherever there were numbers of the residents and talked to as many as possible. That was how they happened to wander into a discussion group in the commons room in midmorning where some teacher from the local junior college was speaking on "How to Grow Old Gracefully," ". . . though what a woman in her forties can tell us about getting old, I can't imagine," Della Ridgeway said out of the corner of her mouth to Caledonia. "Honestly! These . . . these *kids*, who think they're experts on what we're already living through!"

In the afternoon, the same commons room featured games—several residents sat at folding tables playing cards, mahjong, backgammon, and Scrabble. There was even one Monopoly game in progress, although as Angela told Caledonia later, it seemed to be merely a continuation of a game that had gone on for a long, long time. "And just watching Monopoly usually puts me to sleep, let alone trying to play. How people can get so intense about it, I've never understood."

"I sat in on a game of Rook," Caledonia said. "What did you join in on?"

"Nothing. They all urged me to play, but I refused. Said I'd just watch and that's what I did. Your friend Nancy Bush was in the game, by the way, and she said trying to get someone to play when they didn't want to was flogogging a dead horse."

"What?"

"Exactly my reaction. That woman's got a short circuit upstairs!"

Caledonia grinned. "Sure sounds like it. Well, short circuits aside, when you were sitting around watching the game players, did you discover anything of interest?"

"Not exactly. I did bring up the subject of strange noises in the night, and one of the Monopoly players agreed she'd heard something in the hall just the other evening, but she said it was footsteps. I mean, she heard a woman walking along the hall in high heels . . . tap-tap-tap . . . tap-tap-tap . . . The sound stopped near her door, so she thought it was a visitor." Angela paused meaningfully, and to her credit, Caledonia let Angela have her dramatic moment. "Well," Angela went on, "she opened the door, and there wasn't anybody there! Just nobody!"

"No kidding! Kind of like Tootsie's experience, in a way, wasn't it? So what about the crying sound. I mean, did this woman . . . this woman . . . what was her name? Did she hear crying too?"

"I never did catch her name," Angela said apologetically. "I'm terrible on names, I guess because I don't really register them the first time and I'm embarrassed to ask later, so if it doesn't really matter, I just let it go. Like this woman's name. When she was introduced, I wasn't paying attention, and . . ."

"Angela! Get to the point!"

"All right! The point is, this woman—whatever her name was—certainly didn't hear a little child weeping. She'd have mentioned it if she did. But all she mentioned was the footsteps."

After a hurried and tasteless dinner that night, Angela and Caledonia joined the residents in the auditorium for a scheduled program, the showing of a "classic" motion picture from the 1930s. They had tried to strike up conversations with the people on either side of them but were *shushed* repeatedly while the audience sat rapt at a performance by the three Lanes (Priscilla, Rosemary, and Lola) and Gale Page in *Four Daughters*.

"This is really awful! And yet, you know, I remember thinking it was so good! How did we ever sit through this, even young as we were?" Angela muttered. "I was, well, maybe not quite twenty when it came out, and I remember telling my girlfriend this film was so beautiful. So sad. I wept, and . . ."

"Shushhhh," Harvey Ridgeway hissed from the row behind her. "Some of us," he said nastily, "are trying to watch the movie!"

"I can't imagine why," Angela hissed back. But she stopped talking till she and Caledonia got back to their guest quarters.

"Wretched acting and a worse script," Caledonia said as they reached her apartment. "Nobody in that cast should have qualified for membership in the Screen Actors Guild. The plumbers' union would be more like it!"

"But I wonder," Angela said, "if the Lanes and those others were any worse actors than the current crop? For instance, just a year or two ago—that blonde who had no underpants on? You remember . . . she crossed her legs and everybody said it was so sexy? It's my opinion that if she'd kept her undies on, she'd be just another starlet today. Why, I can't even bring her face to mind when I try."

"Neither," Caledonia smirked, "can anybody else. It isn't her face that got her noticed!"

"To me, these youngsters all kind of blend together," Angela complained. "They act alike and some of them even look alike. So . . . so ordinary."

Caledonia nodded. "I don't even remember the kids' names! Johnny-come-latelies, all of them. Of course, I still think of Robert Redford as a newcomer."

Angela sighed. "Oh, I've seen Robert Redford. I haven't even seen most of these other kids in a film. Hollywood certainly isn't making films to appeal to people like me, these days. So I've just about stopped going."

"You wouldn't go anyway," Caledonia grinned. "You'd wait till the movie was on tape and then ask Trinita to rent it to show in the . . . Uh-oh! Did you hear that?"

"Hear what? I didn't hear any—"

"Hush!" Caledonia's voice dropped to a whisper. "Listen. Didn't you hear something?"

"No." Angela was puzzled. "Nothing but *you* going on about . . ."

"There it is again! Shut up and listen!" Caledonia held her big hand up like a crossing guard's stop sign, and Angela obeyed. Faintly, and as though from far away, they heard a hoarse little cry . . . silence . . . and then again, a bit closer, another rasping little sob of a sound.

"That's it, that's it!" Angela was vibrating with excitement. "The crying child!"

"But I thought it would sound like . . . well, like a child sobbing. That's like a little baby bawling!"

Waaaaaa . . . There was a pause, a kind of choking, gurgling gasp, and then from a bit closer yet another bleat of that sound— *Waaaaa* . . .

Caledonia was on her feet in one fast, swooping motion. She might be huge, but she could move when she wanted to. She strode rapidly toward the hall door and flung it open, stepping out to look left and right. And as she pulled the door open, there was an additional little blip of sound followed surprisingly by the sound of what seemed to be a woman's high heels tapping quickly off down the hall. "But Tootsie's right!" Caledonia said in an awed voice. "There's absolutely nobody out here!"

"Yes, there is! Look!" Angela whispered excitedly. She had crowded into the doorway beside her huge friend. Or rather, she had pushed her head and one arm through the little space left by Caledonia, who all but filled the door frame. "There . . . look there . . ." Angela whispered, pointing down the hall toward the receding sound. Her finger, however, was not aimed at body height but toward the floor. "Look . . ."

Caledonia's eyes, adjusting at last to the darker hallway, picked up a hint of movement, a low shape scuttling along near the floor, and as she looked, the movement ceased and a pair of glowing eyes appeared as the creature slowed to a stop and looked back toward her. The light from the doorway reflecting from its almond eyes gleamed like two tiny glowing sparks.

"A cat!" Angela, in her excitement, raised her voice to normal level, and the eyes disappeared as the cat, startled once more, headed away again and turned the corner toward where there was a row of less expensive apartments that looked out at the side of the municipal office building. The tick-tick-tick of the cat's claws against the composition flooring faded away as the cat rounded the corner and passed out of sight. Faintly they could hear a scratching sound as the cat reached its home base and signaled its owner for admission. There was a glow of light, faint to their eyes, as a door around that far corner was opened and the cat—they supposed—was admitted. Then the light went out simultaneously with the sound of the door closing.

Caledonia moved back inside her own room, and pulled Angela after her. "Wow! A cat!" she said. "Of course, I never believed it was ghosts, mind you. I knew there was some perfectly rational explanation for Tootsie's noises and lights . . . but a cat? All the same, I'd never have guessed a cat walking along could sound like a person walking along. And that eerie, crying sound it made . . . like a baby in distress." She shook her head.

"It's not so strange, Cal. The cat's obviously a Siamese," Angela said. "You're not a cat lover, so . . ."

"You can say that again!"

"Well, my point is, Siamese—and some mixed-breeds with Siamese in them—sound completely different from other cats. Their voices are very hoarse and when they are annoyed they complain vocally, as that one was apparently doing. They sound like a baby with a cold. Sort of."

"The footsteps . . . I thought cats had soft paws."

"They do. Except for Siamese. I mean, they don't seem to retract their claws completely the way other cats do, and they really make a pretty noticeable clicking on a surface like that hall. Well, you heard it. They even run differently. Other cats run silently, but I've heard a couple of Siamese, when they were in a big hurry, pounding along on a wooden floor. You'd swear Siamese were shod like ponies, they make so much noise."

"How do they sneak up on a mouse then?"

"Well, they *can* move quietly, you know. It's just—sometimes, they don't seem to *want* to."

"That voice of theirs . . ." Caledonia shook her head. "Well, it certainly solves Tootsie's ghostly mystery. Her rooms are in that other first-floor hall, and I guess sometimes that cat was mad and grumbling as it passed her door. And when she looked out, she didn't see it any more than I did!"

"I wonder why I never thought of a Siamese, after I discovered people here owned cats," Angela said mournfully. "My brains must be starting to atrophy. Years ago I owned a pair of Siamese cats, you know, and . . ."

"Well, there's no mystery about why Tootsie didn't think of it. She's lived at Camden-sur-Mer for so long she's forgotten what a cat sounds like, let alone a Siamese. And . . . hey! That means we can go home tomorrow!" Caledonia beamed. "First we'll tell Tootsie that her ghosts aren't ghosts at all, and then we'll tell the management we've seen enough to make our decision, so we're going off to talk it over and make up our minds. Then we'll call the limo service, and . . ."

"Why not just tell the management here the truth? Why not tell them," Angela said, "that we don't like the atmosphere and we hate the food. Tell them . . ."

"Tell them no such thing. You said it about the dining room staff, and I'll say it about the rest of the management: why make enemies? Let's just tell 'em we're still thinking it over. Okay?"

Angela sighed with longing. "My own dear little apartment, and my comfortable bed."

Caledonia nodded. "My own wonderful place where I can look at the rose garden and the sea, instead of staring at the traffic going by in the street . . ." She waved a hand toward the windows of the guest quarters.

"And the meals! Back to Mrs. Schmitt's cooking," Angela said in a half-whisper, and her voice sounded reverential. "You've always loved the meals but I never really appreciated . . ."

"Well, I did. I do. And I always will! You're probably disappointed that the big mystery turned out to be a very little mystery, but I can't wait to get out of here myself. Come on, Angela, start packing! We're going home!" And Caledonia pulled her big suitcase from under her bed and started throwing clothes into it.

Angela nodded joyfully. "If I had Judy Garland's ruby slippers, I'd click my heels for joy. There *is* no place like home!"

6

IN LATER YEARS WHEN he looked back on the week—the same week that began with the return to Camden-sur-Mer of Angela and Caledonia—Torgeson, a man not afflicted with undue modesty, liked to think of it as "Torgeson's Triumph." He conveniently blotted out from his memory the facts that first, the week was really more like two weeks, and second, the events in which he took such pleasure were within days to be overshadowed (at least for other people) by a murder. In fact, for anyone else remembering this particular period of time—if they remembered it at all—it would be characterized merely as a sort of gathering of the cast of characters.

Angela and Caledonia began the week with unpacking, of course, but they could hardly wait to tell their friends what they'd been up to, and the lobby was a lively place in the half-hour of gossip and greeting just before their first lunch back home, with a dozen friends and acquaintances gathered around them, listening eagerly to the ghost story and to the description of The Golden Years.

"Well, I never!" Tom Brighton said. "I mean, I don't believe in ghosts, but I'd never have guessed . . . well, well, well—flashlights and a Siamese cat and eyes not adapted to look out into the dark . . . Very clever of you ladies!"

"So brave of you to sit out in the courtyard at night, Angela," Mary Moffet murmured. "I can hardly bear to go down the garden walk to my apartment after dark, unless somebody's with me. And investigating ghosts! Oh, you're both so courageous."

"Glad to have a full report on The Golden Years," Emma Grant said. "I don't think I'll bother to investigate that cut rate on rooms that Tootsie was telling us about."

"Tell us more about that handsome man with the cat . . ." one of the Jackson twins simpered. "Yes," the other chimed in. "You say he might come down here to live?"

"Croquet?" Trinita Stainsbury said. "What a good idea. I've been searching for something new we could do around here, and a croquet tournament might be the very thing." Trinita chaired not only the Residents' Council but the Entertainment Committee, and an activity she could not only promote for the pleasure of her fellow residents but perhaps preside over personally was a treasure. But even her beloved committee work could not compete for her attention during the visit of Conrad Stone three days later—looking into a possible move, just as he said he might.

Clara, the redheaded clerk who managed among other things the front desk, the switchboard, the mail distribution, residents' complaints, and Gossip Central, spread the word that Stone would be visiting in midmorning. The Jackson twins twittered their anticipation and posted themselves in the lobby early, craning their necks and sighing audibly as he finally passed, towed along by Torgeson to inspect an available unit. Trinita Stainsbury was not quite as subtle as the Jacksons had been. She dashed right over to Stone, grasped his hand, introduced herself, fluttered briefly as he kissed her fingers in greeting, and expressed the hope that he would be "a joiner-inner, not a stander-asider—we get both types, Mr. Stone, and we need all the active folks to do their part to raise the level of participation, serving as a good example to . . . Oh my goodness!" She gasped and giggled as he raised her fingers to his lips once more and assured her he intended to attend programs and would even serve on committees, "'. . . especially if the other members are as charming as you, dear lady." Mary Moffet, entering the building as Stone and Torgeson were heading out the garden door, grew weak in the knees just looking at Conrad's handsome head of hair and devastating smile, though of course she said nothing.

Torgeson had high hopes as he brought Stone down the garden walk toward the vacant apartment. Mrs. Berger, its former tenant whose arthritic joints no longer allowed unassisted movement, had recently taken permanent residence across the street at the little health facility. "Just in time for us to hook Stone," Torgeson was thinking, although he had better sense than to say aloud anything of the sort. Instead he chattered guilelessly as they moved down the walk toward the bungalows that were called the cottage apartments.

"You'd be our first tenant to bring in a cat, Mr. Stone, and we're most anxious to begin our little experiment with the . . . uh . . . the animals. So obviously I'm delighted that there's space available for you and . . . Puddin', did you say? Ah, yes. For you and Puddin'. We don't often have a vacancy in such popular units as these garden apartments." But if he thought Stone would jump at the vacancy, Torgeson was doomed to disappointment.

"Oh, no," Stone said at once, even before inspecting the interior. "This won't do at all. It's surrounded."

"Beg pardon?"

"It's the center unit in the bungalow—an occupied apartment on either side. Puddin' sometimes cries in the night. All cats do, I suppose. But I'm not going to take a place where I have to worry about waking people on two sides. Look, sir, there's the perfect place, down there . . ." And he pointed to the two cottages at the very end of the garden, each bounded on the inward side by the garden, on the outward side by the small city streets that hugged Camden-sur-Mer left and right, on the third side—the side to the west—by Beach Lane, the narrow street that paralleled the sea cliff and cut across the end of Camden-sur-Mer's garden, and on the back of each by a grassy strip.

"Don't you see it?" Stone said with enthusiasm. "That back entrance into the utility area would be the perfect place for me to put in a cat door. And I'd have a wonderful view of the ocean from my living room—which for me is one of your big selling points."

"And each apartment is slightly larger than those further up the garden toward the main building," Torgeson said enthusiastically, "since each of those bungalows contains only two apartments, not three or four."

"Wonderful," Stone said, his enthusiasm matching Torgeson's. "Then Puddin' and I would run less risk of disturbing a neighbor. It would help, I suppose, if my neighbor's hearing was failing . . ." He laughed jovially to let Torgeson know he was speaking partly in jest, then went on, "If either of those two places is available, I'll sign a contract today!"

"Oh, dear," Torgeson said, his enthusiasm ebbing swiftly away. "I regret to say that none of those four units is currently vacant. Three of the places are occupied by couples who are long-term residents in excellent health, and one—the one on the street side there in the right-hand unit—that one was just rented a couple of weeks ago to a Mr. Cherry from Moose Jaw, Saskatchewan. A widower. He seems to be happy here and settling in well. And he too is perfectly . . ." He hesitated a moment. "Well, to be candid, he has heart trouble. And Mr. Jefferson in the adjoining unit has diabetes. So I shouldn't say either one is completely healthy. But I couldn't in fairness suggest there'd be a vacancy any time soon. Look here, Mr. Stone, I tell you what. Why not rent the Berger apartment for the time being, and if one of these end units becomes available, you can be first on the list to take it?"

"Hmmmmm . . ." Stone considered the suggestion for a moment. "Let me think about that. It's a possibility, of course. But the cat door I will have made—and Puddin's comfort is one of the big reasons I'm moving here, that and your marvelous ocean view—that cat door will be expensive. I wouldn't want to have the job done twice. Let me think . . ."

And so, to Torgeson's disappointment (and the disappointment of Trinita Stainsbury, the Jackson twins, Mary Moffet, and Angela Benbow), Stone went back up the hill to The Golden Years without signing a residence contract. "But it would be so nice to have him here," Angela sighed. Caledonia just shook her head and said nothing.

Torgeson's disappointment was at least partly soothed on the very next day, however, when Della and Harvey Ridgeway appeared at his office. The cast of characters was beginning to take shape, although of course Torgeson was not aware of it.

Torgeson showed the Ridgeways a handsome double apartment overlooking the garden from the second floor, a set of rooms that seemed to please them very much. Torgeson invited them to lunch as his guests, where they sighed over a splendid Chicken Marengo. After lunch the Ridgeways sat in the garden enjoying the sunshine and the roses, chatting to whatever residents strolled past, and in midafternoon they came back into the lobby to attend a silver tea, an event staged every other week by ladies from various churches in the area. Today it was the women from The Church of the Eternal Covenant with the King of Heaven and Earth, over in Temeculah, who bustled cheerfully among the residents, refilling cups and offering seconds on the food they had brought, making bright, friendly conversation as they worked. Ordinarily a bit forbidding—dark and cavernous with outsized, overstuffed furniture—the lobby seemed romantic and even cozy today, with candles along the length of a serving table set up in the center of the room and the gleam of the dim overhead lights reflecting off an antique sterling service which shone above the lace cloth dressing the table, both the cloth and the tea service having been gifts from one of Camden-sur-Mer's first residents, years ago.

"Look, Della," Harvey Ridgeway whispered, giving his wife a huge nudge to be sure she obeyed him. "Look. They're giving us real china plates and cups. And cloth napkins!" Before they left that day, the Ridgeways had signed on the dotted line and paid their entry fee.

On the next day of Torgeson's Triumph, Torgeson fielded a phone call from Nancy Bush inquiring about the availability of single apartments. "There's been some trouble up here," she said cautiously.

"Trouble?" Torgeson's ears pricked up. Trouble imported from The Golden Years he didn't need.

"Well, nothing major, you understand, but I've had a quarrel with one of the women here, a Mrs. Madison, who's being most unpleasant. I've tried to avoid her, but it just isn't possible, and it's got to the point that I don't like to attend meetings or go into the commons room because I'm always running into this Madison person. Maybe it doesn't sound like much to you, but . . ."

"Oh, dear lady, I quite understand," Torgeson lied. He had quarreled with a number of people, but always felt it was up to them to avoid him, not the other way around. "If you feel that coming here would make your life easier and happier . . ."

"Oh, undoubtedably," Nancy said. "So if there were any way I could move right in . . ."

There was a largish studio apartment on the northeast corner of the building, vacant at the moment because it had no view of the ocean. But when Nancy Bush visited later that same day, she assured Torgeson the view was of secondary concern—peace and quiet were more important. Torgeson rubbed his hands in satisfaction as she signed a contract and wrote a check. His list of vacancies was getting shorter and shorter; things were definitely looking up.

Then, only two days later, Mr. Cherry was so obliging as to drop dead in the night. The dining room waitress who had Mr. Cherry's table at breakfast marked his absence from the meal and quietly notified the head nurse, who went down the garden to check, finding the unfortunate Mr. Cherry in his pajamas, lying dead in the middle of his living room clutching a bed pillow to his scrawny chest, his television playing softly, the couch-side lamp on, and all the shades drawn. It was assumed that he had been unable to sleep, perhaps feeling unwell, and he had gone into the living room during the night to watch some television from the living room couch. "And it was there," Doc Carter said judiciously when he came to make a preliminary examination, "that his heart trouble caught up with him. I've examined him twice since he arrived here, you know, and his heart was an absolute ruin. But at least the dear man appears to have died peacefully. It would have been quick, and he wouldn't suffer, you know." He sighed. "I'll write out the death certificate, of course. Tell Mr. Torgeson to make the necessary arrangements."

And Torgeson did, after contacting Mr. Cherry's only remaining relative, a cousin in Regina, who authorized Torgeson to take charge. Within another twenty-four hours, Mr. Cherry's furniture and possessions were packed and moved out, a refund check was written to the cousin (Mr. Cherry's passing having come at the four-week mark in his residency, the check was for just half of his entry fee). Then the handymen's schedule was altered to have them start at once to freshen up the Cherry apartment, although, as Pete Lopez the head carpenter said, it hardly seemed necessary, since Cherry hadn't lived in the place long enough to track sand onto the carpet, let alone get dirty fingerprints on the walls.

"It's sad, of course," Torgeson remarked to his secretary Juana Ortega as he beamed out over the May garden from the window in his office. "Terribly sad." He smiled again. "Still, it clears the way for a new tenant who will be a real asset," and as his lecture made clear to the long-suffering Juana, the profit to his bosses would be significant. "This has been a remarkably successful year so far. Five new tenants. And the best of it is, four of them have come from The Golden Years. Or will come," he added. "We'll need to notify Conrad Stone that the unit he wanted has become vacant, of course. And then . . ." and he ticked off on his fingers all the steps needed to finalize the change in tenants.

Torgeson wasn't quite so happy the next day when Conrad Stone came to discuss the alterations he wanted made in the place. Pete Lopez called Torgeson down for a three-man conference by the apartment's back door. "It's gonna be a bigger job'n you thought, Mr. Torgeson," Pete said. "This guy wants a hole cut in this back door that's so big it's gonna make the door buckle. I mean, it'd weaken the whole structure. Wouldn't be surprised if the door warped just hanging there."

"What do you mean, a big hole? I thought you could just cut a . . . like a flap. And put hinges on it, of course."

"Huh-uh," Lopez said. "He wants it like maybe two feet by two feet, or thereabouts."

"Two feet by . . . What is this animal of yours, Mr. Stone? A cougar?"

"No-no-no. He's big, all right, but not quite that big. It's just so Puddin's whiskers don't brush the edges," Stone explained. "Cats hate to feel a narrow opening rubbing their . . ."

"I don't know," Torgeson said, clearly worried. "A hole that big might make the door as useless as having no door at all. I mean, a burglar . . . all he'd have to do is level one swift kick at it."

"Okay, okay," Stone said. "You've convinced me." He narrowed his eyes and walked back and forth, staring at the door. "Okay, how about this? Suppose you didn't cut into the door itself. Suppose you cut the flap into the back wall? Neatened it up with a frame all around, of course. How about that?"

It was Lopez's turn to think a moment. "Well, we could do that I s'pose. But it's gonna come out behind the cabinets, isn't it? The cabinets and the counter run right across that kitchen wall to the door frame."

"Cut it up at counter height!" Stone said. "Puddin' loves to be up high on things. It'd suit him fine to walk across that counter to get to his door. And he could jump right down to the stoop here, and . . ."

"But how about getting back in from outside? That door would be at least three feet up from the stoop," Torgeson protested.

"You don't own a cat, do you, Mr. Torgeson?" Lopez grinned. "A jump of three feet would be nothing for any self-respecting cat, provided he had someplace to land. And I could build a kind of shelf on the outside, so he has a place to light when he jumps up, if you see what I mean. I could do that real neat."

"Well, then," Stone said. "Then what's the problem?"

"A hole in the wall, though," Torgeson said.

"Pete'll put a bolt on the inside so I can close it tight whenever I'm not there, right?"

"But what if you change your mind and move out? We're stuck with an apartment with a big hole in the wall, and . . ."

"Well," Stone said, reaching into his pocket to withdraw a checkbook, "suppose I gave you $1,000 right now as earnest money? Over and above the entry fee, of course." Torgeson's eyes lit up. "I don't know what the whole job will cost," Stone went on, pulling out a thin, gold ballpoint. "But it doesn't matter. Now, I want you to make a neat, professional job of it, Mr. Lopez."

"You betcha," the carpenter said, pulling a steel tape from his pocket and starting to take measurements.

Stone smiled. "Well, then, it's settled."

"Indeed it is," Torgeson said, restraining himself with difficulty from rubbing his palms together in glee. "It won't take Pete long, and we'll have you and Puddin' here with us in just a few days." He went back up the garden path beaming, a smile that broadened when he realized that a moving van had arrived and a crew was busily bringing the Ridgeways' possessions through the lobby and upstairs. Angela and Caledonia were already standing casually around, as were a number of other residents, all trying to pretend they were there for some other reason as they watched the moving men come and go. Looking · over newcomers was one of the activities of which the tenants never tired: estimating their net worth from the apparent value of their possessions, commenting on their taste, speculating on what might be an heirloom and what a garage-sale acquisition, trying to see how the newcomers might fit into the "extended family."

"Can't imagine why anybody'd want to move in here," a gravelly voice came at Angela's side. It was Mr. Grogan, a little bleary as usual, but relatively sober, though suffering from the hangover that seemed to be his in perpetuity. "It's none of my business, of course, if one of our fellow residents wants to ruin his own liver," Angela said frequently to Caledonia. "But Mr. Grogan can be so unpleasant when he's drinking."

"He's not much better when he hasn't had a drink," Caledonia reminded her. "The man is just a natural-born grouch, and that's all there is to it. The thing to do is stay out of his way, Angela. When you see Grogan coming, drunk or sober, just move out of the line of fire."

But this time, Grogan had caught Angela and Caledonia unawares by coming through the garden door behind them, so that he was standing next to them talking—or rather grousing, whining, carping, finding fault—even before they knew he was approaching. There was no escape short of downright rudeness. "This place ain't exactly a barrel of laughs," he went on. "Look around you. Sick people, old people, people dying in the night . . . What makes these folks from up on the hill think this is one bit better'n the place they're coming from?"

"Oh, but it is!" Caledonia said. "This place lives up to its name— it's a retirement home. That place on the hill is just a . . . a geezer factory!"

"Huh?"

"A place that makes old geezers out of people. I mean, you start out perfectly all right, but you move in up there and they regulate you and starve you and bore you . . . and pretty soon you're just another old geezer."

"Hah! And of course that wouldn't suit that man with the movie star face, would it?" Grogan said sourly.

"He is good-looking, isn't he?" Angela breathed. "That wonderful hair, that perfect complexion, that firm jawline . . ."

"Oh, for Pete's sake, Angela!" Caledonia's reproof was impatient. "He wants a place he and his cat can be happy together," she told Grogan. "Angela's hoping he'll make room in his life for her as well as for Puddin' . . . that's the cat." Angela blushed but said nothing.

"I've seen the type before. There's always something wrong with these guys who are too pretty for their own good." Grogan nodded wisely, then clutched his temples in both hands. "Oooooh, shouldn't jostle my head like that in the morning. Anyhow, he puts me in mind of a fellow I used to know back when I was in the newspaper business in Seattle. So good-looking that the girls fell all over themselves trying to get him to notice them. That guy turned out to be a woman."

"What!"

"Masquerading as a man, you know? Handsome ol' gal nearly six feet tall with broad shoulders. Like you, Mrs. Wingate."

"Hey!"

"Not that I think you're a man in disguise. Or that you should disguise yourself as . . ."

"Oh, Grogan, hush up!" Caledonia was impatient. "I've talked to Stone, and he's not a woman, trust me."

"Not right now, he's not, maybe, but he could have been at one time, couldn't he?" Grogan said. "Saw something like that on *Geraldo* the other day. On TV, you know. I say you keep an eye on him. Or her." And he stumped off toward the main desk to pass the time of day with Clara, the redheaded clerk.

The fourth day of Torgeson's Triumph saw yet another vacant

apartment rented. Howard and Harriet Gould, a couple from Min-neapolis, visited Camden-sur-Mer, looked over the Berger apartment in the garden, and signed a contract on the spot. "We haven't been retired too long," Howard explained, "and we're both in excellent health, but we know Janice Felton, one of your residents, and she's been recommending this place for ages. And Janice says people shouldn't wait till they're ailing to join a community like this. She told us we should move in while we can still enjoy the company and the activities . . ."

"It's true," Torgeson said with obvious pleasure, "that most of our folks don't come in till they're alone and perhaps starting to fail a bit. You'll be younger than the average resident here by as much as . . ." He hesitated, looking at the unlined face and red-gold hair of Harriet Gould. To himself he was thinking, "Dye job. Face lift." But he wasn't about to say that. Instead he said, ". . . you'll be younger than the average by perhaps ten years. So I recommend that you look around and be sure you're going to feel comfortable here." Juana Ortega, listening from her desk outside Torgeson's office door, could hardly believe her ears. No high pressure, no bending the truth . . . Torge-son's recent success in filling his vacant spaces had made him both more gracious and more considerate. She smiled quietly and went back to her work.

Tact and honesty didn't seem to hurt Torgeson's success record. The Goulds exclaimed happily over everything they saw, and though the Berger apartment was a bit smaller than they'd hoped for, they insisted it would do until something larger came along. "And one of the most important things, I can keep my Desmond with me. My cat," Harriet Gould said with delight. "I've been so worried what to do if we should go into a home. So many of them don't allow pets. We were delighted to hear about your new policy. I couldn't wait to tell Desmond!"

Behind her back, Howard whirled one forefinger around his ear and made a face to Torgeson that implied that "telling Desmond" was just some lunatic aberration of which he did not approve. Tor-geson merely nodded. If Howard wanted to think that meant Tor-geson understood and sympathized, well and good. Aloud Torgeson explained that this new rule allowing cats was, after all, only an ex-periment, begun by vote of the Residents' Council. "Your Desmond will be our second pet—well, our second of the four-footed variety—and we're most anxious to see if this is a good policy or not."

"Residents' Council, eh?" Howard Gould said. "Now there's something I might be interested in joining. I was on the school board back home and I was appointed to a citizens' planning council. Knew the mayor, and he chose me. I liked the work. Kind of thought I'd be a good politician. Anyhow, I think that council sounds like my kind of thing. Besides," he added with a wink aimed at Torgeson behind his wife's back, "I'd like to have a vote about this cat experiment, when it comes time to decide whether to keep the policy or not."

Torgeson nodded and thought to himself that if Howard had his way, perhaps the days of the grand experiment were numbered. Puddin' and Desmond might well be the first and last feline residents ever to live at Camden-sur-Mer. But all Torgeson said aloud was, "We like to have residents who want to participate, and we always welcome the council's suggestions."

"We've already sold our house back in Minneapolis and our stuff is out here in storage," Howard Gould was saying. "So we'll be in here within the week. If that's okay."

"Better than okay," Torgeson said. "I look forward to your arrival most eagerly." He was beaming as the Goulds departed, and his mood was not dampened when Clara came bustling in to tell him that The Golden Years had hit the newspapers with unfavorable publicity—"At last!" Torgeson breathed—because one of their residents had fallen to her death from a second-story window.

"It's time they had some bad publicity," Torgeson said gleefully. "Every time we've had a little bad luck of that kind, it's hit the newspapers and we hear about it for weeks. The number of new residents goes down and all people can talk about, when they do check us out, is that somebody got themselves killed here." He shook his head in disapproval of such tenderhearted sentimentality. "Well, now it's their turn up at The Golden Brick Pile, and it serves 'em right. I bet you that Calvin Bugle and Tootsie Armstrong wish now that they hadn't moved up there!"

He was half right. Tootsie Armstrong was in his office the next afternoon to talk about taking her old apartment back. "Unless you've already rented it?"

"Oh, no, it's still vacant, but I don't know . . ." Torgeson hesitated, but inside he was jubilant. Tootsie's place had not yet been renovated for a new tenant; that chore had been delayed in favor of doing up the old Cherry place for Conrad Stone's move. If Tootsie came back to Camden-sur-Mer, the renovation on her apartment need never be done at all, saving an expense that . . . "You realize you'd have to pay another entry fee," Torgeson said cautiously.

Tootsie's eyes filled with tears. "But I just paid the fee up at The Golden Years, and they won't give it all back to me. I paid an entry fee when I came here . . ."

"Years ago, Mrs. Armstrong. Years ago. Though, I'll tell you what . . ." Juana Ortega stopped rattling the keys of the computer long enough to be sure she overheard every word. "Tell you what," Torgeson went on expansively. "You're a longtime resident, and we really want you back with us. So I tell you what. If you'll move back into your old apartment, and if you understand that we're not repainting or putting in a new carpet, I'll waive three-quarters of the usual entry fee. I'm sure I can talk my bosses into that concession."

"Oh, Mr. Torgeson!" Tootsie's tears flowed in earnest. "How wonderful. Thank you! I made such a dreadful mistake moving up the hill. It's so . . . so stiff and rigid. Some of the residents there joke about it. They say 'No dust, no germs, no fun!' "

"How about Mr. Bugle?" Torgeson said. "You think he might want to come back here? We only just started doing up his place. We haven't got very far, and if he were coming back . . ."

"I don't think so," Tootsie said. "He was never really happy here, you know. Not that he's happy up there, mind you, but somehow having all those rules seems to suit him better than it did me. He says he likes to know exactly what's going on all the time and rules do that for you. I had an uncle like that; Uncle Trevor didn't like people to change arrangements once they were made. So I understand Mr. Bugle. Once things are set, he wants them to stay that way. Here, he told me, we were always changing things."

"Improving things," Torgeson corrected her. "Listening to our residents' suggestions, and modernizing procedures, and . . ."

"Oh, yes," Tootsie said. "But that doesn't suit Mr. Bugle, all the same, so I don't think he'll be coming back."

And that was the week of Torgeson's Triumph. New tenants appearing, old tenants returning, The Golden Years losing residents to Torgeson and having trouble worthy of several column inches in the Camden *Daily Gazette* . . . it was all too wonderful to be believed. Torgeson checked his office door to see that it was truly shut tight, he checked the blinds on his window to be sure no one could look in from the garden, and he went to the bottom drawer of the oak file cabinet to take out a bottle of excellent bourbon and pour himself a small, congratulatory toddy. "Torgeson, old fellow," he toasted himself, "you've done well! Here's to you, my man!"

He sipped, he sighed, and he sank back into his chair with delight, holding his tiny shot glass up so that it caught the afternoon light. The amber glow in his hand reflected the golden glow of happiness in his heart. Torgeson's Triumph indeed! If there were clouds gathering on his horizon, Torgeson couldn't see them. Yet.

CHAPTER

7

I N THE MANNER OF good friends everywhere, Angela and Caledonia often disagreed and found themselves wrangling about things that mattered very little—whether to take the retirement-home van downtown or hire a limousine; whether Mrs. Schmitt's Beef Burgundy was better than her Chicken Kiev; whether or not to go into the lobby for the twice-monthly tea. So it was not surprising that they wrangled over whether or not to attend the memorial service that was to be held for the late Regina Madison.

"You never even met her," Caledonia protested. "And I barely did. We talked for maybe five minutes one afternoon out in the courtyard. And you know I'm not really anxious to return to Alcatraz-on-the-Freeway. I had enough of that place in two days, believe me."

"But if we go up there," Angela said eagerly, "we might be able to ask questions. Find out . . ."

"Oh, Angela, don't be so silly. We only went exploring up there to help Tootsie, and she's moving back here. Besides, we've solved her mysteries. What would we be asking questions about now that we know there aren't any ghosts up there? I can't imagine . . . Oh, wait! I get it. It's Conrad Stone, isn't it? You want to see the stunning Conrad again, don't you? Angela, you're absolutely the end!"

"Now, Cal, don't be so judgmental." Angela turned her tiny nose skyward. "Not about me; I'm used to that. About Conrad Stone. I'll repeat, you don't really know him. Besides, this has nothing to do with him. And even if it did, why would I want to go to this memorial? The renovation of his apartment will be finished tomorrow, and he'll be moving in almost at once, and . . ."

"You've been nosing around down at the end of the garden?"

"Certainly not. I asked Clara. She knows everything, and she says they've really pushed because Torgeson thinks Conrad Stone is such a desirable new tenant. Besides, he gave Torgeson a check for $1,000 extra, and that was wonderful motivation for Torgeson to push the crew and have them put in a little overtime. So if I wanted to know anything about Conrad Stone, I'd only have to wait another day or two. No, it isn't that. It's . . . well, I was thinking we ought to ask a few questions about how Regina Madison died."

"Oh, for Pete's sake! Her head cracked when she hit the ground after falling from a second-story window, that's how she died."

"No-no-no. I mean, who pushed her!"

"Angela! Nobody pushed her. She fell!"

"Well, they don't know that, do they? They just think so! And we should certainly ask around a little bit, shouldn't we? Please, Cal . . . you know you're as curious as I am. Besides, we always pay our respects at the memorial for people we've known, don't we?"

Finally, grumbling and groaning, Caledonia agreed, and that afternoon at 3:00 the women clambered from the limousine Caledonia had insisted they hire and came through the antiseptic lobby of The Golden Years, down the sterile hallways and into the tiny and entirely utilitarian chapel. They were just in time. The loudspeakers overhead crackled to life with a recorded rendition of "The Children's Hymn," and as the two women slipped into a vacant place in the next to last row, a middle-aged man they did not recognize came to the podium to speak. Reading from a card that he took from his breast pocket, he extolled Regina Madison's involvement in the life at The Golden Years ("Caught every bit of it through her binoculars," Caledonia whispered), her generosity to her friends and relatives (Caledonia thought of the afghan Regina had been crocheting for her sister), her love of small creatures ("She was cat-sitting for neighbors," Caledonia whispered. "Must have been a cat lover, to do that, I s'pose . . ."), her sense of responsibility, her lively good spirits . . .

Just when Angela was starting to fidget and leaned over to Caledonia and whispered, "How long is he going to go on? He obviously didn't know her personally. You could say those things about half the people here!" the recorded hymns began again—"Onward Christian Soldiers," "Harvest Home," and "The Little Brown Church in the Dell"—and the memorial was over. "I bet the Chapel Committee just bought a ready-made tape of religious favorites to play," Angela complained as they edged their way out into the main aisle. She complained softly, however, since people who might overhear and be offended were pressed close around them on all sides, as people do cluster when they leave a church.

"You're right," Caledonia whispered back. "There isn't a one of those that's a funeral hymn, and I'm not sure the last one qualifies as a hymn at all!"

As they inched their way toward the chapel door, they recognized a few faces among the crowded audience: Tootsie with her friends the Dusenbergs; Conrad Stone; and the Ridgeways, obviously back just for the occasion. Then someone behind them spoke: "How good of you two ladies to come back for the service," and they turned their heads to find Simon Peterson moving up the aisle directly behind them. "Recognized you from your two days here. Made up your minds? Going to join us permanently?"

"Oh, we don't know yet," Angela lied hastily. "I don't believe I had the chance to meet you while we were here. You're . . ."

The man introduced himself to both women. Caledonia didn't bother to tell him she already knew who he was, though he looked a great deal less bulbous and bloated in his jacket and trousers than he had in his swim trunks. Instead she said, "I'd heard about your arrangement with Mrs. Madison—to check on you because of your heart. What will you do now?"

"So good of her to look after me that way," Peterson said. "Mrs. Ashmore—perhaps you met her while you were here?—she's up on the third floor, so she can look across at my windows, and she's agreed to train her binoculars on me from time to time just as Regina used to do." He smiled wanly. "I'm grateful to Mrs. Ashmore, but I shall miss Regina all the same. She was such a bright conversationalist and she had such a lively interest in the world, besides playing guardian angel to me." He sighed. "Friends are terribly important, in this tired old world. I ought to know—I've reached the age where I seem to be losing my friends left and right. Regina's gone, and now Conrad Stone is leaving too . . . Now, that was an unpleasant shock. Oh, I'm sure he's got good reason for the move. But he's been my next-door neighbor as long as he's lived here, and we'd got quite chummy. It'll be lonely around here, till I make new friends." And he moved off, shaking his head.

"What now?" Caledonia growled. "Who'd you figure you'd grill about the cause of Mrs. Madison's death?"

"What about asking a policeman?" a man's soft voice sounded behind her. "They say we know everything." Caledonia turned to find herself almost eye-to-eye with the handsome face of Lieutenant Martinez, their favorite policeman in all of San Diego County, and her own face blossomed into a welcome.

Angela saw him too and beamed every bit as broadly. "Oh, Lieutenant! How lovely!"

"All right, Lieutenant! I'll bite. What're you doing here?" Caledonia challenged, though she smiled as she asked.

Martinez grinned. "Just the question I was about to ask you! But considering the kind of mischief you two get up to, I think I'd better ask it somewhere besides the entrance to a crowded chapel. Goodness knows what the answer might be. How about the small room next to the lobby? Is it a writing room? I don't know. It's got two desks and a supply of official stationery . . ."

The women followed eagerly along and easily located the small room, though Caledonia groaned to find the only chairs in the place were of the small, straight type most often stationed near a secretary's desk or at a telephone stand—designed to match the decor, not the user's anatomy, and guaranteed to be uncomfortable for a woman of Caledonia's queenly proportions. "Not so much as a cushion in the place," she sighed. "Oh, well . . ." and with a groan she spread her caftan—and her ample self—onto the largest seat available.

"All right, then. Since you asked . . ." Angela said, seating herself gingerly in a second chair, ". . . we're here to find out why Regina Madison died, and don't tell me it was because she hit the ground with her head. Caledonia has already said that to me. What we mean is, did she jump or was she pushed? And naturally we thought that, if she was pushed, perhaps we could take a hand in finding out why. And who. We didn't know Mrs. Madison well, but perhaps . . ."

Martinez held up a graceful, well-manicured hand. "Mrs. Benbow, I know your overwhelming interest in puzzles and mysteries. And of course I came here originally with the same questions you have. But everything we've discovered so far is consistent with the theory that her death was an accident."

"Was she faint or dizzy?" Angela said. "Was she ill and . . ."

"Not that we can determine. The autopsy shows no evidence of disease or physical abnormality and her general health was excellent for her age. No, apparently she overbalanced trying to lean far out to one side. It seems she had set herself the task of checking with her binoculars on a neighbor with a ground-floor apartment also facing the courtyard . . ."

"Simon Peterson. We know about that, Lieutenant," Caledonia said.

". . . and this particular evening," Martinez went on, "someone had moved one of the big tables down in the courtyard—the ones with the umbrellas mounted on them. Anyhow, someone had moved one of those tables so that it was between her and Peterson's window. She would have had to lean way, way over to peek around it. She'd even pulled off the screen and set it inside the room so she could lean further outside."

"Surely someone else could have pulled that screen off."

"Of course. But if another person did it, wouldn't she have become suspicious? Unlatching the screen and lifting it inside the room takes several seconds and she'd have had time to run away or call for help. No, removing the screen must have been something she did herself, which we consider very significant. We believe she leaned out as far as she could stretch and apparently that put her so far out of balance that she fell."

"Exactly what I thought," Caledonia nodded.

"But weren't there any marks on her?" Angela asked. "Like . . . well, I don't know about those things, but . . . something?"

Martinez nodded. "We did find some traces of . . ." He hesitated and decided against being specific. "Well, I don't think you'd want to know the specifics, but our medical examiner says she had torn fingertips as though she'd clawed at the brick. Except for the marks consistent with her striking the ground and some bruising on the legs—perfectly natural for a woman fighting to regain her balance—there were no other marks on the body." He hesitated and noticed that both women were tense and silent, their imaginations working overtime. "You don't want to hear any more of these unpleasant details, I'm sure. Just take it from me, we believe the death was accidental."

"But if that's the case, what are you doing here today, Lieutenant?" Angela said.

"Oh, I don't mean we've finished our investigation. We're still asking questions and looking things over. But about today specifically, well, I get to know the people I investigate," Martinez said with a soft smile. "And I got to thinking that except for her sister back east, this woman had nobody left in her family. It occurred to me that the chapel might be relatively empty for her memorial, so I thought I'd pay my respects."

"How nice of you!" Caledonia beamed at him, forgetting momentarily about her uncomfortable chair. "You are the kindest person! Of course you couldn't know that absolutely everybody in the place comes to these memorials. We often go to memorials for people we didn't even like very much. I mean, someday it will be our memorial service needing to fill the seats. So we feel an obligation of sorts, you see? But that doesn't keep yours from being an especially thoughtful gesture."

"You're kind to say so," Martinez said. "But don't give me too much credit. After all, a memorial service is a good place to look over the potential suspects. All the same, accident is the most likely answer. Murder by defenestration is relatively rare. It's been used as a tool of political assassins—some Austrian premier, I believe, in recent history. And not long ago, two pubescent Fagins in New York threw a younger child off the top of a building because he wouldn't steal for them. But it's not a good choice if you really want to kill, because people have been known to live through a fall—at least they've lived long enough on some occasions to bear witness against their attackers. Even shooting and stabbing aren't all that certain. Amateurs sometimes miss the vital spots, you know."

Martinez warmed to his subject, as he sometimes did, and lapsed into his lecturer's tone. "No, if you want to murder someone without their being able to survive and identify you to the police, you have to do something like knock them down with a club, hard and quick so they're dazed or unconscious—so they can't yell for help. Then just keep on clubbing till you're sure. And when you're done, wipe the club clean of fingerprints and—assuming you haven't been silly enough to use something that can be identified as yours, something like say your favorite 9 iron—just leave the weapon behind with the body. If you try to carry it away to dispose of later, the risk is too great someone will see it and remember."

"And another thing—" Martinez was immersed in his subject now. "Don't stick around trying to find out if anybody discovers a clue you overlooked. We often find killers in the crowd standing behind the yellow crime scene tape, gawking while the police are searching for clues and interviewing potential witnesses. So my advice would be, do your killing, go away, and stay away."

"But, Lieutenant, if one of the residents here had killed Mrs. Madison, it would be suspicious if they just up and left, wouldn't it? I should think they'd be more likely to stay right where they are, to keep up their daily routine so that nobody could say they'd acted oddly, let alone tried to make a getaway."

"Well, yes," Martinez conceded. "If it were a resident of a place like this, he—or she—would be wiser to stay put and keep up normal appearances. But since there is no killer here, we're just making idle conversation. And, Mrs. Benbow, don't you go getting people here excited and nervous by letting them think Mrs. Madison's death was anything but a natural death."

Caledonia smiled. "She's naughty, Lieutenant, but I'll see that she behaves. It won't be hard now that she's assured there's no crime needing her services as a detective. That's really why we're here, you know. To reassure Angela that there's no call for alarm."

Martinez got to his feet, and it was obvious to both women that the pleasant visit was at an end. "By the way, I hope we'll see you down at our place one of these days," Caledonia said. "Remember that sherry time is anywhere between four-thirty and supper time, and you're always welcome."

"If I ever have the time, it would be my pleasure," he promised and glided away.

"He moves so quietly," Angela said admiringly. "I never really notice him arriving till he's right beside us. And when he goes, he just sort of disappears, doesn't he?"

"Like a dancer, I always think," Caledonia agreed. "Well, come on. The limo's waiting to take us home again." She grinned as they moved off down the hall toward the front entrance. "Angela, I hate to say 'I told you so,' but I did tell you so. Except that we got to see Martinez, this whole memorial was a waste of time."

Angela shrugged. "Well, it might have been a crime, mightn't it? And wouldn't we have felt awful if there'd been a real murder case and we had let the opportunity to investigate slip away? Wouldn't you feel disappointed?"

"Not really. I enjoy our excursions, I suppose, and I certainly enjoy the breaks in routine. But by and large, I'm comfortable with my life, Angela, and I don't go looking for trouble, the way you do."

But whether they looked for trouble or not, trouble came and found them. To start with, the trouble was neither exciting nor glamorous, of course; in the everyday world where real people live, there are more annoyances than high tragedies, more mosquitoes than rogue elephants.

Two weeks after Regina Madison's death, well after all the new residents were in place at Camden-sur-Mer and settling in, the first trouble descended in the form of an unexpected rainstorm in the night. Whipped by a wind off the sea, the rain found its way into every crack and hole in the roofing and the stuccoed walls of the old building, and many residents of Camden-sur-Mer woke the next day to find that water had dripped through ceilings and fingers of moisture had pried in around windows facing south and/or west. The wind had snapped off flower heads; leaves, twigs, and dried palm fronds had been blown everywhere, every which way, so that by morning, the usually gracious gardens of Camden-sur-Mer looked like shaggy parkland instead of cultivated space.

By lunchtime, however, most of the damage from the overnight storm had been repaired. Gardeners had raked and brushed and scooped and stacked till a semblance of order had been restored to the grounds. Maids had gone to various apartments with mops and brooms and vacuum cleaners so that most of the residents were only temporarily inconvenienced by small leaks in walls and ceilings. But two of the rooms had been badly affected—Nancy Bush's studio apartment on the top floor and Angela Benbow's little suite on the first. Angela's living room drapes were a stained and sodden ruin, while Nancy's ceiling had come down in one corner, big chunks of wet plaster falling onto a little table and all over a velvet-covered easy chair. Torgeson inspected the damage and, with nothing better he could do, offered the ladies temporary quarters while repairs were done.

"There is only one vacant apartment right now," Torgeson told Angela. "We're putting Miss Bush there for the moment and getting started on her place at once. Then when Miss Bush has been able to return to her own quarters, we'll get started with your window frames. Yours is not the greater damage; that is to say, you can continue to live here. Miss Bush couldn't possibly occupy her unit until we get the ceiling up off the floor. All the same, yours is the more complicated job. That window will have to be pulled out and reset." He ran a probing finger over the frame, and his face drew itself into unhappy lines. "Perhaps we'll even have to get an entirely new frame here. This wood is in bad condition." He sighed. There went another chunk of the profits for the year. The owners would not be pleased, but there wasn't much he could do about it.

So all morning long the maids helped Nancy Bush transfer her clothing and personal articles to the new apartment—on the second floor of the south wing, overlooking the garden—and the handymen took down Angela's ruined drapes and sheers. "Nothing to be done with these except throw 'em out, Mrs. Benbow," Pete Lopez said. "This fabric ain't gonna clean worth a nickel. I'll take 'em to the cleaners for you, if you want, but . . ."

"Yes, do let's try to save them," Angela said. "I wouldn't mind new drapes, of course. But you don't know how long it took me to find this material that matches my couch and the carpet. I dread thinking of . . ."

"Mrs. Benbow, how long has your window been this way?" Pete pushed the lower half of the window up, then took his hands away and watched the window slowly slide back closed again. "It's supposed to stay open where you leave it, not slip back shut. But the whole window, frame and all . . . it's kind of loose in the outer frame, if you see what I mean."

Angela laughed. "Pete, I reported it that very first day I moved here. Furthermore, I've reported it every time I've thought of it ever since. I'm absolutely sure that if you look back through your work orders, you'll find a dozen complaints about this window."

Pete grinned at her. "Oh, no, Mrs. Benbow. Mr. Torgeson never gave me a work order on this window or I'd have been here and fixed it, sooner or later. Probably later, of course, because I gotta get to things in the order of how serious they are. But Mr. Torgeson, I guess he doesn't even pass along word on chores that can wait. Is that why you got this ruler sitting here on the sill?" He picked up and brandished a wooden, foot-long ruler.

"That's right. That's my window pole."

"Your what?"

"Remember when we used to have window poles to unhook and push open the tall windows in schoolrooms? Long wooden rods with a kind of metal hook on one end to catch hold of and unlock the latch, and then you propped the window open with the rod, one end on the floor, the other end holding . . ."

"I never even heard of a window pole, Mrs. B."

"Oh, dear. You're too young, I suppose. That goes back to my day.

Well, anyway, now that you know about my window being defective, I expect you to see that it's fixed. It's so difficult to open it, once it's slid shut."

Pete was struggling to pull out the spring-loaded pin locks that had snapped securely into their holes on each side of the frame and to push the window up at the same time. "Damn! Oh, gosh, I'm sorry, Mrs. Benbow. I shouldn't have said that, but this window takes three hands to get open, once it's slammed shut—one hand on each lock and a third hand to push up on the . . . How do you ever manage it?"

Angela laughed. "I get help. It's a two-person window, all right. And then once I have it open, I usually just leave it open, rather than struggle with it. I prop it up with my makeshift window pole."

"You don't close it at night?"

"No need, with our gentle weather here. Except for those few times it rains, of course."

Pete smiled proudly. "Well, you sure don't have to worry about burglars or anything, with the security grill on every window. That was my idea, Mrs. B. We needed a way to keep these ground-floor places safe and I thought the wrought iron would look real Spanish. Turned out to be real pretty, I think."

"I think so too, Pete," Angela assured him. "Listen, you see what you can do about getting me a whole new window, will you? I'm so tired of just fixing things up. They only break again right away." She sighed. "With this old place it's just patch, patch, patch . . . Kind of like the humans who live here, right?"

Pete Lopez just smiled and with tact born of experience said nothing.

"How are you liking the new apartment?" Tom Brighton asked Nancy Bush that noon, as the residents gathered outside the dining room before lunch to exchange descriptions of their storm damage and compete as to who had the most to complain about.

"Really nice," she said with enthusiasm. "I didn't realize that overlooking the garden was so pleasant. I can see the fountain—and if I lean way over, the ocean as well. Perhaps I'll ask to stay there instead of going back to my other room. The problem is that the new place has two rooms, and though I love having the space, it's more costacious than my one-room apartment was. So I'll have to consider carefully. Is it worth the extra money? That's what I have to think about."

By the very next morning, Nancy had made up her mind that the view was worth the expense. What remained of her furniture in the old apartment was moved to the new, and Torgeson came with Pete Lopez in tow—presumably for moral support—as he informed Angela that when repairs began on her place, she would have to move to the studio apartment that had once been Nancy Bush's.

"Go into a one-room apartment? Oh, dear, I don't think I'll fit. I'll have to leave most of my things here!"

"But that's all right. You can move a few changes of clothing and toilet articles . . . we'll put in a bed and dresser. The rest of your things will be just fine here while we work. And it's only for a few days, Mrs. Benbow." Behind Torgeson's back, Pete Lopez shook his head and grinned, flashing ten fingers in Angela's direction. "In fact, we're almost finished upstairs, and we should be ready to start your place after this weekend. We're on top of everything," Torgeson finished.

As usual with all changes, Nancy's decision to keep her new apartment was a source of discussion for the prelunch crowd. "So you're permanently in the place facing the garden now, eh?" Tom Brighton said. "I know it well. Right upstairs from me. It belonged to a Mrs. Benton before. Nice lady, but she fed wild birds up there . . ."

"Oh, dear. Wasn't that messy for you, down below?" Nancy asked, and Tom Brighton smiled.

"Glad you understand the problem without my having to tell you about it in detail, dear lady. I've never found a polite way to talk about bird droppings. I really don't know why I brought the subject up at all, come to think of it, except I suppose I was trying to ask tactfully whether or not you intended to feed the birds too."

"No-no-no . . . I have several hobbies, but birds aren't one of my enthusiasms. I prefer people."

Emma Grant, tall and slim, looked down at the tubby little Nancy Bush and nodded. "I quite agree, my dear. And there are fascinating and charming people here for one to study. But take my advice: be friendly, but don't become friends. At least, not too soon. Wait till you know who's who and what's what. Some of us might seem all right at first, and then you'd find out we have . . . peculiarities."

Caledonia Wingate, joining the group, rumbled her thunder of a laugh. "Peculiarities? Some of us are downright eccentric. And sometimes you have to get to know us before it shows. I mean, you wouldn't guess that Trinita Stainsbury is obsessed with lists and with making announcements over the loudspeaker, would you?" She gestured down the lobby to where Trinita was standing talking to the Jackson twins. On this particular day, Trinita was dressed in suede squaw boots and an aqua, ankle-length broomstick skirt topped with an off-the-shoulder blouse with a ruffle—obviously going Southwestern—and her hair, which she had drawn back into a large bun secured with huge, decorative silver hairpins, had now been dyed an odd shade of pale blue-green.

"Well," Caledonia said tolerantly, "maybe the aqua hair is supposed to remind you of a turquoise or something. Frankly, I liked last week's color better. A nice reddish brown. But I admit this dye job's an improvement on the time Trinita dyed herself purple. Now there was a sight, and . . ."

"Get outa my way," a voice growled, and heads turned to see Grogan push his way into the lobby past three other people just entering. Conrad Stone had waited at the garden door to let the Goulds come in before him, and Grogan simply elbowed his way between them. "Don't just stand there," Grogan said with a ferocity that made the other three cringe. "Dad-blasted people who want to pass the time of day and keep other people from getting where they're going!"

"Another case in point," Caledonia said, nodding toward Grogan. "Talk about eccentric . . . Listen, you newcomers. I apologize for Mr. Grogan. Don't judge us by the worst of us."

Fortunately for the sake of harmony, the Goulds and Conrad Stone merely smiled politely and joined the group without comment. "And how's my favorite little girl today?" Stone smiled, putting an arm around Angela's shoulders to give her a little squeeze in greeting. "And Mrs. Grant, Mrs. Wingate, Mr. Brighton . . ." He touched each woman's hand and gave a tiny bow toward Tom Brighton.

"We were surely sorry to hear about your misfortune with the rain, Miss Bush," Harriet Gould said. "What bad luck."

"No, actually it turned out to be good luck," Nancy said. "The new apartment has a fine view and I get to watch people come and go up and down the walk, and I get to look at the flowers . . . There's always something to see. Much nicer than the place I had, and I intend to stay where I am now."

"But I thought you liked that first apartment," Stone said.

"Oh, sure I did. But this is better. I feel as though I'm part of everybody's life. I was a little . . . a little isolitated in that first apartment. But now I can tell you all kinds of things about people in the garden apartments—for instance, who visits them at teatime, how much junk food they order in after hours, what time they take their morning walk, whether they sleep with their windows open or closed . . ."

"Well, then. No need to commiserate with you," Harriet Gould said, her voice a bit tight. "You're doing just fine, aren't you? Come along, Howard . . ." and she took her husband by the hand and literally pulled him away from the group. Fortunately, the double doors opened at just that moment and it was natural for them to move off and into the dining room.

"What did Nancy Bush say that could have got Mrs. Gould so upset? I wonder," Angela said later to Caledonia, "if Mrs. Gould was put out because she offered her sympathy where it wasn't needed? She certainly stiffened up there." But it didn't seem worth investigating and the subject didn't come up again.

As the week drew to its close, repairs in Nancy's old apartment neared completion, and Angela let Torgeson know that she had resigned herself to using a temporary bedroom while the work was done on her place. Torgeson took a deep breath of relief, as he always did when by a stroke of good luck he avoided direct confrontation and conflict. Perhaps things would settle down now and he could relax awhile and enjoy the luxury of having an almost full house.

Three days later Howard Gould was found dead in the garden, his head resting on the curled tail of one of the giant seahorses that made up the center of the fountain, and Torgeson, swallowing one antacid pill after another, found himself in the midst of another police investigation.

CHAPTER

8

ANGELA AND CALEDONIA WERE absolutely delighted to learn that their Lieutenant Martinez (and that is always how they thought of him, as *their* lieutenant) had come back to Camden-sur-Mer and would be interviewing witnesses (of whom there seemed to be none yet), friends (again almost none, since the Goulds were so new to the retirement home), and neighbors (except for Grogan, who as usual would be of less than no use, for even though his apartment was next door to the Goulds', he had viewed them most often through a haze of gin-and-tonic, rum-and-Coke, bourbon-and-branch, and assorted wine coolers). Once again Torgeson had reluctantly extended the hospitality of Camden-sur-Mer to Martinez and his gangly young partner, Shorty Swanson, till they had completed investigations. They were invited to share the bounty of the dining room and to take over the sewing room on the second floor as a temporary headquarters, and all morning long Angela and Caledonia had waited to be invited up to that room to talk about the Goulds and then—as they hoped— to be invited to join the fun.

"Well, not fun exactly," Angela said apologetically to Caledonia. "But you know what I mean. To be a part of things. To ask questions on behalf of the police, to run errands for the lieutenant, even to be interviewed so we can tell him everything we know . . ."

"Ah, but there's the rub," Caledonia sighed. "We don't know any-thing. How could we? The Goulds were newcomers . . . the newest of the newcomers, if you don't count Tootsie's return."

"All the same," Angela said, "the lieutenant realizes how useful we've been to him in the past. He knows that we're better at interpreting senior citizens and their motives than he would be. And of course we know our own neighbors here and we can even find out things he can't. I'm positive he'll send for us soon and perhaps even give us an assignment."

But they waited and they waited, and they weren't sent for until after lunch, by which time they were both on edge with anticipation. They were greeted warmly by Martinez and Swanson, a greeting they returned with enthusiasm. But Caledonia was a bit grumpy after what she considered a longish wait for attention, and she hadn't had time for her usual nap after lunch. So she spoke sharply. "We may not have a lot to say about this," she began, "but one thing I'm certain of. You'll have to look outside Camden-sur-Mer for a killer. He wasn't murdered by any of us. None of us is dippy enough to kill a man who's practically a total stranger."

"Wait! Wait a minute!" Angela protested. "Janice Felton knew the Goulds. They said she recommended this place."

Caledonia's expression was scornful. "You're not implying that Janice killed him, are you?"

"Well, no, of course not, but you said he's a total stranger and that's not true. Somebody knew him. Just not us. We didn't know him, you and me. Or is that 'you and I'? Or maybe 'you and me' . . ." She stopped and began to whisper to herself for a second and then said aloud. "All right. I've got it. It's 'you and I.' I just had to say it out loud. When I was in grade school my teacher used to drill us on pronouns like . . . well, she'd have us say the sentence over again with the 'you and me' as the subject and then we had to say it aloud without the 'you' . . . to see if it sounded right, you know? Because the 'you and I' actually stands for the 'we' that's the subject. We'd sit there muttering 'You and me didn't know him,' then 'Me didn't know him,' and of course it sounded so bad we knew that 'I' was right and 'me' was wrong. "See?" she finished triumphantly. The others were staring at her with blank faces.

"Mrs. Benbow," Lieutenant Martinez finally said with a sigh, "I not only don't see, I lost you about at the first 'you and me.' Do you suppose we can get back to the point? You came here to tell me what you know about the Goulds, and . . ."

"And we don't know a single thing. We can't be of any help, and that's the long and short of it," Caledonia said. "Of course we're pleased to have the chance to visit with you awhile, because we don't get to see you that often, though we often see young Swanson. He comes to visit his fiancée whenever she can get away from her waitressing at the same time he's off duty. Don't you, Officer Swanson?"

Swanson, seated at the end of the big table in the sewing room, his notebooks open before him, a supply of pencils ready, blushed crimson and looked fixedly downward at the scarred oak tabletop when Caledonia mentioned his frequent visits to Camden-sur-Mer. "Canoodling with the girlfriend!" Caledonia's laugh was a trumpet call. "Not that we don't approve. We love Chita and we're very fond of you, too, Swanson."

"Now who's off the point?" Angela interrupted. "Lieutenant, Caledonia's excessively negative about our being of help. The truth is that being insiders here at Camden-sur-Mer, we still know our neighbors better than you do, even if we didn't know the victim himself. I'm absolutely certain we'd be of use to you. Besides," she cooed, in her most wheedling tones, "we really treasure the chance to work with you again." Martinez gave her a half bow of acknowledgment, and she plunged on with her appeal. "I mean, it's a murder, after all, and we've been pretty helpful in other murders."

"Mrs. Benbow, I've been grateful to you in the past, it's true. But I really don't know what you can do in this case, if you have no information to pass along about the Goulds. Or rather," he added quickly, as he noted Angela's patent disappointment, "I don't know yet what you might be able to do for me. The truth is, nobody's been of much help and we have very little to go on, so far. We'll find clues as we go along, I'm sure. But right now . . . you'd think the perpetrator was listening to my lecture the other day. You remember my telling you that the best way to commit murder would be to bash someone hard enough that they couldn't call for help, wipe the weapon clean of prints, and just walk away? Well, Howard Gould was killed almost instantly by a blow from one of the hammers taken from a toolbox left near the cottages, which was then wiped clean of fingerprints and dropped right there beside the body."

"A toolbox near the cottage?"

"I don't think the toolbox itself has any significance. Pete had sent one of his men down to sandpaper some rough edges on a door frame they'd just installed."

"That would be the frame on the cat door," Angela said.

"Cat door?" Swanson was startled enough to interrupt again. "You're letting people have cats here now, Mrs. Benbow? Oh, excuse me, Lieutenant," he apologized hastily. "I didn't mean . . . I mean, I meant to, but I didn't mean . . . I mean, Chita didn't tell me about the cats." He blushed again and ducked his head. "I don't suppose it's important, but it's something new."

"Officer Swanson," Angela said, eager to be the one to offer the information, "they're trying the policy out and there are two cats here: Puddin' and Desmond. Puddin' belongs to Conrad Stone and Desmond belongs to the Goulds."

"Clara told us," Caledonia put in, "that Conrad Stone went on and on about the sloppy job the men had done with the framing. He was arguing that the rough edges snagged his jacket when he reached through, and he said that Puddin' scraped against the raw wood, too. That Puddin's one fat cat, Lieutenant—wait'll you see him! Anyhow, I suppose eventually Torgeson got tired of the complaints and sent the carpenters down to fix it. The squeaky wheel gets the grease around here, all right."

"Careless of the workmen to leave their tools lying about," Martinez said. "Because that toolbox was lying there in plain sight from the walkway, it furnished a weapon of opportunity for whoever killed Mr. Gould."

"Murder in the first degree!" Angela breathed with obvious delight.

"Well," Martinez said cautiously, "we don't know the degree yet, do we? It might even be manslaughter, though it surely doesn't look that way. Anyway, we're in the process of investigating right now, and . . .

"We know. We could see the yellow crime-scene tape around the fountain. We could sit at our table in the dining room and watch all your people working—taking pictures, measuring, marking, searching for clues . . ." Angela's voice vibrated with excitement.

"Glad you took poor Howard away before we got up and walked through the garden this morning, Lieutenant," Caledonia said. "It's hard enough to face breakfast—even the thought of breakfast—before my coffee's taken effect, but to have to look at a body as well . . ."

"Nobody says you have to look, Mrs. Wingate," Martinez said. "Besides, the fountain's at the far end of the garden from your apartment. If you caught sight of Howard Gould's body, you went out of your way to do it. All the same, I'm glad we could clean things up a bit before you and the other residents saw anything unpleasant. Well, enough of this. We have interviews scheduled, and . . ." He got to his feet and made a small gesture to indicate this interview was at an end. Swanson took the cue at once, folding away his notebook and setting down his pencil.

Reluctantly, Angela and Caledonia headed for the door, escorted by the lieutenant, who said, "It seems to me you're right. Your connection with the Goulds was a merely casual acquaintance, so there's nothing you can do to help me yet. Don't look so disappointed, ladies. I said 'yet' and I meant it. If there's anything you can help with, you know I'll be in touch at once. And now . . ." He ushered them out with a little bow and closed the door behind them.

Angela said nothing as they walked down the hall to the elevator, but once safely inside, after the heavy door had slid shut and the car began to creak and groan, lowering them gently to the lobby level, Angela smiled widely and said with satisfaction, "Well, Cal, we're on the case. I'm not sure what the first thing to do is, but probably we should . . ."

"Beg pardon? Did you hear something I didn't?"

"You know Lieutenant Martinez wants us to ask a few questions of our friends and watch and listen for anything unusual or odd. He doesn't have to say it."

Caledonia grinned herself. "Provided he doesn't say 'Don't' you assume he said 'Do.' Well, I'll admit it usually works out just fine. Question is, who should be talked to first? And of course, what should we ask? I haven't really got a feel for this yet. All I know is that Howard Gould was found facedown in the fountain this morning, and . . ."

"That's what I was about to say, Cal, if you'd just wait and let me finish. I thought we should go first and talk to Harriet Gould. It would be perfectly natural, of course, because everyone will be stopping by her place to offer condolences. She wouldn't be suspicious of us if we stopped by and then just casually dropped a few questions into the conversation. There's no telling how much we could find out."

"Well, why not?" Caledonia led the way out of the elevator toward the garden door. "It can't hurt. And we certainly do need to stop by to extend sympathies, right? I won't even have to walk very far, since their place is right across the garden from me," Caledonia said.

"Oh, dear. It's a wonder the Goulds didn't move right out, the first time they realized that their very next-door neighbor was Grogan," Angela said. "Has Grogan been singing lately?"

"Opera," Caledonia nodded. "The love duet from *Madama Butterfly* last night. 'Ridi, Pagliacci,' the night before. It used to be folk songs and Irish ballads. Where he got the notion he was a classical tenor . . ."

Harriet Gould answered their knock almost immediately, her thin face woebegone, her iron-gray hair straggling loose from its knot at the nape of her neck. It had been a chilly morning, and though it had warmed up beautifully by lunch time, she still wore a cardigan over her simple blouse and skirt, the sweater pockets jammed with Kleenex. From time to time she dipped into one of the pockets and pulled a tissue up to her eyes to dab at the tears that welled up almost continually.

"My dear," Angela began, "I'm sure you're not really up to visitors yet, but we did want to offer our sympathy."

Harriet didn't speak, merely nodded, but she did step slightly aside, all the invitation Angela needed to pull Caledonia after her into the small apartment: a living-dining room combination with a kitchen wall across one end, partially shielded from their view at the moment by a long folding door. Off the tiny hallway stood the bath on one side and a bedroom on the other, as Angela knew from having seen the apartment when it was occupied by Mrs. Berger, the bedroom walled on one side by floor-to-ceiling windows and a patio door opening onto the garden.

"I . . . I suppose . . . I mean, please do sit down," Harriet Gould said, seemingly helpless to do less than give a lukewarm welcome to her uninvited guests. Harriet chose a small, straight chair and sat with her ankles crossed, her hands lying limply in her lap. She looked inquiringly at the two visitors, but said nothing.

"I've always liked this little place," Angela began, seating herself on a small couch. "That bedroom window is wonderful. My own apartment faces east like this, and sometimes it's nice just to lie in bed and let the morning sun warm the room before I get up. But your apartment is even better, because of course," she babbled on, "I don't have the view of the roses. If I lived here, I'd lie in bed for hours looking out at the flowers."

If the purpose of Angela's talk-talk-talk was to get Harriet Gould started talking too, it worked. "Howard always got up as soon as he woke," Harriet said in the voice of sad reminiscence. "He didn't like to lounge around. Said it was a waste of his time. It didn't matter whether it was morning or the middle of the night, he'd get right up as soon as he opened his eyes. So full of . . ." she choked and whispered, "so full of life."

"I suppose," Caledonia ventured, "that's what happened last night, is it? He woke up in the night and slipped out the patio door. Did he slide it shut behind him?"

"I guess so. It was shut this morning when I woke up," Harriet said, swallowing hard. "Howard was so considerate. He wouldn't have wanted the draft to get on me. I've had a stiff neck from drafts, and . . ."

"But that's not the point," Angela said. "The point is, what woke him? Why did he go out there in the first place?"

"I really don't know," Harriet said. "I didn't hear anything, but my hearing's not all that good these last few years. Probably he got up to let our cat out, but maybe he just woke. Since we've been here, Howard hasn't been sleeping well—getting used to a strange place, I suppose. So he often got up at night. Sometimes he'd go into the living room to watch TV. He'd listen through earphones, so as not to wake me. I kept telling him I wouldn't hear it, but Howard never liked to take chances, you know? So he used the earphones and . . ." Her voice got thick with tears again and she broke off her narrative. "I don't know why I'm talking about that."

"No-no-no, dear," Angela assured her. "It's good to talk about all sorts of things. It'll make you feel better. For instance . . ." Her face took on a foxy look, and Caledonia turned quickly away, appearing to take in the view of the garden. She could read "I'm about to spring!" written all over her friend's features, but perhaps, Caledonia thought, it wasn't so obvious to Harriet Gould, who didn't know Angela well.

"For instance," Angela went on craftily, "you need to think about the reason this might have happened. Who Howard's enemies were . . ."

"Enemies!" Harriet was indignant. "How could we have enemies? We'd just arrived here."

"But how about enemies from back home? In . . . you did say Minneapolis, didn't you?"

Harriet made an exasperated noise. "Howard was the sweetest, most considerate . . . We got along with our neighbors. I don't recall any time he had a quarrel with a customer or a competitor. His employees adored him . . ."

"How about relatives? Family can get madder at you than strangers can, and . . ."

"Nonsense. Dear old Aunt Edna an enemy? Her son Roald? My

sister Letitia? Besides, Edna's in Boston, Cousin Roald is a lieutenant colonel stationed in Europe, and Letitia lives in Alaska. None of them could come here to attack Howard even if they wanted to! Which they don't!"

"You never know," Angela began, but Caledonia, who had recognized the tone of finality in Harriet Gould's voice, nudged her little friend hard.

"That's wonderful," Caledonia said, ignoring Angela's annoyance at the interruption. "I wish everybody got on with their relatives and business contacts and neighbors as well as you and Howard did, my dear. And of course, as you say, you're new here, so you hadn't time to rub anyone here the wrong way. Even," she added hastily, "if you'd been so inclined."

"What sort of thing was Howard especially interested in?" Angela said, trying another tack.

"Interested in? I . . . I don't know what you mean," Harriet said. "He collected United States stamps. He was a golfer . . . oh, and he liked to read historical novels."

"I was thinking more of the sort of thing that might have taken his attention during the night and beckoned him to walk out into the garden," Angela said. "I was thinking . . . Oh!" A small, furry object had landed squarely in the middle of her lap.

"Desmond," Harriet said, scooping up the gray-striped cat in a practiced motion and bringing him to her own lap and away from Angela. "Don't be naughty, Desmond. Perhaps Mrs. Benbow doesn't like cats."

"Oh, I adore them. It was just—I was startled, that's all."

"Actually," Harriet went on, stroking Desmond as she talked, "I assume that's what woke Howard. Desmond having to—you know, do his business. That happens at least once every night. Howard wasn't happy about being Desmond's designated doorman, but I just don't wake that easily, and Howard was wide awake at the first little meow. Desmond certainly knows to go to Howard's side of the bed to make his request. Howard just gets up, lets him out, stands there and waits, and in a few minutes, when Desmond comes back in, Howard gets back into bed. But last night . . ." Her voice choked and she wiped away another tear. "The paper boy found him, you know. I didn't even wake up. Not till the police knocked at my door." Her breath was a tremulous sigh. "Oh, dear, what will I do without Howard? And poor Desmond's going to miss him so much too!" Desmond squinted his green eyes balefully from the shelter of Harriet's arms and snuggled himself down even more firmly.

"It seemed obvious to me," Caledonia told Angela later when they were alone, "that Desmond couldn't care less about Howard's departure, as long as Harriet continues to manage the can opener and to let him out when he needs a trip to that great big toilet surrounding his home."

"That's a very prejudiced remark, Cal," Angela said. "Why can't you accept the fact that cats are affectionate animals and they really do care about their owners? If Harriet Gould says Desmond will miss Howard, you ought to take her word."

Caledonia just shook her head. "He wasn't in mourning that I could see. But we didn't get a single sensible question asked after the conversation turned to Desmond, did we? All you did was *ooh* and *aah* over him, and encourage Harriet to talk about his cute tricks . . ."

"Well, but at least we did get her to suggest a reason for Howard to be up and about in the middle of the night, didn't we?"

The point was amplified when Conrad Stone joined Angela, Caledonia, Tom Brighton, Tootsie Armstrong, and Mary Moffet in the lobby a few minutes before supper that night. Since his arrival, he'd made it a point to join first one group and then another, to the delight of the female residents. Tonight, as Caledonia sneered to Angela later, ". . . it was just our turn to bask in his radiance."

Inevitably the conversation was about Howard Gould and the police investigation. "Mrs. Gould thinks he may have got up to let the cat out," Angela said. "But we still can't think why he went out into the garden. His wife says he usually just stood at the door until the cat was ready to come back in. Why would Howard go outside in his bare feet in the dead of night?"

"Ah, well, that's easy," Conrad Stone said. "Being a cat owner myself, I know perfectly well why he pattered out in his pajamas and bare feet. He got tired of waiting for Desmond to return and went out to fetch him."

"Why didn't he just call?" Caledonia said. "Well, I grant you he wouldn't yell. Harriet says he was very considerate and that would have waked his neighbors. But if he just whispered 'Here, kitty, kitty, kitty' it wouldn't have roused most of us."

Tom Brighton spoke up. "Mrs. Wingate, let me enlighten you, since you seem to be a woman who's never been owned by a cat. They just don't come when they're called, and unless it's raining or something, they can get to wandering around and thinking of other things besides coming and going promptly. Howard might have got tired of standing there, barefoot and shivering in the chilly night air, and he might have gone all the way outside, trying to fetch Desmond in, instead of waiting for him to be sensible and come home on his own."

"Oh, I agree," Conrad Stone chimed in. "I've done it a dozen times with Puddin' when we were living up at The Golden Years. Here, of course, Puddin' can come and go as he likes through his own door. Otherwise . . ." he shook his head dolefully ". . . otherwise it might have been me out in the garden last night, you know? And if some drunken drifter were there, trying to find a place to sleep . . . or some burglar was interrupted sneaking in to rob the apartments . . . Well, what I mean is, it might have been me lying facedown in the fountain, instead of Howard Gould!" He shuddered broadly.

Nancy Bush wandered up at that moment. "Everybody . . ." She nodded left and right. "So sad about Howard Gould, isn't it? Ah, well, life is only temporary, and we never know, do we? Has anybody," she went on, "figured out why he was in the garden in the middle of the night?"

"We were just talking about that," Tom Brighton said. "These folks think he got up to let his cat out and then maybe went out to fetch the cat back in."

Nancy nodded. "I've seen him out there quite a few times, even in the few days I've had a view of the garden," she agreed. "Night as well as daytime. Howard, I mean. Well, of course I've seen the cat, too. And your cat, for that matter, Mr. Stone . . ."

"Connie, please," he said. "I thought when we were both up at The Golden Years, you'd agreed to call me Connie."

"Connie, then. By the way, uh, Connie, uh—I meant to ask you why you're feeding Puddin' outside. I was on my morning walk yesterday and I saw you put food down on the back step for him. At least, I think it was his food. It was an opened can, and . . ."

"Puddin' is such a messy eater," Stone said apologetically. "He takes a bite and shakes his head so that food splatters left and right. So I . . ." He hesitated. "Is there something wrong, in your view, with putting his food out on the back step, my dear?"

"Oh, no-no-no," Nancy said hastily. "Except that it seems to me it would attract a lot of bugs. Don't you think ants and cockroaches and all are likely to come, and . . ."

"I never thought of that," Stone said. "I mean, there are so many

insects in this warm climate, it never occurred to me I'd be increas-
ing . . . well, perhaps you're right. Perhaps I shouldn't do that. Actually, it's only his breakfast I've been putting out, and then only after
he's been out roaming all night. Not just because of the mess, you
see, but also to kind of lure him home. Puddin' can smell food from
the other end of the garden, and I know the scent will bring him if
I just open a fresh can of that fishy kind and put it on the step. But,"
he went on with one of his little bows to Nancy, "he can have all his
meals in the kitchen, from now on. I don't want my neighbors saying
I bring more bugs around here, and . . ."

He was interrupted by the Westminster chimes, sounding through
the loudspeaker system. The diners began to move toward the double
doors, now pushed open by one of the waitresses, beaming a welcome.

"Nancy," Angela said, putting out a hand to keep the chubby little
Nancy from moving forward toward the dining room with the others.
"Have the police interviewed you yet?"

"Goodness, no," Nancy said. "Why would they?"

"Well, it just occurred to me while you talked about seeing Desmond and Puddin' that you have a wonderful view of the garden, and
you might have seen something else—something important—something that you aren't even aware of. Tell you what, Nancy. What if
I come up and talk to you tonight after dinner?" They moved toward
the dining room on the heels of the others of their group and pushed
from behind by a press of hungry residents. "I'm helping out with the
police investigation, you know, and I've got a few ideas . . ."

Caledonia was not encouraging when Angela told her of her inspiration as they walked through the lobby after supper. "Nancy Bush
didn't know the man any better than we did, Angela. And Martinez
will have talked to her already, along with everybody else he's interviewed."

"But he might not realize the view she has from her window. A
perfect view of the garden, and . . ."

"You know, for once I agree with Conrad Stone. Isn't he the one
who said it was probably some drifter or some potential burglar, who
got scared when Howard caught him out in the garden?"

"Oh, I think it was Tom Brighton who said that part," Angela
responded. "Or maybe it was Tootsie. Does it matter? The point is,
I'm going to have a little chat with Nancy!"

Standing in the path of a big Caterpillar tractor would have had
more effect than trying to stand in Angela's way, once her mind was

made up, so Caledonia simply smiled, murmured, "Okay. You go ahead. It's a good TV night, so I think I'll just go on home." She waved cheerfully and went on her way, leaving Angela to do her investigating all on her own.

Nancy answered the door immediately to Angela's knock. "Come in, come in. I'm so anxious for you to see my little place. You haven't been here before," she said eagerly, her jiggling walk seeming to express her pleasure and excitement. "I wasn't all that anxious to have visitors in my little studio apartment on the other side of the building, but here . . ."

"Very nice," Angela said with a glance left and right. "And you do have a wonderful view, don't you?" She walked straight across the room to the windows and peered out. "Oh my! I can see right into the windows of the garden apartments across and over there to the left. Does Harriet Gould know you can look right into her living room and her bedroom?"

"I can only see a foot or two in," Nancy protested. "Just the edge of the room. Because of the angle. But if you think it would bother people . . ."

"Well, it wouldn't bother Mr. Grogan next door, but Harriet Gould . . . Oh, and look how clearly you can see who's sitting on the terrace under the bougainvillea! Well, well, well, it certainly is a fine view, just as you say." Angela turned back from the glow of sunset into the lamplight within the room. "Now, my dear, what all did you see last night?"

Nancy shook her head. "I wish I had seen something important. But last night it was just like it is every night. People coming and going from dinner or ambabbling along on an evening stroll."

"Let's see," Angela said. "Last night there was a bingo game in the community room across the street, wasn't there?"

Nancy nodded. "And I have terrible luck at bingo, so I left early."

Angela laughed. "My dear, if you'd stay long enough, you're bound to win. Don't you know how they arrange those games? Once you've won, you can't win again. You can go right on playing, but they won't give you a prize after the first one, and sooner or later, as the winners are eliminated, every player will get a little prize before the evening's over. Our activities director seems to think we senior citizens are going to get our feelings hurt if we don't win a roll of scented toilet paper or a cake of glycerine soap or a Kennedy half-dollar . . . that's the kind of prize she gets for us. So I would stay and play, dear, if winning is really important to you. But anyhow, since you did leave early, you must have seen who came and went through the garden. Tell me about it."

Nancy thought hard. "Let's see . . . well, Mary Moffet, your little bitty friend, came down the path with Conrad Stone escorting her. She was almost pulling him along, she was trying to move so fast."

Angela smiled. "Everything frightens Mary, and she hates being out at night. I'm glad she had someone to help her along. I wish, of course, she wouldn't choose Connie . . ." Nancy Bush looked surprised, and Angela hastily amended her words. "Oh, just so she wouldn't be a nuisance to him, you know. If Caledonia were here, she'd say I was being jealous. But that's nonsense. I just think you can take advantage of a man, and . . ." She bit her lip. "I'm babbling, aren't I? Cal would say I'm off the point. So let's get back to it. The people in the garden last night?"

Nancy might not have followed all of Angela's comments but she returned gamely to her own narrative. "Oh, all right. Let's see . . . there was your Mrs. Armstrong—the one who was up with us at The Golden Years. She came strolling along with Mr. and Mrs. Ridgeway, and they disappeared down the garden, out of my sight. Oh, and then Pete Lopez came along with a ladder and replaced the bulb in one of the floodlights on the second cottage down."

"Really. I didn't know he worked after five," Angela said. "Very industrious. Well, go on. Anyone else?"

"Well, there was Mr. Torgeson. I have no idea what he was doing in the garden. He didn't seem to be in a hurry, you know. Just strolled along. He greeted Mrs. Armstrong as she came back along the path heading for the main building, and he sat on a bench beside the flower bed there just where the path dips, beyond the . . ." Nancy's tic, that hiccup of extra syllables, was working overtime ". . . the eucalypipticus."

"I know the place," Angela said. "They've planted stock and nicotinia there, and the scent is strong and wonderful. I wonder if Torgeson was just out, like Ferdinand the bull, breathing in the wonderful smells? Who'd have thought he was the kind to appreciate beauty? Well-well-well . . . Sorry, my dear. Torgeson's character is really a side issue. I don't suspect him of killing anybody, naturally. Not someone whose death wouldn't mean a profit, at least. He won't even get to rent the Goulds' place out again, the way he did Mr. Cherry's apartment, because Mrs. Gould is still there. At least, I suppose she'll stay on. Do you know her plans?" Nancy shook her head mutely. "All right then," Angela went on, "who else did you see?"

"Well, nobody, really."

"Of course you saw the Ridgeways coming back up the path . . ."

Nancy thought a moment. "No. Oddly enough, they never came back at all. Not that I saw. Mrs. Armstrong did, but not the Ridgeways."

"I suppose," Angela said, "they could have circled the building and come in by the front door. I must ask them. But go ahead, my dear. Surely that wasn't all you saw. Usually one of the nurses comes along, making her night rounds, and . . ."

"Oh, you mean the staff? That kind of thing? I thought you meant residents. Or menacing strangers. Like that. I've told you about the people who belong here. And there weren't any menanacing strangers. But I did see one of the nurses. Two, in fact. One had a medicacation tray, and she must have delivered pills and shots up and down the garden, because it was nearly an hour before she came back to the main building. Another nurse came hurrying down much later. I supposed somebody was sick in one of the apartments."

"You watched a long time, didn't you?" Angela said curiously.

"Oh, my, yes. I do every night. I see the delivery men come and go . . ."

"Delivery men?"

"Well, like that boy from the drugstore. Sometimes he brings a prescription for someone. And the kids delivering for some of the fast-food places . . . there were two or three last night. And the soft drink man who refills the machine, just outside the library there. And sometimes a gardener works late or a handyman, like Pete Lopez last night. There were a lot of what you might call business trips."

"You know, that's fascinating," Angela said. "I'm on the other side of the building, so I had absolutely no idea the garden was so busy at night."

"Well, it wasn't busy every minute," Nancy said. "The traffic goes by fits and starts. Like last night, the Chicken Shack boy brought a box to someone on this side of the garden, down to my left—I saw him turn in there. And the fellow from the Chinese Dragon came in with possibly twenty cartons. I wish you could have seen him staggering down the garden. Chinese has so many side dishes and so much trimming."

"That's amazing. I mean about the fast food. The food here is so good, I can hardly believe people are ordering in. I had no idea . . ."

"Oh, healthy is the thing these days, of course—and here it even tastes good. But don't you ever get a longing for something that isn't quite as good for you? I do."

Angela shook her head and got to her feet. "Well, I'll take your word for it. And now, if you don't have anything else to tell me about . . ."

Nancy shrugged. "I wish I did. But as for Howard going and getting himself killed, I'm afraid I have nothing important to tell."

Angela was gracious in her thanks, but privately she wasn't sure she agreed with Nancy's assessment. A garden full of suspects all evening long! Angela could see all kinds of possibilities for questions and investigation, and she hummed as she walked down the hall.

CHAPTER

9

"**W**ELL," CALEDONIA SAID, "IT'S all very interesting. But I'm not sure what it means." Angela had gone straight from Nancy Bush's apartment to her own, on the first floor, and phoned Caledonia immediately to report.

"It means," Angela said loftily, "that people were coming and going through the garden all evening long. It means the woods are full of suspects. Like the Ridgeways, for instance."

"Harvey and Della Ridgeway are suspects?"

"Well, think about it. They disappeared somewhere after they walked the length of the garden. Where were they? What were they doing?"

"Surely they just strolled around the building and came in the front door."

"Ah, but we don't know that."

"Besides, all these people were running around in the garden in the early evening hours, long before poor old Howard got beaned with that hammer. We could have had a troop of trained elephants come parading through, and it wouldn't have any bearing at all on who killed Howard Gould."

"Well, but we can surely ask the Ridgeways where they went after Nancy Bush saw them."

"I guess we could," Caledonia said. "But I think you're following a dead end with that one. However, one thing does strike me. There's an awful lot of fast food floating around our garden at night, isn't there? If this was The Golden Years, that wouldn't surprise me at all. Those people have to order takeout to stay alive! But Mrs. Schmitt here creates wonderful meals. Why would all these people have food brought in, for Pete's sake?"

"I made exactly that same point to Nancy," Angela said. "I wonder if something odd *is* going on. That chicken, for instance. What are people doing with it? They can't be eating it. It's so greasy you can feel your arteries getting stopped up while you just look at it, before you take a single bite."

"How do you know?"

"Well," Angela said reluctantly, "before I moved in here, when I was still living down in San Diego, I used to get food brought in. Sometimes almost every night."

"Angela! You've always claimed you're a gourmet cook!"

"I am. But it's really hard to cook for just one, you know. They never just pack two chicken thighs, to make a single serving. Besides, all my recipes serve six, and they never taste the same if you just cut the amounts by two-thirds. So I cook the recipe as is, and end up with a refrigerator full of leftovers."

"Angela! Get to the point!"

"I don't remember what the point was. Oh, yes, I do. The point is, I've tasted that stuff, and most of it—well, I can't believe people are really ordering it to eat it."

Caledonia barked out a short laugh. "What do you think they're doing, Angela? Hanging it from strings in the middle of the living room and calling it a mobile? Of course they're eating it. Though I can't imagine why any more than you can. Well, if you think that's of any genuine interest, why don't you find out more about it?"

"Oh, I intend to. I was thinking . . ."

"Listen, is that all you had to tell me about? Because my TV program is just about to start, and . . ."

"Cal, won't you help? I can't get everything done that needs doing, without you. You could take the Ridgeways, and I'll go along the garden asking who had the food brought in."

"But not tonight," Caledonia said. "And certainly not right now. Tell you what . . . I'll do it, if it'll make you happy, but right after breakfast tomorrow morning. How would that be? Just for now, you relax and let me watch my program, okay?"

And with that Angela had to be satisfied. The next morning seemed to Angela to drag its way to 9:00, when—just before breakfast was over and the waitresses set up places for lunch—Caledonia sailed into the dining room. Angela was waiting at their table near the windows to the garden, bouncing up and down in her chair with impatience. "How could you wait till the last possible minute? Suppose they wouldn't serve you? You know you're no good at all without your coffee, not to mention how cross you get. And aren't you anxious to get started talking to . . ."

"Mmmmmph . . ." Caledonia may have meant to respond, but no words came out—just muffled sound, as she peered over the rim of her cup. "Wahmmykfee. Leafmilone."

After the first cup was finished, Caledonia's speech cleared slightly. "Wait," she said. "L'me ham eye secon' cup. Kay?"

When the second cup had been tossed down, Caledonia's eyes focused at last and she was able to communicate as she sipped at her third cup. "Just don't push me," she said, her speech clear at last. "I'm going to finish my breakfast before I do anything." In actual fact, Caledonia had thought it over during the evening before and had decided that interviewing their fellow residents, who had almost certainly been interviewed at least once already by Martinez, was probably an exercise in futility. In consequence Caledonia had also decided to cut her own participation today to a minimum. But one didn't say to Angela with impunity that her ideas were without merit. So Caledonia lied by indirection. "Verbal sleight of hand," was what she called it. "Now, I'll just finish my breakfast," she went on, "while you can get started. Then we'll meet just before lunch, at about eleven at your place, okay?"

It seemed to Angela that it would be the most sensible step to start with the source of all information, Clara at the front desk, and Clara was only too glad to oblige. "Sure, I know some of the answer. Even local calls have to go out through the switchboard, after all. Usually one of the night shift would have the board, but I've filled in a couple of times, you know, and I remember . . . Well, there's your friend Mary Moffet, who's had burgers brought in sometimes from Fat Boy's downtown. Then there are Mr. and Mrs. Spangler in the first cottage. The same building as Mrs. Wingate, you know? They order from the Golden Dragon downtown because they're crazy about Chinese, and Mrs. Schmitt won't make a Chinese dinner, not in large quantities like for our dining room here. She says it's too hard to do. So the Spanglers skip dinner and order in Chinese every week, one night or other, especially if the evening meal is lamb. Mr. Spangler says he just hates the taste of lamb."

"Honestly, some people can be so picky. Mrs. Schmitt does lamb beautifully! Of course she does everything well. Okay, I've made a note—the Spanglers. Now who else?"

"Miss Spring orders frozen yogurt brought in once in a while," Clara said. "And Mrs. Harland has a boy who'll go fetch her an order from Marie Callender's . . . they don't deliver, but they'll do a takeout box for her. I think she gets one of their pies, eats a slice fresh, and freezes the rest. And that's all I know about."

"How about pizza deliveries? People at The Golden Years ordered in pizza."

Clara shrugged. "Oh, there've been pizzas ordered. It's just that I didn't place a call to any of the pizza places through our switchboard this week. One of the others could have, when I was off duty, of course. How is this going to help?"

"Well, you can keep a secret, I hope . . ." Clara nodded solemnly, even though both she and Angela knew that was a faint hope. "Caledonia and I are looking into poor Howard's death . . ."

"Just like you always do! That's great!" Clara's grin was broad and approving. "Boy, you and Mrs. Wingate do get up to more mischief!"

Angela smiled and started for the garden, then stopped as a thought struck her. "Clara, is the trash from the garden apartments emptied the same way ours is? I mean, we empty full wastebaskets into the big containers in storerooms on every floor and the staff takes the stuff out of those big bins. What do they do in the garden apartments?"

"They have a large trash bin for each cottage," Clara said. "And those are emptied sometime in the morning, every other day. In fact, I think today's trash pickup day. What do you have in mind?"

Angela came back to the desk and spoke in low tones. "Well, it'd take so awfully long to talk to everybody who lives along the garden, I just had this terrific idea. I thought maybe it would be better if I . . . Clara, what would people say if they saw me going through the trash bins?"

"They'd say you'd lost your mind, of course," Clara responded promptly with a huge grin.

"But it'd be one way to find out who had some sort of delivery night before last, wouldn't it? Nancy Bush gave me the idea. She said there were food deliveries, and Billy from the drugstore brought something. And whether the boxes and bags went into the trash immediately or not till this morning, they'd still be there, wouldn't they? Till the men come to collect . . ."

"Say! I think I know what that delivery from the drugstore was," Clara said. "I'm pretty sure that was a prescription for Mr. Jefferson. He has diabetes, you know, and he's had problems lately. New medications almost every other day. I'm not sure that it helps you any, though. And I still don't understand why you're checking on deliveries."

"Because there seem to have been a lot of people wandering around the garden after dinner night before last, and one of those people might have seen something odd going on, you know. For instance, if a thief had decided to rob some of our residents, he might have been hiding in the shrubbery early in the evening, casing the joint. That's police talk, Clara," she said loftily.

"Why hide in the bushes? He might just have walked right up through the middle of the garden, right on the sidewalk, and nobody would think to ask him any questions. A lot of visitors come and go before we lock down for the night. The night Mr. Gould was killed, people were up and around till maybe nine-thirty because of the weekly bingo game, you know. So your burglar could be right out in the open and everybody would have assumed he was somebody's guest, if you see what I mean. He wouldn't have to skulk in the shrubbery."

"Good point, Clara. You'd make a fine detective yourself," Angela said.

Clara beamed. "Oh, by the way, maybe you'd like to have a plastic bag," she volunteered. "One of those grocery store bags. I brought an orange and an apple to work with me to snack on. I'll just park them under the desk here . . . and there you are, a nice clean plastic bag to collect your trash in."

Angela took the bag. "These aren't a speck of good for carrying heavy groceries like glass juice bottles, but they ought to do fine helping with my empty cartons, so thank you. And thank you for your brilliant suggestion, too." Clara blushed deep crimson with pleasure. "When I find out who those delivery men were," Angela went on, "I won't just ask them about dark shapes hiding in the shadows. Thanks to your idea, I'll ask them who they met on the paths, too. Especially if they've been here several times, they'd recognize some of the regular residents. So all they'll need to tell me is if they saw someone they didn't recognize, and give me a description. Then I'll . . ."

A buzzer sounded. "Oh, 'scuse me," Clara said, "that's the switchboard. I need to answer. Hello, front desk . . . Oh, yes, Mrs. Felton?

... Gee, I'm sorry—breakfast is finished. They just closed the doors. But if you want, I'll ask Mrs. Schmitt to make you some toast. That might hold you till lunch, and . . . All right, I'll do that, and . . ."

While Clara was busy arranging a snack for a late riser, Angela hurried out into the garden. She had a vague memory of the workmen rolling a gigantic trash barrel up the walkway, stopping behind each cottage and its nestled apartments as they moved along toward the main building. It made sense. It would be a lot easier than to start gathering trash at the top of the garden, with the huge barrel getting heavier and heavier as they worked, then having to trundle the filled barrel all the way back up from the end of the garden. "I bet that was Pete Lopez who figured out they should move the empty barrel down the walk and bring it back as it gradually filled," Angela muttered to herself. "He's so clever. Well, if I want to sort through two days' worth of trash, I'd better start at the far end of the garden myself. So as to beat the crew to the bins."

True to her own conclusions, Angela started behind the first build- ing on the left, where Mr. Jefferson and his wife occupied the inner- most apartment and the Pyms the street-side quarters. But when she opened the big trash bin, she was horrified to find wet coffee grounds loosely wrapped in newspaper filling the top layer. "I don't know why," she told Caledonia later, "but I never realized there'd be . . . you know, wet stuff like half grapefruits and slimy old bits of half- eaten cheese toast in there. Our trash inside the building is usually nice and dry!"

"That," Caledonia said loftily, "is because our apartments have kitchens and you don't, up inside the main building."

"Oh, I knew that. But I bet you don't throw out eggshells and cartons of sour milk and . . ."

"That's just because I seldom use the kitchen, Angela. I prefer to take my meals from Mrs. Schmitt's hands, since she's a much better cook than I ever hoped to be. And being as I'm lazy." Caledonia grinned. "I can see you now, pawing through discarded banana peels and sticky, half-empty cans and . . ."

In fact, Angela had taken one look at the contents of the trash bin and decided that only the topmost layers could possibly interest her. She rationalized that if there had been fast food or a drugstore deliv- ery, the evidence would be tucked in with the most recent materials to be dumped. "I'm really not interested in what was thrown out the day Howard was killed," she told herself, wrinkling her nose with distaste as she reached into the first bin, "only in what was thrown out yesterday, after he was killed." She pushed aside the soggy newspaper with its coffee grounds and with the tips of her fingers moved a copy of *Newsweek* that had been immediately beneath. The next layer revealed a broken plastic comb, a pile of direct-mail ads (unopened), and a lot of crumpled Kleenex.

"I should have worn gloves like they do in the movies," Angela said unhappily. After a moment's thought, she went over to the garden area behind the Jeffersons' cottage and broke a branch off one of the bushes. She peeled most of the leaves off it and then went back to forking through the trash, using the stick as a probe. Raking the odds and ends aside with her stick made for slow work, but shortly she found the evidence she was seeking. Lying beside the discarded carton that had held a tube of toothpaste was a small cardboard box with a typewritten label on it. "Jefferson, Phillip W." it said. Angela pounced, and the small carton went into her plastic bag.

As she replaced the cover on the trash bin, she was sure she saw the window curtains near the Jeffersons' back door move. Someone was peering out at her. She smiled and waved, just in case, and crossed the garden to the building that housed Mr. and Mrs. Taylor on the garden side, Conrad Stone on the street side. Using her stick as a rake again, she pushed aside three magazines, two half grapefruit shells, an emptied carton that had held granola, two brown glass bottles (one that had held hydrogen peroxide, according to its label, the other nose drops), a squeezed-out toothpaste tube, a broken toothbrush, three emptied cans of cat food, and then she saw an empty pizza carton. "Ah-hah!" Angela crowed, grabbing at the carton and stuffing it into her plastic bag. "I just knew someone had ordered pizza!" She straightened up again, glad to rest her back, which ached horribly while she remained bent over the bin, and as she did so, she saw movement in both the Taylor and the Stone apartments. She certainly was not, she thought ruefully, escaping unnoticed in her detecting efforts.

In fact, Gerald Taylor popped his head out through his back door just as she replaced the lid on the trash can. "What're you doing, Mrs. Benbow? Can I help you with anything? You lost something?"

"No, no, Mr. Taylor. I'm . . . I'm trying to make a list of who was in the garden last night. Besides just us, you know. Besides the regular residents, I mean."

"Good night!" Taylor seemed mystified. "Whatever for?"

"To help out the police, you know."

"How is my trash going to help with that?" He was clearly skeptical.

"Well, if I found a carton here that showed you had a delivery last evening, I'd know without bothering you in person that I should talk to that paticular delivery boy. Or man. Or woman, of course," she amended hastily. "In my day, delivery persons were all male. Nowadays . . ."

"We haven't had anything delivered for days," Taylor said. "I hate to disappoint you, but . . ."

"Gerald!" Mrs. Taylor's whining voice came from deep within their apartment. "Do your gossiping outside or inside, but don't stand in an open doorway. There's a real draft coming through and you know I'm trying to avoid catching cold. I have the solo in Sunday's choir anthem and . . ."

Taylor made an apologetic face in Angela's direction and swung his door firmly closed, leaving Angela awash with relief. She'd been afraid Gerald Taylor would somehow believe she was accusing him of something. It would be so hard to explain . . . She briefly blessed the peremptory command in Mrs. Taylor's voice and turned back to her task, lacing her way left and right across the garden, up the path to the rear of each of the apartments to gingerly examine the top layer of the trash. At Mary Moffet's building, where three apartments shared a single cottage, Angela found a bag from Fat Boy Burgers. "I'm going to have to tease Mary about this," she said as she popped the telltale bag into her carryall. "Imagine eating a burger after Mrs. Schmitt's roast lamb dinner! I can't imagine . . . oh, YECH!" Angela's probe had just twisted in her hand as it met something slippery and . . . but Angela relaxed as she realized it was only leftover face cream, a glob of which clung to the side of a nearly emptied jar. She scraped the cream off the end of her makeshift rake by rubbing it against the side of the bin and hurried on to her next trash barrel.

At the cottage that contained the Goulds' apartment and that of Mr. Grogan, Angela had to nudge aside four whiskey bottles before she could reach into the bin to lift out a red-and-white-striped cardboard bucket with THE CHICKEN SHACK printed large on its side and grease stains deeply embedded inside. "Those are Grogan's bottles, of course, but it couldn't be Grogan who ate the chicken," Angela told herself. "He's a scrawny thing, and I'm sure the alcohol kills his appetite. Must be that the Goulds ordered this as a late snack." She lifted the container gingerly and put it into her carryall, then replaced the trash lid and hurried across the garden to the rear of the Spanglers' place, the same building that housed Caledonia's apartment. That trash barrel was nearly empty—not surprising, since Caledonia never used her kitchen, and her apartment was really two apartments with the partition wall between knocked out, so that there was only one more place under her roof, the apartment owned by Fremont and Katerina Spangler. And there, just as Angela had expected, were the white paper cartons with the thin metal bales that always marked Chinese food. These too went into Angela's collection, and she slid the lid back onto the Spangler-Wingate trash barrel and headed for the main building with her little sack of treasures.

"At least," she told an amused Caledonia when they met in Angela's apartment just before lunch to compare notes, "at least I was only caught once. And Mr. Taylor didn't seem very upset. Well, to be fair, he didn't have the time. His wife is an awful nag, have you noticed? And she whisked him back inside before he could ask many questions. I really didn't much want to tell the whole story, and it would have been too humiliating to lie."

"What kind of lie," Caledonia grinned, "would you have made up to cover going through a trash barrel and grabbing out empty food cartons? They *were* empty, weren't they?"

"Oh, yes. And I'd have dumped out any . . . you know, any garbage. But there wasn't a speck of food left. Anyhow, I just told the truth. Some of it. It's much simpler."

"The truth is always best, Angela, especially for people like us who don't lie very effectively. And now, don't you want to know what I found out when I talked to the Ridgeways?"

"Oh . . . Oh, yes, of course. I'm sorry." Angela was genuinely contrite. "Please, tell me . . ."

Caledonia might think Angela's investigations were futile, but she knew she ought to do at least her one assigned task, and since when she finished breakfast she had the time, and since she was already in the main building, she headed straight from the dining room to the Ridgeways' apartment. "I was curious anyhow," she told Angela. "It was my first chance since they'd moved in to see what they'd done with the place." The Ridgeway place occupied the center-back of the building's second floor, directly over the lobby's garden entrance, and it had a living room that extended forward, so that the room itself formed a kind of canopy over half of the patio area, the patio's other half being shaded by an overhead trellis holding brilliant fuchsia bougainvillea. From their living-room window, the Ridgeways could look down into a sea of bright pink blossom. Theirs was the only apartment in the main building that had a full kitchen and two separate bed-rooms—one left and one right, as one entered from the hall. "This must be the biggest place in all of Camden-sur-Mer," Caledonia said admiringly. "Too bad it wasn't vacant when I first moved in. I could have saved the expense of having two apartments combined into one. Not that I'd give up my place now, you understand, but this is charm-ing."

The Ridgeways beamed. There's no soothing syrup like having somebody envying your good fortune. Their mood became so mellow under Caledonia's flattery that they asked few questions and certainly raised no objections when Caledonia finally got around to asking about their rambles through the garden the night before.

"So different from The Golden Years," Della Ridgeway said con-tentedly. "I mean, that courtyard was nice, I guess, but it was just a recreation area, you know what I mean? The pool, the shuffleboard court, the croquet game. No flowers, no trees . . ."

"And the view here!" Harvey said. "Walking down between rows of flowers to stand beside that cliff . . ."

"Not a cliff, Harvey," Della corrected. "Just a bluff. 'Cliff' sounds so big and menacing. It's maybe ten or twelve feet high is all. And there are steps you can use to get down to the beach . . ."

"In fact, that's what we did last night," Harvey Ridgeway said. "We go down the garden to look at the sea every night, but it's been kinda chilly, and we come right back. But last night it was warmer, less breezy, so we climbed down the steps to the beach."

"We won't do that again," Della said. "Not that it wasn't beautiful. But you can see a lot better from the top of the steps. And the sand got into my shoes and all. I had to call the maids this morning to vacuum the carpeting, I tracked in so much last night."

"How'd you get back to the building?" Caledonia asked. "That's what I was curious about. Nancy Bush says she saw you going down the garden, but never coming back."

"Oh, her! That Nancy Bush has always been a nosy thing. Nice enough, I suppose, but nosy. Haven't I always said so, Harvey?"

"Nice enough, but nosy," he nodded his affirmation. "And she's often mistaken about things. I mean, we came back up to the main building last night exactly the way we came down. Right up the garden walk. You can ask Nurse Bingham, if you don't believe me.

She was coming along with her medication tray and we stopped to say hello. We must have been just about under Nancy's windows when . . ."

"Well," Caledonia soothed, "Nancy probably just turned to look at the TV or something and missed seeing you, you know? I don't think she meant anything by saying you hadn't returned."

"Don't be so sure," Della said. "She has a mean streak in her, Nancy does. Didn't she tell you why she moved here? She got into an awful argument with that woman who fell out the window. That Regina Madison. They said nasty things to each other every time they passed in the halls, and Regina said it had got so bad that *she* was thinking of moving. Instead, Nancy beat her to it. I can tell you I wasn't too happy to hear that Nancy was coming here, after we'd signed the contract to come here ourselves."

"And that," Caledonia said as she reported later to Angela, "is all I learned. Not much, really."

"Not much! Oh, I disagree! I disagree! This is awfully interesting. I had no idea Nancy wasn't just a well-padded, pleasant little woman with some kind of strange glitch in her speech. But if she was feuding with Regina Madison, there's more to her than meets the eye. We have something we can legitimately investigate," Angela said, her pleasure making her voice almost girlish. "I'm going to turn this plastic bag full of empty cartons over to Lieutenant Martinez after lunch, and we can give our attention to Nancy. And of course the Ridgeways, who don't like her one little bit, I take it. Fascinating."

They moved from Angela's apartment into the lobby as they talked. "I wish you'd leave that plastic carryall behind in your place," Caledonia muttered softly. "People are going to ask questions."

"No, they won't. They have no idea what's in the bag or why," Angela said. "And if the lieutenant comes in to lunch, I can hand it to him right there. Or if he doesn't, I can go find him right after lunch without stopping back at my place, right?"

"Okay, okay . . . I'm all for saving a few steps myself, of course. And I think . . . Hey! What's that?"

Ahead of them, between the garden door and the entrance to the dining room—still closed to keep everyone out till lunch was actually ready to serve—a little knot of residents had formed, and the buzz of their conversation was audible the length of the lobby. "Oh, how cute!" "Does he mind if we touch? What soft fur!" "Oh, I adore . . ." "Let me—let me—"

Caledonia led the way, breaking a path through the circle of residents, Angela pattering along in her wake. "What's all the excitement?" Caledonia trumpeted. "Oh, for Pete's sake, a dog!" She moved forward, but Angela stepped hastily backward as Caledonia continued to exclaim. "A dog! I don't believe it!"

It was indeed a dog. Standing in the midst of a group of residents— Tootsie Armstrong, Tom Brighton, the Jackson twins, Janice Felton, the Ridgeways, and the Jeffersons—was Officer Swanson, attached by a long, woven leather thong to a handsome golden retriever. "Well!" Caledonia seemed deprived of words. "Well!"

"Ooooh, isn't he simply lovely, Caledonia?" one of the Jackson twins breathed.

"And his fur is soooo soft," the other said, though as usual Caledonia could not distinguish one twin from the other.

"His name is Roderick," Swanson volunteered.

"He's not moving in here, is he?" Caledonia asked suspiciously.

Swanson laughed. "Oh, no. He's a policeman, temporarily off duty. His regular handler, Joey Flynn, has the flu and Roderick needs his regular shots from the department's vet. So Lieutenant Martinez said I should take time off and chauffeur Roderick—as a favor to Flynn."

"A member of the K-9 patrol?" Tom Brighton said. "He's certainly amiable for a police dog. He doesn't seem to mind at all if we touch him." Brighton ran a hand over Roderick's silky ears, and the retriever's mouth opened as though he were laughing, his plumey tail wagging just a bit more rapidly than before. "He's so gentle . . ."

Swanson nodded. "He's not an attack dog, he's a drug dog. They're different from other police dogs—different breeds, different training, different commands. One of our patrol dogs shouldn't be touched without permission. But these drug dogs are just friendly old fellows most of the time, unless they're in the middle of a job. You shouldn't interfere then."

"How fascinating," Janice Felton said, edging forward to run a hand through the red-blonde fur. Roderick's tail moved into overdrive as she let her fingernails scratch against the skin on his rump and his smile seemed to grow broader. "Tell us all about how a drug dog does his work."

"I really don't know, ma'am," Swanson said, and he seemed faintly embarrassed. "I suppose I should, but that's not my department, and all I know is he can sniff 'em out. I have no idea . . ."

"This is all very well, young man," Caledonia said. "But if you're delivering the dog to the vet for shots, what are you doing here?"

Swanson's embarrassment grew even more apparent. "Well, I thought you would all like to see him, since you can't have dogs here yourselves. And I thought I'd show him to Chita, too, as long as it was on my way."

"His girlfriend! It's an excuse to have a minute with his girl—" Caledonia laughed, explaining to the Ridgeways, who, being new, might not be up on the gossip, "—you know, that pretty little waitress in our dining room, Conchita Cassidy? They're engaged."

Della Ridgeway beamed, as women will whenever engagements or weddings are mentioned. Harvey Ridgeway shook his head. "Watch out for the marriage trap, young man." But he was smiling.

"WOOF!" The lobby erupted in noise and confused motion! It all began when Roderick suddenly went stiff, his gaze—like that of a pointer finding quail for his master—fixed on Conrad Stone, who had just entered by the garden door. "WOOF!!!" In the same moment with that first, frantic bark, an unholy screech exploded and a round-ish black blur shot violently away from the region of Conrad Stone's chest, heading back out the door toward the garden and leaving Stone half bent over in the door, moaning and cursing.

"The Alien! He's given birth to the Alien!" Grogan bleated from his bench near the dining-room door.

"I'm bleeding!" Stone shouted. "That damn cat! He got me with his claws when he . . . What the hell is a dog doing in here anyhow?"

The object of his interest gone, the dog in question had stopped barking and straining at his leash and had resumed his placid, friendly air. Still clutching his injured arm, Stone strode closer to the group, his face a thundercloud. "Now Puddin's taken off—taking some of the skin on my arm with him, I might add—and heaven knows how long it will take to round him up, scared as he was. I would never have brought him if Mrs. Felton hadn't asked to see him, and I would never have brought him at all if I'd known . . . Isn't anybody going to tell me what that dog is doing in here?"

"Geeze, I'm sorry, Mr . . . Mr . . ." Swanson's memory for names deserted him along with his aplomb. "I never dreamed somebody would bring a cat in here. I'm so darned sorry, I can't tell you . . . Did he gouge you bad?"

Stone took out a clean handkerchief and pushed it up under his jacket sleeve, then brought it out again with a single spot of bright blood on it. "Just got me in one place, I guess. Hurt like he'd taken an inch of skin, but maybe just one claw went in. Sorry I yelled so loud, young fellow, but you can understand . . ."

Trinita Stainsbury had joined the group and quickly moved next to Stone. "Let me help," she said briskly. "I studied first aid, you know. Push your sleeve up . . ." She took Stone's handkerchief and wrapped it deftly around the nick on his forearm, the area where he'd been holding Puddin' when the cat decided to use him as a launching pad.

"And look at dear Roderick," Tootsie Armstrong said. "He was as upset as Puddin', I think, but he's calmed right down . . ."

"You can't really blame him," Swanson said, still apologetic. "He was just sort of shouting a greeting, I think."

Harvey Ridgeway nodded. "I agree with you. It was just excitement. A greeting. Or maybe a warning. I mean, dogs will be dogs."

"And cats will be cats," Stone muttered crossly. "Puddin's never done anything like that before, but . . ." Trinita was taking an extra long time bandaging Stone's arm, as Caledonia noted with cynical amusement. Another of Stone's conquests, just like Angela.

But at that moment, Angela was paying no attention at all to Conrad Stone. She had finally moved cautiously in from the far edges of the group, had come around Caledonia, and moved close to the beautiful retriever. Very timidly, she stretched out a hand toward him, and then, very gingerly, began to pet him. "You know, I've always been afraid of strange dogs after I was bit when I was a little girl. But Roderick seems so . . . so civilized."

"And this pretty boy can root out heroin and cocaine and things like that?" Tom Brighton said wonderingly.

"Oh, absolutely," Swanson said. "You're hunting a hidden supply of illegal drugs? Count on Roderick to find it."

Angela moved closer to Roderick, running a finger down his jaw line, and as he lifted his chin slightly as though to help her reach the tender spots on his neck, he sat down at her feet, looking upward at her as though in admiration. "What a nice dog. I wouldn't have been so reluctant to pet him, if I'd realized. Oh, look, here comes Chita. Your girl is here, Officer Swanson."

Chita Cassidy had swung open the dining-room doors as the Westminster chimes sounded from the lobby's overhead speakers and, spotting Swanson, had moved over to him with a delighted smile.

"You staying for lunch, Officer Swanson?" Caledonia said.

"No, no . . . I'll just speak to Chita for a second. I know she's got work to do. Then I'll get Roderick to his doctor's appointment. I suppose I really shouldn't have taken the time for this stop, except I knew all of you would enjoy seeing him. All right, that's enough, Roderick. Good boy . . . Come here . . . Stop bothering people . . ." The golden retriever trotted obediently back to Swanson, reaching him at the same moment as Chita did, and to her obvious dismay, the dog reached upward and took hold of one end of the tea towel she carried.

"What is he doing?" the girl said. "Stop that, you silly dog . . ." and she pulled at the towel, trying to detach it from the dog's grip. But her pulling on the towel only seemed to excite the dog, who hung on for dear life, lowering his head and pulling back.

"He wants to play tug of war," Caledonia said, amused. "Isn't that cute?"

"That's enough, Roderick," Swanson said. "Drop it, that's a good boy." The retriever obeyed immediately.

"Gosh, he's good about obeying, isn't he?" Caledonia said. "Look, Officer, we're delighted you brought the dog but it's our lunch time and we're having braised short ribs. So we'll just get moving and let you two have a minute to yourselves." And she moved off after Angela toward their lunch. Looking back over over her shoulder, she saw the two young people greet each other shyly, aware of the presence of so many observers.

"Bet they wish we'd all get on into the dining room so they could have a quick kiss," Angela said as she and Caledonia joined the other residents moving from the lobby to the dining room. "Oh, look. Look. Roderick is trying to come into the dining room with us."

Caledonia laughed. "Wants some of Mrs. Schmitt's short ribs, I suppose," and she went on to her lunch, leaving the golden retriever standing yearning silently after the diners, still wagging his strawberry blonde plume of a tail.

CHAPTER

10

"**W**HY DIDN'T YOU GIVE your plastic sack of garbage to Officer Swanson?" Caledonia asked Angela, as they left the dining room after lunch. "He could easily have carried it to Lieutenant Martinez for you, but I see you're still dragging it along with you."

"I thought," Angela said, bristling slightly, because she took Caledonia's question to be an attack on her own good sense, "I thought I'd do better explaining what all these cartons were for if I talked to him in person. I certainly didn't want to tell Swanson in front of all those other people that I'd spent the morning rummaging through trash bins. It would have made me look ridiculous."

"Oh, that's certain," Caledonia agreed. "Well, you don't really need me, so I won't bother going upstairs with you on this little trip. It's nap time, after all. What do you plan to do with the rest of your afternoon after you talk to Martinez?"

"Well," Angela said, "if the lieutenant will let me, I'd like to be the one to interview the delivery boys. I've done all the preliminary work on this idea, so why shouldn't I be allowed to go on with it? If you like, you can come along with me when I do. I'll get in touch about two-thirty, when you've done with your nap, and we can plan our strategy."

She made approximately the same argument to Martinez a few minutes later. "I'm the one who found out about all the deliveries into the garden last night, so I should be the one to talk to the delivery boys, don't you agree?"

"Absolutely not. Mrs. Benbow, haven't you stopped to think that it's possible one of those delivery boys might be the killer of Howard Gould?" She started to answer, but he held up a hand for silence and hurried on, "Oh, I grant you it's not likely. Billy from the drugstore has been delivering for them for five years at least; everybody knows him." Martinez reached a hand into the plastic bag and abstracted a white carton with the silvery bail. "As for Charlie Lee, who runs food over from The Golden Dragon, he's a respectable fifty-year-old gentleman and part owner of the business since 1975. I can't imagine anybody less likely to murder a customer than Charlie Lee."

"Well," Angela said petulantly, "if my idea is so far-fetched, so trivial that you make fun of me, you needn't bother with following it up. But I intend to go ahead and talk to . . ."

"No! Please, Mrs. Benbow. I will do the initial interviews with everyone on my list, which now includes these delivery boys." He stirred a finger gingerly through the bag. "At least these treasures you brought me are nice and clean," he said. "You haven't handed me a crumb of used rice or a shred of secondhand pepperoni."

"We're neat around here," Angela said, and her voice was sulky. "It's just the considerate thing to do, to clean out food cartons, when we all have to share the same trash bins."

"But these cartons are so clean, I thought you must have washed them just for me," Martinez said lightly. He waited, but she bit her lip and said nothing. "Look, please don't be annoyed with me, Mrs. Benbow. I'm genuinely in your debt for your ingenious idea of figuring out who to ask by checking the trash. We may get really useful information if, as you suggest, any of these people," he gestured at the plastic bag, "actually saw something like . . . well, something like you suggested, someone hiding in the shrubbery or a suspicious stranger or even a quarrel between two residents. I shall profit by your hard work, and I am grateful. But until I've talked to—let's see, Billy from the drugstore, Charlie Lee, the burger delivery kids from Fat Boy's and The Chicken Shack, and whoever's delivering for The Pizza Palace—till then, I don't want you to approach them." He was aware that thunderclouds were forming on her brows and hurried on. "Later, perhaps, if I want some follow-up data, I'll at least consider assigning you to one or more of the interviews."

"Truly, Lieutenant? You wouldn't just say that?"

Martinez took a deep breath, smiled, and lied in his perfect white teeth. "Absolutely. But now, if you don't mind . . . I have another interview scheduled with Mrs. Gould, and she might be intimidated by seeing you in such friendly conversation with me."

"I should think you'd want her to see me chatting with you, all relaxed and easy. She might be more comfortable if she knew other residents liked and trusted you."

Martinez smiled. "You forget that your reputation has spread, Mrs. Benbow. I think everybody here, even the newest resident, knows that from time to time you've been—how shall I say—informally deputized, as it were. You're too modest, when you say you're just another resident."

Mollified at last, Angela smiled. She couldn't stay angry for long at Martinez. "So handsome," she sighed later as she reported to Caledonia. "And so charming. But now, let me tell you about my afternoon, and how embarrassing . . . Oh, Cal, it was so humiliating!"

Angela hadn't felt in the least like resting in her room, but there was little to help her while away an hour or so after lunch till Caledonia awoke. The hallways were quiet, most of the residents having gone straight from lunch to nap, just as Caledonia did. The library was empty, and Angela had long ago read most of its holdings— largely books donated to Camden-sur-Mer by incoming residents who realized (too late for them to hold a garage sale) that there was scant space in the new quarters for shelf after shelf of books. Thus, in addition to row on row of mysteries, Westerns, and romances, the little library boasted two unabridged dictionaries, a copy of Gray's *Anatomy*, three *Complete Works of Shakespeare*, twelve world atlases, *The Guinness Book of World Records*, and four encyclopedias, but none of these could furnish light reading to help pass the time till Angela could confer with Caledonia. She did kill ten minutes or so leafing idly through the daily newspaper, but she'd read all the news before breakfast, since like many other residents, as she reminded Caledonia later, she had her own subscription delivered to her door before dawn. "A newspaper is a nice way to pass the time before the dining room opens each morning."

"I get my morning scandal from the TV while I dress for the day," Caledonia said. "Besides, doesn't the noise wake you up? It's bad enough to have the thump-thump-thump up and down the garden as that kid slings rolled-up papers at my neighbor's doors. I've learned to ignore that. But if there were a thump at my own door every morning, it would rouse me even from the soundest sleep. Or I'd wake up and wait for it every morning, because . . . Hey! There's an idea. The paperboy. How about him for a suspect? I mean, you just said he comes here before dawn, and . . ."

"But he's the one who found the body," Angela said. "Harriet told us. If he'd killed Howard, why would he go up to the office to tell them somebody'd been killed and ask them to call the police? That's what Clara says he did."

"He'd do it to throw off suspicion, of course," Caledonia said promptly. "I know I would."

"Well, you may be right at that," Angela said. "Though I hardly think so. All the same, I'll try to talk to him—maybe even before dinner tonight, if there's time. I'm sure that back in my place somewhere or other I have a card with his name and address. One thing's certain, I'll speak to him before I mention this to the lieutenant. Otherwise he'll just tell me not to. And that really wouldn't be fair, because it was my idea."

"Our idea, Angela. The paperboy belongs to both of us, and you remember that, okay? Now get back to your story. You started out saying something embarrassing had happened to you, and that intrigued me, to say the least. So why not tell me . . ."

"Oh. Oh, yes. Oh, my! Embarrassing is not the word! Here's how it happened. Let's see, I told you I couldn't find anything I wanted to read to kill the time. And you know I don't want to use the exercise equipment. There wasn't anything good on TV, and somebody'd worked the big jigsaw puzzle and just left it out there on the library table, all finished, for the rest of us to admire, so there really wasn't room to start a new puzzle, and admiring somebody else's cleverness doesn't take me long . . ." Caledonia grinned but said nothing.

"So I went down the garden and took in the view for a while. Watching the ocean always soothes me, but after just a few minutes in the midday sun, you can feel sunburn coming on. I mean, the reflection off the water alone would be enough to fry you. So I gave up and started back up the garden."

Angela had walked slowly. It was still only 1:15 and it would be nearly an hour till she dared to stop at Caledonia's apartment. Suddenly, in the shrubbery near one of the cottages, there was a disturbance that made the leaves rustle sharply, and she stopped in her tracks. "Is someone there?" she called out. There was no answer, but the leaves rustled hard again and she could see a shadow of movement. "I couldn't tell exactly what was in the bushes there, not from where I was on the path," she told Caledonia, "so I went across the grass to . . ."

"You just went right over there? Angela, you have absolutely no common sense at all."

"Oh, for heaven's sake, it was broad daylight. I figured nothing too bad could happen to me in bright sunlight, don't you agree? And the truth is, I'd already sort of figured out what it was."

Moving slowly across the grass, she edged past a bed of scarlet salvia bordered by bright blue lobelia. "Here, kitty-kitty-kitty," she ventured, bending double to see under the lowest branches of the hydrangea, where the leaves were wobbling frantically in response to her voice. "Is that you, Puddin'?" she asked softly, coaxingly. "Don't you know your owner's been looking everywhere for you? Poor baby, I know you were frightened by that nasty big dog. Oh, dear, I shouldn't even say that word, should I? But you can come out now. He's gone, and I'll protect you, because I love kitties . . ." She continued talking in a low, soothing voice as she tiptoed closer and closer to the quivering hydrangea. "Incidentally, he was really a very nice you-know-what, after all. Not nearly as nice as you, of course, but . . . Oh! You're not Puddin'!"

She had finally got to a point where she could see a cat's eyes, narrow and glowing chartreuse in the shadow of the lowest leaves. But even as she made out the cat's form, heavily shaded as it was by the overhanging bush, she realized that the cat was definitely neither fat nor black. It was sleek and gray with darker gray stripes. It was Desmond, glaring out at her with deep suspicion and moving a few inches away as she tiptoed forward.

"Desmond," she said to the cat, "what are you doing hiding there? I hope you weren't scared of me, were you? Be good and come out from under there." Now that she knew it wasn't the terrified Puddin', still hiding from Roderick's loud barking, she didn't bother to keep her voice in its low, soothing register, but addressed the animal in her normal tone and reached her hand over toward him, but much too fast—certainly faster than would have been recommended by any "how to" book on making friends with cats.

Desmond reacted violently to her quick gesture. He flinched broadly and shied sharply away, and as he did so, he backed into a second hydrangea behind him. The leaves of that second bush shook for a moment, even more violently than Desmond's bush had, and out from its shelter shot the missing Puddin', who headed hell-for-leather down the garden.

Desmond's nervous flinch may have startled Puddin', but the sight of Puddin', streaking away as though he had a cadre of pursuing fiends on his heels, seemed to scare the living daylights out of Desmond in return, for he instantly took off away from the unknown danger, ears flat back against his head, body low to the ground, hard on Puddin's heels. Angela, moving as fast as she was able, puffed along behind them. At the little utility area behind his owner's apartment, Puddin' turned hard right, Desmond not a dozen steps behind him. Angela, gasping, turned the same corner just in time to see Puddin's cat door flopping back and forth, having been hit hard by Puddin' as he headed for safety, and to see Desmond diving through the same door.

"They both went into Stone's apartment?" Caledonia said. "My gosh, what did Conrad say about getting a strange cat inside his . . ."

"He wasn't home," Angela said. "I knocked at his back door, and nobody answered. And that really worried me. You see, he might stumble over Desmond, and it might give him a terrible shock."

"You just wanted an excuse to talk to Mr. Perfect again, didn't you?" Caledonia said scornfully. "You used Desmond as an excuse to . . ."

"No, not at all. Let me get to my point. After I knocked and called out for Conrad and he didn't answer, I figured I better see if I couldn't do something about the situation myself. All I could think of was Conrad—Connie—coming home and walking into his kitchen, all unsuspecting, and Desmond springing out and giving him a shock that would knock him out—maybe even send him to the hospital, and . . ."

"Oh, honestly, Angela!" Caledonia's exasperation was only half serious, and she grinned. "What a load of my-eye that is!"

"No, truly. So what I did then was, I tried to lure Desmond outside again."

"How did you figure to do that?"

"I just went up to the stoop and stretched over to the cat flap—it's right beside the back door, you know, not very far—and I pushed the flap open and called Desmond, very softly so as not to startle him again."

"Did it work?"

"It didn't do a bit of good," Angela admitted ruefully. "So next I went back to the trash bin and found a piece of string that wasn't too yucky to handle, and I tied a little stick to one end and stuck it inside through the cat door, and I wiggled it around awhile and kept calling Desmond. And pretty soon, I felt a little tugging at the string from inside . . . very lightly, like a fish just nibbling at the bait on a line. I mean, you've been fishing, haven't you, and felt that first, gentle tug-tug-tug, and . . ."

"How do you know that wasn't Puddin' pulling at the string?"

"Well, I didn't, of course. So what I did next was, I leaned way over that railing that runs along beside the stoop, and I poked my head through the cat door to see if I could see which cat it was, and if it was really Desmond, I was going to grab him and haul him out—provided I could reach him. So there I was, almost halfway inside that cat door, kind of half off balance, standing on my tiptoes, bent way over the railing beside the back stoop, with my arms and head inside the flap . . . and Conrad Stone came home!"

"Can I help you, Mrs. Benbow? Give you a boost, perhaps?" Stone sounded amused, but Angela thought she sensed an undercurrent of annoyance. She pulled herself out of the cat door and turned to face him, hastily straightening her hair, which had been considerably ruffled by her efforts, and yanking down her blouse and sweater, which had climbed upwards to spring free at her waist and hang crookedly over her belt on one side.

"Oh, dear. Oh, Mr. Stone! What can you possibly think of me!"

"Well," he said, "my dear lady, it depends entirely on what you were planning to do, once you got through that hatch. If you were coming to visit, I applaud your enterprise and I'll invite you in right now. But if you had decided to rob me of my few treasures, I shall have to deal harshly with you!" But he smiled as he said it, and Angela dimpled in return.

"I really wasn't trying to get in," Angela said, with one more pat at her hair and one more push downward to the now captured blouse hem. "Truly. I was trying to get Desmond out before you saw him."

"Desmond?"

"I accidentally startled the cats, and Puddin' headed straight home. But Desmond followed him. And I was afraid that if you found a strange cat unexpectedly, the shock . . . Well, do you have a weak heart or anything? I've never asked you, and . . ."

"What a kind thought." If Stone had been annoyed, it no longer showed. His composure had been completely restored. "To answer your question, this old heart's as sound as a dollar. I'd be able to withstand even the surprise of finding Desmond in my house. But it surely was considerate of you, worrying about me like that, to say the least."

"Oh, I'm so glad you understand. I didn't know what you'd think, especially after you saw me this morning going through the trash. I mean, that was you looking out through your kitchen window, wasn't it? I thought you saw me and . . ."

"Yes, I wondered about that. I thought that perhaps you were collecting aluminum cans to sell and might be embarrassed to admit that you needed money. So I didn't ask. I've had otherwise perfectly respectable people going through my trash for aluminum before, and that was the first thing that occurred to me." He reached out, took Angela's hand in his, and gave the hand a little squeeze. "I say, Mrs. Benbow, as long as you're here, won't you come in for a few minutes? I could make a pot of tea . . ."

Angela was still a bit flustered. "And besides," she told Caledonia, "I thought it would be better if we came for a visit with him together. I remember my mother always saying that a lady never enters a bachelor's apartment by herself until they have been friends for a long, long time. And even then it doesn't really look . . . well, you know."

"By the way, is Stone a bachelor?" Caledonia said. "We've kind of taken it for granted, but I don't believe I've ever been told one way or the other. Most of the men living here alone are widowers or divorced, if you've noticed. There just aren't many men who've remained bachelors into their later years . . . not in our generation. What is Stone's status?"

"I don't believe I've heard," Angela said. "I think I'll ask Clara. She knows everything. But in the meantime, what I did was just beg off the invitation and tell him to ask us both together sometime soon. I hope you don't mind if I spoke for you. I told him we'd love to come down for tea, and . . ."

"Oh, I don't mind. I just won't love it very much. By the way, whatever happened to Desmond?"

"When Connie Stone opened his back door, Desmond strolled out as though nothing had ever been wrong at all. He wasn't frightened or anything. And he didn't seem to remember it was me that had startled him. He came and wound himself around my ankles and purred . . . Cats are strange creatures, aren't they?"

"I wouldn't know," Caledonia said. "I really wouldn't know, but . . ." She was interrupted by the telephone. "Now you wait here and don't go anywhere. We still have to talk about—Hello . . . Well, yes she is, as a matter of fact, Clara. Here, Angela, it's for you . . ." and Caledonia handed the receiver across to a startled Angela.

"I wonder," Clara said, "if you could stop up at the office on your way back through the building, Mrs. Benbow? Sometime before we close at four-thirty. Mr. Torgeson would like to talk to you."

Torgeson was beaming as he ushered Angela into his office. "It's very good news, Mrs. Benbow," he said. "We could all use some good news, of course, couldn't we? What it is, Pete Lopez says he and his crew are ready to start work on your window frames tomorrow. So if you approve, we can help you move a couple of suitcases full of personal belongings up to the studio apartment on the second floor, where you can stay for the time it takes Pete's men to get your place in good shape. Just a couple of days, as I said . . ." Angela said nothing, remembering Pete's signal to her that in this case "a couple" really meant something more like ten. "We've put a bed and dresser and mirror into the studio apartment . . . oh, and a TV and a couple of chairs and a little table. We even remembered," he said proudly, "to put some hangers into the closet for you. I know it's an inconvenience, but you'll be happy having a brand-new window in your place. Perhaps," he went on in a hopeful tone, "things will get back to normal around here now. I mean, get back to where they were before poor Mr. Gould was taken from us. We could all use a little 'business as usual,' couldn't we? Well, now, if you'll just go and pack those bags, the maids say they'll be happy to bring your bags upstairs and hang your things up for you."

Back at her own apartment, Angela phoned Caledonia the news, then packed three cases full of clothing from her crowded wardrobe and bureaus. Two maids carried the clothing away and a third waited while Angela packed yet another case for her makeup and medicines: comb, brush, lipstick, curlers, powder, toothbrush, toothpaste, aspirin, antihistamines, foot powder, antacids, complexion soap, deodorant soap, deodorant, nail file, tweezers, magnifying mirror . . . The case grew heavy, but as Angela explained apologetically to the waiting maid, "Better take everything right now instead of having to come back and disturb the workmen right in the middle of . . . At least, I'm packing everything I think I might need," Angela said. "I hope it's not too much for you." The maid shook her head with a grim expression, and said nothing as she lugged the big case to the elevator and then down the hall to the studio apartment in the far corner of the second floor.

Angela pattered along behind and supervised as everything she'd packed was unpacked again and hung or placed into drawers and shelves. It didn't take much more than an hour altogether, and Angela was ready for the little sherry that Caledonia offered down in her apartment as a prelude to dinner. "I figured you needed a chance to relax tonight," Caledonia said. "Goodness knows moving is tough any time. But you've had to pack and unpack three times within a month . . . first to go up to The Golden Years, then coming home again, now to take temporary quarters while your place is patched up . . . It's enough to unsettle anybody. My recommendation is that you just take it easy this evening, go to bed early, and . . ."

"No. Oh, no," Angela said. "Because one thing I picked up when I was in my place was the card with the name and address of our paperboy. Ricky Sherman, and he's just over on Cedar Street beyond the Presbyterian church. I think we should go over and talk to him tonight. Before . . . well, just before."

"Before Martinez knows what we're doing, like you said before. Right?" Caledonia grinned. "You know, for once, I'm on your side. I mean, what harm can it do to talk to the boy? And we might find out all sorts of interesting things. The kid was right there in the garden, after all, and he found poor old Howard, didn't he?"

"And one of the nicest things is," Angela said, her good humor quickly restored, "it isn't in the least dangerous! I mean, you don't really think he's a suspect, do you?"

"Of course not. I was only teasing you. The paperboy it is, right after we eat."

Caledonia's cooperative mood, the warmth of that tiny glass of sherry, and the prospect of adventure blended like soothing syrup to wash away fatigue and temper alike and Angela smiled.

So it was that after dinner, the two called a taxi to take them fourteen blocks, past the tiny downtown area and into a neighborhood of modest homes decorated with bougainvillea and trumpet vine, most surrounded by eight-foot-high screen fences built so close to the houses on their tiny plots of land that one could hardly squeeze between house and fence. Dwarf lemon and orange trees stood in some yards, some were heavy with flowers and boasted perfect little lawns, while others had substituted ivy for grass. This was a neighborhood with pride, even if it showed little in the way of wealth.

"I hate taxis," Caledonia was saying as they arrived. "I wanted the limo service, but we waited till too late to call them and they didn't have a driver. In a limo there's space for me to spread out, but I always feel cramped in a taxi. Now you," she addressed the driver imperi-

ously, "you remember you're waiting for us, not driving off somewhere."

"I remember, lady," the driver said tolerantly. "Suits me to sit here
running up your bill. I don't care as long as you pay me."

Caledonia started to respond, but Angela intervened. "Hush, Cal.
How about being cheerful while we do this interview? There's nothing we can do about the limo service now, and if you're thinking
about the taxi, you won't be giving your full attention to Ricky and
what he has to say." Angela pushed the doorbell. For several minutes
there was no answer.

"Nobody home?" Caledonia said suspiciously. "I thought you said
the kid would be waiting for you."

"Well, when I phoned him, that's what he told me. He said . . ."

Caledonia was reaching for the bell again when the door finally
swung open, revealing a pleasant-faced, middle-aged woman carrying
a wet frying pan and a dish towel.

"So sorry. The bell's hard to hear in the kitchen. Did you wait
long? Ricky told me you were coming. You must be Mrs. Benbow."
The woman looked left and right, first at Angela, then at Caledonia.

Angela put on her friendliest manner. "And you're Ricky's mother,
I suppose." The woman nodded, and Angela introduced herself and
Caledonia. "We're so sorry to interrupt your evening . . ."

"Oh, it's all right. Ricky told me it was questions about the . . . you
know, what he saw up there at the retirement place. Please sit down.
But you know, I don't really understand what you . . . I mean, I
thought the police had talked to him already."

"Oh, dear!" Angela was clearly disappointed. So much for their
having an original idea. "Oh, dear. Lieutenant Martinez has already
. . . Oh, dear."

Caledonia was not at all downcast by that news. "It's natural," she
told Mrs. Sherman. "Your son found the body of the late Mr. Gould,
and of course they'd want to ask about that. But it occurred to us,
Mrs. Sherman, that your son might have seen other things of interest."

"The police . . ." Mrs. Sherman began.

". . . will want to know everything we find out, of course," Angela
said quickly. "But they've gone on to other more urgent matters. So
we are just filling in the holes, so to speak. Picking up a few loose
ends. And your son . . . is he home? He said he would be."

"Oh, yes. He's in his room," Mrs. Sherman said. "Homework, you know. He's a junior in high school. I'll get him. He won't be a minute."

As his mother had promised, Ricky Sherman stumbled into the room within moments. A weedy young man with enormous feet and large, round, dark eyes that peered out from beneath a shock of black hair straggling over his brow, Ricky looked extremely ill at ease. He swallowed hard, several times, his Adam's apple bobbing hugely. "You—you want to talk about that . . . you know, like that dead fellow in the garden?"

"Not exactly, young man," Angela said. "More about what you saw and did in the garden that night."

"Did?" He was clearly puzzled. "I delivered the papers. I didn't do a thing. Except for that."

"She means," Caledonia said, "what did you see, where did you go, what did you hear . . . Anything that wasn't just the ordinary sort of . . . well, and the ordinary things, too, I suppose."

"Tell us exactly what you did that night," Angela said kindly. "In your own words. Do you deliver the papers in the main building first?"

"Oh, yes, ma'am," he nodded. "I try to be real quiet up there and lay the papers down in front of every door, like I saw in a hotel once. I start up on the second floor, then I do the ground floor, and I end up going out the door into the garden. I go down the walk and throw those papers, so I usually sit down before I start and fold some."

"Is that what you did just before you found Howard Gould?"

The boy nodded. "Got nineteen folded and pitched 'em. Well, I didn't get to pitch the last four, because those four places are past the fountain, you know, and when I got that far down the walk I saw him. The guy. Like, you know, facedown in the fountain, with blood on his head. Well," he shuddered at the memory, "he wasn't really all the way into the fountain, you know, but . . ."

"Don't think about it," Angela said kindly. "Think about something else. Anything else. Try to remember . . ." She assumed a soft, coaxing, musical tone. "Walk down the walk again in your mind's eye. Tell me what you see . . . Now, you're at the main building, and you have your newspapers rolled up and ready . . ." She was imitating the voice of a hypnotist she'd seen in one of those old Charlie Chan movies from the '30s, movies she absolutely doted on. "Look at the crystal ball," he'd intoned, "and think back. Tell me what you see . . ." and the blonde starlet had become glazed and obedient. Angela didn't have a crystal ball, but she could assume the steady stare and the singsong voice the hypnotist had used. "Think now . . . you stand up from the chair on the porch and you have your fifteen newspapers tucked under an arm . . ."

"Huh-uh. Nineteen papers, and I put 'em into like a bag," the boy said.

"All right," Angela said, a bit annoyed at the break in the mood. "Nineteen then. In a bag. Okay, once more . . . you come to the first little building with three apartments on your right . . ."

"I pitched at the place on the left first," he said. "Then I turned around and threw to the apartments on the right. The lights were on in the first apartment, and I could see . . ."

"The lights were on?" Caledonia pounced. "That would be the Goulds' place. Was one of the doors open?"

He thought a moment. "No, I don't think so."

"Did you see Mrs. Gould?"

"I told you, I didn't see anybody outside at all. There was just me and that dead fellow out in the garden."

"No-no-no, I meant inside the apartment. Did you see Mrs. Gould moving around in her place? Was she up and around?"

"I don't think so. Like I said, I didn't see anybody inside or outside. Well, just a cat. It was outside the door of that place with the lights, and I could hear it meowing to get in. But nobody came, so it would like 'Meow' again and wait some more. I noticed 'cause we got, you know, a cat, and what I wanted to do was go let it in myself. But I was afraid if I opened the door, somebody inside would think I was trying to come in myself. Like a burglar, you know? So I just went on and threw more papers. First to apartments on the left, then to apartments on my right . . . Hit 'em all square on, too," he said proudly.

"Wasn't there anybody else in the garden at all?" Angela asked, disappointed.

"No, and no lights on in any other apartments, either. At least, not out in the garden. There were some lights on in the big building, upstairs where people live."

"Well." Angela took a deep breath. "No strangers walking on the street outside the garden?" He shook his head. "None of the staff moving around?" He shook his head. "No things lying around that you remember? Objects, I mean. We know there was a toolbox somewhere near the fountain. But anything else?"

He shook his head once more. "I didn't even see the toolbox. All I saw was a bag."

"What kind of a bag?"

"You know, like just a little white paper bag. From Fat Boy's burgers. I picked it up and carried it over to the nearest trash bin, and then I turned around and started back toward the fountain and that's when I saw the dead guy. And I didn't see one other thing. Nothing. Nowhere."

"Well," Angela said, obviously disappointed, "I suppose that's it then, and thank you very much, Ricky." She stood and started for the door, then turned back so suddenly that Caledonia, coming along directly behind her, nearly ran her down. "Oh, one more thing. If you think of anything else, something you forgot or something we didn't ask that seems important, you'll let us know, right? Here . . ." and she scribbled her name and phone number on a scrap of paper from a tiny leather-covered notebook in her purse.

"Okay." He took the paper and shoved it into a pocket of his stained jeans.

"That's the last anybody will see of that paper," Caledonia said, as they reached their taxi, "till it comes out of the washing machine next week—or next month—whenever he gives those jeans to his mother for the laundry. Your paper will just be a water-soaked ball she'll throw out along with the used Kleenex and old movie ticket stubs he'll have squirreled away by that time. What'd you bother with that for?"

"It's was what the detective always does on TV—hands over a card and tells the person to call him. He'd have been disappointed if we didn't do something like that, and who knows? He might think of something else."

"But more likely not," Caledonia said. "Come on . . . home we go . . ." The driver pulled smoothly away from the curb and headed westward, toward the ocean and Camden-sur-Mer.

"You know," Angela said, "I'm interested to hear about that burger bag. It had me worried."

"How so?"

"I couldn't believe Mary Moffet would be eating Fat Boy burgers. She's too sensible to take aboard all that cholesterol. But the bag wasn't hers. It was just dumped into her trash by Ricky, tidying up."

"What makes you think it wasn't hers?"

"Because," Angela said loftily, "Mary would absolutely never have thrown trash away on the lawn. Somebody else littered up the garden." They paid off the driver and were starting into the lobby when Angela stopped short. "Oh, dear! Oh, dear!"

"What's the problem? Lose something?"

"No. It's just that I only this minute remembered that I'll be upstairs in the studio apartment tonight. A strange bed in a strange room . . . I won't sleep a wink!"

But of course she did.

CHAPTER

11

"OH, BOTHER!" ANGELA HAD hunted three times through her new medicine cabinet and twice through the bag in which she'd carried cosmetics without finding either a tube of mascara or her shower cap. She'd discovered the omission of a shower cap the evening before when she tried to wash off the dust and the cares of the day before retiring, and ended by wrapping her head in a towel to keep her hair away from splashes. The mascara wasn't needed till morning when she went to put a light coating on her pale lashes, lashes that had turned white at the same time her luxuriant hair went from blonde to silver, and which she customarily darkened each day, ". . . otherwise I wouldn't have any eyes at all," as she said defensively, when Caledonia teased her about her "war paint."

This morning, however, she was annoyed with herself, rather than defensive. "With all I carried here with me," she scolded herself, "I can't believe I forgot the mascara and the shower cap! Well, I'll just bring this little tote bag down to breakfast with me, and right after I eat, I'll go in and get the things I need. Before the men get started working." And indeed, immediately after she finished toast, bacon, and coffee, she hurried to her own apartment on the first floor, unlocked the door, and stopped dead in her tracks, taken aback for a moment to see an expanse of white cloth thrown over her bookcases, her desk, a couple of chairs . . . Another stack of white canvas lay folded in a corner, ready to cover the couch, the remaining chairs, the side tables. Of course she realized at once that the maids must have returned—after they got her bags unpacked on the second floor but before going home for the night—to cover her things because of the dust the carpentry crew would raise. She stepped back into her

living room again and stopped once more. She had caught an unpleasant scent, alien yet half-familiar. She couldn't place the smell,
but it tickled lightly at her throat and made her want to cough. Once
more she stepped backward into the hall.

"Whew, Mrs. Benbow, what'd you spill in there?" It was Harvey
Ridgeway, coming along the hallway with his wife Della just behind
him. They had stopped at the open door, and as Angela stepped back,
Harvey pushed himself forward, nostrils flared. "It really smells awful!"

"Harvey," Della admonished, "don't be rude." She sniffed deli-
cately, her nose wriggling like a rabbit's. "I don't smell a thing." To
Angela's annoyance, Della pushed right past both Harvey and Angela
and entered the living room. "No, I don't smell anything. Tea, maybe.
Faintly. But it's not really unpleasant."

"Oh, please, Della!" Harvey marched into the center of the room,
turning his head slowly, sniffing here, sniffing there . . . "Surely you
can pick that up. It's . . . kind of like the stuff we used to swab out
latrines with, way back when I was in the army. What the Sam Hill
was that? My memory's getting so bad . . ."

"They say," Della said pleasantly to Angela, as relaxed as though
she and her husband were invited guests, "that our sense of smell
becomes less acute as we get older. Maybe Harvey can still smell it,
but I surely can't. By the way, what are all these dust covers for,
Angela? Are you going traveling?"

Angela was growing more and more annoyed with the intrusion,
but she simply had no idea—short of being rude herself—how to rid
herself of the invaders. "I'm not traveling anywhere," she said shortly.

"But what's with the white cloth?" Harvey pursued the subject.

"Oh, the staff put the covers on my things to protect them while
repairs are done," she said, waving an impatient hand toward her
water-stained wall and the windows. "They must have brought in the
drop cloths after I left last night because the men are supposed to
start work today. Anyway, I imagine that's how the furniture got itself
covered. I wasn't here."

"We know that," Della twinkled. "We came calling last night after
dinner. Knocked and knocked, but you didn't answer."

"We're making the rounds," Harvey said. "That's what we're doing
here in your hallway today." He walked to a little chair and tweaked
its white canvas covering slightly aside.

"What're you doing!" Angela's voice was sharp. ("I thought," she told Caledonia later, "that he intended to sit himself down right then and there for a visit. The last thing I wanted.")

If her annoyance was obvious, it certainly wasn't so to Harvey Ridgeway. "Just trying to see if it's these covers that have the odor. I thought they might have been stored down in the carpentry shop and picked up a smell of paint remover or something. But," he went on, holding a corner of the cloth to his nose, "I guess not." He carelessly threw the cloth back in the general direction of the chair, leaving it partly uncovered, and Angela hurried over to pat the cloth into an orderly position.

"Just guess, Mrs. Benbow," Harvey went on with a mischievous twinkle. "Just guess who it is we're coming to visit this morning. Who would you think was next on our list?"

"Not me!" Angela was dismayed. "I'm only going to be here a moment while I pick up a few things."

"Heavens, no," Della laughed merrily. "We're on our way to call on Tom Brighton. That's how we happened to be passing your door. Very fortunate to get to see you at all, you seem to be such a gadabout." She laughed again, as though she'd said something frightfully witty. "Where were you last night?" she went on, in an accusing tone. "We have a list, you know, and we're going to visit everybody in turn—get to know everybody here—and we were going in alphabetical order."

"Systematic, see?" Harvey said. "We don't want to miss anybody, but the old memory's not what it used to be. Maybe with Della it's the sense of smell, but with me it's the memory. So I gotta do things in some kind of order, you know? So we were starting with the B's. Benbow, then Brighton, see?"

"There were four A's up at The Golden Years," Della put in helpfully. "Appleby, Anthony, Alexander, and your Mrs. Armstrong. But of course she's moved back here now. Did you realize she's the only A in Camden-sur-Mer? Of course, we'd already visited her up at The Golden Years, because we started our program of getting to know our neighbors when we were up there. So we didn't need to do Armstrong again down here, did we? And we just started with the B's." Angela was shifting her weight impatiently from one foot to the other, trying to think of a way to interrupt and get her uninvited guests started on their way again, when Della went on insistently, "So where were you last night? It's really frustrating to come to see someone and find they're not at home."

"I had an errand after dinner," Angela said shortly. She didn't bother to explain about the move to the temporary room upstairs. "Next time I go out," she added sourly, "I'll post a note on the bulletin board. I wouldn't want anybody to be annoyed with me for going about my business."

"How thoughtful," Della said cheerfully. Obviously sarcasm was quite beyond her comprehension. "Well, we'll just move you to the list for later in the week. Maybe Thursday."

"Oh. Thanks! That'll be charming!" Once more, the sarcasm passed way over Della's head.

"We'll look forward to it then," Harvey said, equally oblivious to any notion that Angela was less than pleased. "Well, now, little lady, you just hunt around and find whatever it is that's smelling up the place, because it really is kind of unpleasant, you know? And we'll be seeing you!" And the Ridgeways went off down the hall with cheerful smiles and friendly waves of the hand.

The forced smile slid off Angela's face the moment the Ridgeways turned away from her, and she stepped quickly back into her apartment and closed the hall door firmly, just in case they changed their minds and headed back her way. Then she went into her little bathroom to pick up the forgotten shower cap and mascara. While she was at it, she picked up some cotton balls, an orangewood stick, emery boards, some blusher—not that she used it very often, but there might be a party, she told herself, and she liked to have a healthy glow to her when she got all dressed up. She swung the bathroom door shut, insulating herself against that unpleasant odor, and went to work in earnest. Into her tote also went hair spray, some styling gel and a few clips to help set straight ends, elbow cream, a comb cleaner, and an extra head for the electric toothbrush . . . before long the little tote bag was bulging and the bathroom cabinet half empty.

"There are a few more thing I maybe could use," Angela said to herself, "but I don't think I have room for them. Maybe a second trip . . ."

She was heading out through the living room, aiming for the outer door, when, just in the corner of her eye, she caught a quick glimpse of something red, a flicker of color that surely didn't belong among the cool greens and sea blues of her decor. She turned toward the couch that sat below the windows. There was a small end table near the arm of the couch, and ordinarily the table held only a lamp and a decorative box in which Angela kept paper clips and rubber bands.

Lamp and tiny box were still there, but there were four additions now as well: four bright red-and-blue cans labeled BOMB 'EM OUT in acid-yellow letters with the picture of a cockroach lying on its back, tiny legs pointed skyward, tiny eyes replaced by big X's. The bombs had obviously been spraying, for the red triggers were in the OPEN position and there was a light, filmy residue on the tabletop, a faint dusting of white.

"Of course!" Angela said, pleased to have solved a minor problem. "That's what the smell is. Insecticide!"

"I should have remembered," she told Caledonia at lunchtime. "From when Douglas and I had a cat that got fleas. We had to set off an insecticide bomb to get those pesky little bugs out of our drapes and carpets. This morning, I could hardly pick up the scent, it was so faint. Just a little reminder of something—oh, like something medicinal. I remember it as being much stronger and much less pleasant. But maybe they've improved the stuff over the years so it doesn't stink the way I remember. Of course different people react to the smell differently. Harvey Ridgeway thought it was terrible, but Della could hardly smell it at all."

"Those two!" Caledonia said. "They aren't people who can take a hint, are they? I think that when they come calling on me, I'll be very direct. I won't say 'I only have a minute.' I'll say 'No, you can't come in.' Period. End of discussion."

"But don't you want to get acquainted with them? They seemed to mean well enough. I felt a little guilty about being so . . . you know, so abrupt."

"Listen, I didn't care for their complaining when I first met 'em up at The Golden Years, and I haven't seen anything that would make me like 'em one bit better. And now they want to be bosom buddies with me? I don't think so!"

"Please pass the butter, Cal. Thank you. I know I shouldn't have any of these rolls, but they're fresh baked . . ." She buttered a moment before she went on. "Cal, I don't think the Ridgeways want to be friends or anything—just to get acquainted. With everybody. In turn."

"And to annoy everybody. In turn. Pass that butter back when you're done, Angela. I've got a couple of rolls to butter too, you know. Ah, thank you." Caledonia spread the butter lavishly and lovingly. "I don't know why you're sitting here defending the Ridgeways. You don't like them either, do you?"

"No, not really. Pass the jar of honey, will you? Thanks."

"There you are. Now. Back to important things. What I really want to know is why you set off the insecticide bombs? Have you got bugs?"

"I don't and I didn't. I mean, the maids set the insecticide going after I left. And I don't think I have bugs, but you never can tell. Anyway, it was very considerate of them. Or of Torgeson. And I've dropped off a note to thank him."

"He doesn't usually think to give the orders so that two jobs get done at the same time," Caledonia said. "When my plumbing was on the fritz and my kitchen needed rewiring, they kept me in a mess for days with the plumbing first, and no sooner were they done with that and I'd settled down than they came back with another work order from Torgeson to do that wiring. I had workmen in and out for two weeks, even if it could have been done in half that, if the plumber and the electrician had worked at the same time. But that never occurred to Torgeson."

"Well, it did this time, and I felt he needed congratulations."

"Good idea. He hears enough complaints—I bet he'll be grateful for a compliment or two. Well, now what do we do toward our investigation? Where are we so far?"

"Our investigation?" Angela's tone carried a hint of reproof. "Does that mean you're going to pitch in and actually do something? All you've done with me so far is to visit the paperboy and to see Harriet Gould. Well, it's true you went and talked to the Ridgeways, but you did that by yourself, and I interviewed Nancy Bush, I collected the trash, I brought the sack of cartons up to Lieutenant Martinez . . . it's really no fun doing things alone. It would be so nice to have you working with me."

Caledonia pushed back from the table, replete at last. "I haven't meant to leave you wallowing on your own, dear girl. It's just now and then you gallop off in all directions at once and somebody should hold you back. I guess I've been trying to slow you down a little. A little subtlety in your approach wouldn't hurt, you know. Going flat-out, slam-bang, full speed ahead just won't work all the time. Sometimes you need to tiptoe up from behind and surprise your prey."

"I have no idea what you're talking about," Angela huffed.

"You wouldn't," Calendia grinned. "But it's especially true in this case, where there aren't any suspects at all yet and you have no idea what it is you're charging at! All the same, I'm perfectly willing to plunge into furious activity, if that's what you really want. Provided we have a plan of action."

So they discussed possible plans as they left the dining room and strolled out into the garden, and at last Angela announced that perhaps it would be as well, after all, to talk to people who had received deliveries on the night of the murder. "Are you sure? At first, you wanted to interview only the delivery boys," Caledonia reminded her, "and not bother the residents here."

"I still think that would be the easy way, Cal, but when I brought him those empty cartons, Lieutenant Martinez specifically told me not to talk to the delivery boys. So we really ought to find another way to get at the same information. Who was in the garden and who saw what."

"Okay. Fair enough. Where do we go first?"

"Before you even take your nap?"

"Oh, come on, Angela, don't be snide. I usually take a nap after lunch. I won't today, that's all. There's a big difference between 'I usually' and 'I always.' Okay, who's first? Want to start out at the far end of the garden and work our way toward home?"

So the two found themselves knocking on an apartment door in the endmost cottage on the garden's southern side, the Jeffersons' place, and greeting a chubby, balding, bespectacled Phillip Jefferson. "Well, for goodness sake, look who's here!" he said, his round little cheeks crinkling into deep smile lines. "Come in, come in. I don't think we've talked since . . . why, it must have been since the big Christmas party. Emmy will be delighted . . ." He ushered the two women into a sparsely furnished living room.

"Here," he said, pulling one chair forward and waving toward the other. "We may not have many chairs but we have a couple that will do. Because of Emmy, you know. Having a lot of chairs and coffee tables and things would get in her way. Oh, here she is now. Emmy, honey, look who's here!"

Emma Jefferson wheeled herself into the room, and suddenly self-conscious, as many people are in the presence of those confined to wheelchairs, Angela jumped to her feet, her hands making little motions as though to help position the wheelchair. Caledonia reached a giant arm over, grasped Angela's hand, and pulled her back down again. "Forgive her, Emma," Caledonia said. "She only wants to help. Emma will ask when she wants you to help, Angela. Quit fussing!"

Emma looked enough like her husband—except for his balding head—to be a sister instead of his wife. Short of stature and spherical of shape, she was full of smiles and seemed perpetually cheerful. "How wonderful to see you both," she said. "Don't scold Angela, Caledonia. I know she only wanted to help, but I'm fine, dear. Well-well-well, you two haven't come to visit since I don't know how long. This is delightful, isn't it, Phil?"

"I'll say. Oh, how about I maybe get you two tea?"

"Oh, let me . . ." Emma rolled toward their kitchenette that had been specially adapted for her use: the stove was one with controls on the front; ordinary faucets had been replaced with eight-inch handles that Emmy could reach easily to turn the water on and off; doors had been taken off overhead cabinets; under-the-counter storage had been removed and counter tops raised so that the wheelchair fit beneath them and Emma could reach the lower shelves unaided.

"I really don't want any tea, Emma," Caledonia called. "We just finished lunch."

Emma came back into the living room. "Well, of course, my dears. I just forget that everyone else goes up to the main dining room for lunch," she said. "We have breakfast and lunch down here in the apartment every day. Because of my chair, you know. But they don't mind if I come to the main dining room for dinner. Of course, I have to wait till everyone else is seated." She smiled tolerantly. "The chair would be just one more thing for some one of our older residents to stumble over."

"And we have some who would stumble over everything," Angela assured her. "Grogan, for instance."

"Oh, Grogan," Phil Jefferson said. "Of course." Then he fell silent while he and his wife looked expectantly at their guests.

Angela cleared her throat and took over. "We did come to ask something. Of course I'm sure the police have already asked what you saw the night Mr. Gould was killed."

Phil Jefferson nodded. "Oh, yes. They sat right here and asked over and over—as though they didn't believe me when I said we went to bed early and didn't see one thing. I mean, nothing unusual. We like to watch our neighbors strolling up and down after supper, and there were plenty of them. Some of the new folks, too. Not Mr. Gould, but Mrs. Gould. And your friend Tootsie Armstrong. And those new folks, the Ridgeways. But mostly it was old-timers like us: the Jackson twins, the Dovers, Mrs. Stainsbury . . . you know . . . the usual after-dinner strollers."

"How about later?" Angela persisted. "I mean, when the light faded and all the strollers went on home to watch TV and go to bed? Did you see anything then?"

"Goodness, no," Emma said. "We watch TV and go to bed early just like everybody else does."

"How about," Angela said, "Billy from the drugstore? Didn't he make a delivery?"

"You know, Em, I do believe he did. Let me think . . ."

"Get your checkbook out, Phil. You wrote him a check for the prescriptions and you'll have the date on the stub."

"Good idea." He got up and fetched a large desk checkbook, the kind that holds three checks to a page opposite a huge stub. At Angela's surprised glance he said, "We don't go out shopping in the malls much, nowadays. Do most of our buying from catalogues. And people are so unpleasant about accepting checks now! Used to be they were glad to have a check. Now they expect you to use those nasty little plastic cards. I don't really need a pocket checkbook at all these days. So I got this big book with the big stubs. There's space so I can write large enough to see it even when I'm tired and the eyes don't focus good. Now let's see here . . ." He thumbed the book open and found the stub at once. "Sure. Here it is. A check to Camden Drugs written on Tuesday night. That was the night that Gould fellow got himself killed, wasn't it? Well, then, you're absolutely right. Billy did come here." He rose and took the book back to his desk.

"So what about Billy, Angela?" Emma asked. "Such a nice boy. He's delivered for the drugstore for oh, maybe four years or more. Saving his money up for college, he tells us. He's not in any trouble, is he?"

"Oh, no, we don't believe so. But we wondered if you might have seen anything about the time Billy came here. I mean, you must have looked out when you answered the door. So did you see . . ."

"Nothing but those cats," Phil Jefferson said. "Blasted animals, sneaking around our trash bins looking for a handout. There's two of 'em, you know. A stripey one and that fat, black thing . . ."

"Phil doesn't much like cats," Emma explained apologetically. "But they weren't doing anything wrong, were they, Phil?"

"Jumping at each other, clawing at the lid of the trash can, running off like they were being chased . . ."

"Nothing wrong with that, is there, Phil?" Caledonia asked. "Cats playing, cats picking up good smells from your discards . . ."

"No. Nothing really wrong," he said reluctantly. "Just that I wish they'd stay away from here. They don't play around other people's trash that way. Just ours."

"Well, Phil, be reasonable," his wife said. "Not many others make their own breakfast and lunch, so not many others have leftovers to make nice smells when they're thrown out! A dog would do the same thing, sniff around the trash."

"I suppose so," he said sulkily. "But there's something straightforward about the way a dog does it. And there's something downright sneaky about the way a cat sniffs garbage. I mean, he always tries to look as though that's not even what he's doing. He just kind of strolls past the can once and then comes back again. A dog, he stops there and lifts his head and you can see what he's up to!"

The last thing Angela wanted was an argument, so she let the remark pass and brought the conversation back to her point. "But what did you see besides the cats jumping and running around?"

"And sniffing garbage!" Phil reminded her.

". . . and sniffing the garbage. Besides that, did you see anything worth mentioning?"

He hesitated and passed a hand back and forth over his balding pate as though rubbing his skull would stimulate his brains. "Honest, I don't think so. Let's see . . . the bell rang, I went out onto the steps when I saw it was Billy, and I took the bag from him. I had my check ready in my hand because they told me on the phone what it would cost, and I just handed it to him. He turned around right smart and kind of jumped off the steps, and he hustled himself off up the garden. Me, I just went back into the house. And those cats ran off toward the fountain, one chasing the other, and that was it, best I could say."

Angela sighed. "You're sure?"

He shrugged. "Sure as I can be."

"Well . . . " Caledonia heaved her bulk upward, her feet set wide to take her weight as she rose. "I guess that's all we wanted to know."

"But won't you stay awhile longer? Just to chat," Phil Jefferson was, however, moving toward the door. The appeal to stay was apparently merely *pro forma*, so Angela quickly got to her feet as well.

"No, not today," she said. "We're asking questions up and down the garden, you see. We'll go across to Conrad Stone's next."

"Oh! That nice, nice man." Emma's voice was a purr. "He came over and introduced himself to us right away, right after he arrived. I appreciated that. Sometimes, you know, people are a little shy about talking to me. Because of the wheelchair. They seem to think somehow I'm going to be . . . well, different."

"You'd be surprised how many people talk to me instead of to Emma," her husband said. "When we ride on public transportation, the driver says to me, 'Is she comfortable?' We go into a store and somebody's bound to say, 'Anything I can do to help her?' I get mad. I always say, 'Why not ask her yourself?' "

"Oh, Phil," Emma said mildly. "It's only natural. I mean, suppose I was senile? It could be real embarrassing if they tried to talk to me and I just drooled at them. They're only trying to be nice."

"But I don't like it," he said, his round little face puckered into ferocious lines. "I don't like them treating you like you're not quite right in the head, just because you're not quite right in the legs."

Emma laughed. "Oh, Phil! Isn't he funny, though?" she went on to her guests. "He takes such good care of me. Well, it was good to see you two if only for a minute, and you come back any day you like. Around teatime maybe. Phil makes terrible tea. But don't you worry, I'll make the tea myself. I'll just let him serve. So it'll be good."

"And if you find out anything interesting," Phil called after them as they crossed the garden, "you let us know, why don't you? You two get into the doggon dest things . . ."

They waved back over their shoulders as Phil closed the door behind them, and they turned toward the fountain and beyond it the cottage in which Stone's apartment was located. His front door being around the building facing Beach Lane, they went without thinking twice to the kitchen door, which opened onto the little service area facing the garden. "See how big the cat door is, Cal?" Angela whispered as they came along the walk. "I could have crawled all the way through it, if I wanted to."

"Can you tell me," Caledonia said, using a whisper as well, "why we're visiting Stone instead of the Taylors in the garden-side apartment? I know you found some box or other in their mutual trash bin, but . . ."

"A pizza box is what I found here."

"Okay, then, pizza. But who ordered it? I mean was there a resident's name on the box? No. So why aren't we calling on the Taylors to ask, instead of calling on Conrad Stone?"

"Because," Angela hissed, "Mr. Taylor told me they hadn't had anything delivered to their place. And because Conrad Stone asked us to call on him, so I figured why not combine two birds in one errand?"

"What a little hypocrite you are. I bet you planned this all the time." But Caledonia was grinning as she scolded. "You'll use any excuse to talk to this guy. That's why you wanted me so bad to come along, so you'd feel comfortable in that man's apartment! If I'd known, I'd just have stayed home and taken my nap." As they whispered to each other, they slowed their walk, but they drew nearer and nearer to Stone's back door. Caledonia was just about to launch into a discussion of her own feelings about Stone when his door popped open and he came out onto the step, a broad smile of greeting making the only lines on his handsome face.

"Saw you coming as I was doing the dishes. I look right out the window as I work, but usually there isn't as good a view as today's." He popped a little bow of greeting to them and added, "Welcome, Castor and Pollux." They looked briefly puzzled, so he went on, ". . . the heavenly twins, you know. You're so seldom apart, I think of you as a team instead of as two separate people. Unless, of course, one of you is trying to crawl through my cat door . . ."

"I explained that," Angela said quickly. "We're here for quite a different reason today anyway."

"You're looking particularly well today, Mrs. Benbow." He smiled a welcome at Caledonia as well, but his eyes came back again and again to Angela. "Rested and happy. It's really grand to see people, especially people of our age, look so . . . so blooming."

"Oh, my! Well," she patted her snowy hair and dimpled her pleasure at him, "one tries to keep oneself up, of course." Caledonia rolled her eyes to heaven, but said nothing.

Stone was standing in a posture that was distinctly welcoming, one hand extended toward them, the other still holding the kitchen door wide open, so Angela took the invitation as explicit and walked in past him. Caledonia, with a little shrug, followed.

"I hope," he said, bowing slightly, "that you've come calling and that you're going to come in and perhaps share some tea? An afternoon cocktail? I have no idea what you two ladies prefer, but I think I can offer . . ."

"How beautiful!" Angela said as she rounded the corner from the kitchen into the living room. "Why, your place is wonderful!"

"My decorator will thank you," Stone said, and held chairs for them. The living room was very much a man's room. Bright Scandinavian throw rugs lay here and there on polished floors, and the furniture was modern without being angular, economical without being Spartan. A tall, simple bookcase neatly stocked with leather-covered volumes stood between the door and a broad window that faced Beach Lane, and nautical odds and ends filled the blank spaces on the walls: a small ship's wheel, a diver's helmet draped with a chain, a brass porthole cover framing a seascape, a miniature anchor . . .

"Yo-ho-ho and a bottle of rum," Caledonia muttered in a sour tone.

"Rum?" Stone picked up on the word. "Maybe you'd like a daiquiri?"

"Oh, no-no-no," Caledonia said quickly. "I was just thinking that your decorator seems to have worked really hard on this place."

"Yes, didn't he?" Stone beamed contentedly and pulled up his own chair to sit closer to them. "And I really needed help planning how to make the move here. My place at The Golden Years was done up a little like an English country home with piecrust tables and serpentine chests . . . You never got to see it, but believe me, those furnishings would have been really out of place in a beach-front apartment. And I certainly feel more comfortable with all of this . . ." He waved a hand left and right.

"I bet," Caledonia said. "Of course it would make more sense if you were a seafaring man yourself."

Angela gave her friend a hard nudge and took over the conversation before Caledonia could say anything too hostile. She explained their mission quickly and finished up, ". . . and so it comes to this; we've been asked to bring the police anything we could find out," she finished quite truthfully, but Caledonia could see Angela cross the fingers on one hand, held out of Stone's sight down beside her chair, as she added, ". . . so you might say we've been assigned to interview everyone about their deliveries."

"Deliveries? What do you mean?"

"I mean, we've discovered that people up and down the garden were getting medicine and fast food and goodness-knows-what the evening Howard Gould died, and we think it's possible that one of them—the delivery boys or the residents, when they answered the door—saw something significant out in the garden." Stone looked puzzled, so Angela went on, "Like Phil Jefferson across the way got his medicine, and he noticed Puddin' playing with Desmond near the trash bins."

"The cats? That's what you call 'significant'?" Stone asked.

"Well, no," Angela conceded. "But at least he saw *some*thing when he looked outside. And we thought the other neighbors might, too."

"First," Caledonia interrupted, "*did* you get a delivery that night?"

"Delivery?" Stone said again.

"Pizza," Angela blurted. "We found a pizza box in the trash be-hind . . ."

"Oh, the pizza! Well, of course. I thought you meant medicine or something. Yes, I had pizza that night."

"But why?" Caledonia said. "I can't imagine anybody not liking the wonderful meals Mrs. Schmitt sets out."

"Well," he said a bit sheepishly, "the truth is I'm not fond of lamb," Stone said. "I don't suppose it's reasonable of me, but when I saw the menu for that night's meal, I decided to order from the local . . ."

"Don't be embarrassed. So did Mr. and Mrs. Spangler," Angela said. "They have Chinese instead of Italian, but the idea's the same, isn't it?"

"Spangler?" Stone said. "I've heard the name, of course, but I don't think I've actually met them yet."

"They live up at the head of the garden," Caledonia said. "In my building. It's quite possible you haven't met. They're pretty quiet out in public."

"But we're told," Angela said in a gossipy tone, "that they have plenty to say to each other in private. The original of the Bickersons."

"Angela," Caledonia warned. "Mr. Stone doesn't . . ."

"Connie, please," he said amiably.

"Connie then . . ." Caledonia said shortly. "Connie doesn't want to hear about all the neighbors and their problems. Just ask your questions and let's go. We really haven't got all day."

"Cal doesn't mean to sound insulting, Connie," Angela said sweetly. "She's just eager to get on with our interviews. It would be terribly disappointing if we had nothing to report to Lieutenant Mar-tinez. But Cal certainly didn't mean . . ."

"No offense taken," Stone said. "Listen, can't I get you two some-thing? If not a daiquiri, then maybe a Tom Collins? Or a gin and tonic? Or how about lemonade? I have some frozen concentrate I could make up."

"No, nothing, thank you," Angela said. "Cal's absolutely right. We do need to hurry along this afternoon. Another time . . ."

"All these pleasantries are slowing us down." Caledonia waved a large hand. "What we want to know is if you saw anything. Anything unusual, I mean, like what you could see when the delivery boy came to the door. He did come to the back door, didn't he?"

"Yes. Or rather no. I mean . . . he did and he didn't. The fellow puts my pizza into the kitchen through Puddin's door. It's an arrangement we worked out one chilly night when I was in my pajamas, and it works beautifully. I have his money on the counter, he shoves the box through and takes the money, and I don't have to open the door or throw on a robe, or anything. And I never even see him, let alone suspicious characters in the garden."

"Lucky that Puddin's a fat cat and you had the door cut wide for his sake," Caledonia said. "It's just about wide enough for a fifteen-inch pizza."

"Yes, that was a bit of luck," Stone agreed. "But it means that I didn't look outside and I don't have information that will be of use to you. Sorry about that."

Caledonia got to her feet. "Well, we had to ask. Come on, Angela. We need to be on our way." She headed for the kitchen and the back door, throwing a grudging "Thanks for the information" back over her shoulder.

"But I haven't given you any information!" Stone protested.

"Yes, you have," Angela said, standing and moving toward the back door much more slowly than Caledonia had. "I mean, negative information can be as useful as positive information. If you didn't see anything, that means we have to go on asking other people if they saw anything. And if nobody saw anything, that probably means there wasn't anything to see. Do you see? I mean, do you understand what I mean? That is to say . . ."

"Angela, give the poor man a break. 'Just say goodnight, Gracie,' and come along," and Caledonia sailed out the door.

Stone gave his polite little bow toward the retreating Caledonia. "Mrs. Wingate . . . or Caledonia, if I may . . ." Caledonia stopped just outside on the back step as he went on, "I don't mind in the least your being eager to get on with your questioning. Especially since I had nothing much to offer. But I want you both to return for a social afternoon very soon. Sometime when you're not running errands for your friends on the police force. Is that a promise?"

"Promise," Angela beamed at him.

"Oh. Sure." Caledonia stumped off the step, out toward the main garden (leaving all the hand kissing that might be forthcoming to be lavished on Angela), and stood glowering by the fountain till Angela joined her.

"Now before you say anything," Angela said, "don't say it."

Caledonia shrugged. "Okay. Who's next?"

"Mary Moffet, I thought," Angela said, and she led the way to Mary's place.

"No," Mary said in her soft, whispery voice, "I didn't get a Fat Boy burger delivered. I do have them sometimes, though. I know they're all grease and gristle, but they're so . . . so good! I get . . ." She blushed shyly. "I get tired of all the healthy food. Beef Stroganoff doesn't taste the same made with yogurt instead of sour cream."

"Gosh," Caledonia said in an awed voice. "You mean Mrs. Schmitt uses yogurt? I'd never guess. Her Stroganoff is so delicious."

"But not as good as it would be if she used real sour cream," Mary insisted. "And once in a while I get so hungry for an old-fashioned meal with old-fashioned ingredients. Like salty things." She hesitated and her voice dropped back to its customary soft tone. "Like a Fat Boy's burger, you know? Except I didn't last week."

"Well, then," Angela said, her disappointment obvious, "you didn't see anything in the garden that night at all, did you?"

"Oh, I didn't say that. I went to bed early, but I couldn't sleep. It was a nice night, so I threw on a robe and slippers and came outside and sat out on a bench for a half hour or so. It was dark," she added apologetically. "Nobody could see me in my comfies. And I was decently covered, you know, so . . ."

"Oh, Mary, for Pete's sake! At our age, who'd care? Now what did you see? If anything," Caledonia said.

"Well, there were a couple people I don't usually see in the garden at night. Like . . . oh, like Nancy Bush coming up the walk. By herself."

"Nancy? But she said she sat in her window and watched the others come and go." Angela was obviously surprised.

"Usually she does. I see her up there," Mary pointed timidly upward at the Bush window, "leaning out with those binoculars up to her eyes, looking us over. But Tuesday night she was in the garden. And let's see—Billy from the drugstore came along, and the woman who runs the frozen-yogurt shop . . . what's her name anyhow? Well, she had a package for Miss Spring." Mary pointed almost directly across the garden from her own place. "I'm not as clever as you two are, but none of this seems very surprising to me. Is it important?"

"I don't know, Mary," Angela said. "But we'll surely find out."

Back outside in the garden, Angela turned toward the main building, but Caledonia stopped her. "Wait a minute. Aren't we going to see the folks who got the Chinese? Mr. and Mrs. Spangler, I mean. And how about Miss Spring?"

"But Nancy Bush seems much more important, to me. She lied to me. I remember distinctly that she said she watched people through her window that night."

"Well, we're out here now, so let's finish the garden apartments." Caledonia checked her watch. "We should just have time to do those interviews before dinner. Talking to Nancy can be our after-dinner treat."

Miss Spring was so thin she seemed almost transparent and she certainly looked unhealthy to Caledonia's eye. The blue veins on the backs of her hands showed clearly through the powdery white skin, and Angela thought she could have wrapped one of her own tiny hands all the way around Miss Spring's upper arm. Miss Spring was reputed to be nearing one hundred, but she refused to discuss her age with anyone but Dr. Carter, and he was sworn to secrecy. But whether she was emaciated from illness or from age, she was not too weak to answer Angela's questions, though her voice came slowly and scratchily.

"Yes," she said after Angela explained the purpose of their visit. "I did have yogurt brought in." Then there was a long pause while Miss Spring apparently thought about what she intended to say next. Angela and Caledonia waited expectantly. At last, Miss Spring spoke. "Peach," she said.

"Oh. Yes. Peach yogurt is good, isn't it?" Angela said. "Miss Spring, what we really want to know is, did you see anything unusual in the garden? Did you see anybody you don't usually see?"

Miss Spring thought a long while. "No," she said at last. "Nothing." Then, after another pause, "Nobody."

They could see her struggle with something she wanted to add, and they waited hopefully. "Peach is better than strawberry," she said at last.

"That lady at the yogurt shop. What's her name?" Angela asked.

There was another long pause. "Easy," Miss Spring said, but neither

Angela nor Caledonia could tell whether Miss Spring meant that was the lady's name or that was a description of her products, and neither cared to ask.

"You didn't discard the carton," Angela said, as they were leaving. "What did you do with it?"

"Still have it," Miss Spring said from her chair; she hadn't bothered to rise to see her visitors out. "Takes me a week to finish a carton of yogurt."

Out in the garden, Angela sighed. "She's bright enough, but she doesn't exactly talk up and volunteer information, does she?"

"I should be half so lively at ninety, let alone at one hundred," Caledonia said.

"From your mouth to God's ear," Angela responded quickly. "Isn't that a good expression? I heard it on television last week and I swore I'd use it the first chance I got. Okay, to the Spangler apartment."

Fremont Spangler and his wife Katerina lived up to their reputation. The only thing they agreed about during the whole interview was that they'd had Chinese food instead of going up to the dining room for Mrs. Schmitt's lamb.

"Nasty stuff, lamb," Fremont said tensely. "Not like beef. Lamb fat is all soft and squiggly under your fork. And it tastes greasy."

"Lamb's perfectly wonderful," Katerina said, her voice equally tense. "If you'd just give it a fair chance. But no, that's your way, isn't it?" Then she added, as an obvious afterthought and perhaps out of deference to their guests, ". . . dear."

"But we didn't see anything different or unusual," he went on, ignoring his wife. Then he had a kind of afterthought of his own and added, ". . . darling," in a sour tone of voice.

"You're wrong," Katerina said brusquely, adding quickly, ". . . sweetheart. I saw a man from Fat Boy's and that youngster from the drugstore. I was looking out the window when he came by and I told you so at the time. But you wouldn't come and look, not you. Mr. Know-It-All here was glued to a TV program. He can't miss his PBS documentaries, can he?"

"Katerina, my pet, there's nothing strange about a couple of delivery boys. Why would I bother to go to the window to stare at them? My beloved here would see something unusual in the sun going down each night," Fremont scoffed.

Katerina's voice was sharp with anger. "If it's not unusual, why are these two here asking about them? Tell me that? Lovey!"

Angela hurried to ask her next question before Katerina could keep the argument going. "Your food was delivered by your usual . . ."

"Absolutely. Charlie Lee," Fremont said loudly. He turned to his wife. "You got something to say about that, angel?"

"No. No argument, honeybunch," his wife snarled. Then she added grimly, "At least, not about that."

A private visit with Mr. and Mrs. Fremont Spangler drew the same reaction from Angela and Caledonia that it drew from everybody: the strong desire to escape. They pleaded another interview to be done and hurried away and across the garden, and through the screen door they could hear Fremont Spangler clearing his throat as though revving up his engine to continue the argument.

Talking to Mrs. Gould didn't take a moment. She acknowledged that she and her husband had ordered fried chicken as a late-night treat. "Two drumsticks and a buttered biscuit for each of us," she said. "I don't suppose it's a healthy snack, but it made a change from popcorn with the movie, didn't it?"

Moving back toward her own place, Caledonia towed Angela along with one hand and held a finger of the other hand to her own lips in a cautionary *Shush*. "Don't say anything till we're inside," she hissed. "Don't let the Spanglers hear you. They might decide to talk to us again." She dived into her living room, closed the door behind them, and quickly produced the sherry decanter and two tiny glasses.

"Tell you what, Angela. If we'd started with the Spangler interview, I wouldn't have been in shape to do one more! Listening to those two makes me terribly, terribly tired! Here . . ." she lifted her own little sherry glass in a toast that Angela echoed . . . "here's to kindness and consideration. Here's to good manners."

"And here," Angela said, "is to us. As opposed to lots and lots of other people that I'd rather not be and rather not see! If you see what I mean."

Caledonia grinned, and they sipped in companionable silence.

12

DINNER DID NOT DELAY them as long as usual that night. "It isn't that I don't like squaw corn," Caledonia said. "But you have to admit it's more like a lunch thing."

"What'd you call that stuff?" Angela asked. She was scurrying toward the elevator with Caledonia puffing along behind her, trying to keep pace.

"Squaw corn. At least that's what my mother always called it when she served it. We loved it as kids. Corn niblets in scrambled eggs, all mixed with crumbled bacon and tiny bits of colored bell pepper . . . Isn't that what you called it? Squaw corn?"

"Never had it before that I can remember. But I agree with you. It wasn't that I didn't like it, it was just that it was more like lunch than dinner."

"Well, I suppose it was an emergency measure," Caledonia said, "after Roderick made off with one of the roasts."

"Roderick? That dog?" Angela stopped dead in her tracks, her indignation obvious. "What on earth was a dog doing in the kitchen?"

"He wasn't in the kitchen. Shorty Swanson had him in tow again. Bringing him back from the vet's to his handler, I suppose."

"And sneaking a chance to visit Chita while he was assigned to an errand, instead of paying attention to poor Howard Gould's murder," Angela said resentfully.

"Well, to be fair, that's how Herman and I got when we were courting. We paid no attention to where we were or to silly things like watching that a dog didn't stray. Anyway, Shorty and Chita apparently met on the steps outside the kitchen's back door. They got to talking and forgot to watch the dog, and Roderick wandered inside. It was just bad luck nobody was in the kitchen at the moment, and Roderick was free to help himself to whatever he thought smelled the best. In a little while, Mrs. Schmitt came in to make dinner and discovered she no longer had enough beef to go around, so she decided to make a substitute dish."

Angela shivered with disgust. "I suppose we're lucky we had squaw corn! At least we weren't served a roast that had been nibbled by a dog before it was cooked. How on earth did you find all this out?"

"I asked," Caledonia said simply. "You jumped up to leave the dining room after you finished eating, but I waited a minute to ask Chita why we got a lunch meal for supper. You're too impatient."

"Well, I want to talk to Nancy Bush before she does something like go play bridge or something, and she'd just left the dining room herself."

Caledonia shrugged. "Okay, then, good point, and let's go." She strode into the elevator and as soon as Angela joined her, thumbed the button for the second floor.

Nancy Bush seemed glad to see them. "How lovely to have callers."

"You weren't going out or watching something special on TV, I hope?" Angela said politely.

"There's nothing good on anyhow till eight, and I start to get sleepy about that time. As for going out, well, I told you, Angela," Nancy's smile looked a little sly, "I love to stay here in the evenings and watch my neighbors come and go in the garden. I prefer to go calling in the afternoons."

"Actually," Angela plunged right into the point of their visit, "that's kind of what we wanted to ask about. One of your neighbors said you were outside in the garden the night Howard Gould was killed."

"Oh, no," Nancy Bush said emphatically. "They're wrong. I hardly ever go out evenings. I like to sit here where I can see everything and everybody. Like a princess on the castle wall, you know? Royalacious."

"Watching the commoners go by?" Caledonia asked with a grin.

"Well, sort of," Nancy admitted. "Anyhow, down in the garden, you see only one or two people at a time. From the window I can see the whole garden. Well, almost as far as the fountain, anyhow. And I like to guess whether people coming down the walk will stop to talk to people coming up the walk, for instance, or will they sail right past . . . That kind of thing. It's much more interesting than being down there myself."

"And you weren't in the garden at all that night?"

"Absolutely not."

"Well, I guess somebody's mistaken," Angela said, and fell silent. In the face of flat denial like that, it was hard to give even a subtle nudge to move the conversation in the direction she wanted. So she tried another tack. "Just tell us again everybody you saw in the garden that night. The night Howard was killed."

"Again? Well, all right, though after all this time I'm not sure I can remember everybody. But I'll try, of course. Let's see . . . I already mentioned the Ridgeways, didn't I? And your friend who was at The Golden Years for a little while, that Mrs. Armstrong. But then you asked about the staff and I got distracticated. I never got to tell you about the other residents who were coming and going."

"Oh!" Angela was dismayed. "I thought you were done. I thought . . ."

"Typical," Caledonia said. "She would jump to conclusions. You just go right ahead and tell us the rest of the list, Nancy."

"Okay . . . Well, let me see . . . There were the Dovers—you know, those people down the hall from me here who are always opening windows and doors, even in the coldest, windiest weather." Her voice was faintly resentful, and Caledonia, remembering the Dovers and their belief in the efficacy of fresh air, grinned broadly.

"They were out for a stroll. Of course with the Dovers, it wasn't a leisurely sort of stroll. More like a leisurely sort of gallop. They were swinging their arms and carrying those weights . . ."

"Weights! Good heavens, why?" Caledonia, whose attitude toward exercise was that it should be kept at a respectful distance, was genuinely puzzled.

"To exercise their arms as well as their legs," Angela explained. "Oh, Cal, everybody knows about exercise weights." Then her face took on a crafty, thoughtful expression. "Of course, an exercise weight could be used as a weapon, couldn't it?"

"Angela!" Caledonia shook her head. "Don't you go imagining things. Mr. Gould was beaned with a hammer."

"How do you know that?" Nancy asked.

"The police," Angela said. "We're . . . well, you might as well know that we're working with them on this case."

"I think somebody told me you were," Nancy said. "I suppose I should be more careful of what I tell you, if these questions are officialous."

She paused and Angela gave her a little verbal nudge. "You were telling us about the people who passed through the garden?"

"Oh. Yes. Well, let's see," Nancy went on. "The Jackson twins were out there, and they were really strolling, not striding like the Dovers. Of course they were walking with that Mrs. Stainsbury, all dressed up so she couldn't have walked very fast. Not with that tight skirt and high heels. So the three of them were going pretty slow. Then a little later there was that Mr. Gorman."

"Gorman? We don't have a Mr. Gorman here."

"Oh, you know who I mean. That man who doesn't walk straight and mutters to himself and sings a lot . . ."

"Grogan?"

"Yes, that's it. Mr. Grogan. He was singing something about a woman being fickle, as he stumbled along. I couldn't catch the words, but the tune was familiable."

" 'La donna è' mobile' in English, I'd guess," Caledonia said. "The man has developed a delusion that he's some sort of operatic tenor. I hope he didn't sit out in the garden and serenade everybody who passed."

"No, he just wobbled on into the first cottage along the walk there . . . the same building the Goulds live in. And I didn't see him again." She thought a moment. "Angela asked me about the delivery boys, too."

"Well," Angela said, "if you could go over that information again . . ."

And Nancy did, faithfully reciting a list that included Billy, a boy wearing a Chicken Shack cap, Charlie Lee, and this time she mentioned the woman from the yogurt shop, although she didn't know that woman's name or exactly what she was bringing. She just knew that some woman carrying a white paper bag had come through the garden at a run.

"Well, did she go toward Miss Spring's place?" Angela asked.

"I really don't know. I can't see the entrance to Miss Spring's place," she said.

"Then how do you know the woman was delivering yogurt?"

"White paper bags aren't that common, are they? I mean, most of them are brown. The drugstore uses little white ones, and I know from bringing home some yogurt myself that the yogurt store does. So I assumed . . . Anyway, that's all the deliveries."

"How about the pizza? And the hamburgers?" Angela asked.

"What pizza? And what hamburgers?" Nancy said sharply. "I'm afraid I don't know anything about those. Especially not hamburgers." Angela and Caledonia waited for Nancy to go on, but she said nothing more—just looked toward the window as though trying to think. At last, apparently conscious of the lengthening silence, she cleared her throat and said, "I wish I could remember something else, but that's about it." She got to her feet. "I'm sorry I'm not more helpful." She edged toward the door, and since both Angela and Caledonia could see that the interview was definitely at an end, they rose and headed for the hall door as well.

"And whoever told you I was out in the garden myself was dead wrong," Nancy said sharply, and she pushed her apartment door abruptly closed behind them.

"Well!" Angela was torn between amusement and indignation. "Well! She got rid of us in a hurry, didn't she?"

"You know," Caledonia said, and her tone was full of speculation, "I bet you anything you like that I know what she's hiding."

"Hiding?" Angela's question was eager. "Nancy's hiding something? Oh, Cal, how clever of you. I didn't catch on that she's hiding anything."

"Well, it's just a guess, mind you," Caledonia said modestly, "but I'd bet she's the one who ate a Fat Boy's burger the night Howard was killed. No big deal, I'm afraid. Nothing to do with the murder, most probably. Still, I'd bet she's the culprit where the burgers are concerned." Angela seemed about to interrupt again so Caledonia hurried her explanation. "Look, everybody's embarrassed to admit they like an old-fashioned fried burger these days, one with all the artery-clogging fat intact. You saw how Mary blushed even talking about it. So what I'm betting is, she got herself a burger and took it down into the garden to eat. Nobody could see her while she sat there in the dark, and she wouldn't leave any evidence of it in her room for the maids to find. Then she just pitched the bag when she finished."

"You always accuse me of jumping to conclusions," Angela said. "But you're doing it too, Cal."

Caledonia shrugged. "Well, here's how I figure it. We were told Nancy was in the garden but she denied it. And we know somebody had a Fat Boy's burger, but though she says she saw everything and everybody coming and going that night, she denies seeing anybody deliver a burger."

"She denies she saw a pizza delivery too," Angela reminded her.

"*Deny* is too strong a word for what she said about the pizza," Caledonia said, as she followed Angela into the elevator and pushed the button for the first floor. "She just said she didn't see a pizza delivery. But she got vehement about the burger. Why? And there's one other clue. Nobody who lives in the garden would just pitch the burger bag out on the grass. I mean, the garden is home. We'd as soon throw trash in the middle of our own living rooms as litter the garden. But Nancy not only lives upstairs, but she's new here. Maybe doesn't feel yet as though this is home. So I think she's one of the most likely people to throw away the . . ."

"Sometimes strangers wander up from the beach and just come into our garden," Angela said. "I suppose they think it's a public park or something. Remember the family that tried to have a picnic on our lawn? Anyhow, my point is, it could have been a complete stranger who threw away the bag. Or it could have blown in from the street, couldn't it?"

"I don't think so. The hedge keeps things from just blowing into our garden, so wind isn't the answer, Angela. And as for it being some stranger . . . well, stop and think. Why is Nancy saying she wasn't even out there that night?" The elevator stopped at the ground floor and the door slid slowly open. "Lieutenant!" The door had opened wide enough to reveal Lieutenant Martinez standing there in earnest conversation with Swanson.

"Ah, Mrs. Wingate. And Mrs. Benbow! The very person I was looking for," Martinez said. "Is there someplace handy we can talk? Perhaps your apartment . . ." He gestured up the four little steps to her doorway.

"I'm temporarily living elsewhere," she told him, "and my regular apartment would be a little chilly, because they're taking out my whole window to replace it, and . . ."

"Well, as it happens, they haven't done that yet, Mrs. Benbow. There was a delay. That's part of what I want to tell you about, and I really don't care to discuss this in the lobby. So let's go to your apartment. Your regular apartment."

Angela shrugged and led the way, turning on the lights and pulling aside the heavy canvas that shielded some of her chairs, so they could find places for all four to sit. Martinez had been quite correct—her old window was still in its place. It looked, in fact, as though absolutely nothing had been done. Angela might have commented, but something else distracted her attention: the care with which Martinez saw that the door was firmly closed suggested real concern about not being overheard, and that intrigued her far more than delayed repairs. "Well?" Her face was bright with interest. "What did you want to tell us?"

As usual, Swanson deferred to his senior partner so that it was Martinez who spoke. "Mrs. Benbow, have you and Mrs. Wingate been out investigating again?"

"Whatever do you mean?" Angela may have intended to play innocent, perhaps even to tell an outright lie, but Caledonia interrupted.

"Angela! Hush. Something's up. Something serious. You come clean with the lieutenant."

"Oh, all right. We've been trying to help, but just a little. We talked to the newspaper delivery boy, Ricky. And we've been up and down the garden today talking to people."

"Before today, I mean," Martinez said. "For instance, how many people saw you going through the trash?"

She shrugged. "Practically everybody who lives in the cottage apartments, I'd say. There were window curtains twitching up and down the line, and we've told people as well."

"What else have you done?"

"Nothing, I swear it."

Martinez looked at Swanson, Swanson looked at Martinez, they both looked at Angela and Caledonia, and Angela and Caledonia stared back. Finally Martinez took the initiative. "I don't think so. There has to be something . . . something that has annoyed someone considerably." He took a deep breath. "Because someone tried to dispose of you last night."

Angela laughed and shook her head. "But that's nonsense. I slept soundly all night long. Nobody even phoned, let alone tried to get into my room, believe me."

"Ah, but how many people knew you had changed apartments?"

"Oh, lots of people. I told everybody about the repairs, and just about everybody I know heard about my having to move."

"No, she's wrong, Lieutenant," Caledonia said soberly. "They phoned from the office at about four yesterday, just before the maids went off duty, to ask her to move. There was so little time left between her move and supper time that we didn't get to the lobby for the usual predinner gossip with our friends. We had a quick sherry at my place and then sailed straight into the dining room. Then right after the meal, we hustled out to get a taxi and go see Ricky—the paperboy. Finally, when we got back here, we went straight to bed. There wasn't even anybody around in the lobby. So I'm positive that neither of us told a soul that Angela wasn't in her own apartment last night."

"I see," Martinez nodded. "That explains it. Well, Mrs. Benbow, someone set off insecticide bombs in here last night, the kind that throw off a heavy fog of poisoned spray, and . . ."

"Oh, that!" Angela smiled. "I'm sorry to disappoint you, but the maids came back here after they helped me move, and they spread out these dust covers and then for good measure set off the insecticide. I wrote a little thank-you note and dropped it at the front desk for Mr. Torgeson. It isn't often he thinks ahead so we can get two jobs done at once."

"The maids didn't set out the insecticide bombs, Mrs. Benbow. Your office tells me the maids are forbidden to handle that stuff. Pete Lopez and his crew are supposed to do any fumigating around here."

"I don't understand. What does it matter whether the maids or the handymen did the fumigating? It was done, and Torgeson had to give the work order. That's why I wrote him the note."

"But it wasn't by Torgeson's order, Mrs. Benbow. Let me explain. This morning Pete came in to check that you were really gone before they started making a mess and to be sure the maids had covered the furniture, and he found those bug bombs on your table." Martinez waved a hand at the little lamp table, where the BOMB 'EM OUT cans had stood. "He knew he didn't set them, so he checked with Torgeson and found there'd been no work order to fumigate. About that time, you dropped off your note thanking Torgeson for being so thoughtful, and it was obvious to Pete, who's a pretty clear thinker, that you hadn't tried to fumigate the place by yourself either. So he came and got me."

"But . . . but . . ." Angela was thoroughly bewildered.

"Mrs. Benbow, they're replacing your window because of rain damage?"

"Yes, and because it won't stay up when I raise it. I have to put a stick in it, or it will slam itself shut. And when the window shuts, the little spring bolts on either side automatically slide into the holes, so that the window locks. Now, that's very annoying, because it really takes three hands to open it again. I've been complaining about that window since I arrived here, but it took a rainstorm . . ."

"Now, let me be sure I have this straight," Martinez said. He walked to the window and pulled at the spring-loaded bolts on each side of the frame, snapping them in and out of their sockets. "You believe these bolts are supposed to stay out when the window's closed? I don't think that can be right. I believe they're supposed to slide automatically into the locked position. That's why they have the spring on them."

"Maybe. But the window's so hard to open again when I have to hold the bolts at the same time I push up on the window, I usually keep it propped open all the time. With a stick holding it up. Unless it's really chilly or unless it's raining or something."

"By any chance did you leave the window propped open yesterday when you moved to your temporary quarters?"

"I suppose so," Angela said.

"Mrs. Benbow!" Swanson sounded shocked. "That's dangerous."

"I've got a screen, and . . ."

"But a screen is no protection. Especially not yours. It just swings out . . ."

"And we've got these security bars on every ground-floor window. Nobody could get even an arm through. Well, maybe a slim arm, I guess . . ."

"They could use one of those grabbits. Those stick things with the pinchers on the top. People use them for fetching things down off a top shelf," Swanson said.

Martinez nodded. "It certainly wouldn't be hard to get one of those cans into a room using one of those. He—or she—pushes in among the shrubbery outside the window so nobody can see him from the street. He sets off a bug bomb, he takes it with the—did you call it a grabbit? He swings your screen aside and shoves the can into the room through the grill. He does that four times and then he takes out the stick that's holding up the window and lets the window slide shut. Very quietly, of course, so he doesn't wake you. Remember, he thinks you're in the other room asleep."

"Why close the window?" Caledonia asked.

"So the insecticide wouldn't air out before Mrs. Benbow suffocated or whatever. We've sent the tins to the medical examiner's office, and he'll analyze the contents and tell us more later about the specific effects. But the point is, those things can really be dangerous. You don't even want to let the solution contact your skin; Pete and his men wear gloves and masks whenever they fumigate. Inhaling the fumes from just one can might do serious damage. Mrs. Benbow would have been breathing in the contents of four cans. Mrs. Benbow, you were supposed to be found dead in your bed, and I suppose your attacker hoped people would think you'd just died in your sleep from the effects of old age."

"But I'm perfectly healthy," Angela protested. "Sound heart, good circulation . . ."

"Unfortunately, you're an exception among people of . . ." he hesitated, ". . . of your age. And haven't you noticed that people—especially younger people—tend to think of all senior citizens as being in fragile health, whether they are or not? But probably the object was just to kill you, and having it passed off as an accident would have been a kind of bonus for the killer."

"If you're trying to frighten us," Caledonia said, "you're doing a good job of it. But you're making it all up from just a few odds and ends, aren't you?"

"Listen, Mrs. Wingate," Martinez said earnestly. "Don't minimize this. If Mrs. Benbow is frightened, perhaps she'll be more cautious than she usually is, maybe she'll be wary of . . . well, for instance, of being alone with someone she doesn't know really well. People are generally, in my opinion, too trusting. Because violence isn't real to most people till they experience it. They think violence is what happens to other people, people they read about in the newspapers. So they put themselves at risk rather than calling for help. I'll give you an example. Suppose there's a knock at your door in the middle of the night. What would you do?"

"Answer the door," Caledonia said promptly, "and find out who it is."

"Suppose it's a stranger. You open the door and there's this fellow you've never seen before. What do you do next?"

"I ask him what he wants. Why is he scaring me to death beating on my door and waking me in the middle of the night?"

"Mrs. Wingate, by that time, you'd be helpless, held at gunpoint while a thief ransacks your home . . . or worse. What you should have done first was to check through a window, or at least keep a chain on the door if you have to open it to find out who's there. And if it's a stranger, phone 911. But no, you figured you'd check it out yourself first, just the way the average householder would."

"Well," Caledonia said, "I'd like to be a good Samaritan, you know. Help my neighbor. Even a stranger. Suppose it was some innocent salesman or something. I'd feel like such an idiot. Imagine calling out the troops for nothing! If the desk phoned 911 for me and got a police car here for a false alarm I'd be so humiliated!"

"Humiliated and alive is better than dignified and dead, Mrs. Wingate. Mrs. Benbow here doesn't believe she could really be in danger. Well, believe it, Mrs. Benbow."

"But, insecticide!" Angela said. "I still think it could have been a genuine effort to debug me."

Martinez shook his head. "If this place had really needed fumigating, a single can of insecticide would have done the job. Two at the most. Someone wanted to make sure you breathed in a lethal dosage."

"Wait a minute," Caledonia said. "I'm with Angela here. First, if a hypothetical villain wanted to bug-bomb her and pass it off as natural death, he'd have taken those cans away once they'd emptied themselves."

"We think he tried to. We found marks—gouges, really—on the outside of your window, Mrs. Benbow, as though somebody tried to pry it up," Swanson spoke up again.

"Trying to get in?" Angela said tentatively.

"We don't think so. This guy had no trouble getting the stuff into your apartment, with your window propped wide open. But then later, when he wanted to get the cans out again to conceal the evidence, he couldn't, because the window had locked itself shut. He tried a pry of some sort, but finally he must have just given up. If he came around and tried your door as well, at least he didn't leave any marks on it. Of course, he'd have had to be really quiet inside the hall. He couldn't exactly use a crowbar on the door. So we can't be sure what all he did to try to get in."

"The point is," Martinez said, "he had to leave the bug bombs inside the room and just hope that if anybody caught onto the real cause of death, we'd all think it was an accident. That you were fumigating the room yourself and overdid it because you're . . . well, again, I'll remind you that a lot of people think the older you are, the less you're able to read and follow directions."

Caledonia snorted her disgust. "At least that part's the truth. The younger they are, the more they try to explain things they're sure we can't figure out for ourselves, and the louder the voice they use to do it. And the slower they talk. Makes me so mad!"

"I'm still not sure you're right, Lieutenant," Angela said. "It sounds like a mighty risky way to try to kill somebody; you couldn't be sure it would work."

"Absolutely right," Martinez said. "But if it didn't work, he could always try again. At the very least Mrs. Benbow might have been made sick enough to be out of action for a long time, sick enough not to be thinking clearly and telling us whatever it is she'd discovered."

"Nothing. I haven't discovered anything important yet. Really. I have no idea what it is I'm supposed to have found out that's so incriminating."

"There must be something," Martinez said. "You think about it again. We believe," he went on, "that you're a very lucky lady. And we want you to stay that way. So first of all, if anybody showed a lot of surprise to see you up and healthy today, we want to know it."

"Nobody. Honestly. Everybody was just . . . you know, just as they always are."

"Even so, for a while, don't leave your windows open while you're gone from your apartment."

"But I'm used to airing it out, and . . ."

"Just don't, for a while. Okay? And keep the door locked, whether you're in the room or not."

"Oh, I always lock the door when I'm home. We have a few residents who . . . you know, they wander. They aren't sure of which door is theirs. So we lock our doors. And of course I lock up whenever I go to meals or go shopping or go out to play bridge or . . ."

"Do you run any short errands?"

"Not many."

"Any?"

She thought a minute. "Well, I take the trash to the plastic barrel in the community-room closet once a day. And dump the newspaper in the recycling bin there."

"And you don't lock the door behind you when you just go a few steps down the hall, do you? But you should. There's plenty of time for someone to slip in while your back is turned and lie in wait for you and attack you when you come back. So lock your door, even if you'll only be gone for a minute."

Angela's little face was sober, but she protested, "But that sounds so . . . so paranoid."

"Paranoid but safe. If I'm scaring you just a little, Mrs. Benbow,

I've succeeded in my mission. I want you to take care of yourself and leave the investigating to us. We'll find out who killed Howard Gould, and we'll find out who tried to attack you. In the meantime, don't go visiting in the middle of the night, lock your doors and windows, and if you have any doubts at all, call someone for help. Clear? Now we'll be on our way. And you . . . you just keep yourself safe."

CHAPTER

13

Despite the lieutenant's dire warnings, Angela spent a quiet night, undisturbed by villains plotting her demise. Breakfast too was uneventful, and though she still looked quickly over her shoulder when she heard someone walking through the gloomy old lobby behind her, no one attempted to assault her, no one attempted to push her down the stairs, and lunch was certainly not poisoned.

"At least," Angela said to Caledonia as they left the dining room, "that German potato salad was absolutely delicious, and I always imagine poison tastes bad, don't you? I mean, I've always wondered how the Borgias could get their victims to drink enough of that poisoned wine to kill them, when it must have tasted really awful. I always imagine the intended victim putting the glass down and saying, 'I guess I won't have any wine, thank you, Lucrezia. It seems to have gone bad or something.'"

"Maybe their guests didn't mention the bad taste because complaining would have been in bad taste. If you see what I mean. Listen, come on down to my place with me to talk awhile. If you try, I bet you can think of what it is that makes you a danger to somebody, and maybe talking it over will help it come clear. Besides, I haven't fed Cesare today. He'll be ravenous."

"Cesare?"

"My parakeet. Didn't I tell you I'd decided to name him Cesare?"

"No. You were calling him 'Tweetie,' the last I heard."

"Well, that isn't very original, and I decided to give him a formal name just last week when I remembered what the color of his feathers reminded me of. The Blue Grotto in Capri. Herman and I went there once when he had a leave out in the Mediterranean. We had a guide named Cesare. The guy talked English, but with a thick accent so we had to strain to understand him, and we were always saying 'What? What did you say?' But that didn't slow him down one little bit. And my little bird reminds me of that guide, you see? Talks all the time without caring if I understand, and his color is that unusual shade of bright, light blue that reminds me of the grotto, not of the guide, of course. The guide wasn't blue. Anyway, I need to give Cesare a little seed and fresh water, so let's go down there to have our talk."

And they had just started out of the lobby when Trinita Stainsbury, entering from the main door, caught sight of them. "Oh, girls . . . Yoo-hoo, girls . . ." she trilled out. "Wait up, girls. I need to talk to you a minute!" And she scuttled over toward them. "Oh, for Pete's sake . . ." Angela was annoyed, but Caledonia gave her a hard nudge. Trinita wasn't a favorite with either one of them, but she was one of the longtime residents of Camden-sur-Mer and therefore, in Caledonia's opinion, a person to be accorded some measure of courtesy.

"Girls, I desperately need a friendly bit of advice," Trinita was saying as she got close to them. Her white hair had a distinctly bluish overtone today, dyed to harmonize with her periwinkle-and-teal slack suit, and the rims of her glasses were a sympathetic shade of soft blue as well. She noticed that Angela and Caledonia were both eyeing her outfit and her hair with fixed gaze, and she patted her hair with a self-conscious simper. "Just got back from the beauty parlor. Do you like this new shade? I thought it made a change."

"You were aqua last week, when you were wearing turquoise," Angela said with a frown. "That was bad enough, but . . ."

"Yes, it was a bit harsh," Trinita said. "This is ever so much softer. I think when we get to be a certain age, we can all use a little help. Like candlelight at our supper. Which reminds me, I've been meaning to ask if we couldn't have candles on the tables at the evening meal. It would cut down on the glare from the overhead lighting."

"Is that what you want to talk to us about?" Angela said impatiently. "Candles at dinnertime?"

"Oh, no. Or rather yes. Sort of. Not the candles, but . . . Girls, can't we go and sit someplace where we can talk privately? Your place, maybe, Angela? Or . . ." She glanced around the lobby, when neither Angela nor Caledonia seemed inclined to invite a move to the privacy of an apartment. "Well, the lobby here would be all right, too. Nobody much is out and around, for the moment. Won't you come over and sit down with me?" She waved toward a couch and chairs far enough from the front desk that nothing could be overheard by the cheerful desk clerk, Clara. "I wouldn't mind Clara's hearing," Trinita went on, as they settled themselves, Caledonia overflowing the couch with Angela and Trinita each in a chair facing her. "It's just that Clara passes things along, and I'd as soon not everybody knew this."

"Okay," Caledonia said, straightening a fold in her caftan. "We're here and we're listening. Now what is this all about?"

"I thought you'd have guessed," Trinita said coyly. "I've been giving you hints . . ." She waited a moment, but neither Angela nor Caledonia spoke. "Go ahead," Trinita coaxed. "Try to guess."

"Oh, for heaven's sake, Trinita!" Angela was exasperated. "Don't be any more of an idiot than you can help! We don't want to guess. Just tell us."

"But try to guess anyway," Trinita persisted. "It's something I've been thinking about doing. Thinking about it for some time, but lately it seemed like a much better idea than ever. My decision to change over to this soft blue shade instead of the bright aqua . . ." she patted her hair again, "and the idea about candlelight at dinner . . ." She waited, but Angela and Caledonia were silent and looking very blank. "Nothing occurs to you? Oh, dear, I'm almost embarrassed to talk about it, but . . ." She took a deep breath and tried again. "Let's put it this way. I've been thinking that I'm not as young as I was."

"Who is?" Caledonia snorted. "What's your point?"

"I've been worried about how I look," Trinita went on. "I mean, I've held up pretty well, you know, over the years. Better than some of the other girls here," she went on. Caledonia looked at Angela and Angela looked back, but neither of them said anything. "But in the last couple of years, I don't know, but I seem to have been sort of . . . well, fading. So what I was thinking was . . . what would you girls think if I was to have a . . ." she hesitated yet again, ". . . a face-lift?"

"A face-lift!" Caledonia's voice was thunderous and Trinita made little shushing motions, glancing nervously over toward the desk, but Clara kept working, not even looking up. "That's what this is all about? A face-lift?"

"But why are you asking us?" Angela said. "Neither of us has ever had a face-lift. What could we tell you?"

"You could tell me what people would think. What they'd say."

"Aren't face-lifts awfully expensive?" Caledonia asked.

"Not cheap," Trinita agreed. "But I can well afford it. No, what I'm worrying about is, would people laugh at me? Would they think I'm extravagant? Would they say I'm vain?"

"Of course," Angela said, obviously not even trying to be tactful. "But why let that bother you? You don't care what people say when you dye your hair a different color every few weeks. You don't care when they comment how much you spend on clothes. Why care what they'd say about a face-lift?"

"I don't know," Trinita said with an apologetic shrug. "Maybe because it's so unusual."

"Not any more," Caledonia said. "There was a time when people didn't admit having their hair dyed, but now they talk about it freely. And the same is true for face-lifts. Actresses are always telling what they had snipped and tucked, nowadays. Phyllis Diller—Roseanne—Bea Arthur—they told everybody."

"Those are all comediennes. Women who want to be taken seriously don't tell. I mean," Trinita went on, "Elizabeth Taylor must have had one, don't you think? But she doesn't tell. And I guess Angela Lansbury did it a couple of years ago."

"Well, they certainly look marvelous," Angela said, "and nobody laughs at them. I don't think people would laugh at the comics who've had it done either, except they invite us to."

"Are you saying I should go ahead and do it?"

"Oh, no," Angela backpedaled hastily. "No, I didn't mean that. It's just . . . Trinita, why are you considering a face-lift? You really look . . ." She hesitated and decided on the judicious lie. "You look just fine as you are, and . . ."

"No, I don't. I used to look as young as anybody here—even younger than most. People were always complimenting me. But lately I've been taking a good look at myself, and I have a few more lines, my jawline is kind of . . . kind of soft, you know what I mean? I have more crow's-feet than ever around my eyes. And my neck looks like five miles of bad road! I have to wear scarves and turtlenecks every day."

"But we're all sagging and bulging and wrinkling," Caledonia said. "Everybody expects it and everybody does it—whether they want to or not. Why do you want to be different?"

"Because . . . Oh, dear, I can't bring myself to say it." Trinita looked modestly downward, hesitated, and then appeared to change the subject completely. "Don't you girls miss your husbands? No, I said that wrong. I should have said, don't you miss having a man in your lives?"

Caledonia laughed out loud. "So that's what it is. You're out to attract a man! Good heavens, Trinita, any self-respecting feminist would have a fit listening to you. Oh, I admit it's lonely without my Herman. Who was it that said the best thing about marriage is having an eye to catch across the room? And even now I find myself hearing a real good story and thinking, I've got to remember the punch line— Herman will appreciate that so much. It's always a wrench to remember that he's gone. Been gone for nearly twenty years now. Two sides to the same coin we were, Herman and me." She sighed. "I never get over missing him." She gathered herself visibly. "But the point is, I have a best friend . . ." she smiled over at Angela, "and I'm not really lonely. The sharing, that's what you miss."

"No." Trinita set her chin stubbornly. "That's not true, because I don't care a scrap what the feminists say, it's not the same. A man's different from a woman—and don't you smirk at me, Caledonia Wingate. What I mean is, having a close good friend who's a man is just plain different from having a woman friend. A man sees things differently, and he knows things women don't know. At least women of my generation."

Angela nodded eagerly. "It's true, Cal. Like cars. And airplanes. And how screen doors work. Funny, practical things like that. Nobody ever told women like me what those words on your insurance policy mean, or when to change oil in the car, or how to fix a leaky kitchen faucet. And then all of a sudden, one day there you are, widowed or divorced, having to figure out a bank statement and how to change a blown fuse and how to use a pliers and a screwdriver . . . Life can be really difficult without a man around."

"And a man's really handy in other ways," Trinita agreed. "Now, Caledonia, don't laugh! I only mean because men are stronger than women."

"Not stronger than I am," Caledonia said.

"Well, stronger than most women. Angela, you know what I'm talking about. Didn't your husband always get the tops off jars for you when they were on so tight you couldn't budge 'em? What do you do now when you can't loosen the top of your new jar of cold cream?"

"Bang it on the floor," Angela said. "That usually works. But I know what you mean," she added wistfully. "It's wonderful to have a close friend, like I have Caledonia here. But there's something missing when you don't have a close friend who's a man, too."

"Well, there you have it. I mean, that's why I want a face-lift. A boyfriend!"

"You've got a boyfriend?"

"Well, perhaps that's overstating it a little, at least for the moment. I mean, I'd certainly like him to be my boyfriend, and I do believe he might be interested. But he doesn't actually say anything. And I've been wondering why? Is it me? Am I . . . you know . . . making the most of my assets? That's why I've got concerned with how old I'm looking." Once more Trinita hesitated, waiting for a reaction.

"Is it someone from here at Camden-sur-Mer?" Caledonia asked. "Of course, it's not really my business, but I can't help but be curious. There aren't many single men here. Of course there's Tom Brighton." She looked at Trinita, but Trinita shook her blued curls. "And there's Doc Colquin, but he's a hundred years older than a goat and not very sociable. And there's Grogan, but you couldn't mean him, could you?"

"And there's Conrad Stone!" Angela snapped her fingers. "Of course. That's him, isn't it, Trinita? Conrad Stone!"

"You've guessed," Trinita said, with what was basically a very silly smile on her face. "Yes, it's Conrad. Connie."

"He's your boyfriend?" Caledonia asked.

"Well, now, that's not quite . . . Please don't go around telling people that," Trinita said, a look of concern replacing the smile. "I just meant it was a possibility. A strong possibility, but . . ."

"But you've only known each other for the time he's been a resident here . . . maybe six weeks," Angela said. "Has he asked you out on a date? Has he said you're . . . you know . . . special to him?"

"Oh, dear. You've misunderstood," Trinita said. "He hasn't said or done anything. Not yet. But the way he kisses my hand . . ."

"Then what's all this about his being your boyfriend?" Caledonia rumbled.

"A possibility! It's just a possibility!" Trinita waved her hands in a damping-down gesture that clearly urged them to slow down. "Anyway," she went on, "that's the reason I'm thinking about the face-lift. Because of Connie. He's so charming and so handsome . . . so different from most of the men here."

"Very different." Caledonia grinned. "He's single! Most of the men here have come in with their wives."

"I know," Trinita said, and her face was dreamy. "And when the single men do come here, they're usually so recently widowed they're still in mourning."

"Is *widowed* the right word to use for men?" Caledonia said. "I thought that only applied to women."

"Besides," Trinita ignored her, "there hasn't been a man, married or single, who's been so charming and so . . . so attentive. At least, not to me."

"Trinita," Angela snapped in obvious annoyance, "you've quite misunderstood Conrad's friendly behavior. He's just as attentive to every woman here!"

"Exactly what I've been saying all along, haven't I?" Caledonia looked straight at Angela. "All that touchy-feely stuff is totally meaningless. He kisses every woman's hand. He even tried to kiss my hand, if you can imagine!"

"Oh, I know he's polite to everybody," Trinita said. "But there's that little special something when he talks to me. I mean, the way he holds my hand when he's standing close by, you know? The way he puts his arm around my shoulders . . . I can tell . . ."

Angela glared. "And just because he holds your hand, you're getting a face lift?"

Trinita still seemed completely oblivious to Angela's irritation. "You're oversimplifying, Angela. But I guess you could say . . . yes. I want him to be my . . ." she hesitated, and to the dismay of her audience, she blushed, ". . . my special someone. And if I were to get a face-lift, I think maybe I'd look more attractive and maybe Conrad . . ."

"Trinita," Caledonia interrupted, "do you really want our advice on this or are you just talking for your own benefit—like thinking out loud?"

"Oh, I definitely want your advice," Trinita said eagerly.

"Then listen to me," Caledonia said. "Don't do it. If he hadn't seen you as you are now—crow's-feet and wattles and all—a face-lift might be effective. But it's a little too late to create the illusion that you're young. By the way, how old is your Conrad?"

"I have no idea," Trinita said blankly. "Around here nobody asks. We guess, of course, but we don't ask. Of course we have a rough idea, since everybody has to be at least sixty to be a resident, and . . ."

"I agree with Caledonia," Angela said quickly. Guessing people's ages was not her favorite subject, since that might lead to someone's trying to guess hers. "I say, don't get the face-lift. Too obvious."

"But it's not as though I'm trying to look sixteen again," Trinita protested. "I was thinking of something a little more subtle. Maybe to take ten years off, that's what I was thinking. Pick things up a bit." She put her hand on top of her cheekbones and pulled lightly up and out, making the deep smile lines by her mouth flatten out. "See? Just to look like I was sixty again. It would be too much to try to look like a young . . ."

"No-no-no, that isn't what Angela meant," Caledonia said. "She meant you don't want to let a man know you're chasing him. You need to sneak up on him, and you can't sneak up if you do things like get a face-lift. He's bound to know you've done that, isn't he?"

Trinita sighed. "Oh, dear . . . Well, maybe you're right. But I do look better with a little antigravity applied in the right places," and she pulled lightly upward on her cheeks again. Then she sighed. "But maybe you're right. Maybe I should go and think about it a little while longer, after all." She sighed again and walked slowly away in the general direction of her own apartment, presumably to spend further time in contemplating the pros and cons of a rhytidectomy.

Five minutes later, down in Caledonia's apartment, Angela felt free to express her annoyance more openly. "The cheek of the woman!"

"Bad pun," Caledonia said absently. She was working at the bird-cage, cleaning out the residue on the sides of the water dish. The bird watched her closely, not bothering to move very far down his perch away from her busy hands. "There. The water will be reasonably clear for a while. And now, Cesare, you be a good boy and move away while I reach in for the seed tray." She unlatched the cage door, but the bird stayed put, close by. "Move, you nasty little pile of feathers," she said, but her voice was rich with affection. "Move, or I'll call in one of our resident cats to give you a lesson on bird deportment . . . There, that's better."

"You're not listening to me, Cal," Angela protested. "Don't you think Trinita is showing even more chutzpah than usual—I mean, to actually make a play for Conrad Stone?"

"Gosh, isn't that word chutzpah a gorgeous word? Just right for what it means. Bet you learned it off television just like I did!"

"Cal! Get back to the point!"

"All right, I will. You're annoyed at Trinita because she's moved in on what you think is your territory. You think you saw Conrad first, don't you? But if anybody has dibs on the guy it's Tootsie Armstrong. She's the one who introduced both of us to him. Or him to us."

"Oh, I don't think Tootsie's the slightest bit interested in him," Angela said. "But there might be others, mightn't there? And you'd think Trinita would at least concern herself with the other people around here. People who might . . . well, you know . . . who might have an interest in this particular man."

"Like you, I suppose? The truth is, I don't suppose Trinita really notices many people besides herself," Caledonia said comfortably, tapping the tray to make the last of the used birdseed fall into the sink.

"Cal, what I'm really wondering is whether or not I should . . . I mean, it would be a friendly thing to do. Maybe I should talk to Conrad about this," Angela mused. "Maybe warn him that his little courtesies are being misunderstood. I could drop in this evening after supper. Just for a little chat, you know."

"Just to keep him aware that you're in the running, you mean. Just to keep him from getting too taken up with Trinita before you have the chance to make your own pitch. Honestly, you're incorrigible." Caledonia brought the freshly refilled seed tray back to the birdcage. "If what you want is company, get yourself a pet. Look at me. I've got a male in my life, Cesare here—and he's all I need. As for my wanting a close friend who's always there when I need 'em, you'll do just fine." She opened the cage door and slid the tray into place. "There you go, kiddo, and *bon appétit*."

"Same to your cat," the bird intoned in his creaky little voice. "Aaawk . . . same to your cat."

Caledonia closed the cage door and watched as the little blue bird dipped his tiny bill into the tray and shook his head violently, scattering seed till he apparently found one exactly to his liking. "Messy eater, isn't he? Oh, well . . . Now, we were going to try to puzzle over what you know that would make you a candidate for murder yourself."

And they did, for the remainder of the afternoon. They talked about secret hamburgers, potential face-lifting, even the possibility of staff grown resentful because of the extra work of helping Angela change rooms, but nothing occurred to either of them that might have been a motive strong enough to lead one to kill. Afternoon blended easily into the sherry hour, and then into dinnertime. Mrs. Schmitt had prepared a tasty beef ragout—"Presumably made," Caledonia speculated, "from the beef Roderick left behind after his raid into the kitchen, but it's delicious all the same"—but Angela's mind was not on her supper. During most of the meal, she craned her neck left and right, surveying the dining room and the diners. Finally, just as dessert was served she spotted Conrad Stone entering the main door with Trinita Stainsbury on his arm. He bowed as he dropped her off at the table that had been hers for at least ten years. Then he made his own way between the diners, smiling at this one, nodding to that one, heading for his own table, which he shared with Doc Colquin, the retired dentist. Colquin was very deaf, so when Stone offered his apologies for arriving so late at the meal, he enunciated carefully and raised his voice enough that his words were clearly audible to Angela and Caledonia, four tables away.

"Hope you didn't miss me, old boy. Just out for a little stroll with a lady friend . . ." and he turned to the waitress who had appeared at his side. He lowered his voice to speak to her, but once Angela and Caledonia had focused on him and his conversation, they could make out the words, "Don't bother if there isn't any of the main dish left. Stew doesn't interest me much. Just a salad and the dessert. And a couple of rolls. That'll hold me."

"Lady friend indeed," Angela sniffed, but said nothing else. But that evening, back in her room, she simmered. "Lady friend!" she muttered crossly to herself again. "I saw him first," she said aloud to the bathroom mirror as she applied dental floss and a toothbrush to the teeth which, as she proudly told everyone who would listen, were still her own. "Poaching, that's what it is. Poaching."

Muttering didn't seem to relieve the pressure of her annoyance and neither did the exercise involved in scrubbing her teeth. She came back into the tiny space of her substitute apartment and began to pace. But it was only eight steps between the foot of the bed and the end of the room, ten steps across from the TV set to the easy chair and the dresser. "This is silly," she said aloud to herself after the third or fourth circuit of the room. "I'm trying to work off my temper and not only is it not very effective, but I'm probably getting furious over absolutely nothing. What if he did call her his 'lady friend'? What if she does think he's sweet on her? She could be mistaken and he could be just being polite. The thing to do," she lectured herself, "the thing to do is go down there and talk to him. There's no point in getting angry here all by myself. Now let's see . . . how can I do this? What excuse can I use?"

She pinched her lower lip tightly. Somewhere she'd heard that helped one to concentrate. Or was that the way you kept from sneezing? No, that was pushing the upper lip against your teeth. Or maybe that was the one that helped you concentrate . . . she couldn't remember which was which. So for a while she alternated pushing against the upper lip and pinching the lower, and whether one of those acupressure points did something useful or whether the idea came out of her subconscious without help, an idea finally did occur to her.

"The way to a man's heart is through his stomach!" she exclaimed jubilantly. "Of course! Mother always used to say that. He's going to be ravenous because he didn't have supper," she added gleefully. "And I know he likes pizza . . ." She went over to the phone and grabbed the local phone book, turning quickly to the yellow pages under RESTAURANTS and then to the subheading PIZZA.

The first listing—Pizza California Style—answered readily enough but denied making deliveries. "Can't compete with them fellers who run 'em out so fast," the man told her. "So we concentrate on makin' 'em better. You come on in and we'll do a hand-tossed crust for you with your choice of toppings. We do 'em all," he went on proudly, "including a few I bet you never tried. You ever had liver-and-onion pizza? Or pizza escargot? How about a guacamole and salsa pizza? Or a Texas chile pizza? We got spinach and escarole pizza and we got a Philly steak pizza, and . . ."

"Thank you, and I'm sure they're wonderful," Angela told him, "but I need a delivery. Another time perhaps."

But her second phone call to Pizza Carry-OK—"Our motto, we make your stomach sing!"—resulted in a promise to deliver within a half hour. "I'm not sure," she told the man who asked her what kind of toppings she wanted. "What's most popular?"

"Pepperoni and mushrooms. Maybe extra cheese. Or you could get the deluxe with onion and chopped peppers and sausages and . . ."

"All right. All of that."

"Okay. About half an hour. "It'll be $19.23, counting tax and the toppings and all. And have the right money ready, lady. We don't let our drivers carry extra cash at night. Nobody does these days. Too many rotten guys out there willing to rob a delivery man just for spare change."

It was closer to a full hour than to a half hour when there was a knock on Angela's door and a pizza delivery boy stood there with a familiar, flat box in one hand, the other hand held out for ". . . that'll be $19.23, ma'am. Thank you, and enjoy." He hesitated, but there seemed to be no tip forthcoming, so at last he just shrugged and left, whistling down the hall.

Angela swung the door closed behind him and checked on the pizza. It looked to be as advertised, with a jumble of meat and vegetables scattered over its top, but the bits of chopped this-and-that lay in wet puddles of melted grease from the cheese, which ran in rivers down the edges of crust while the remaining white strings of cheese glued the slices to the box. "I hope he likes this," Angela muttered. "It doesn't look too appetizing to me. But he likes pizza," she reminded herself, "and he certainly didn't have much to eat for supper . . ." She paused long enough to give her white hair a smooth-and-pat in the bathroom mirror; then she wrapped the pizza box in a layer of newspaper, partly because the box was still hot to the touch and partly so she could have the enjoyment of watching Conrad's pleased surprise as he unwrapped it, and she headed for the garden walk.

It was already past nine and most of the residents were in their own apartments for the evening, watching television or reading or getting ready for bed. Angela glanced upward at the second-story windows on her left, but she didn't see Nancy Bush at her hobby of people-watching. In fact, the lights in Nancy's apartment seemed to be out. "Well, maybe she went to bed early tonight," Angela told herself. "If not, if she is sitting there in the dark looking at me, she'll have something to say about this tomorrow, I suppose. And I hope Cal doesn't look out here either. She'd tease me so . . ." but Caledonia did not appear. All the same, Angela's steps slowed the farther down the garden she got. An observing Nancy or a mocking Caledonia or not, Angela was getting cold feet.

But she kept going, even though she walked slower and slower till she got to the fountain. Then she caught sight of the black cat Puddin', sitting on the raised edge around the little pool, silhouetted in the pale moonlight, industriously grooming himself. She moved even more slowly as she approached. He raised his head and considered her, then went back to licking his sleek fur. "Hello, there, chubby little boy," she said soothingly, stretching out a hand. "Let's be friends." For a wonder, Puddin' seemed perfectly willing and rose to come close to her and rub his back against her outstretched hand. "Now there's a good kitty," she said, and stroked him firmly, neck to tail, the way cats like best to be stroked. "What a good boy he is," she went on as Puddin' stretched himself upward into her touch and made appreciative noises. "I wouldn't have seen you at all if you hadn't been sitting upright. It certainly is dim out here. The little walk lights just throw their light downward, and Torgeson wouldn't think of putting overhead lights out here, of course. Oh, here . . . let me use both hands . . ."

She started to put the pizza box down on the edge of the fountain and thought better of it. If Puddin' should step on it and overbalance the box, it could easily tip into the water. She bent and put the box flat on the ground, and seated herself beside the cat, noticing that she and the pizza box were almost completely invisible in the heavy shadow of the fountain's structure. "Well, now, Puddin', let me use one hand on your chin and the other on your back, and we'll have a real cat-stroking here. I suppose I'm just stalling," she said. Puddin' purred harder. "I'm shy about going to see your master because it's pretty bold to call on a bachelor alone. At least, my mother would have had a fit if she knew. But you don't care, do you?"

Puddin' lay down and rolled onto his back, his four paws trustingly raised into the air. For a moment Angela stroked his pudgy tummy, and then she felt his muscles tense under her hand and he craned his neck upward, his ears cocked into attentiveness. In a single motion, he rolled over, belly side down, his tail twitching nervously, his feet gathered beneath his crouched form, his eyes focused on the darkened area behind Angela, the area where Conrad Stone's back door stood.

"What is it, kitty?" Angela said. She peered off in the same general direction where Puddin' was staring with such concentration and saw Stone's back door swing open. She recognized Stone's handsome head of white hair as he stepped out from the lighted kitchen, and saw with dismay that he was carrying a flat, square box which he popped into the big trash can before going directly back and closing his door behind him.

"Oh, dear, Puddin'!" she said. "I'm already too late. He's gone and ordered himself a pizza and he won't need anything more to eat. And it was such a good idea, too. Well, I suppose I might as well throw this one away. I certainly don't want it myself." She sighed and got to her feet, and Puddin' seemed to mimic her, rising with a sigh. "Poor Puddin'," she said, giving his chin another little stroke. "Poor me . . ."

And she picked up her pizza box, and walked over to the same trash bin Stone had just closed, picked up the lid and threw her box in, newspaper wrapping still intact around the useless gift. She had already set the lid back down when she had a second thought. "I wonder . . . Pizza would still be a good excuse for a visit. Not tonight, of course, after he's just had one. But I ought to check and find out exactly what it is that he likes on his pizzas." It was her second inspiration of the evening, and she acted on it quickly, opening the trash bin again and pulling out Stone's discarded pizza box. But squint as she might, it was far too dark in the garden for her to read the signs.

"Signs?" Caledonia asked. Angela had come straight up the walk to knock on her friend's door, carrying Stone's pizza carton in to the coffee table while she explained her evening's mission. "Signs?" Caledonia asked. "What signs?"

"You know, signs of what Conrad might order for himself. Sausage crumbs or a stray shred of mushroom or onion or whatever . . ."

"And you brought it in here for me to see? Good night, girl, I don't care what the man likes for a snack. If I wanted to talk to him, I'd just go talk to him. I wouldn't need fast food for an excuse."

"But I do. You know how I feel about calling on him by myself without a good excuse. Anyway, I knew there'd be enough light in here for me to see clearly. Honestly, the amount of light Torgeson has out in the garden these days is hardly enough to keep from tripping over your own shoelaces. So I thought of your place. I knew you'd still be awake—you stay up so late."

"And you thought I'd be as interested as you are in what trimmings Stone wants on his pizza."

"Well, maybe not exactly, but . . ."

"Oh, all right. I suppose I am mildly curious. So let's open the box and find out." And Caledonia walked over to the box and flipped its top up. "Well. This isn't very helpful, is it?"

"I don't see anything at all," Angela said. "The box is empty."

"Exactly," Caledonia said. "No crumbs, no shreds." She lifted the box to her nose. "Not even any smells! So you still don't know what Stone wants in the way of toppings, right?"

"I guess that's right." Angela took the box and examined it more closely. Her little face was creased into lines of disappointment. "Well, at least," she said, pointing to the big red logo on the box top, "we know he orders from the Pizza Palace—for all the good that does us."

CHAPTER

14

ANGELA'S KEEN DISAPPOINTMENT ONLY served to amuse Caledonia, and the more Caledonia chuckled, the harder Angela frowned. "You threw away a perfectly good pizza," Caledonia chortled, "because you assumed your Conrad already had a snack, and here it was just an empty box. You trashed twenty bucks for nothing!"

"I guess I could go back and get my pizza out of the bin," Angela said sulkily. "I mean, I'm sure it's still there. And it'd be clean. I mean, it's in the box, and the box is wrapped in newspaper, and . . ."

"Oh, don't be so silly. It's got cold by now and the cheese will be all gluey. Just forget it. It was a rotten idea anyway. If you want to talk to him, just go and do it. No subterfuge, no coy excuses, and no snacks."

"Right now, you mean?"

"Right now I *don't* mean! Wait till tomorrow, if you still feel by then that you must. It looks too eager to pop in on him in the middle of the night. Well, at least it's the middle of the night for people our age. Remember what we told Trinita—you want to sneak up on a man, not look overanxious. Wait till there's some excuse like . . . well, like tomorrow afternoon's program. I bet you he'll be there just like everybody will . . ."

"What makes you so sure? He skips a lot of our entertainment programs. The Tall Ten came in to play their harmonicas the other day, and he wasn't there. And I don't remember seeing him at the community sing last week. Nor at that ten-year-old who did show tunes . . ."

"Well, maybe he's got a tin ear for music. He came to the lecture on astronomy, didn't he? And when the ladies from the local book club had readings from a Jackie Collins novel. And when the man from the camera shop demonstrated how to use a camcorder . . ."

"Maybe he's just interested in more serious stuff."

"You take Jackie Collins seriously?"

"You know what I mean. Lectures and things like that. What is tomorrow's program?"

"I've got the listing of this month's programs somewhere," Caledonia said, groaning as she hoisted herself to her feet once more to go and rummage through her little desk. "Oh, sure, here it is. Let's see, what's tomorrow? The twentieth? Okay, here it is . . . Ah-hah! One of the faculty from Camden Junior College is talking about sexual role reversal in classical Greek drama. Whatever that may mean."

"Oh, I'm sure you remember plays like *Lysistrata* from your college lit. classes. You know, that's the play where the women took charge because they wanted to stop the war and . . ."

"Never ask an English major a question about literature," Caledonia sighed. "You don't get an answer, you get a lecture! My point is, our fellow residents may not like to admit it, but they'll all come to tomorrow's program. Put the word *SEX* into the title and some will come to tut-tut-tut, some will come hoping for a thrill, but they'll attend. All the same, a critical analysis of Greek dramas? Listen, the lobby'll be Snore City before the first twenty minutes are up. All the same, I'm betting that your little buddy Connie will be there tomorrow afternoon. You want to talk to him? Just slip into a seat next to him in the audience. It's a lot more natural way to start a conversation than trotting down to his apartment in the middle of the night carrying a pizza! Take my word for it."

"Well . . ." Angela was clearly reluctant to abandon what she had thought was a clever plan, but finally she agreed. "All right. I'll try to think of some excuse to start talking and . . ."

"Never mind the excuse. Just start talking. Talk about the weather. Talk about the other people in the room. Don't worry, it'll come to you. And hey! Come back here! You take this stupid, empty box along with you, okay?"

After Angela skittered off to her own room, Caledonia settled back for her usual evening of television viewing. She started with a remote-control tour of her favorite stations, the ones showing old movies, but nothing attracted her. She had seen all of them except a worse-than-B feature starring Richard Arlen and Rochelle Hudson, not exactly actors of renown. For a while she stayed on the rerun of a tennis match recorded earlier in the day in Calcutta, but it made her yawn. "Too many baseliners playing these days. It may be effective, but it's dull to watch. Where are John McEnroe and Martina Navratilova when you need them?" she muttered, and stabbed at the remote control again. At last she settled on a cooking show, Graham Kerr galloping through his kitchen with a wooden spoon and a quip. But as she watched him brown some onions and deglaze the pan with a little white wine, she became aware that her stomach was rumbling.

"I could stand a late-night snack myself, I guess," she said to Cesare. The little bird didn't answer, but eyed her wisely and nibbled at his seed dish. "All very well for you, kiddo. You've got a steady supply of goodies. But I know what's out in my kitchen cabinet—a bottle of mineral water and a box of soda crackers. If I'd realized Angela was ordering pizza for her boyfriend, I'd have asked her to order one for me. What a waste for her to throw that whole thing away!" Cesare swung gently to and fro on his perch and said nothing.

Caledonia returned to her TV watching, but she fidgeted in her chair. After a few minutes, she began muttering to Cesare again. "It's just sitting down there in its original box. It'll be cold, but it'll be clean and I could heat it up in the microwave." Cesare eyed her and kept swinging. "It isn't as though it's really become garbage just because it's been set down with the garbage," Caledonia went on. "I mean, it wouldn't hurt to check it out, now would it?"

After a moment's thought, Caledonia slid her feet back into the scuffs she had kicked off earlier, pushed herself up out of her chair and out her front door, and set off down the garden path, shuffling silently except for the slap-slap-slap of her slippers against the concrete. There was no trick at all to finding the right trash bin and to lifting out the pizza, still resting safe and dry in its wrappings. There was no trick at all to whisking it back to her apartment and to setting the box gently on the kitchen counter. And there was definitely no trick at all to heating up a slice and wolfing it down. "Delicious!" she sighed, slipping a second slice into the microwave. "And don't you glare at me," she warned Cesare, who swung silently back and forth, staring at her. "You eat seed that's fallen out of the dish onto the floor of your cage, and that can't be nearly as clean as this pizza is. All the same," she cautioned the bird, "don't you tell anybody or I'll wring your little feathered neck. Nobody but a fat lady could understand; other people would be horrified. But to paraphrase the TV ad, a pizza is a terrible thing to waste!"

The next day, in midafternoon, Angela came down the main staircase into the lobby to look for Conrad among the audience seated in ragged rows facing the lobby's far end where the grand piano was located. The staff had done their best to create good sightlines and a neat arrangement, putting folding chairs at regular intervals and in slightly curved rows. But the residents had immediately destroyed all symmetry and order by dragging the more uncomfortable of the folding chairs away and replacing them with better padded seating from around the lobby. Thus it wasn't easy to sight down a row and see who was seated where, since some rows terminated in a cluster of chairs around a love seat and other rows broke in half around a pair of deeply upholstered easy chairs. Angela stood behind the last row, shifting from one foot to another and peering anxiously over the audience till Caledonia, who had been sitting at one end of the back row, rose to stand beside her.

"He's over there," Caledonia whispered, pointing down the room toward a tapestry-covered wing chair in the second row from the front. "You can't see him unless you move forward a little because he's sitting back in the chair. But you can certainly see Trinita buzzing around him. And the Jackson twins. And . . . yes, there's Mary Moffet. She's too shy to push herself forward, but she's there . . . in the little folding chair on the other side of Stone's chair. And . . . Angela, what have you got that for?" Caledonia pointed at the box under Angela's arm, the empty pizza box from last night's little fast-food mystery.

"I thought," Angela whispered back, "that I'd use it as a way to start our conversation. There's no point in my wasting my gesture entirely. I mean, I didn't actually feed him last night, but he might appreciate that I thought of it. And I could ask him what he likes on his own pizza, and I could explain . . ."

"How come you didn't arrive earlier? The program's almost over."

"Well, I didn't care whether I heard the lecture or not," Angela admitted sheepishly.

"You can say that again! What a monumental bore! I've been trying to decide if anyone would notice if I just walked out, back to my own place, and . . . Hey!"

A buzz of sound had begun at the front of the room and spread, whispers and small noises registering pleasure. The lecturer, a slim woman in a tailored suit, seemed confused. No audience had ever before reacted with such delight to a comparison of characters in *The Trojan Women* with *Medea*. But she gamely kept going, talking about strophe and antistrophe, the masculinity-femininity scale, and the subtleties of symbolism, even though her audience was looking past her and to her right at two figures that had just entered the shadowy lobby from the side door to the street and now stood quietly near the grand piano, just waiting.

"Hey, look! It's Roderick!" Caledonia grinned. "I don't recognize his friend, but isn't that dog a beauty!" The golden retriever stood patiently, lightly restrained by a short leather leash held in the hand of a square, dark-featured man in gray slacks and a lightweight blue coach's jacket.

"And thus, in conclusion," the slim woman at the lectern said, "we can all agree that the ancient Greeks anticipated the tenets of the feminist movement by more than two thousand years. I thank you."

There was a smattering of halfhearted applause from the dutiful audience. "Any questions?" the woman said hopefully. A hand shot up from someone in the front row. "Yes, sir? You wanted to know . . ."

"Yeah. What's that dog doin' here?" It was Grogan, slightly muzzy from his day's work, which had consisted of emptying bottles that needed to be cleaned out before being discarded. A less hardy soul might simply have poured down the drain the last drops of gin, the half-teaspoon of Scotch. Grogan was made of sturdier—and more absorbent—stuff. Whatever was left in each bottle went straight into Grogan before the bottle went to the trash bin, and there had been a lot of bottles that cried out that day to be tidied up. "What's with the dog?" he insisted again.

The man attached to Roderick stepped forward and spoke quietly to the woman at the lectern for a moment, and she moved aside, tucking her lecture notes into her briefcase. "There's a little surprise addition to your program for the day," she said. "Mr. Flynn here has brought you a friend. I thank you for being such a pleasant and attentive audience to my little presentation . . ." a muffled snore came from the far side of the audience, where Mr. Dover had nodded off, ". . . and I'll turn the program over to Mr. Flynn."

"I've been told," the dark man said, "that Roderick turned thief and burgled your kitchen the other day, and by way of apology I thought I'd bring him back to visit . . ." Roderick's plume of a tail waved lazily in greeting, ". . . and we'd give you a little demonstration of his skill. He's a full-fledged member of our county police force, but unlike our other K-9 policemen, he's not trained for attack. There's not a ferocious bone in Roderick's body. For instance, if a K-9 Corps dog jumps on you and takes your arm in his teeth, stand absolutely still and do whatever his handler tells you if you value the use of your arm. If Roderick jumps on you, he wants you to ruffle his ears. He's an old softy, this boy . . ." and he slipped Roderick's leash off the collar ring. Roderick just stood there, making a little breeze with his tail and showing his teeth in that wide, doggy smile.

"Well, what good is he then?" Grogan spoke up from his front-row seat. "What does he do besides look handsome?"

"Roderick's a drug dog," Flynn said. "He's trained to sniff out drugs of all kinds."

"I saw that on television," Mrs. Dover spoke up. "The dog was at a border station and there was this pile of luggage, and you should have seen him pawing away to get to the suitcase with the whatever-it-was hidden in it that was on the bottom of the pile."

Flynn smiled. "That's not Roderick's technique," he said. "Want a demonstration?"

And with a delighted group of seniors watching and applauding, Roderick located a tiny plastic packet of marijuana that Flynn hid first in the piano bench, then under a wrought-iron lamp, and finally in Tom Brighton's shirt pocket. And each time Roderick went about his labors quietly and cheerfully as soon as he was given his working command, "Find it, boy. Go on, find it . . ." Smiling his toothy, doggy smile and wagging his tail with enthusiasm, Roderick quartered back and forth across the room and at last zeroed in on the correct place, sitting down abruptly and smiling when he at last located his quarry. Then he returned to Flynn for his rewards, his tail going happily. Each time, Flynn praised him for his success—"Good boy, Roderick. Good boy!"—and then extended a hank of graying terry cloth, knotted hard at each end, and he and Roderick indulged in a brief but enthusiastic tussle, each pulling hard, Flynn hauling Roderick this way and that as the dog gripped the cloth with bared teeth.

"Don't you give him a treat?" Tom Brighton asked. "I thought trainers used dog yummies or milk bones or . . ."

"Oh, he'd rather play tug-of-war with me than have any snack you can name," Flynn said. "This is part of the reward he looks for . . Okay, boy, that's enough. Good job." And Flynn once more tucked away his frayed piece of toweling.

"I don't believe he smelled that stuff inside the plastic," Grogan groused sourly. "He saw you put the envelope of marijuana in those places. He knew exactly where to look."

"Well, let's try it another way then, sir," Flynn said patiently. "Someone take the dog's leash . . ." and he reattached the leather lead to Roderick's collar, "and take him outside. We'll have someone else in the audience take the package and just sit on it. Then we'll bring Roderick back in, and he'll find it, even when the scent is muffled by someone's person on one side and a chair on the other."

"I'll do it," Tom Brighton volunteered eagerly. "He looks just like my Zippy. That's a dog I had once, years ago. Come on, boy . . ." and he led Roderick outside through the side door while Flynn held up his tiny plastic demonstration envelope and called out, "All right, who wants to play drug smuggler this time? How about you, little lady?" And he moved through a gap between first-row chairs, straight to little Mary Moffet.

"Me? Oh, dear, I don't know . . ." Mary's blush covered her face and neck completely. "What do I have to do?"

"Nothing. Just take the little envelope, put it on your chair, and sit back down."

"Oh. Oh, dear . . ." Mary did as she was told.

"That's no good," Mr. Dover called out from midway back in the audience. "The dog isn't blind, you know. Any moron could see that she's turned beet red."

"Dogs are color-blind, sir," Flynn said patiently. "She could be painted bright green, and Roderick wouldn't notice. His best sense is his sense of smell and that's what he's using." He went over to the side door and stuck his head out. "You can bring him back now, sir," he said, and Brighton came back into the lobby with the cheerful Roderick at his side, reluctantly turned the dog back to Flynn, and took his place again next to Grogan.

Once more Flynn slipped the leash off the collar ring and bent down to say in the same, upbeat tone of voice as before, "Find it, boy. Go find it. Can you find it?" Roderick started his circling of the room, quartering back and forth through the open area first, his tail still waving his pleasure in his task.

"Does he really enjoy his work?" Mrs. Dover asked. "He seems so happy."

"I really believe he does, ma'am," Flynn said. "Not just the tug-of-war at the end, but the hunting out of the drugs, as well." As Flynn talked, Roderick had turned his attention to the audience at the side of the room where Mary Moffet sat. Back and forth his head went for just a moment, and then he crowded between Mr. Brighton and Mr.

Grogan, pushing toward the second row of chairs, his head pointed squarely at Mary. With a waggle of his rump to make a little room in the crowded space, he sat down and looked back toward his handler, then back directly at Mary.

The audience laughed and applauded while Flynn gave his praise, "Good boy. You see?" Flynn turned to the audience and his satisfaction was obvious. "That's enough, Roderick, good boy!" He hesitated a beat and then said more briskly, "Roderick, come!" The dog stood up again, backed out, and returned to Flynn, who gave the dog's ears an enthusiastic ruffle, let the dog fight him over the towel for a few moments, and then patted his beautiful golden retriever once more and put the knotted toweling away. "And now," Flynn went on, "Roderick is off duty again. And I think that's the end of our little demonstration. Once more, we apologize for Roderick's bad manners and we hope he's forgiven."

There was enthusiastic applause and then the audience began to struggle to their feet and mill about, leaving the lobby. A number fumbled for canes and walkers, holding up everyone behind them, but patience is a virtue much cultivated in a retirement home, and there was no complaint. Several came forward to pet the dog, who seemed delighted with the attention. "It's all right," Flynn assured them. "When he's not on duty, he's just a love sponge, our Roderick. Feel free . . ."

"Are you sure it's all right if I pet him?" Mrs. Dover asked. "I have all my pills and prescriptions with me in my purse. He isn't going to jump all over me and get his paws on my silk dress, is he?"

Flynn smiled. "He probably won't hunt unless I give him the command, and ordinary medicines like aspirin and antibiotics aren't among the things we trained him to look for. Besides, Roderick's signal that he's found drugs isn't to paw wildly, the way some dogs do. That's a matter of who trained the dog and how. Roderick here was trained in Belgium, with English commands of course, as you saw, especially for work in airports and bus depots and like that. Where there are going to be a lot of people around, most of whom are completely innocent, we prefer it if the dog signals quietly the way Roderick does. By just sitting down when he's found drugs."

"Interesting . . ."

"Fascinating demonstration."

"What a beautiful dog . . ."

"Oh, isn't hims just the tweetest . . ."

The people milled around Flynn and the golden retriever, then after a few minutes began to move slowly away. Only the knot of people (all women) around Conrad Stone did not seem to move at all. Or rather, the group jiggled and pulsated and twittered and fluttered—but it made no progress toward one of the exits. "Reminds me of a bunch of sparrows when someone's thrown out a handful of bread crumbs," Caledonia said. "Look at 'em. Angela, better give up for today. You're never going to be able to get near your Conrad, let alone being able to have a few minutes of quiet conversation."

"But you're the one who said this would be a perfect time to . . ."

"I meant perfect compared to the middle of the night. I reckoned without Trinita on his arm there. And with the Jackson twins guarding his other flank, the man is as secure as a Mafia don among his bodyguards. Even Tootsie Armstrong and Mary Moffet can't get close. See? They're part of the group, but sort of attached to the outer edge. Angela, don't you make a spectacle of yourself by joining the crowd. There's plenty of time to talk to him later."

"But I'd like to remind him I'm . . . you know, interested. I don't want Trinita to have the inside track. Or Sadie, or Janice, or any of those others . . ." She waved a tiny hand toward Stone's harem.

Caledonia took Angela's little elbow and propelled her firmly toward the garden door. "Come on, girl. Down to my place, away from the competition for the moment. It's a hot day and before I came here to the program, I got Mrs. Schmitt to give me a pitcher of lemonade. We can pull two of the redwood chairs from the lawn over onto my front stoop so that we're in the shade, sip lemonade, and you can cool off awhile. Trust me . . ."

It wasn't really one of those days—happily rare—when the Southern California winds blow straight out from the desert toward the ocean, bringing with them the unbearable heat of a Santa Ana, but it was unseasonably warm all the same. Angela slid into the redwood chair and sipped her cold lemonade with satisfaction. "Maybe you're right," she said with a hint of contentment in her voice. "Today's not the time for me to get into a cozy conversation with . . . I mean, I'm not at my best when I'm worried about whether there are wet stains under my arms and whether my skirt will stick to me when I get out of my chair. Another day will be better. Oh, look . . . even ol' Puddin' is trying to get a little relief from the heat." She pointed to one of the nearby rosebushes, and there, just under its lower branches, lay the big black cat, one eye open just a slit as though he were trying to determine whether or not the women offered any threat to his peace and quiet. Apparently deciding that they did not intend to interfere with his rest, he dropped his head again and let out a tiny thread of sound. But whether it was a purr, a snore, or just a groan marking the return of sleep, it was impossible to tell.

"I kind of wish he wouldn't hang around here," Caledonia said, pouring herself a second glass from the lemonade pitcher. "Because of the bird, I mean. Oh, Cesare doesn't seem to mind him. He just eyes old Puddin' through the window and keeps right on swinging. But I keep thinking maybe today's the day the cat would get hungry and might attack."

"I suppose," Angela said lazily, "that Cesare has seen cats before. Maybe in the pet store he came from originally. I wonder if he'd feel as nonchalant about Roderick?"

Caledonia sighed. "Beautiful dog. But this place gets more like a zoo every day. I think it's probably a mistake to encourage having all these animals around. In six months when we take a final vote on whether cats should stay here or not, I think I'm going to vote against it. In the meantime, I guess I'll have to find a way to live with the menagerie."

"Just don't think about the animals, Cal. We have plenty to keep us busy with the Gould case. Except . . . well, in spite of all the work you and I have put in, we don't seem to have anything to show for it."

"Nonsense. You've had a load of fun rummaging through your neighbors' garbage. You've presented Lieutenant Martinez with several new ideas—the delivery people, the paperboy—like that. And even if you don't think you're getting anywhere, somebody does, because they tried to kill you, didn't they?"

"You'll forgive me," Angela said sourly, reaching to pour herself another glass of lemonade, "if I don't find that thought very comforting."

"And we even went ghost hunting," Caledonia went on lazily. "Now that isn't something we do every day, is it?"

"But that doesn't have anything to do with the Gould case, does it? At least, how could it? Because that was before Howard Gould even moved here. Before any of us knew him. And before any of the things I especially wonder about even happened."

"What do you mean, the things you wonder about?"

"Well, you know, like why would Nancy Bush lie about being in the garden? And who pushed Regina Madison out the window?"

"Angela! Nobody pushed . . ."

"And why Conrad Stone had an empty pizza box? And who set the insecticide cans in my room to . . . Wait a minute. I've had an idea. I mean, why *was* that box empty?"

"Because Conrad Stone ate the pizza. All of it."

"No, that isn't it. Because there were no tomato stains or cheese stains in the box. Look. I have it right here." She lifted aloft the empty box she still carried with her, and slid the top open so Caledonia could inspect the inside.

"Oh, Angela, come on. There are lots of pizzas that don't use to-mato sauce. There's pesto sauces. There's all-vegetable pizzas. And not all cheeses leak grease, either."

"But suppose there never was a pizza? Suppose the delivery boy brought the box to Conrad by mistake. The question is, why would a delivery boy have an empty box with him in the first place?"

"Well, maybe he wasn't a boy. Maybe he was an older man. Old enough to be absentminded. We're certainly used to absent-mindedness, you and I—we live with enough of it around us. And lots of businesses are hiring senior citizens lately. I've had an eighty-year-old bag boy at the supermarket, I've seen an old coot of nearly ninety serving burgers, so why not an ancient and forgetful pizza de-livery guy?"

"Well, of course that's one possibility. There are others."

"Like what?"

"Like . . . like . . . well, like I don't know. And that's the point. If you have a question and you don't know the answer, what do you do? You don't leave it a mystery. You just go and ask somebody who is apt to know what's what. So I think we ought to go and ask the pizza people themselves." She checked her wristwatch. "There's plenty of time before supper, provided we leave right now. Pizza Palace, that's the name here on the box." She waved it aloft once more. "And their shop is just two doors away from the drugstore. I've seen it often when I'm downtown. It's not far . . . maybe four blocks altogether. We could walk it easily."

"You could. I don't walk anywhere, remember? And I'm not the one who's curious about the box, you are. So if you want to go ask, you do it on your own. I'm going to sit right here with the shade and a cool drink . . ." She emphasized the point by pouring herself yet another glass from the sweating, icy pitcher. "I'll be dying to hear all about it when you get back. Of course I'll make you a bet right now . . ."

"A bet?"

"That there's nothing unusual about it at all or even very interesting. That it's just some kind of silly mistake."

"I'll take that bet," Angela said huffily. "If I win, you owe me coffee and chocolate-chip cookies at the Dutch Cafe in town. And you have to walk there with me." Caledonia groaned. "And if you win . . . well, if you win, what do you want for a prize?"

Caledonia grinned. "Just the satisfaction of proving you're wrong. You're always so sure of yourself when you take off chasing some wild goose or other, and you're always making mysteries where none exist. Hearing you admit that you're mistaken will be prize enough for me."

Angela's little nose rose another inch into the air as she rose to her feet and picked up her empty box again. "Well, all right. I'm on my way, and if you'd rather just sit here and do nothing . . ."

"Oh, I'd much rather. Much."

"All right," Angela said. "You'll see . . ." and she bustled off toward the lobby, heading her steps ultimately toward town.

Caledonia just leaned further back into the shade and sipped happily at her lemonade. "Fool's errand, that's what she's on. A fool's errand."

"SHE'S ON A FOOL'S errand," Caledonia repeated as she emptied the last of the lemonade. If anyone had overheard her, they'd have thought she was talking to herself, and in a way she was, for the only ears within many yards were the two pointed black ears belonging to Puddin'. "Empty boxes? Absentminded delivery boys? It's all nonsense. Who cares—except for Angela? Of course you wouldn't know this, pussycat," she went on, and Puddin' cocked his head in her direction as though he were really listening, "but when Angela makes up her mind to do something, she's hard to divert. So I let her go. But you and I, we know better than to really stir ourselves on such a hot afternoon."

Puddin' had pulled himself to his feet and begun an elaborate stretching routine, first bending deep at his shoulders, his forelegs extended full, while he yawned so wide it looked as though his jaw would unhinge, then pulling his back up into a high arch and yawning again. At last satisfied that all the joints and ligaments were in their proper places and in good working order, he glided lazily over toward Caledonia. "Oh, no," she said, pulling her feet aside and tucking them under her chair. "No need your trying to make up to me with all that rubbing. I don't dislike cats nearly as much as I let on, mind you, and it's certainly nothing personal. But the truth is, I own a bird. See through the window there? So it's natural I wouldn't care for the bird's enemies. Like you." Puddin' paused at her feet and looked up at her with narrowed yellow eyes. He appeared to be thinking about what she had said. "You're a pretty fellow, aren't you? As cats go, I mean. Lovely soft fur . . ." She put a pair of fingers down to his head and he raised his head to meet her touch. "Mmmm, you like that, don't you?"

He let a purr rumble from his throat and pushed his head against her hand again. "You're not such a bad old boy. Mind you, you made a mistake not being born as a dog. But all considered . . ."

She stroked again and Puddin' looked up at her a moment and then, without warning, he was in her lap. He didn't seem to have jumped, or indeed to have expended any effort at all. One minute he was on the ground, looking up, and the next he was standing in Caledonia's lap, making himself round, tucking his legs under him, and settling himself into a thick black ball of contentment. "Fast work, Puddin'," Caledonia said. "You don't fool around. You're like most pretty boys . . . just take what you want, right?"

She chuckled and smoothed the cat's fur again. "I don't really dislike cats at all, you know," she told him. "I just always had dogs, and they're so different." Her fingers lingered on Puddin's bright red elastic collar. "Hey, fancy stuff you got here." Idly she turned over the little tag that hung from it. "PROPERTY OF PETS-N-MORE, WILLOW STREET, CAMDEN. Well, for goodness sake, fellow. Stone should have had his own tag put on here after he bought it for you. This store tag isn't any use as an ID."

Her fingers gently stroked Puddin's head and back a moment, and then they stopped. Puddin' looked up at her, wary again. "Look, fat boy," she said, "I've got something I'm going to do and I can't, with you attached to my lap. Time to get back down and . . ." To her surprise, Puddin' got gracefully to his feet and allowed himself to flow quietly to the porch floor, where he sat cleaning his paws, one at a time, as though that was really what he'd meant to do all along—as though the detour to her lap had been incidental to his real purpose.

"Well," Caledonia said to him, "you read my mind. Do all cats do that?" Puddin' licked his paw with increased fervor, nibbling hard at the tough membrane around the claws and ignoring her completely as she hoisted her bulk into motion, heading to her living room and the telephone, and rang up her limousine service. There was still, she noted, glancing at her wristwatch, plenty of time before dinner for what she wanted to do.

Angela, of course, had wasted no time pet-petting, but went directly off on her own errand. The Pizza Palace was only four blocks away, just across the railway tracks that divided the town of Camden, as it did many of the beach communities north of San Diego, cutting the business district and major residential areas off from their beach-front properties. Angela might not walk as fast as she once did, and she might take more care to avoid stumbling than she once did, but she didn't mind a short walk—especially when, as she would have put it, she had a mission. And she was scarcely out of breath at all when she arrived at the Pizza Palace and seated herself across from the manager in his miniscule office located behind his kitchen.

The manager was a youngish man with sandy hair, dressed in the California uniform of chinos and a polo shirt, the sleeves of which were short enough to show off the bulging curve of his biceps. Obviously when he was not on duty at the shop, he was not just studying better ways to make a pizza—probably pumping iron instead, Angela thought, pleased with herself that she remembered the term she'd heard now and again on television. "Now, ma'am, you wanted to ask me something?" the manager said. He was so excessively polite that Angela was convinced he suspected she was one of those customers who pretend to find a bug in their mozzarella and threaten suit. He certainly didn't look like a young man who would willingly take time out of his working day to answer casual inquiries. So Angela decided quickly that it was time to improvise. Not to tell a real lie, mind you. Just to . . . to improvise.

"Yes, it's about a pizza party we want to give," Angela said mendaciously, looking up at him with round, innocent eyes. "We're shopping around for the best prices and the best guarantee of delivery. It's a birthday party for one of our residents, you see, a Conrad Stone. He's crazy about pizza, but we don't have the kind of ovens in our retirement-home kitchen that would do a good pizza, like your old-fashioned brick ovens here . . ." She waved a hand at the brick wall behind them through which the heat was radiating into the little office, making the air uncomfortably close in spite of the shop's air conditioning.

"All right," the manager said, "we can certainly furnish pizza for your party. Of course the total cost will depend on what toppings you want, but in quantity, I'm sure we could make you a very attractive price. How many do you think you might want?"

"I'm not sure," Angela said. "Maybe . . ." She hesitated, realizing she had absolutely no idea how many pizzas it might take to feed three or four people, let alone a crowd of party guests. "Maybe . . . twenty-five?"

The manager beamed at her. "That's a lot of pizza, but we can handle it, provided you don't want it during our busiest time. If your party were, for instance, in the middle of the afternoon, I think we could handle it rather nicely."

"Oh. Oh, yes. I could schedule it for the afternoon, all right."

"Now . . . about those toppings . . ."

"Well, that's another reason I needed to talk to you. I'm not sure about those toppings," Angela said, her eyes rounder and more innocent than ever. "I'm not at all sure what Mr. Stone would prefer. The party's for him, you see, so we ought to order what he likes best."

"You'd better ask him, then, and . . ."

"Oh, goodness no! This is supposed to be a surprise party! And if I ask the guest of honor his preferences, there won't be any surprise, will there?" She snapped her fingers in an elaborate pantomime meant to show that she'd had a sudden idea. "I know. Why not look it up on your list of customer preferences? Find out what he usually orders."

The manager shook his head. "We don't keep records like that. Maybe some gourmet restaurant does, but we're just a small pizza shack, and . . ."

"But when people phone in orders, you write down what they want, don't you?"

"Oh. Of course," the manager said. "And we do keep phone order slips for a week or so." He waved his hand at a cardboard box file lying on one corner of his desk. "Our accountant compares them to our register tapes and our deposit slips to kind of check up and see if our drivers have turned in all the money they get. We used to have a big problem . . . a couple of these young sharpies who thought they could skim some of what they took in. So now we keep a duplicate of each slip we send out with the pizza. But when the accountant finishes, we pitch the sales slips out. So they don't go way back."

"Well, has your accountant been through the receipts recently? Our friend Mr. Stone ordered pizza earlier this week, and his name should be in that file somewhere. So you can look up what it was he ordered last time."

"That should be easy," the manager said, and he opened the box file and started through the green-and-white sales slips inside, most of them grease stained or marked with tomato sauce. "Stone, you said? What's the address?"

"Camden-sur-Mer, 1003 Beach Boulevard . . ."

He thumbed through the stack . . . "Stone, you say?" I have a Rumford on Beach Boulevard here. Number 351 . . ."

"No, that's not us. We're at the retirement home, you know."

"Okay . . ." He went on through the stack. "Oh, here's a Stone, over on Rutherford B. Hayes Circle, but that's a long way from Beach Boulevard . . . Gee, I'm sorry, ma'am, but are you sure he got his pizza from us?"

"Well, no, except . . ." She hesitated. "Well, to tell you the truth, I saw the box. With your name right across it. And he threw that box out only a couple of days ago, so he must have ordered rather recently."

"Not necessarily. I mean, could be the pizza was delivered the week before and he was just now pitching the box out," the manager suggested. "Let me try this bundle of receipts from the week before . . ." and he pulled out another stack of sales slips held together with a rubber band, and he hummed as he thumbed . . . tunelessly . . . arhythmically . . . "Dum-de-dum . . . PAUSE . . . Dum . . . PAUSE . . . Hmmm-de-dee . . ." Angela was biting her lip to keep from telling him to shut up by the time he finished the stack and spoke again.

"Sorry. No Stone at all, yours or anybody else's, last week. Guess you'll have to ask somebody who knows him better'n you do what he likes to trim his . . . Or wait!" It was the manager's turn to snap his fingers to indicate the arrival of an idea. "How about this? How about if you get our deluxe pizzas with all kinds of toppings? You'd be pretty safe with mushrooms and pepperoni—your guests can pick those off if they don't like 'em—and most people like sausage and peppers and onion. And I'll throw in a little container of anchovies, in case anybody wants 'em, though they're not nearly as popular, and . . . Here, let me give you a price. You said twenty-five altogether, didn't you?" He pulled a little scratch pad from his top drawer, a pencil from a ceramic desk-top holder, and a calculator from his pocket, and then began punching figures into the little machine.

"Wait!" Angela said. "Or rather, go ahead and work, if you can write and talk at the same time. I have another question . . . Not important, just something I wanted to know about."

"Go ahead," he said, continuing to poke at the calculator.

"Well, the aunt of a friend died a couple of weeks ago . . ." Angela was improvising again, ". . . and while we were clearing out her things, we found something rather odd in her kitchen. She had this empty pizza box," and Angela reached down into her tote bag and pulled out Stone's empty pizza box. "See? And I was wondering if you could think of any reason she might have had that empty box lying around."

"She ate the pizza that came in it," the young man said, not even looking up from his calculator. "What's the problem?"

"No, the box is clean and dry, see?" She flourished the box and flipped open the top, but he barely glanced at it, even though she prodded, "Look. It never had any pizza in it at all. At least, it has no crumbs and no stains . . ."

The manager finished his calculations and copied the results onto the scratch pad. Then at last he looked squarely at Angela. "Well, of course it might have been a pizza without cheese or tomato, though even so you'd think there'd be some kind of staining anyhow. Let's see . . ." He picked up the box and looked idly at the cover. "You know, there might be one thing . . . We had a guy come in and buy a stack of these empty cartons from us about maybe four, five months ago. He was telling me he'd gone shopping at the flea market and bought some beautiful decorative plates he wanted to give as Christmas gifts and he needed something to put 'em into. Before he wrapped them, you know what I mean? I mean, it's kind of hard to wrap a plate without a box around it. So maybe your aunt wanted to give somebody a plate as a gift, you think? Well, now, about your party . . . I think I can work things around to give you a good total, okay?" He pushed the little scratch pad toward her, and Angela, to her dismay, could see no way to avoid examining the figures scribbled on it, even though she loathed numbers and calculations. And so, even though she had made little progress in her real inquiry, she made progress toward her imaginary party.

Caledonia's errand, in the meantime, took her to Willow Street in the heart of Camden's tiny downtown, where her limousine pulled up smartly in front of the store marked Pets-N-More. "You wait for me," she commanded her limo driver, who just nodded and pulled out a pencil and a newspaper folded open to the crossword puzzle. He was used to waiting and he had come prepared.

Caledonia swirled off into the pet store, wrinkling her nose as she entered; the faint smell of wet animal fur and of litter boxes was strong, despite the best efforts of the staff and the pungent odors of the disinfectant that swabbed out the cages daily. She was the only customer, and her entrance set off a cacophony of sound, a blur of movement; the puppies in their wire mesh apartment house set up an eager yipping, leaping at the bars of their cages, clawing frantically in their efforts to attract her attention, and a red-feathered macaw began to swing back and forth on its perch to shout, "Hello, beautiful! Hello, beautiful!" Even the fish seemed to swim faster in their aquariums. Only the several kittens, penned together in the center of the shop, paid absolutely no attention to Caledonia's entrance, absorbed as they were in frantic games of chase-the-ball, chase-each-other, chase-my-tail, chase-your-tail, chase-a-fly . . . around and around, bumping into and tumbling over each other. Caledonia stood and watched them, ponderously amused.

"Can I help you?" A thin young man with thick glasses came out from behind the counter.

"Do you sell cat collars?" Caledonia asked, getting right to business.

"You bet," the clerk said, brightening up. "And if you buy a cat, we'll give you a collar free. That's one of our gimmicks here . . . a free collar with each puppy and kitten."

"A red elastic collar for the cats?"

"Right. We give a woven collar for dogs, but cats climb trees, you know, and they might get a collar snagged or something. A cat should wear a collar they can slip out of in an emergency. Can I show you a kitten? We have some nice domestic shorthairs, two Persians, and a lovely little blue-point Siamese in stock at the moment." He gestured into the pen where a furry lump of kittens was rolling over and over, fighting over a tennis ball. All of them, except for two who had fallen into exhausted sleep—one in a corner, the other draped across the food dish—had become tangled together in a wriggling mat of multicolored fur from which miscellaneous tails and ears protruded.

"I hate to disillusion you, but I'm here for information, not for a kitten." The clerk shrugged and stayed silent, waiting for Caledonia to explain. "I'm interested in a particular cat named Puddin' . . . a big, fat, black creature . . ."

"Domestic shorthair, probably mixed with some Persian, in my opinion," the clerk nodded. "What about him?"

"Well, he was purchased here, wasn't he?"

"Sure was. I remember it real well because the guy who bought him didn't seem to care about the cat's color, or whether it had long fur or short fur, just so long as it was fat. Big-boned and fat. And that struck me as odd."

"Strikes me as odd, too," Caledonia said.

"Well, when I asked, he said he'd owned a cat that recently died, and he was trying to replace it with one just like it," the clerk said.

"But then he said he wanted a leash to walk the cat with. I know of some trainers can teach a cat to walk with a leash, but hardly anybody else. Then he asked for a stiff collar instead of this stretchy one— because, the way he said it, when he needed to tie the cat outside, it could get out of a stretchy collar. Tie the cat up outside? What kind of nutty . . . Well, what I figure, he knew something about dogs, but not a thing about cats. In fact, I don't think he ever owned a cat before in his life, no matter what he said about buying this one to replace another."

"I see. That is interesting. Well, did you find him what he wanted?"

"Sure," the clerk said. "Took some time, and I showed him two or three others he turned down before we located Puddin'. They were good cats, but they weren't big enough to suit him."

"Well, when was this?" Caledonia said. "You do keep records, don't you?"

"Not exactly, but I might be able to find . . ." and the clerk went to a cubicle at the back of the shop where there was a desk littered with papers, cans of flea spray, bottles of worming pills, nail clippers the size of a ticket punch, a tangle of leashes . . . Nestled in the midst of the clutter were a keyboard and monitor, and the clerk seated himself in front of his screen and started tapping out instructions for his computer.

While the clerk worked away at his keyboard, Caledonia moved over to the kittens' pen and reached inside, trying to separate the frolicking youngsters so she could get a good look at them while she waited, and reaching into the pen, she discovered what cat owners since ancient Egypt have known: that making a cat do something it doesn't want to do is, to understate the case, difficult. The kittens regarded her hand as one more toy to be attacked, ducked, dodged, pounced upon, nibbled, kicked . . . but not one of them would willingly allow her to pick it up. At last, just as Caledonia was able to abstract a single kitten, struggling and protesting, from the middle of the pack, the clerk was back.

"It was about four months ago," he said. "I'm working on inventory control, now that we've got a computer, and I've got records of the sales of the animals we stock regularly and of the pet food and the medicines and the leashes and the chew toys and all that stuff, but Puddin' wasn't here to begin with, you see. I mean, he was never really 'in stock,' properly speaking. So he wasn't on my computer, and I didn't have an exact date on that sale. But I remember that about that same time I was looking for a supply of that bran-new antiflea pill. They're back ordered from the warehouse, so I used one phone call to the other shops to ask about both the pills and whether or not they could furnish a fat cat. And that means that I've got a record on Puddin' after all, even though it's really a record on the flea pills, see?"

"No, I don't see. But if it gets me the answer I need . . ."

"Well, I remember that I located Puddin' the very next day after I located a supply of flea pills, so I looked it up, and it was the twentieth. Just before Christmas. So I got hold of Puddin' on December twenty-first. That what you wanted to know?"

"You bet. I can't thank you enough."

"If you really want to thank me, you could buy something. Like how about you buying that kitten you're holding?"

Caledonia replaced the kitten, still milling its little legs and yowling its complaints, in the pen with its brothers and sisters. "No, sorry. But, tell you what, how about a big sack of that premium birdseed you've got on display?"

The clerk grinned again. "Sure thing." He moved quickly to take her proffered payment and write down her name and address. "Seed'll be at your place no later than tomorrow afternoon. So you've got a bird, eh? Well, I guess that explains why you don't want to buy a kitten."

Her limousine returned Caledonia to Camden-sur-Mer exactly as the Westminster chimes sounded on the overhead speakers and the double doors to the dining room were swung open, so Caledonia marched straight from the limousine into the dining room, where she found Angela just seating herself. "Oh, Cal," Angela said breathlessly, "I've had the most interesting visit with the people at the Pizza Palace. I can't wait to tell you . . ."

"Dinner first," Caledonia said, puffing a little from having hurried. "Let me catch my breath and eat . . . and then we'll exchange reports. I've got something interesting to tell you, too," and each time Angela's natural tendency to bubble out her news surfaced and she started to explain what she had learned, Caledonia motioned her into silence, saying, "Not yet, not yet . . ." In relative silence they dined on stuffed pork chops, rice, and English peas. "Amazing what an appetite detective work gives me," Caledonia said as they waited for dessert. "You'd think Lieutenant Martinez would weigh a lot more than he does. Oh, dear, speak of the devil . . ."

And there he was, Lieutenant Martinez, threading his way through the other tables and straight up to them. "Ladies, good evening," he said. "I need to talk to you, and I'd be very obliged if you'd join me in the second-floor conference room after your dinner is over."

"Oh, of course," Angela said eagerly. "We have so much to tell you. I've been down to the Pizza Palace and learned something really unusual."

"And I have some interesting news myself," Caledonia said. "I meant to tell Angela first, but I can tell you both at the same time."

Lieutenant Martinez gave a little bow of acknowledgment. "Excellent. I'll be grateful. Till after the meal then," and he hurried away.

Angela was torn between irritation and smugness. "I could have told you this would happen. You insisted we wait till we finished eating before we talked over our news and sorted things out . . . and now we won't even have a chance to reach our own conclusions. He'll preempt us the way he always does and thank us and go look into everything we've discovered and tell us not to interfere, and it's all your fault. If only you'd done what I asked . . ."

Caledonia reached across the table and got a tiny pitcher of vanilla sauce to pour on her dessert, a small blackberry tart. "It wouldn't matter whether we reached conclusions or not," Caledonia said and poured the sauce lavishly over the berries. "We always planned to tell the lieutenant everything we've found out in any event."

Angela started to protest and then appeared to think better of it and lapsed into silence while she demolished her own blackberry tart.

Later, as they took the elevator to the second floor and headed down the hall toward the conference room, Angela cleared her throat. "There is one thing, though, that I really need to talk to you about before we see the lieutenant. Slow down a minute. I have something I want to discuss. I mean, this wouldn't interest him, but I really need your advice."

"My advice?"

"Yes. You see, I was pretending to be a customer at the Pizza Palace so I'd have time to ask about the empty box."

"How would being a customer help?"

"It got me in to talk privately to the manager. What I did was, I told him we were giving a party and wanted to check on what Conrad Stone usually got on his pizzas." She hesitated.

"Sounds harmless enough. What's the problem?"

"Well, the problem is, it got awfully complicated before I was finished. He did a lot of calculations and made a special price, and he was so nice about it, I was ashamed to turn him down. So . . . so I ended up ordering a delivery for next week."

"A delivery of what?" Suspicion was rich in Caledonia's voice.

"Well . . . of . . . of a pile of pizzas."

"A pile? How many is a pile?"

"Twenty-five," Angela whispered.

"That's a lot of pizza, all right. What exactly are you planning to do with all of them?"

"Oh, I was planning to cancel the order. But I was hoping you'd do that for me. It'd be so embarrassing, after all I said about . . ."

"Oh, no, you don't. I'm not going to pull your chestnuts out of the fire! Or rather, pull your pizzas out of the oven! This is one little jam I refuse to help with. And it serves you right, telling all those lies!"

"I wasn't lying! I was . . . I was improvising!"

Caledonia led the way down the hall, grinning widely. "Improvising or lying, I'm looking forward to hearing you try to get yourself out of this one!"

"I SEE." LIEUTENANT MARTINEZ WAS disappointingly calm as Angela finished her recital of her visit to Pizza Palace. "You get notes on all that, Swanson?"

His young partner nodded. "I always get 'em, Lieutenant. No fear."

"And you have Mrs. Wingate's information in your notes as well?"

"Yessir, sure have. Pet store, cat collar, fat cat acquisition, the works."

"All right, then." Martinez hesitated. Caledonia waited politely, supposing that he was organizing his ideas and would tell them what he'd wanted of them when he was good and ready, but Angela was impatient, as usual, and leapt into the conversation with conclusions of her own devising.

"I find this very disappointing," she said. "All this hard work we've gone to, all these leads we've developed for you, and all you can say is 'All right'? Surely you can see where all this points. Someone at the Pizza Palace is involved in Howard Gould's murder!"

"That's quite a flight of fancy, Mrs. Benbow," Martinez said gently. "But you have a tendency to do that—to connect things that have very little connection. How do you get that from an empty pizza box?"

"Not just the empty box. Oh, I know that's why I went down to Pizza Palace to begin with. But I thought about it all the way home, and . . . well, doesn't it strike you that there's an awful lot of pizza in this case? Conrad Stone, for instance, gets pizza so often he even has a special arrangement with his delivery man to push the pizza through the cat door onto the kitchen counter. Conrad just leaves the money inside and the fellow takes it, so Conrad doesn't have to open the door in the night air, standing there in bare feet and pajamas and all.

And he can't be the only pizza lover living here. There must be plenty of others. It seems logical to me that the pizza delivery man is as good a suspect as . . ."

Martinez shook his head. "But surely not everybody orders pizza from the same place, do they? There must be a half-dozen different people delivering here. Besides, why would a pizza delivery man kill Howard? As far as we can tell, Howard was just standing around in the garden trying to retrieve his cat."

"All right," Angela said, "then maybe it wasn't the pizza man. Maybe it was somebody who was lurking, waiting to waylay the delivery man and steal the pizza, and Howard just accidentally got in the way."

Caledonia barked out a laugh. "Somebody who's addicted to pepperoni, maybe? Angela, that's so silly. Why wouldn't he just buy his own pizza? Besides, there are more deliveries to Camden-sur-Mer from the drugstore than there are from all the pizza places put together. If mere frequency is your measure of suspicious activity, all this is probably connected to Billy and the drugstore! Maybe Howard stumbled over a killer who was lying in wait to hijack a delivery of Ex-Lax and Tums. Your theory makes absolutely no sense at all. Just to begin with, nobody's that nuts about pizza."

"Of course they are. There isn't a human being alive who doesn't like pizza! Even animals. Roderick, for instance," Angela said defensively.

"Roderick the dog?" Swanson waded into the conversation, but from his tone it was obvious that he was wading over his head.

"Didn't you see him come over and wag his tail at me that first time you brought him into the lobby?" Angela said. "I was a little afraid of him, but he was so sweet to come and greet me that way, sitting right there at my feet and letting me rub his ears while he inhaled my leftovers and crumbs . . ."

"Crumbs?"

"Of course, Lieutenant. That was the day I'd picked through the trash. I had that plastic bag with me . . . the bag I gave to you, with all the containers in it. When Roderick came right over to me, out of that whole crowd, I knew of course that it wasn't just me. It had to be because of some scent from the leftovers in those cartons and boxes. And he was so cute about it . . ."

Martinez shook his head. "I thought everything you salvaged from the trash that day was emptied out. There wasn't anything left inside.

Still, if his nose is as sensitive as it's supposed to be, maybe he could pick up the scent of mozzarella or moo shu pork or . . ."

"That's not the point anyway," Angela said. "You always accuse me of getting off the point and this time it's you! The point is that . . ." She paused and passed a hand over her forehead. "I've kind of lost the point. Where was this discussion going, anyway?"

"Angela." Caledonia shook her head. "You weren't making your point anyhow, so why not give it up? And let the lieutenant tell us his news. I mean, you did call us up here for some reason, Lieutenant."

"Indeed I did," he nodded, and smiled at her. "Don't feel guilty, Mrs. Benbow," he told Angela, who was looking abashed. "We were very interested in your information and even in your theories. But we do have a new piece to the puzzle, or so it seems. We had a visit from your new resident, Nancy Bush, this afternoon, and since you two know Miss Bush better than we could hope to in such a short time, we thought you could set us on the right track about her."

"But we don't know her very well either. You said it yourself—she's new here," Angela said. If she had been contrite about monopolizing the conversation earlier, she had recovered completely from her contrition. "We only met her briefly up at The Golden Years, and then shortly after we came back home she moved down here too. But that's not the basis for a close friendship or anything. Look, hadn't you better go ahead and tell us what she wanted from you?"

Swanson grinned at her businesslike tone, and Martinez gave that graceful little half-nod, half-bow that was his unique way of acknowledging and agreeing, and he started his story. Martinez and Swanson had been sitting in the conference room in the late afternoon, the lieutenant told the women, going over notes and trying to make sense of what they already knew, when there was a diffident knock at the door. "May I come in?" Chubby little Nancy Bush had poked her head around the door with a hopeful expression on her face. "I . . . I have to talk with you two . . ."

"It took her a while to explain what she wanted," Martinez went on. "We certainly didn't push her into saying anything. That doesn't work. Or rather, it sometimes works too well. People are tremendously anxious to please, and if you suggest they have information, they'll work hard to come up with something, even if they have to make it up. So we tried to be patient."

"This is so embarrassing," Nancy went on, as the two policemen waited politely. "I don't really know how one goes about things like this . . ." She cleared her throat and looked hopefully around the room. "Would you mind terribly if I had a glass of water?"

"Swanson . . ." Martinez gestured, and Swanson untangled his gangly legs from under the table and loped off down the hall to the community lounge for the second floor north, where there would be a paper cup and bottled spring water in a cooler. Nancy accepted the little cup and sipped daintily for a moment, but said nothing but "Oh, thank you." At last Martinez spoke again. "Miss Bush," he said gently, "you have something you want to say to us, am I right? Please, go ahead. We won't scold you or be shocked, if that's what's worrying you. The best thing is just to come out with it."

"No-no," she said, carefully wadding up the emptied cup and gingerly dropping it into the wastebasket Swanson kept nearby for note pages that were no longer worth saving. "It's only that it's a very hard thing for me to say. I didn't expect you to be shocked. I mean, policemen hear all kinds of things, don't they?" She cleared her throat. "Well, all right then, I'll just say it. You can stop trying to find out who it was that killed Howard Gould. It was me."

"I see." Martinez kept his voice calm and noncommittal. "And exactly how did you do it?"

Nancy smiled slyly. "That sounds as if you're trying to test me. But it won't work. Everybody around here knows that Howard Gould was killed with that hammer from the toolbox. That's what I did, all right. I hit him with the hammer."

"I suppose you're right . . . everybody here does know about the weapon," Martinez said. "There certainly aren't many secrets at this place, and we didn't try to keep it quiet. But, Miss Bush, a hammer's not really what we call a woman's weapon, you know, and that was an awfully hard blow. You're not very big, and I wonder . . ."

"I'm pretty strong, though," she said smugly. She reached out and grabbed his hand. "Feel my grip! I didn't have any trouble hitting hard enough. Besides, the hammer was the only thing handy. It isn't as though I planned to do it, you know. It was completely spontanacious. If I'd planned to kill him, I'd have carried something that fit my hand better. My cast-iron paperweight, for instance. I have a nice heavy one on my desk. In fact, it didn't even occur to me until I saw the hammer. Then I just grabbed it and used it."

"All right, then, Miss Bush. I see. Well, now to another important question. Why?"

"Because I didn't have the paperweight. I just looked around and saw something heavy, and . . ."

"No, I didn't mean why the hammer. I meant, why did you kill him?"

"Oh. Oh, I see. Oh, dear . . ." She hesitated. "Do I have to explain?"

"I should think you'd want to."

"He was a bad man," she finally said. "A very bad man."

"How so?" Martinez was gently insistent.

"He . . ." Her voice dropped to a whisper. "He leered at me. I could tell what he was thinking. Bad thoughts. Nasty thoughts. About . . . you know . . . about women. He wanted . . . dreadful things. Do I really have to say it out loud?"

Martinez caught Swanson's eye and sighed. "No, Miss Bush, you don't need to say anything that makes you uncomfortable, but can you be more specific? For instance, when did he do this leering?"

"Oh, whenever I walked by. He couldn't keep his eyes to himself. And when I sat in my windows in the evening. He'd glance up there and he'd wave and smile at me, and I knew what he was thinking."

"I see. And is there anything else?"

"Anything else?"

"About killing Mr. Gould."

"Oh, I thought you meant had I done anything else. To someone else. I thought you meant like killing Mrs. Madison."

"Mrs. Who?"

"Regina Madison, sir" Swanson said softly. "You remember. The woman who fell out of the window up at The Golden Years."

"That's right." Nancy Bush nodded vigorously. "I thought you meant had I killed her, too. I'm impressed that you worked out that was really a murder and not just an accident. I mean, it's a wonderful way to kill somebody. Because when somebody falls out of a window, there's no clue or anything, is there?"

"Are you telling us you killed Regina Madison?"

"That's right." She nodded again.

"You pushed her out of her window?"

"Oh, no. I rearranged the lawn furniture so she'd have to overbalance and she'd fall all by herself. And it happened just the way I planned."

"You rearranged . . . You dragged that table with the umbrella to a new place on the lawn?"

"Oh, yes. At the time, I only wanted a place to read my book and watch the croquet game at the same time. But when it was dinnertime and I went to drag the table back to its place, I had to stand up, and when I did, I was kind of sighting past the umbrella, and I realized that it was blocking the view from Mrs. Madison's window. She would have to lean way over if she wanted to see the apartments across the courtyard. You know she checked up on Simon Peterson every night."

"We've heard."

"Of course, that was a good thing. The bad thing was her nosing into what all her other neighbors were doing, too. She had no reason to do that except to be nosy. And that's why I decided to leave the table out of position. It was poetic justice. Her spying was evil, and it was her spying that killed her. The murder weapon wasn't the umbrella table. It was those field glasses of hers!"

"But, Miss Bush, you use binoculars yourself," Swanson said. "The first time we talked, you told us you watched the gardens from your windows."

"Yes, but I just look at people walking up and down. I don't look into their apartments. Well, not much. Besides, I wouldn't dream of talking about what I saw if I did happen to glance into a window. That Regina Madison—she didn't just peek into other people's windows—she told everybody what she saw there!"

"But she didn't look into your windows. You lived on the other side of the building there in The Golden Years, didn't you? So she couldn't have been looking at you, and I don't understand . . ."

"But looking into windows is an invasion of privacy," Nancy Bush insisted. "And that's criminalacious, isn't it? The woman bore false witness! Well, some of it was false, anyway. She gossiped about this one, gossiped about that one . . . And you know, people don't seem to be able to defend themselves against that kind of thing. They just suffer in silence. I was taught, on the other hand, that we must not only stand up for ourselves, we must help weaker people who can't take care of themselves," she said smugly.

"So that's what you were doing when you left the umbrella table blocking Mrs. Madison's view? Defending other people?" She nodded but said nothing. "And you hoped she'd fall out the window trying to peer around it?"

"And it worked, didn't it? So now you know. And you needn't go around blaming other people. That wouldn't be fair. I believe in fairness above all else." She got to her feet with a big sigh. "I can't tell you how much better I feel. Like a great weight off my chest. I was always taught to tell the truth no matter what." And she left the room, her head held high.

"You let her go!" Angela asked. "You didn't arrest her?"

"Well, Swanson followed along behind her," Martinez said, "and she just went straight to her own apartment, as I assumed she would. She's not going to try to escape or anything."

"Sounds dangerous to me," Angela said. "You're taking an awful chance, letting her roam around free, now that you know she's guilty."

"Well, maybe, but I'm not at all comfortable with her confession," Martinez said. "And that's why I called you two in. Oh, we're investigating her statement, of course. For instance, we'll take another look at the grounds up there at The Golden Years. We've got a police-woman who's just Miss Bush's height, and she's going to stand there in the courtyard tomorrow trying to see if she can really judge the sightlines from the Madison window while she's down below by the umbrella table in question. And naturally we're checking much more closely into Miss Bush's background. I want to see if there's any record that she's been confessing to other murders. A lot of people who give false confessions don't stop at just once, you know. If she's made a habit of it, we should be able to find a record. But I also wanted to hear about her from you two who know her personally."

Caledonia shook her head. "Not well enough to evaluate that confession, I'm afraid. Except, if you want a gut reaction, Lieutenant, I just don't believe she's guilty. I have nothing solid to go on, but to me it doesn't fit together. And what about the attempt on Angela's life? Nancy didn't say anything about that, did she?"

"Not a word."

"Well, assume for the moment she is guilty," Angela said stubbornly. "She did say so, so assume it's true. Doesn't that go to prove that the insecticide was put into my apartment for innocent reasons, just the way I thought? Somebody trying to do me a favor . . ."

"If that were the case," Martinez said, "somebody would own up to leaving the aerosol cans on that table. But nobody admits to placing them in your apartment—not for innocent purposes, not by mistake . . . and in all this time, with all the questions we've asked, somebody would have said something, if it was done innocently. I'm afraid, dear lady, that someone was indeed trying to do away with you."

Angela shook her head. "I've always been a bit skeptical of that theory. More so as time goes on, because they haven't tried again. Nobody's tried to bug-bomb me again. Nobody's hit me over the head or pushed me over the cliff. Why haven't they, if they really want to get me out of the way?"

"Well," Martinez answered, "perhaps you said or did something that convinced him you weren't as dangerous as he'd thought."

"Her. If it's Nancy Bush," Angela said, "it's her, not him."

"But it just can't be Nancy," Caledonia said. "It just doesn't make sense, all that stuff about Gould and Regina Madison being bad people. Howard Gould was just a friendly man and Regina Madison was completely harmless."

"But if she didn't do it, why did she say she did?" Angela protested.

"We get at least one confession to almost every murder we investigate," Martinez said.

"That doesn't make sense either," Caledonia growled. "What kind of nut would confess to a murder if he didn't do it?"

"Well," Martinez said, "we've found some people who just craved attention—even unfavorable attention. More rarely, we've run into people who have delusions, who really believe they've killed someone, even though they haven't. Then there are pathological liars who enjoy the experience of fooling others. And though we don't often see it except on television dramas, we've run into people who've had something to gain by a phony confession—for instance, they might hope to clear another person of suspicion."

"I'm confused. Which of those fits Nancy Bush?" Angela asked.

"I have no idea," Martinez conceded. "I'm not sure she fits into any of those categories. Perhaps she's telling the truth. I just don't know. We really hoped you could tell us."

"Well," Angela said judiciously, "if it's any help, I don't think she's a pathological liar. I mean, I don't think she's crazy."

"Just because she doesn't wear a Napoleon hat or have straw sticking out of her hair?" Caledonia was scornful. "Listen to what she says, for Pete's sake! Men ogling her? Defending her fellow residents against pernicious invasion of their privacy? The woman's obviously a fruitcake!"

"But even fruitcakes can be killers," Angela insisted.

Martinez sighed and got to his feet. "I can see we'll have to look further for the answer, but I thank you ladies for your advice."

"Advice?" Angela said. "We didn't give you any advice."

"Well, I suppose you implied it: that our job isn't done and we have to go on asking questions. A lot of questions. Of course I could hope that just for once the answer might have been handed to us on a platter. But it's never that easy, is it?" He smiled and moved toward the door, indicating that the interview was at a close. "Swanson," he was saying as he swung the door shut, "we have a few things we can do tonight before we head home . . . a list to look into . . ." and then the door cut off his words.

"How are the repairs to your apartment coming along? Do you know?" Caledonia asked as she and Angela strolled along the hall.

"Very nicely, I think," Angela said. "I saw Pete Lopez going through the lobby this morning and stopped him long enough to ask. He says only a couple more days. It'll be wonderful to get back. I'm bored with that one room . . ."

"Exactly why we're going to my place now to talk for a bit," Caledonia said, and put a hand under Angela's elbow to turn her toward the elevator, instead of toward her temporary quarters. "It'll get you out of that stuffy little room for a while before bedtime."

"Oh, Angela! Yoo-hoo . . ." A shrill voice sounded as Caledonia and Angela stepped out of the elevator and into the cavernous, shadowy old lobby. "Caledonia! Angela!"

"Oh, gosh!" Angela cringed into Caledonia's shadow. "Oh, help! It's the Ridgeways."

"Your good buddies?" Caledonia grinned.

"How fortunate to find you both!" Della Ridgeway was bearing down on them, waving a hand so they couldn't miss seeing her as she hurried over with her husband Harvey trailing along behind her, beaming every bit as broadly as Della was smiling. "Girls, we're giving a party," she began.

"A party," Harvey seconded, nodding emphatically.

"To show off our new apartment, now that it's fully decorated," Della said.

"Just showing off a little," Harvey agreed.

"Next week on Tuesday," Della went on. "We're sending along little notes to everybody, but we're telling people in person as well. I've had people miss our parties because they've forgotten our invitations . . ." Della said.

"No!" Caledonia said, pretending surprise. "You don't mean it."

"So we wanted to be sure everybody got the message in two ways," Harvey said. "Once in writing and once in person."

"Tuesday, you say?" Angela said, taking the leash off her improvisational skills again. "Oh dear, not this coming Tuesday! What a shame. I have a friend coming in from Pittsburgh."

"Well, just bring her along," Della said cheerfully. "The more the merrier."

"Oh, but she's so shy she wouldn't feel comfortable with a group of strangers," Angela said hastily. "And I did promise not to inflict strangers on her."

"Then just leave her at your place! She can watch TV or something while you drop in on the party. You needn't stay, and she won't mind if you take just a few minutes away," Della said.

"We insist, little lady," Harvey said jovially. "We won't take 'No' for an answer."

Angela sighed in surrender. "Well, all right, maybe for a few minutes. We'll—we'll see. It'll depend on how she's feeling and all . . ." she finished lamely.

"You'll be there, of course, Caledonia." Della, her first objective achieved, turned to her second.

"No visitors from out of town for you, I trust," Harvey brayed.

"No. I suppose I'll be at your party, all right," Caledonia said quickly. "But for now you'll have to excuse us. The truth is, we're in a bit of a hurry, and . . ."

Her alibi for a quick escape was unnecessary, for just at that moment, Della spotted Trinita Stainsbury coming across the lobby from the garden door and turned to intercept another victim. "Trinita . . . Look, Harvey, there's Trinita Stainsbury. Yoo-hoo, Trinita . . . We're giving a party, and . . ." and off they rushed, jet-propelled spiders in pursuit of their next fly.

Caledonia led Angela in a wide, circular path that avoided the Ridgeways and Trinita by at least ten feet, but even as they left the lobby, heading for Caledonia's place, they could hear Trinita's voice, high-pitched and rapid in a hypocritical expression of regret. "Oh, dear, Tuesday? What a pity. I have an appointment with my oculist, and you know how hard it is these days to get an appointment. I couldn't miss that . . ."

"A friend from Pittsburgh?" Caledonia said, as they cleared the garden door. "A friend from Pittsburgh! You don't know a soul in Pittsburgh and you never did. What a fib!"

"Well, it didn't work anyway, did it?" Angela said sadly. "I can't believe we're stuck with that stupid party. I wish I'd thought of a doctor's appointment like Trinita did."

"Won't do her a bit of good, either," Caledonia said. "That Della Ridgeway isn't going to let up till she gets what she wants. I didn't even bother to struggle, when I saw how easily she handled you." They had reached Caledonia's apartment, and with a grand gesture she flung open the door. "There we are . . . Come on in," and she led the way into her living room, flipping the switch on a lamp as she entered. "Soft drink or anything? No? Suit yourself. Now . . . what's the next step? For us, I mean. I have a sort of halfway idea . . ."

"So do I," Angela said eagerly. "Not that I don't credit Nancy's confession, mind you. I suppose she did it, don't you agree?"

Caledonia frowned. "No, I don't agree. And you wouldn't either, if you were thinking straight," she began, but Angela rushed on, not really listening.

"What I was thinking was that this might have something to do with the pizza delivery boys. And what I was thinking is that we need to go back and get a list of them from that young manager at the Pizza Palace. I thought we'd get him to tell us when each delivery boy was on duty and where they all live so we can talk to the ones who might have been here the night . . ."

"That dumb pizza again! You worry about pizza more than a mozzarella salesman does! I had in mind something a little closer to home," Caledonia said. "It occurred to me that not everybody owns a grabbit, and . . ."

"What?"

"You know, that long stick with the pinchers on top. What somebody must have used to get those insecticide cans into your apartment."

"But we're not even sure somebody meant me harm!"

"*You* aren't sure. You refuse to admit the obvious. Martinez is sure and so am I. And I don't know why I didn't think of this before. Who owns the kind of instrument that could reach between those narrow bars with an aerosol can? We need to look around this place for . . ."

"All right," Angela said earnestly, "I get the idea. But you know I disagree. So I'll tell you what. You follow your hunch and I'll follow mine, and we'll just see who's right." She yawned in spite of herself. "Oh, dear . . . well, of course I mean we'll get to work first thing in the morning. Right now I think I'd better get some sleep. Maybe I can dream of a way to avoid the Ridgeways' party."

CALEDONIA SHOOK HER HEAD and eased the door shut behind Angela, closing out the growing chill in the evening air. With her weight, she felt the heat terribly and welcomed lower temperatures, but the May evening was just a degree or two too cool for her tastes, so before she flipped on her television set and sat down to browse through the evening's entertainment potential, she threw a shawl around her shoulders. Television was a disappointment: sweeps week was over, so the networks had relaxed into reruns, and even CNN, apparently having no news at all to report, had fallen back on yet another retrospective of the O. J. Simpson trial.

Caledonia sighed, punched on the mute, and took up a book of acrostics and a pencil, but she had filled in the easy blanks already— Juliet's boyfriend; the oldest city in the USA; the assassin of a Secretary of the Treasury . . . The remaining clues would require her to do a little serious thinking. "And I'm not in the mood for making an effort over things that don't matter," she muttered.

Cesare, sitting quietly on his perch, nodded sleepily, and though it was probably just a product of his swinging motion rather than agreement, Caledonia beamed at him. "So," she went on, "I propose to do something that does matter. I'm going to see if anybody else is still up and about, like I am, and I'm going to check on those grabbits. The question is, how? How do I do that, eh?"

At the question, Cesare opened one bright eye and contemplated the world around him. Nothing especially frightening or unusual appeared, however, and the eye slid closed again. "That's the answer, of course," Caledonia said to him. "Sneak up on 'em. Don't alarm 'em. So I can't just say, 'Do you own a grabbit?' I need a cover story.

I wish Angela were here. She's good at creative whiffling. Oh, well . . . I expect I'll think of something."

She rose heavily to her feet. "Let's see. Who's likely to own a grabbit? Well, invalids and people in wheelchairs, right?" Cesare swung and nodded, swung and nodded . . . "We've only got one person in a wheelchair at the moment, Emmy Jefferson. And there's Miss Spring, who must be feeble enough to need a grabbit. Neither of them is likely to be a killer, nor Emma's husband Phil, but they might have loaned the gadget to somebody, or it might have been stolen from them. Oh, and of course I should ask people who are already suspects in the Gould murder, like nutty Nancy."

Putting her idea into immediate action, she stepped out onto the garden walk, craning her neck upward. Sure enough, a light glowed dimly from Nancy Bush's windows and Caledonia thought she caught sight of a shadow moving behind those windows. Nancy was still up and around, and that was enough to send Caledonia into the main building and up to the second floor.

The door swung open at Caledonia's very first knock, and she realized that Nancy must have been not only wide-awake but standing just inside the door as though waiting for a visitor. But Nancy's voice was thick with disappointment as she greeted Caledonia. "Oh, it's you! Oh . . . sorry . . . I don't mean to be rude. Actually, I'm glad you've come by, because I'm under a little bit of stress tonight, and having someone to talk to will take my mind off it all. You see, I was expecting the police. They'll be coming to arrest me soon, and I'm busy getting my bag packed. Because I'll need clothes, naturally, and I'd surely hate to have to spend the night in jail without my comb and brush. And my own toothbrush and toothpaste, of course. I can't use just any old toothpaste, you know. Too much peppermint flavor makes me gag in the mornings before breakfast, but all these companies seem to use peppermint flavoring. Why do they do that, Caledonia? Why not citrus? Or wild cherry?"

"Nancy, you're babbling. Just the way Angela does when she gets anxious."

Nancy giggled nervously. "I guess I am. Babbling, I mean. I haven't even asked you to come in and sit down."

"Well, I wish I could," Caledonia said. "But I'm in a real hurry . . . You see"—she launched into the story she had devised as she waited for the elevator—"I dropped my wristwatch down into the drain near the fountain. You know, that iron grid in the sidewalk there?"

"But you're wearing your watch!" Nancy protested.

"My everyday one," Caledonia ad-libbed. "The one I dropped was a gold dress watch I don't wear often, so I didn't realize the catch was loose. Anyhow, I can't lift the metal grill over the drain, and my arm's too short to reach far enough in. I thought maybe somebody might loan me a grabbit."

"A what?"

Caledonia explained.

"Oh," Nancy said, her voice bright with enlightenment, "a long arm! At least, that's what we used to call them. Mother had one in the kitchen. She was very tiny and she couldn't reach things on the top shelves without it. As a matter of fact, I do. Here . . ." She bustled over to the closet and took out an aluminum pole that had been standing in one corner behind the hanging garments. "Clever things, aren't they?" She worked the scissors grip on the handle, and the two little claws on the other end opened and closed. "Nice, firm grip. You should be able to get the watch with . . . Oh, dear, I can't think straight, I'm so nervous. Here. You take the long arm. In fact, you can keep it. I really don't care. I . . . Oh dear, where *are* they?"

"Look, Nancy. Calm down. The police will have to look into your confession before they take any action. Do some investigating," Caledonia said soothingly. "I know all about that confession, by the way, and . . ." She hesitated and decided against amplifying that statement. Instead she finished a bit lamely, "Anyhow, I wouldn't expect the police to come here tonight. Maybe tomorrow."

"Well, I hope so," Nancy said. "I thought perhaps they weren't listening closely and I'd have to go and confess all over again. But you may be right. Perhaps they'll come tomorrow. That would be nice. I really think we should get it over with, don't you? Of course, not till I've finished packing. Cal, should I carry a pair of pajamas, or do they give you something to wear at night? Hospitals do, but I have no idea what they do in a jail. Oh, dear . . . At this rate, I'll be busy packing all night. I'm so sorry . . ." and she bustled off into the bedroom. Through the opened door, Caledonia could see piles of clothing and cosmetics laid out on the bed around a large pullman case. "Forgive me if I get back to work . . ." Nancy called out.

Carrying the aluminum pole, Caledonia retraced her steps to the first floor and back out into the garden, leaving her prize propped against the wall just inside her living room door, for want of anything better to do with it. From there, she marched straight on down the walk to Miss Spring's apartment. Ordinarily she might have waited until morning to talk to a woman of Miss Spring's advanced age, but the apartment blazed with light, which seemed a sure sign that Miss Spring would be awake.

"Come in, whoever you are." Miss Spring's cracked little voice rustled out an invitation as soon as Caledonia knocked. Or rather, shortly thereafter, since Miss Spring did nothing in a hurry any longer. She was sitting on her couch, bundled from toes to earlobes in a comforter against the chilly evening, her television set blaring.

There was a moment's silence while Miss Spring took in her visitor and registered identity. Then she smiled thinly but warmly. "Sit down, dear," she said, nodding toward a nearby chair. There was another moment's silence. "Turn off that racket," Miss Spring said, looking at the television. "Please." The remote control was on the table right next to her, but her hands were hidden inside the cocoon.

Caledonia did as she was instructed and in the ensuing silence told her manufactured story. "My watch," she said. "Down that drain thing in the garden . . . too narrow to reach . . . so I wondered if you had a grabbit?"

There was a long pause while Miss Spring thought about the request. Finally she spoke. "What's a grabbit?"

Caledonia explained.

"Oh," Miss Spring said. There was another silence. "A long arm." Then she was silent so long that Caledonia wondered if the old lady had slipped into a coma with her eyes wide open. "Yes," Miss Spring finally spoke up again. "In the kitchen. Broom closet."

"Oh. Oh, how lucky for me," Caledonia said, feigning enthusiasm, and then, carrying on her charade, "May I?" She went to the broom closet and took out a wooden pole a little over three feet long and sporting metal claws on one end, the requisite scissors grip on the other. "May I borrow this for a little while, Miss Spring?"

Miss Spring's answer was, as usual, a delayed response but perfectly sensible. "Mmm-hmm," she said. Another pause. "Never use it. Great-grandniece gave it to me." She caught her breath a moment and went on, "Good idea, but too heavy. For me."

"I see," Caledonia said, rising to leave, her prize clutched in her hand. "So you never use it yourself? Well, have you loaned it to anyone recently?" Caledonia waited patiently for an answer.

"New lady. One who lost her husband."

"Mrs. Gould?"

Miss Spring nodded. "And that other new woman—Barbara Reagan."

"You mean Nancy Bush?"

Miss Spring nodded again. "Whatever." Her eyes closed and Caledonia thought the tiny woman might be drifting off to sleep, so Caledonia tiptoed toward the door, but Miss Spring opened her eyes and spoke again. "And Pete."

"Pete? Pete Lopez? The head of maintenance?"

Miss Spring's little shoulders moved under the quilt in a shrug. "Don't know, but he works here. Said he wanted it for his sister. She was laid up. She broke a leg." There was another pause while Miss Spring appeared to be struggling to bring out a few more words, and at last she actually did speak again. "That's it. Goodnight," she said. And this time her eyes did close and didn't open again.

Caledonia knew the nurse would come by to tuck Miss Spring into her bed and she needn't stay herself, but she still felt guilty as she carried the grabbit up the walk to her own apartment and stashed it beside the first pole. "Another bit of good luck, Cesare," she spoke to her bird, who had opened his eyes as she entered, and she checked her watch. "Just eight-thirty, so I think I can squeeze in a couple more calls before I quit for the night. You keep on swinging there, and Mama will be home to cover your cage for the night pretty soon." And she whirled off down the path to the Jeffersons' place, where she had noted that the lights were still on.

Phil Jefferson had already gone to bed, Emmy told her, but Emmy had wanted to watch Mary Tyler Moore on Nick at Night. What could Emmy do for her visitor? So once more Caledonia explained her errand and told her elaborate lie.

"I'm really sorry about your watch, Caledonia," Emmy Jefferson said. "But we don't own anything like that, I'm afraid. Would a pair of kitchen tongs do? You know, the kind you serve spaghetti with? Would they help?"

"What a good idea! But not long enough, I'm afraid," Caledonia said. "And probably not strong enough."

"To lift a watch?"

"Well . . ." Caledonia couldn't think of an answer to that, and moved toward the apartment door.

"Wait!" Emmy said. "I have an idea . . . if spaghetti tongs won't do, how about barbecue tongs? They're certainly long enough. Over two feet long, some of them. And they have a good grip . . ."

"Hey! I never thought of barbecue tongs," Caledonia said. "Do you have some?"

"No, we don't," Emmy said, "but several people in the cottages barbecue now and then, and they might have tongs. Like Mr. and Mrs. Taylor over there." She waved a hand, pointing straight across the garden at the cottage directly opposite, the building the Taylors shared with Conrad Stone. "The Taylors keep to themselves, as you know, and they do things by themselves a lot of the time. And one thing they like to do, they cook out every now and then. They never invite anybody else, but you can tell what they're cooking by the wonderful smells." Emmy's voice pinched down tightly, and then she burst out laughing. "Oh, dear, listen to me . . . jealous because my neighbors eat barbecued chicken and smoked pork chops and don't invite me!" She shook her head. "I never used to be so petty. I must be getting old."

"Aren't we all, Emmy dear? Aren't we all? Well, thanks for the bright idea . . ." Caledonia took her leave and went straight across the garden, past the little fountain, and into the grassy service area that separated the Taylor/Stone cottage from its nearest neighbor. She located the trash bin, of course, but she could see no barbecue equipment. But next to the cottage wall, in the shadow of the hedge that sheltered the yard from the street, there was a squarish shape, something shielded from dust and sea air by an expanse of canvas. Caledonia tweaked the cover aside and exposed a Texas smoker and beside it a rolling cart on which there stood a small barbecue grill and two racks, one holding outsized salt and pepper shakers and plastic bottles labeled CATSUP and MUSTARD, the other holding an assortment of cooking tools—brushes, a long fork, an outsized pancake turner ("Barbecued pancakes?" Caledonia muttered. "Surely not!"), and . . . yes, there hung a pair of tongs, long metal tongs fitted with a wooden grip to dissipate the heat.

Caledonia grabbed the tongs and pulled them out of the rack to where she could see more clearly. Yes, she told herself, these would go into her collection of implements, right beside the grabbits. They were more than two feet long, they would fit between the bars of the window grill, they were very strong and would undoubtedly hold an aerosol can with no trouble, and they had some kind of stain or discoloration. She rubbed a finger inquiringly over the redwood strips that formed a handle. Was that a slight, ashy white residue? She licked the finger to wet it and rubbed at the whitish area again, put the finger into her mouth—and spat violently! Whatever the faint white powder was, it tasted strongly medicinal and so nasty that if it wasn't actually poisonous, it might well make you sick just from the taste.

"Yech! What *is* this stuff?" She rolled her tongue enough to gather some saliva to rinse the spot where the taste lingered and spat again. "*Yick!* If it's that insecticide, I need water!"

She didn't even stop to think. Conrad Stone's light was on and she charged straight over to his kitchen door and knocked loudly. "Mr. Stone! Mr. Stone! Conrad . . ."

He opened the door cautiously. "Uh . . . yes? Uh . . . Good heavens, it's Mrs. Wingate! What on earth . . ." He took in her puckered face, the flecks of saliva around her mouth, the barbecue tongs she waved in one hand and stepped aside automatically.

"I need some water," she said. "Quick!" She half stumbled, half charged over to the kitchen sink, turned the tap on full, and bent over as far as she could reach to push her mouth half under the stream of water, letting it gush into and straight out of her mouth. "Oh, boy, that's better. That stuff seems to be washing out. I can still taste it, but . . . Oh, wow! I could have made myself sick with that nasty . . . I know better than to do that, too, but it's almost an automatic way of testing things."

"What on earth . . ."

"Oh, I was silly and wanted to test the residue on these tongs . . ." she waved them high so he could see them clearly, "so I tasted it. Dumb!"

"Yes, I'd say that was pretty dumb," he agreed. His voice was as silky as ever, his smile as warm. But his words made Caledonia stop still in her tracks. "I don't think it's as poisonous as they say on the warning labels, but it's supposed to make you mighty sick if it doesn't kill you. The question is, how did you guess to look for the stuff on the tongs?"

"I didn't," she said cautiously. "Although the spray left a white powder all over everywhere in Angela's room, and it seemed to me it might have got on the thing that reached the cans into the room as well. The question is, how did *you* know about the insecticide? I don't think the police told anybody. Anybody but Angela and me, of course."

"The police? Oh, I see. They've caught on to the bug bombs. What a pity." Stone said. His voice was the same voice he had used when he kissed the ladies' hands and flattered the staff, low and smooth and creamy, but somehow, to Caledonia's ear, it sounded more menacing than soothing. "It really was a mistake to try to do away with Mrs. Benbow, and I worried about it at the time. But I'd hoped it would be taken as an accident, whether the attempt succeeded or not. Of course I'd meant to retrieve the little canisters, but that wretched window locked. I suppose there was no hope then that the police wouldn't work it out." He made a tut-tut noise with his tongue. "And then, wouldn't you know it, Mrs. Benbow really hadn't figured out my pizza delivery scheme after all! I could have avoided all this trouble by just doing nothing! Ah, well, I shouldn't be annoyed. After all, I've done it to myself, haven't I? Oh, I had realized time was probably getting short here, but it's such a convenient arrangement that I'd hoped . . ." He sighed and his tone became businesslike. "You will do me the favor of coming along, too, of course. As a rather substantial insurance policy . . ." and from the pocket of his tweedy jacket he pulled a small but apparently all-too-functional automatic.

"Please don't make any sudden moves, Mrs. Wingate. You're big enough to intimidate me, but I fancy I have a little bit of an edge with this." He waved the little gun as though to be sure she had seen it.

Silently Caledonia told herself to move very slowly and keep her voice casual. Aloud she said, "I'll behave, I assure you, so don't get nervous, will you? I mean, if you must keep a finger on that trigger, keep the finger steady. I've got a few good years left in me, and I want to enjoy them."

"Very sensible. We'll wait, I think, until it's completely dark outside and most of the residents are asleep before we leave. Maybe another hour. I'm expecting a delivery, and we'll surprise the driver by hitching a ride."

"Where are we going?"

"For now, just to the living room, Mrs. Wingate. Please move slowly and walk ahead of me. That's the idea . . . All right, now sit down carefully . . . Good girl. We have a little time to kill and we might as well be comfortable." He eased onto the edge of a chair himself, but didn't sit far enough back to indicate the slightest relaxation. "Let's see, you asked a question, didn't you? Where will we go? Well, I have no idea where *you're* going. That depends on how you behave. Speaking for myself, I will be going to Mexico and then, as soon as I can arrange it, to Colombia. I have a fine apartment in a good district of Baranquilla, I have a Mercedes convertible just waiting for me in a garage there, I have friends . . ."

"Colombia? That sounds like drugs."

He laughed. "Oh, Mrs. Wingate. You sound so ingenuous. I'm sure you've figured that much out. Of course, I'm no big-timer . . . just a middle-sized middle-aged middleman. They bring me frequent deliveries of a fair amount of material that I mete out in small packets to individual buyers."

"You're a dealer!"

"I prefer to say I'm a redistributor. That's all."

"And you tried to kill Angela!"

"Yes," he conceded, "and that was a mistake, as I said. But I thought when I saw her going through my trash that she'd worked out my system. Of course she hadn't. I was still safe, and I certainly didn't make a second attempt. No point in stirring things up and drawing any more attention to this place. It was bad enough when I had to get rid of that Gould fellow."

"So it was you!"

"Well, what did you think?" His tone was that of a patient teacher pointing out an obvious truth to a slightly slow pupil. "Nosing around the garden in the middle of the night that way right when I expected a delivery . . ."

"The pizzas!"

He beamed at her, the teacher delighted that the student had finally caught on to the point. "Of course. Isn't it perfect? Using pizza boxes to hide my stuff as it's brought to me."

"Angela was right," Caledonia said with disgust. "It had to do with pizza all along! The Pizza Palace had us all fooled. We thought they were a legitimate business."

"Oh, they are. So far as I know. We just use their boxes, and we borrowed their name to put on the side of our van."

"But why kill Howard Gould? Surely he was fooled by the pizza box like everybody else. I'm sure he thought you were getting a fast-food delivery . . ."

"Alas, no. Unfortunately the delivery boys are not the brightest . . . We had them come in late at night, so very few people saw them, of course, and . . ."

"And that's why nobody seemed to know that pizza was delivered the night Gould was killed. Nobody was awake to see it."

"Right. But then the idiot making the delivery on that particular night tripped and dropped the box. It spilled onto the sidewalk, and even an innocent like Howard Gould, who'd come out into the garden chasing his cat, couldn't mistake a large number of small zip-lock bags containing white powder for pizza. Even so, I think he didn't quite catch on. He tried to play the good Samaritan," Stone went on scornfully. "The fool was actually trying to help pick up the packets and put 'em back in the box. But when I saw him, I realized he'd think it over later and realize how odd it all was, and he'd have told someone. So I had to take care of the problem, didn't I? It was kind of Pete Lopez to leave me a weapon."

"So you grabbed the hammer, killed Gould, and then you went right on selling drugs."

"Well, not right on. Police were prowling the garden at night for three or four days. My customers were getting really anxious by the time the all-clear was sounded."

"I'm surprised nobody's noticed and asked questions about all those people knocking on your door all night."

"That's the beautiful thing," he said smugly. "You just said it yourself. Nearly everybody goes to bed early around here. And as for knocking at my door . . . you know better. I've told everybody about my delivery system, with pizza boxes slid into and money picked up through that cat door. Well, customers do the same only backwards. They slide money in and I slide their stuff out. Nobody ever sees anybody else. It's a fine safety measure. None of us could honestly identify any of the others in court."

"But they know where you live, don't they?" Caledonia said reasonably. "They'd say, 'Who's our supplier? Why, that man in the outside corner apartment!' wouldn't they?"

He smiled. "Ah, well, if it ever came to that, the police would be searching for Conrad Stone. And by the time they were, I'd be somebody else. I'd be in Colombia with a new name, a new look . . ."

"Don't tell me you're planning plastic surgery again."

"Again?" He seemed surprised. "I haven't had plastic surgery."

"No face-lift to hide the wrinkles?"

"What wrinkles?" He smiled and preened as though to let her admire his firm, unlined face. "You're too influenced by my gray hair, but you'd be surprised how little peroxide it really takes to turn a whole head of hair from brown to white. I'll look completely different with my hair and brows back to their own color. I'll just use dye, of course, till the bleach grows out. Just like your Mrs. Stainsbury, eh?" he said cheerfully.

Caledonia squinted at him hard. "You're really not as old as you've made yourself look, are you?"

"Oh, you're catching on very well, Mrs. Wingate, even if the pieces of the puzzle go together one at a time. I always knew you were one of those who still had all their wits about them. I really hope you'll continue to behave. I'd hate to have to dispose of you. Besides, I think three deaths are quite enough."

"Three!"

He got to his feet and moved over to his window, pulling aside the blinds and peering quickly out, then returned to his chair. "Another few minutes, Mrs. Wingate, and then we'll move out. The delivery's due just after dark. A few more minutes . . ." He came back and perched on his chair again. "But I'm quite enjoying this little chat, you know. It's been a long time since I was able to relax and talk about myself, and I find it remarkably pleasant. Now let's see, where were we? Oh, yes. Three murders. Can you . . ." He beamed coyly at her. "Can you guess who?"

Caledonia shivered, but persevered. "Well, Howard Gould, of course. And I suppose you're telling me you killed Regina Madison?"

"Very good! You worked that out quickly."

"Well, she's the only other one who died recently, and although everyone says she just fell . . ."

"In a way that's true. When I came into her room, she had already taken away her screen and was perched on the windowsill, and she was leaning way, way over the edge, looking through those wretched binoculars. She didn't hear me come in behind her and it hardly took a touch to push her over."

"But why would you . . . Oh, of course. The binoculars! That fellow with the heart trouble she used to check on, he lived right next door to you, and so . . ."

". . . and so," he picked up the narrative, "when I began to get such frequent deliveries of pizza, she noticed. And when a few times my man brought in more than one box, she noticed that, too, and unfortunately for her, she teased me about it. Told me I'd get fat eating that much cheese and pepperoni. I had to do something, didn't I? I had already decided to leave, of course, but I still couldn't take a chance. That woman talked about everything she saw, and it was just a matter of time till she talked about me to the wrong person."

"Why did you leave up there and move here, anyway?"

"Oh, surely you can work that out, Mrs. Wingate. The Golden Years turned out to be a mistake for me. There was no good way for me to contact my customers there. I could get my deliveries, disguised as pizza, but I had to arrange with a third party to pass the stuff on to customers. Very inconvenient. This place is much better for business. More profitable, you know, when I'm the only middleman I need. Because this garden is open to the street, so customers can come and go and nobody even notices. There's even plenty of parking space for my customers right out on the street. I was really fortunate in this location."

"Yeah, fortunate," Caledonia said sourly. "What would you have done if the man who lived here before hadn't passed away? You know, Mr. Cherry . . . that dear little man from Canada with the bad heart?"

"I'd have done just what I did," Stone said. "Put a pillow over his nose."

"I don't believe you," Caledonia said. "The doctor would have caught on if he was suffocated!"

"Oh, he didn't suffocate. He had the heart attack everybody expected him to have. I suppose it was the shock of an intruder coming into his living room in the night—the struggle to breathe under that pillow. But I didn't hold it over his face for long. He went limp and I just took the pillow away and let him die on his own."

"You sound proud of it."

"Not really. It didn't take any special ability to frighten the old man to death. What I am proud of is my idea of moving into a retirement home. It makes a wonderful cover. People really think old folks do nothing but rock and play cards. It never occurs to them that a resident might have a life outside of eating and sleeping and just staying alive. This is an excellent plan, if I do say so myself. And I really resent your interference . . . you and Mrs. Benbow. All the same, if this weren't an emergency situation, if you hadn't become a danger to me, you wouldn't be sitting here now. I seldom make an important mistake like trying to get rid of someone who doesn't matter. All it does is turn a spotlight on . . ."

"That isn't true. You tried to knock Angela off!"

"I told you that was a mistake. She wasn't as much of a threat to me as I'd feared, and I was really relieved she hadn't been hurt. Incidentally, why didn't Mrs. Benbow tell us she was going to be in another room that night? She could have saved me no end of trouble.

I really struggled with that window, and . . . What was that!" There had been a soft *FLAP-SLAP* from the kitchen that made him jump nervously, as in fact Caledonia did as well. But Stone relaxed at once. "It's just that damned cat coming home," he said. "Now there's one thing I won't miss when I move on. Pretending to like that animal . . . Making a fuss over him . . . Talk about feeling like a fool!"

"Why did you go out and buy a cat, anyway? I really don't get that."

He nodded. "Why, he was part of my cover. People tend to think warm, cozy thoughts about you if you have a dog or cat. And the softer and rounder the animal, the more people take to him. I couldn't have a dog because of all the strangers coming and going. Besides, retirement homes don't admit people with dogs."

"I should think not!" Caledonia said indignantly.

"So I wanted a cat, and preferably a cat that looked like a harmless blob," he went on smugly. "Anyway, as it turned out, when I realized I could get this place as a headquarters, having that cat was twice as good an idea, because I could insist on getting that extra-big cat door, you see?"

Caledonia sighed. "Poor ol' Puddin'. You didn't even like him, did you? No wonder you fed him outside on the back step."

Stone shuddered. "Really a messy eater, throwing bits of food all over. Disgusting."

". . . till Nancy Bush complained about it, of course. Incidentally, would you eventually have pushed her out the window, too? She certainly looked the whole garden over with her binoculars, just like Regina Madison did."

"Ah, but she couldn't see down this far. She said she could only see just barely to the fountain," he reminded her. There was a longish pause in the conversation. Stone flicked the window blind slightly aside to check on the level of darkness and nodded his satisfaction but didn't speak.

"You're going to shoot me, aren't you?" Caledonia said at last, and she slid a little forward in her chair as she spoke. "You have no intention of letting me go. As soon as you've made a safe getaway you'll dispose of me."

"Oh, come, Mrs. Wingate," Stone said. "That might be true, of course, but I might also be planning to release you. And you can't take a chance, can you? I think you'll continue to behave as long as there's the slightest chance of surviving, and . . ."

And the room exploded in sound and motion, everything seeming to happen at once. Actually, it started innocently enough. Without giving a warning, and of course with no sound at all, Puddin' appeared, sailing gracefully through the air—a round, black, fuzzy projectile aiming itself for Caledonia's lap. Taken completely by surprise, Caledonia let out a shriek and jumped up, pushing the huge cat outward from her. Puddin' let out a yowl that was just as loud and leapt for a firmer platform—unfortunately for Conrad Stone, Stone's lap. Stone jerked backward while Caledonia, having lurched to her feet off balance, stumbled forward toward Stone. Almost simultaneously there was a deafening BANG as the little gun in Stone's hand went off, and in the same heartbeat, Puddin' screamed, Caledonia screamed, and Stone screamed! At the sound of the shot, Puddin' had once more launched himself outward, yowling, and this time his extended claws tore into Stone's legs at the same moment that Caledonia fell forward onto Stone, her arms flailing as she tried to catch her balance. Caledonia was yelling because she was startled by the shot, but Stone, his trousers shredded, his thighs bleeding, had his scream of anguish cut short as his breath was knocked from him by the impact of Caledonia's full weight landing squarely on his chest.

At almost the same moment, a voice outside shouted "Police!" and Stone's front door flew open. Lieutenant Martinez burst into the living room, Swanson on his heels. Both men had guns drawn, both men were booming out "Police! Police!"—as well as "Nobody move!" and "Drop your weapons!" and "Hands up and behind your head" and other expressions appropriate to the moment.

"Are you hurt, Mrs. Wingate?" Martinez shouted. "Don't move, Stone . . ."

"I've got him," Swanson was yelling, a handcuff already out and working. "Give me your other hand, Stone. Now! That's right."

Stone, who was struggling to breathe, said nothing as Caledonia, a little dazed, levered her weight off him. He no longer had the little gun with which he had menaced her; it lay several feet away on the floor, where it had flown as he was hit by the full force of Caledonia's accidental body block. Stone appeared to be every bit as dazed as Caledonia, and Swanson rolled him over in the chair so that his hands could be firmly cuffed behind his back.

"Where did he shoot you?" Martinez insisted. "Are you all right?"

"I think he got me in the barbecue tongs," Caledonia said wonderingly, holding up the implement she still held in one hand. The wood on the handle was splintered and the metal beneath it de-formed. "I guess I threw my hands up and this got in the way of that little bullet. It's not very clear . . ."

"You're all right then!" Swanson said, from where he was carefully picking up the little gun. "Boy, am I glad to hear that. When that gun went off . . ."

"We were right outside," Martinez said. "We were listening at the door. We intended to come in, eventually, but you were doing just fine and we were certainly interested in the conversation, I can tell you."

"Well, thanks a lot," Caledonia said. "You could have felt free to interrupt just anytime. I was absolutely scared stiff, and when he got into all that bragging about how he'd killed three people, I figured I'd had it. I'd have been lucky if he let me live as far as the Mexican border! If it hadn't been for the cat . . . I . . . I . . . Gosh! You know something? I don't feel too steady. I think . . . I think I just might faint."

"Mrs. Wingate!" Martinez said with alarm. "Hang on . . . don't do that!"

But she did.

CHAPTER

18

LIEUTENANT MARTINEZ LEFT THE cleanup details to his men, under the direction of his partner Swanson, and insisted on being the one to help Caledonia back to her apartment, where he immediately phoned for Angela and for Doc Carter, in that order.

"She's perfectly all right," Martinez assured them, after a brief explanation of the circumstances.

"I'm perfectly all right," Caledonia insisted, trying to brush off the multitude of helping hands that were patting and fluffing and fluttering around her couch pillows, her shoulders, the afghan drawn across her knees.

"She's perfectly all right," Doc Carter agreed, tucking away into his little black bag his stethoscope and his sphygmomanometer. "Heart's ticking over steady, blood pressure normal . . . remarkable woman."

"She is *not* all right!" Only Angela stubbornly held out for Caledonia's invalid status. "That was a horrible experience. She'll need to rest up. She could have some kind of delayed reaction. She hides her real feelings, and you can't tell how upset she is." And by sheer force of will she pushed the others out and bullied Caledonia into going to bed for the night.

The next morning Angela sat on Caledonia's front porch until she heard sounds from within the apartment that suggested Caledonia was up and moving around. Then she raced up to the dining room in the main building, borrowed a large thermos for coffee, fixed up a breakfast tray, and hurried it back to Caledonia's place. They had long since exchanged extra apartment keys—just in case of an emergency, they had assured each other—so Angela let herself in without difficulty and set up breakfast on the living room coffee table. When Caledonia emerged from her bedroom, showered and fully dressed, she was pleasantly surprised to find she need walk no further toward the dining room.

"I told you I'm all right," she reminded Angela. "This is awfully nice of you, but really unnecessary."

"Well, I disagree. I do believe all this has affected you more than you show, and I certainly don't mind playing nursemaid. Besides, this is the only way I can feel a part of things now. I mean, all the good part is finished! You went off and had all the fun without me!"

"If you call being held hostage fun." Caledonia poured herself a cup of coffee. "Actually, I didn't mean to get into matters deeply enough to get shot at or anything. I only meant to look into the matter of the grabbits."

"I don't understand why you collected those things." Angela waved a hand at the two grabbit poles propped against the living room wall.

"Well, after I'd told people I dropped my watch down a grate and needed something to fetch it out, I had to borrow the grabbits to make my story ring true. I'll return them . . ."

"You just stay put," Angela ordered. "Tell me where they go and I'll take them back for you. And tell me what you want for lunch. You have a choice of macaroni-cheese or Swiss steak. I'll bring it to you on a tray. In fact, I should bring you a tray for dinner, too, because there's no use taking a chance, is there?"

"Angela, please don't make such a big deal out of this. I've told you and told you I'm perfectly all right."

"You're not," Angela said firmly. "Now just be a good girl and behave yourself. Sit down, put your feet up . . . let me get another pillow to put behind you . . ."

"Well, I'll do it. For now." Caledonia's grumpy voice showed plainly how much it annoyed her to be fussed over and bossed around and how reluctant her capitulation was. "But I'm not going to like it. Not going to like it at all."

"Will it make you feel better about staying in this morning to tell me all the details of last night? I've only had the barest outline, re-member . . ."

"Oh, I don't mind talking about it. I've been waiting for the chance! You see, it all started when I put that insecticide residue onto my tongue and needed water . . ." Angela could not complain that Caledonia was at all reluctant to share every detail of the story, and although from time to time Caledonia paced the floor fretfully while she talked, she seemed slightly mollified by having such a willing and attentive audience.

"And that's it!" Caledonia finished her narrative in a rush. "I think I've remembered everything Stone told me before the police charged in and took him away. Well," she checked her watch, "it's almost lunchtime, and I see no reason why I can't just walk up to the dining room with you and . . ."

"I think not," Angela said sternly. "Next thing, you'll want to go charging around as usual, shopping or playing bridge or whatever, wearing yourself out. I want you to rest this afternoon too. Just to be sure. Now I'm off to get you . . . you did say you wanted the Swiss steak, didn't you?" And Angela pranced off to the dining room so that once again Caledonia could dine off a tray perched on her coffee table while Angela stood guard.

"You go ahead and eat, Cal," she said as she put the tray down. "Keep your strength up. I brought myself this little cucumber sandwich and I'll just nibble along and keep you company." She took a dainty bite. "You know, I still can't believe it. To think it was Conrad Stone. That nice, nice man. I'll say it again, I just can't believe it!"

"Oh, I can believe it, all right," Caledonia said, piling into her Swiss steak. Annoyance at Angela's fussing hadn't diminished her appetite one bit. "Remember, I never liked him. Not from the first."

"And you were quite right, Mrs. Wingate," a man's voice spoke from the open doorway. "He wasn't really what you'd call a likable man." It was Lieutenant Martinez, standing just outside Caledonia's screen door. "I'm sorry to interrupt. If this isn't a convenient time . . ."

Angela hopped up to let him in, and the women assured him that he was both welcome and that the timing could not be better. "Caledonia needs something to take her mind off being confined to quarters," Angela said. "I've told her she's to take it easy today, and she's not one bit pleased about it. So a visitor is very welcome indeed. Besides, there are still gaps in what I know, and maybe you'll fill them in."

Between Martinez and Caledonia—when her mouth wasn't full of lunch, which Martinez insisted she continue eating—the whole story of Stone and the drugs and the murders was reviewed and brought to its climactic close once more.

"I still find it hard to believe. He wasn't really an old man, then?" Angela said with wonder. "How old was he?"

"Fifty-two," Martinez answered.

"Amazing. Everybody just assumed he was older, because who would want to live in a retirement home if they didn't have to?"

"Plenty of people," Caledonia said defensively. "Twenty-four-hour security, a comfortable apartment, wonderful meals, maid service, a beautiful view and a lovely garden, medical services close by and as needed, built-in friends and activities, and complete freedom to go wherever we want without having to hire a house sitter or worrying about someone to take in the mail. I tell you, only the very wealthy live as well as people in a retirement home like this. I mean, there's so much that's bad about getting old, there have to be a few rewards, too, don't there? And a place like this is one of the best."

"I'm sold," Martinez said with a smile. "Sign me up."

"You're not old enough yet," Caledonia reminded him.

"And apparently," Angela said, "neither was Conrad Stone." She had a sudden thought. "Wait a minute. He deceived us about his age, so perhaps he wasn't Conrad Stone at all. I mean, was that his real name?"

"Of course not," Martinez said. "He's Carl Seymour, wanted for questioning by at least two federal agencies. They had a tip on him from an informer some months ago, but when they went looking for him, he seemed to have disappeared off the face of the earth. They could never have guessed he was still doing business under the excellent cover of a senior citizens' residence."

"But he wasn't a geezer like us at all," Angela said. "He was really an ante-geezer."

"An antigeezer?" Martinez said.

"No-no-no . . . *ante* with an *e*. A *pre*-geezer, if you'd prefer." Angela shook her head as she thought that over for a moment, then became businesslike again. "Now, there's one thing that I don't understand, Lieutenant, and that is how you and Officer Swanson came to be right outside his apartment, so you could burst in and save Caledonia."

"I wish I'd known you were out there. I wouldn't have been quite so scared," Caledonia said. "And if he'd known, maybe he wouldn't have shot at me. I still don't know how he missed me, at that close range."

"He swears he didn't do it," Martinez said.

"Oh, come on, Lieutenant. You heard the shot almost as plainly as I did."

"Oh, he fired a shot. He just claims it wasn't fired at you. He says the gun went off accidentally. And I believe him, because the tongs were not enough to keep the bullet from hitting you, Mrs. Wingate, if it hadn't been fired at an angle, partly away from you."

Caledonia nodded. "I agree. He couldn't have missed, if he'd been aiming at me. I'm a pretty big target. I'm glad you were able to come rushing to my rescue so he didn't have a chance to try again. How come you were eavesdropping, by the way?"

"Well, to tell the truth, what pushed us to go after Stone was Roderick."

"Roderick! Roderick the dog?"

"That's right. He pointed out that you had been carrying drugs, Mrs. Benbow."

"I don't know what you mean! I was not!"

"Oh, but you were. That first time Roderick came here to Camden-sur-Mer, he singled you out and sat down in front of you, and then he went to pull on Chita's towel—a clear signal that he'd located drugs and expected his little game of tug-of-war as his reward. You must realize that now, too, after the demonstration Flynn put on in your lobby. Of course I know better than to think you'd carry drugs on purpose, but by accident perhaps? You had that sack full of empty cartons with you at the time. The one you brought to us to investigate. So last night we got Flynn to bring the dog back here, and we let Roderick sniff at that plastic sack."

"You still had that sack, Lieutenant?"

"Oh, we don't throw things away till we're positive they're of no use. We set the empty cartons out on a table and brought Roderick in. Flynn gave him his working command and he did just what he'd done with you. He sat and pointed right at the pizza box, then went over for his reward, his little game of pull-the-towel. So we decided that we ought to interview Mr. Stone again, and the sooner the better. Of course when we arrived at his place, he was in the middle of telling you all about himself, Mrs. Wingate, and we had the pleasure of listening in. Well, now he can tell it all over again. To us and to the federal agents. Although," Martinez added smugly, "they're going to have to take their place in line to get at him. We're holding him now on the charge of murdering Howard Gould. And we may be able to get him indicted on three murders altogether, on the strength of his confession to Mrs. Wingate."

"What about his trying to kill me?" Angela said indignantly. "How about that?"

"Well, it'll do for a backup if by some miracle he could escape the first three charges," Martinez said.

"You know," Caledonia mused, "this was about as strange as anything we've been involved in with you. It started as a ghost story and it finished with murder and drugs, but not till it had wandered through pizza and hair dye and fumigation and cats and dogs . . . And speaking of dogs, I hope the department will reward Roderick properly for his efforts. A nice thick steak ought to do it."

Martinez nodded cheerfully. "Exactly what I thought. And arrangements have been made."

"And once again, speaking of arrangements and of cats," Caledonia said, "what's going to become of poor old Puddin'?"

"Oh, yes," Angela said. "Poor Puddin'. I feel so sorry for him. The cat that wasn't really loved. And he's such a very nice cat. So affectionate . . ."

"He is," Caledonia agreed, "and you can believe me when I say that, because I don't even like cats. Most cats. Well, I don't *dis*like them, you know, but . . ."

"You should adopt him, Cal," Angela said, "since you've taken to him so strongly."

"You know I can't do that. Not with Cesare." She gestured over toward the little blue parakeet swinging contentedly in his cage. "He's safe enough behind bars, I suppose, but it'd be cruel to tempt fate. All the same, I wish we could be sure Puddin' would have a good home with someone who'd love him, for a change."

"If that's your concern," Martinez said as he rose to take his leave, "I think I can put your mind at rest. I've found him a good home already. With someone who is really extremely fond of cats."

"How wonderful. Who took him in?"

Martinez smiled. "I've adopted Puddin' myself. It may not be strictly legal just to take over the property of an accused felon, but no one need ever know of my little act of petty larceny."

"Oh, Lieutenant, how wonderful!" Angela said. "To give that lovely creature a good home at last . . ."

"I said it before and I'll say it again," Caledonia beamed at him, "you're a nice man."

"We're going to need statements from you both," Martinez reminded them. "Especially your statement, Mrs. Wingate. And if we don't have enough evidence on Stone concerning the murder of Howard Gould, we may need your testimony in court as well, you know."

Caledonia shrugged. "Why not? It'd be something new for me. And a way to break the routine around here. Although lately I'd say this place has been anything but monotonous."

"Wait!" Angela cried. "What about poor Nancy Bush? What about that confession of hers?"

Martinez hesitated at the door. "We're going to try to get her some help," he said. "Your Mr. Torgeson is anxious to assist in arranging some kind of long-term, outpatient treatment for her, so she can stay on here. He says he's lost too many tenants already this month and it would look better for all concerned if she didn't have to be carted away. One thing your Mr. Torgeson understands is enlightened self-interest."

"He's still got fifty percent of his new tenants," Caledonia said. "That should cheer him up, when he stops to think about it."

Lieutenant Martinez smiled, gave his little half bow, and swung the screen door open. But he stopped halfway through and turned back with a broad grin. "You know, I liked that term you invented, Mrs. Benbow. But you applied it to the wrong person. Being young is not a matter of chronology. It's not how old one is in years, but how old in spirit. And you two . . . you two are the most *ante* ante-geezers of all." And he bowed again and moved gracefully away through the sunlit garden.

"Isn't he just the sweetest man!" Angela said. She rose and stretched. "Well, all our mysteries are solved now, and I suppose it's time to relax again."

"Well, almost. There is one more thing." Caledonia was grinning wickedly. "Have you decided what to do about all that pizza you ordered up for your imaginary birthday bash?"

"Oh, Cal! I hoped you were going to phone up and cancel it for me."

"I already told you I wouldn't do that."

"But, Cal," Angela's voice took on the wheedling tone she'd used to get her way since she was a child, "it'd be so embarrassing for me to phone in myself. What could I say? That I lied about the birthday in the first place? That would be completely humiliating."

"Serve you right to have to embarrass yourself a little. But you won't have to, Angela. I've been waiting for a chance to tell you that I've come up with an idea to take care of the problem."

"You have? What is it?"

"Well, I told you not to fuss me, but you went right on fussing. Tucking me in, bringing me trays, bullying me into staying in all morning . . ."

"It's all for your own good, Cal."

"I suppose so, but I was fed up with it last night, I'm fed up today, and I decided to find a way to get even. Nothing bad, but just to teach you a lesson. And I found it. While you were up getting my lunch tray, I phoned the Pizza Palace."

"You did? And you canceled?"

"Oh, no. What I did was tell them time and date of the Ridgeways' party next week and asked them to deliver all your twenty-five pizzas to the Ridgeway apartment."

"Cal! You didn't. That's not funny!"

"Oh, I think it is," Caledonia said. "I think it's the perfect practical joke! First of all, you brought it on yourself. Maybe now you'll think twice about fussing and interfering when I ask you not to. And maybe you'll be a little more careful when you think of a story to tell somebody . . . like that poor pizza guy. You got his hopes up for a big sale, you know, and it really wasn't fair."

"Oh, dear." Angela was dismayed. "I didn't even think of that."

"Well, now he'll get his big sale. And the second good thing about this . . . nobody's hurt by it. In fact, the Ridgeways will be delighted. Imagine giving a party and having someone else furnish the food! And you certainly can afford it. Oh, yes, this is perfect. Twenty-five pizzas!" and she chuckled massively.

"Oh, Cal," Angela said reprovingly. "It's not the expense I mind. It's having that dreadful Della Ridgeway pursuing me with cries of gratitude. You've practically insured that the Ridgeways will consider themselves my bosom buddies from now on."

"Oh, but they won't," Caledonia said, smiling even more broadly, "and that's the best part of all. Because I managed to make two practical jokes out of one, and the second joke isn't on you. You'll love this part. I dictated a note over the phone . . . a note that the pizza folks will bring along with the pizzas. It says, 'Thank you for the invitation. I look forward to being with you,' and I had them sign it *Trinita*."

"You didn't!"

"Ah, but I did. Trinita Stainsbury will get the cries of gratitude and she'll be the one to have Della for a bosom buddy . . . and you'll pay for it! Now that, I think, is a truly elegant practical joke!"

She beamed, and after a moment Angela began to smile in spite of herself. "You're right, Cal. In fact, I can hardly wait for next Tuesday to see the look on the Ridgeways' faces. Twenty-five pizzas! And Trinita won't have the least idea what they're talking about when they thank her. Oh, I like it! I really like it!"

There was a moment of contented silence before Caledonia yawned and raised her huge arms up in a monumental stretch. "Well, now," she said, "I've had my lunch and I'm going to take my usual nap. And after my nap, I might even go for a short stroll in the garden—and don't you start fussing again, Angela. I'm through taking it easy. I'd say everything is back to normal."

Angela smiled lazily. "Perhaps today I'll take a little nap myself," she said. "Why not? Cal, you're right. Everything is back to normal."

And outside, the sun shone, the roses nodded gently, and the sound of the sea at the foot of the garden whispered along as the breeze took its own afternoon nap. Life was serene once more, and good—as it had always been.